... A man she could not live without.

BOUND AND GAGGED, MORLAIX'S HEIRESS REMAINED DEFIANT . . .

"She was unwilling, Fulk," his cousin explained. "She does not want to be married."

Even in the dim light, Fulk could see the Lady Alwyn was not old, at least not as much as he expected. Her linen headcloth had been knocked askew, but under it dark, curling hair cascaded from the top of her head, almost covering her face. He could just make out her mouth, stuffed with a cloth gag.

Inwardly, Fulk cursed. Delivering his intended bride to the altar in such a condition was not desirable, but neither was it illegal—Norman law allowed that heiresses could be married even if they were notably resistant.

"By the saints, be quick about it," Fulk growled. "Once we are tied in holy wedlock, I see I will have a lifetime to regret it."

BLOOD RED ROSES

KATHERINE DEAUXVILLE

ST. MARTIN'S PAPERBACKS

**For Edward Novak III, Jennifer Weis,
and most particularly Harrison.**

BLOOD RED ROSES

Copyright © 1991 by Maggie Davis.

Cover photograph by B & G Associates.
Illustration on cover stepback by Leslie Pellegrino.

ISBN: 0-312-92571-9

Printed in the United States of America

St. Martin's Paperbacks edition/ September 1991

10 9 8 7 6 5 4 3 2 1

Prologue

THE TALLY REEVE CAME LOOKING FOR her along the walk at the top of the curtain wall, threading his way among the men-at-arms who hunkered down out of sight of the Earl of Chester's archers. From the look on his face, Alwyn supposed he had more bad news. Probably the cook had sent him to nag at her again about food for the evening meal.

At any time now, it was to be expected that Castle Morlaix would surrender. At least that was the way their attackers reasoned it. No woman, except one other that Alwyn had heard of, had ever defended a siege of a castle.

She took another bite of bread, sitting on a water cask, elbows propped on her drawn-up knees. She'd been on her feet since dawn, and now the sun was setting. As she put the piece of bread to her mouth Alwyn noticed it was gray with smoke and dirt. She looked down and saw her filthy hands. The bread had been clean before she picked it up.

"My lady," the tally reeve called, sidling along the parapet. He did not raise his voice; the bowmen encamped below the portal gate shot at any noise. "The cook wishes

1

to know if you will come down now and see to the people who wish to be fed."

Alwyn stuffed the last of the bread in her mouth and nodded yes, so that he would go away. After thirteen days of siege she had learned they would not have another assault on the walls so close to nightfall. But in the dark the sappers would work on their tunnels again, digging under the outer walls and the ward and making for the stone tower of the keep to set underground fires in the hope it would collapse.

The Earl of Chester's knights made much of their beleaguered condition.

Three times a day, in early morning, at noon prayers, and at sunset, a herald in elegant silks rode up under a white flag of parley and blew his horn. When he was sure they were listening, he exhorted the Welsh and English men-at-arms and the garrison of Norman knights to overthrow the Lady Alwyn and bargain for terms of surrender. Which, according to him, were extraordinarily generous: the Earl of Chester, Hugh of Avranches, would pardon all inside Castle Morlaix and allow them to depart with safekeeping. The Norman knights would retain all their arms and their horses. The Welsh and English men-at-arms would be allowed an escort out of the marches. And the villagers who had taken refuge inside Morlaix could return to their lands in the valley without fear of punishment.

All they had to do was turn over Fulk de Jobourg's wife to his rightful liege lord, the Earl of Chester.

It was about time for the herald to make his sundown visit; they could hear his horn in the distance.

One of the Welsh bowmen sitting with his back to the wall said, "Don't you pay no attention to what that fancy horn tootler says when he comes, milady. Especially about it being unnatural and all for a woman to lead us. Lord love us, I'd give a good penny to send an owl-feathered shaft through that poppinjay's throat."

Alwyn shook her head. It was not allowed to shoot a herald. They all knew that.

"If your lord husband was here," one of the English pikemen put in, "we'd show them what's what. He'd raise this bloody siege and send that earl's dirty scavengers packing right off."

She managed a smile. If Fulk de Jobourg would come to their relief. She heard it a thousand times a day. Even now, the castle people believed she'd welcome him. This husband who had never wanted her.

Who perhaps did not want her now.

Under the wall, Chester's herald was shouting his opening remarks. He was very skillful, Alwyn thought, standing up so that she could see him. Or perhaps someone else had composed his flowery, persuasive words.

The earl's archers did not shoot while the herald was under his flag of parley; it was almost as though the castle people were encouraged to come out in the open. Perhaps, Alwyn had thought, as a means of counting them to see how many of them were left.

The past few days, the herald had begun his speech by reminding his listeners that the Lady Alwyn's father had been a Breton traitor, hanged for his treachery against King William. It followed, then, that her supporters had best not expect trustworthiness from his daughter. She would betray them all, as they would find to their sorrow, since treachery was in her blood.

A few of the men-at-arms listening along the wall growled under their breath. Farther down, the Norman knights who owed their loyalty to Fulk de Jobourg were silent.

Alwyn leaned her arms on the parapet and looked down. The herald, who was tall, fair-haired, good-looking in his colorful clothes, rode his horse back and forth as he shouted. His banner with the earl's device of a leopard rampant whipped behind him in the evening breeze.

Alwyn studied him thoughtfully. If only Morlaix's people knew why the Earl of Chester wanted her. The part about treachery was not far wrong—Hugh of Avranches had another husband for her, better, he had promised, than the one she now had.

In addition, she was assured she could give up the futile defense of her castle. That too would be hers by Chester's grant if she agreed. It was certainly better than what she'd had when Fulk de Jobourg had seized Morlaix and claimed it for his own.

Alwyn sighed. To hear them talk you would think her husband had no friends; at least they didn't count his wife as one of them. It seemed the whole world knew the truth of their marriage.

Holy Mary, she thought suddenly, she was sick of senseless warring and killing and siege-making. They had fought all day from sunup to sundown and four times had beat the attackers back from the walls with fire and arrows and heated stones dumped on them from red-hot buckets. Men had died. She had seen with her own eyes the sorely wounded carried away. And Morlaix's hall was full of their own. It was madness.

She watched the herald ride back, not at all downcast at his reception. It was plain that the earl's knights were sure Castle Morlaix's surrender was not many more days away. The sun had gone behind the horizon; it was almost dark. Alwyn knew they would have to set a guard for the night to listen for sappers tunneling under the walls.

What the Earl of Chester did not know was that if she wished, she could appeal to King William herself. With any luck she supposed the king would agree to it. Then she would need no husband at all.

She thought of Fulk de Jobourg.

It was cursed from the beginning, she told herself dispassionately. She had always wondered what he'd been thinking when he rode through the snow that night to Morlaix to marry her.

A dew of blood dripped from our swords,
The arrows whistled as they went seeking helmets—
For me a pleasure equal to holding a girl in my arms.
                    —Battle Song of Ragnar Lodbrog

Chapter One

THE SNOW WAS DEEP, WITH A THIN crust of ice on it. As they made the last rise of hills, the horses plunged into a deep drift to their knees. With a curse, Fulk de Jobourg reined in his floundering destrier and called the others to a halt.

"Can you see?" his squire asked, squinting against the thickly falling snow.

Bundled in ice-stiffened cloaks and sheepskins, the knights were dim shadows on horseback. Through the snowfall Fulk could barely make out the pennant that dangled from the castle's outer wall, the signal that his knights Bocage and de Bais had arrived with their men and secured the place by King William's order. By now, Fulk thought with a distinct lack of enthusiasm, they had also notified the rebel Lesneven's daughter that she was about to be married. Also by William's command.

He drew back his hood and felt a whisper of snowflakes settle in his hair. "It is Morlaix," he assured them. He thought of the five tortuous miles since they had crossed the river. "And, by God's bones, none too soon."

The castle before them was an unwelcoming pile of

gray-black stone against the snowy mountainside. The wooden fortress that it had replaced had been called something long and unpronounceable in the Welsh tongue, but all here had been under Norman rule for years. The Breton ally that King William had given the fortress to, Bruse Lesneven, had renamed it Morlaix for his home place in Brittany.

Fulk hunched his shoulders against the wind. The movement sent a small shower of snow under his sheepskin and into his neck. He had sweated with the exertion of long travel, then grown cold, and the padded shirt underneath his mail was now like a suit of ice. He felt like an old man, every muscle in his body aching with tiredness. It was hard to remember that he was barely half a score years older than the downy-faced squire who rode beside him.

The gale moaned in the mountain passes, carrying another gust of snow over their heads. It was a cursed bad day to be married. In all his years in William the Bastard's service, Fulk had never given the possibility of a royal order to wed a passing thought, although it had become common enough: a rich widow or young heiress was a fitting reward for a knight's loyal soldiering, and the king acquired Norman-held castles and Norman-held lands without bloodshed and the expense of war.

From what Fulk could see through the falling snow, Castle Morlaix looked like a strong, advantageous holding. The former baron, who had fought with William at Hastings, had been given, as his reward, this fort in the Welsh hills. Unfortunately, or fortunately, according to how one looked at it, Lesneven had been tempted to treachery by his countrymen, and was among the first to be hanged when their revolt against William was discovered. Now that he was dead, Fulk had been commanded to rush to Wales, reclaim the castle for King William, and wed Lesneven's heiress, whether she wished it or not.

Fulk had no argument with binding property through

marriage, especially when it was to one's own gain. But he had as little stomach for this particular married state as he supposed did the rebel knight's daughter.

"Sound the horn," he told his squire.

The boy put it to his lips and the horn's thin bray addressed the silent stones of the castle.

Fulk had been told in London that Lesneven's daughter was older than most maids, a spinster neglected and unwed because of her father's part in conspiracies. It had occurred to him during the long hours of travel from Wrexham the lady might feel—being elderly, the family name in disgrace, and with all her estates forfeit—that she was fairly well served to take any sort of husband King William thought to provide.

Such as, he thought, somewhat wryly, a worthy and valorous knight of undistinguished Norman family, now wanting rewarding; some tried and true but impoverished soldier, son to an unlucky liegeman of William's who had somehow lost his promised share in the cutthroat frenzy after the conquest.

Now, regarding the castle before him with a critical eye, Fulk judged it was not bad, something any landless knight would covet. It was deep in Welsh country, but that was all to the good; fortunes, both military and otherwise, were to be made in the marches where an ambitious man could fare well. If there was anything wrong, it was having to take an unmarriageable female as the price of possession. Fulk had told himself that since he traveled far on the king's campaigns, he need never be at home much here at Morlaix.

The horn's hail died in the frigid air and the knights kicked their horses forward. The big destriers, sensing shelter and feed in the castle before them, lumbered to a trot.

As his mount half slid down the steep roadway, Fulk considered that the fate before him as a new bridegroom was God's will—or if not God's, at least King William's. A

9

bare month ago, to hold a castle and barony was what he could only dream of; he was suddenly surprised he found himself hoping the woman waiting to be married was not impossibly ugly. Or old as sin.

Perhaps it was the weather and his own frozen condition, but he couldn't help thinking a little luck would not be amiss when he was called upon to perform his marital duties. The saints knew his powers in bed had never failed him, but as he was now, tired, hungry, and aching with cold, he hardly felt equal to the challenge of an elderly or—God forbid—overly timid virgin.

Let come what may, he thought resignedly. In the past few days he'd hardly had time to concern himself with such things. At King William's summons, he had covered hard miles to London from a thankless campaign seeking out rebels in Huntington and Bedford and, once at the king's court, a place Fulk had never liked, he'd found himself crowded in with a pack of nobles anxious to disavow their part in the revolt. As he was herded along with petty Norman vassals from the rebellious east, he couldn't help wondering how William felt to suddenly find so many protesting they loved him. For the first time in years, the Conqueror was faced with a serious threat to his power.

The Bretons' revolt had begun when the young firebrand Roger Fitz-Osbern, Earl of Hereford, turned against William with Ralph of Wader, the half Breton, half English Earl of Norfolk. Fulk learned of the king's concern for his Welsh borders when he was stopped on his way to the White Tower by a clerk, who told Fulk he would be ordered to secure a castle, Morlaix, that was not only the farthest west of the marcher forts, but had been held by a Breton traitor.

In an anteroom packed with knights, King William sought Fulk in the crowd and, with his typical impatience, ordered him to force-march to Castle Morlaix, marry Lesneven's daughter before some outlaw seized her and her castle, consummate the union to the satisfaction of church and king, and then go with all due haste to Chirk township. Fulk was needed there to deal with a splinter of Hereford's forces going to meet other rebels in the south. As the king moved on, a clerk bestowed on Fulk a writ proclaiming his barony. It was the lowest of titles, but enough; Fulk hardly heard the monk when he told him a ceremony must need await a time when the war was not so pressing.

Now, he gazed at his holding through the falling snow. He was pledged to hold this piece of the marches for William and make his fortune here too, if he was diligent. Now that he was a titled knight, it would be better, although God and all the saints knew William was not an easy man to serve. The Conqueror was not called the Crippler for nothing: at the battle of Cambridge when Ralph de Wader had fled, leaving his men to be taken, William lived up to his reputation by having his Normans cut off the right foot of each luckless captive.

Fulk was about to tell Aubrey to hail the castle once more when there was a clatter of chains and the drawbridge banged down across the moat, hitting the far bank in a puff of snow.

"God's wounds," he growled into his hood, "are they trying to break it?"

His squire spurred his horse ahead, crying a halloo for Bocage, de Bais, and the knights who had ridden to Morlaix the day before. Fulk, with his third in command, Yerville, at his back, proceeded more cautiously. As he rode past the rubble of the castle's partly completed curtain wall and into the cobblestoned yard, he saw the place looked a shambles.

His knight, de Bais, came running across the snowy yard to meet them. "There was no one to answer our hail from the wall," Fulk shouted. "Post a guard before I break your thick skull."

"Fulk—*m-milord*!" De Bais stumbled over the title, still new. "The guard left to lower the entry. I was in the

11

chapel, as you ordered yestreen. Preparing for your marriage."

Fulk remembered his orders to have the priest and Lesneven's daughter ready on his arrival. Sweet Mary, they'd probably rushed the woman to the church the moment they heard young Aubrey's horn.

From outside, Morlaix had seemed a goodly place. Inside, the seat of his new baronage looked like the devil's own backside. There was garbage underfoot, not to mention the stink of offal from the stables. His own men were not in much better condition. De Bais's tethered horses, their rumps turned to the wind, had a gaunt look from months of fighting. Geoffrey de Bocage's knights huddled about a fire and hardly looked up as he rode past. Morlaix was a far cry from London and William's court, where all was silken display and fawning upon the king. But even in his present mood, Fulk thought he might prefer it. It was different when it was one's own.

"The villeins fled," de Bais explained as he helped a stiff and aching Fulk to dismount. "Also, we found the storerooms but not the keys; the chamberlain is gone with them. The kitchen is empty, we've had to forage for the horses, and there's nothing in the village. The people are hiding there and will not come out, like the damned Welsh they are."

Fulk hobbled after him. "Holy mother, what's *'fled'*? Do villeins disappear like smoke?"

The young knight looked affronted. "These Welsh are devils, Fulk, even the castle servants are treacherous. And Lesneven's daughter, Lady Alwyn, is half Welsh, so you must watch your own back. When we arrived, the servers threw a shower of rocks and refuse over us from the walls and then disappeared. There was a castle guard loyal to Lesneven, mostly Welshmen. We had to fight them to gain the keep."

So her name was Alwyn, he thought. He followed de Bais across the snow-drifted yard to the castle chapel.

The church was no more than a shed stuck against the uncompleted curtain wall. Geoffrey de Bocage met them at the door.

His cousin was almost as tall as Fulk, with the same dark red hair and long Norman nose that were, as with King William himself, the evidence of their mixed French and Northman ancestors.

Fulk stuck his head forward and shook off the hood, making snow fall in a shower. "God's blood, do we marry or not?" he wanted to know. The church was dark and cold with only a few candles; he could hardly see if anyone was there.

Geoffrey scowled at him. "There were difficulties."

"Difficulties?" Fulk could make out an unwashed-looking cleric in monk's clothing, probably the local priest, waiting at the altar. The old man looked terrified. But then Geoffrey was not the most tender of knights. Two of his cousin's men, still in mail and swords, held the bride.

They held her, Fulk saw, because the woman was so tightly bound with ropes that she could not stand alone. Lesneven's daughter, the spinster heiress of Morlaix, was trussed like a Martinmas pig. Her hands were tied behind her back and for good measure a length of rope was run around her waist, circling her legs and feet. One shoe was missing. The other foot, which did not touch the ground because of the men holding her, still wore a small leather bootkin.

Fulk swore softly. The old monk's eyes were rolling up in his head; he looked as though he might break and run.

"She was unwilling, Fulk." His cousin looked down his nose at him. "She does not want to be married."

"Unwilling" was hardly the word. Bound and gagged, Morlaix's spinster reeked defiance. Her eyes, a silvery color, bulged with fury. Even in the dim light Fulk could see the Lady Alwyn was not old, at least not as much as expected. Her linen headcloth had been knocked askew, but under it dark, curling hair cascaded from the top of her

13

head, almost covering her face. He could just make out her mouth, stuffed with a cloth gag.

Inwardly, Fulk cursed. Delivering his intended bride to the altar in such a condition was not desirable, but on the other hand, neither was it illegal. Norman law, William's law, allowed that heiresses could be married even if they were notably resistant. At least, he thought, it was better than kidnap and rape. Or even murder.

Unfortunately, the Lady Alwyn was not impressed with her good luck. She glared at him, making enraged noises through the cloth gag.

A wave of tiredness suddenly swept over him. God's bones, but he was spent. He could scarce believe he was standing where he was, in a mud and wattle church inside a half-built marcher castle, surveying a totally unknown, struggling woman his king would have him marry. He resisted the urge to lift his hands and rub his frozen face.

"She is not bad looking." This was young Yerville, at his elbow. "It's dark in here, Fulk, but certainly she is not foul to the eyes. I see that myself."

He must look more worn than he thought, to have his knight want to comfort him. In the silence, Lady Alwyn gave another angry squeal under her gag.

Fulk peered at her. He did not know what he expected to find after their hellish journey from Wrexham. Some faceless woman, some shadowy form he was pledged to serve in the marriage bed. But not this. He found himself wondering what a man could hope for under all those bulky woolen clothes. She was black-haired like the Welsh and her skin was, from what he could see of it, smooth, milky-white. He wondered how old she really was. With the silvery, rain-colored eyes, at least one could not call her ugly.

Fulk caught himself. The woman looked like a captive of war. This was no way to marry, even by King William's orders. If she'd fought like a hellcat every step of the way to the church, Geoffrey still ought to have been able to manage something more seemly than binding her head to foot. But then he could never fully trust Geoffrey.

Throwing back his wet cloak, Fulk said, "Come, let us take this thing from her mouth."

It was a mistake, they knew instantly. When he reached out to withdraw the balled cloth her mouth snapped open, showing little white teeth.

Then the Lady Alwyn screamed.

The sudden noise made even Geoffrey start. The two knights holding her shuffled their feet in surprise.

The Lady Alwyn had an amazingly strong voice, furious and vengeful. She lunged about in the knights' grip, delivering herself of a condemnation, at the top of her lungs, of Normans, devils and murderers all, in fairly passable French.

Fulk stuck the rag back in her mouth quickly.

Rotten luck, he told himself. Nor did he know quite what to do with her.

However, he was under William's order.

"Marry us," he told the priest. He was suddenly in need of a fire to warm himself, bone-weary enough to throw himself into any bed, with or without a bride. God knows he needed something to eat; his stomach was rumbling loudly.

"By the blood of Christ, be quick about it," Fulk growled. "Once we are tied in holy wedlock, I see I will have a lifetime to regret it."

Chapter Two

GUY DE BAIS FOLLOWED FULK AND THE two knights carrying the Lady Alwyn up the narrow tower stairs.

"It is a bad thing not to have a wedding feast," he commiserated, "but the fact is, there is not even bread to be had in the castle. This chamberlain, one Bedystyr, took the plate, flour, salt, and meat, and all that there was to drink, and melted away like a mist. There were not even pony tracks to follow in these cursed hills."

Geoffrey's knights carried Lady Alwyn like hunters with a trussed deer. They deftly flipped her on her side as the staircase wound to the second story. Fulk stepped down a step to avoid being hit by her feet.

"As we stormed the keep, this supposedly trusted steward then deserted the Lady Alwyn, leaving only the guard in the tower and a few of the thieving Welsh to protect her." De Bais was full of scorn for the Bretons, whom he felt were inferior to even the Saxons. "Fulk, I did not tell you this before, but we discovered sickness in the wards among the castle guard, which naturally they did not tell us at first, thinking perhaps to test us with the

16

plague. But Geoffrey de Bocage sent them to the village, heedless of it, and burned their beds and the straw."

"In there," Fulk told the knights. He bent his head at the low lintel as he entered the tower room. It too was freezing cold, but had a bed with tapestry hangings. "The Lady Alwyn was hiding in here?" he said, eyeing the bed.

"Hiding? Oh, no. At first we thought she was one of the Welsh, as she was dressed plainly and running about throwing stones with the wild serving maids and urging them on against us. Such behavior was not what we expected from the daughter of a Norman knight."

"Lesneven was a Breton," Fulk told him. "One of William's early allies. You said the daughter is half Welsh."

The young knight considered this. "There was a dog too, of the type they use to hunt wolves here in the marches, running with the women. A fearsome beast that sought to attack everything in its path. It was hard to manage the horses in such a wild fray."

Women and wild dogs, Fulk thought. The storming of Castle Morlaix did not sound like a battle de Bais and his cousin could boast of. He stepped aside to let the knights carry the girl to the bed. Fulk heard her groan. He would not untie her, he told himself, until he had time to deal with her. If there was any water at all in Castle Morlaix, he wanted a bath. Steaming hot. He needed to know if his sore, frozen limbs could be restored to life, or if the condition was permanent.

De Bais looked dismayed. "A hot bath? Fulk, have you not heard what I've been telling you? Castle Morlaix is a pigsty, neglected all during the revolt. The Welsh run in and out of it like rats in a cheese. Look about you." He gestured indignantly. "The old baron had not even finished the outer wall. Does King William know how it is?"

If William knew the condition of Castle Morlaix, he'd not told Fulk of it. *My miraculous good fortune,* he thought as he looked around the stone bedchamber. With hard work, and building onto the castle, which could perhaps be paid for by a levy settled on the Welsh, he supposed he could bring the fort up to what the king wanted of it. It would take years.

Fulk pulled up a stool and sat down on it. Sweet Jesu, what a rat's nest. And this was King William's grant to him. The girl, too.

Aloud, he shouted, "Will you see to a fire here?" Geoffrey de Bocage had come in. Fulk indicated the two knights who had carried the girl with a jerk of his head. "Get them to hauling water before I perish of cold. And send up my squire. I want out of these stinking wet clothes."

He saw the two knights stare at each other. Fighting men disliked what they considered base work; even the squires were slow to fetch and carry unless one drove them to it. Lofty Norman pride had increased by leaps and bounds now that England was under the Conqueror's heel.

Or considered to be so. The Bretons' revolt should have shaken them all, Fulk was thinking, as he bent his head and began to work at the lacings under his arms. Not to mention the ever-seething Welsh. Normans had still much to learn. As he'd found during his stay at William's court.

"And fetch me something to eat." If he didn't get fed, he would not be able to face the night's marital chores. "Raid the village, if that is what it takes, or storm the nearest Welsh fort. But beer or wine, at the least, if you can find no food."

De Bais darted forward to push Fulk's hands away from the fastenings. "Let me do it, Fu—milord." The two knights, galvanized by shouts from Geoffrey, clattered down the stairs to fetch the bath and search for something to put in Fulk's stomach.

His cousin came to kneel by Fulk's stool. "I know where the stores have gone. There's a local nuisance named Powys who leads the Welsh brigands hereabouts. They think him a military leader."

Fulk squinted at him as de Bais inched the heavy mail shirt toward his face. "And the missing chamberlain?"

"Carried all castle stores to the Welsh rebel, including the plate, such as it was, and Lesneven's treasury. Did they not tell us in London that here in the borders there is a Welsh traitor in every bed? Apparently there is one in every pantry, too." Geoffrey eyed Fulk's bare upper body as de Bais peeled away the padded undershirt. "Sweet Mary, I had not seen the new wound. If you were not built like a horse, Fulk, you would be all scar. Who dealt you such a blow?"

Fulk put his arms over his head and stretched. His cousin never forgot the three inches of height that overtopped him, nor Fulk's strength. Geoffrey had never won a practice bout against him, though he'd tried desperately. Now, Fulk realized, not looking at him, Geoffrey had even more to envy: Castle Morlaix and the title of baron that William had bestowed. Perhaps even Lesneven's daughter, through whom all this was accomplished, who was now waiting for him in the curtained bed.

Fulk planned shortly to give Geoffrey a place to advance his ambitions. But not soldiering with him in the field.

"Find the butler and hang him," he said.

"Fulk, we go to Chirk on the morrow," Geoffrey pointed out. "Do I chase Welsh butlers here, or the rebels in Chirk?"

Fulk realized he'd lost track of time. Half a day and time to sleep here at Morlaix was all he had. It was to be a damned short marital bedding. He stood up so that de Bais could strip away the mail chausses and the padding under them.

Guy de Bais stepped back to view Fulk with mock awe. "Man, there is nothing small to you. The talk in the castle

19

began the moment you entered the gates. A bull for a heifer. And pity the poor heifer."

Geoffrey looked sly. "She's surpassing old for a heifer."

The other knight snickered. "But not yet a cow; we must leave that to Fulk."

It was the sort of wit associated with weddings, but Fulk turned a cold eye on them. "You speak of my wife. If I am your liege lord, the woman is your liege lady."

De Bais reddened. "Fulk—*milord,* it was meant in jest." Hastily, he went to the room's ransacked wardrobe for something to put about Fulk's bare shoulders.

Geoffrey got up from his crouch by Fulk's stool, sword and mail jingling. "I am no expert on virgins, but I have found they weep torrents when they are bedded, bleed copiously, complain bitterly. But recover miraculously at the word 'marriage.' "

Fulk refused to be baited. "Then I shall have no trouble, as marriage has already been accomplished."

De Bais cast them an apprehensive look, but at that moment the squire entered the room with an armful of wood. Fulk took the low stool again, although his temper was not improved by sitting naked in the frigid air. It further drained his patience to hear de Bais shout the knights into hurrying with the tub and the water.

Aubrey had found a white woolen tunic somewhere below. He threw it about Fulk's shoulders. An iron kettle had also been located, but it was so large it took four knights to drag it up the stairs, and it stuck between the walls midway. The cursing and running for more knights to work the kettle free wore on Fulk's nerves. He sat with his shoulders hunched, waiting for the hot water that was eventually brought by knights running up and down the stairs with much clamor, perhaps to demonstrate they were not lowly fetchers and carriers. By the time Fulk eased himself into the bath the water was tepid, not hot.

He sank into it with a fervent groan, nevertheless. The wound that Geoffrey had remarked on had been gotten in

France the past year, a reminder that with some Christian knights of King Phillip it was still wise to protect one's back. The fire leaped, sending out warmth on his shoulders. As he soaked in the warmish water, Aubrey brought in a flacon of beer.

Fulk's eyebrows went up. "Where did you find this?" He sipped the yeasty-tasting brew cautiously, then grimaced. "Well, it could be worse."

The young squire smiled. "I traded for it, Fulk. From a maid I found here in the castle."

Fulk gave a sudden bellow of laughter that made him feel better. A young maid and Aubrey? The knights tormented the boy constantly. "Don't tell me what you offered for it. Did she accept?"

The squire's face turned crimson. "Milord," he murmured, eyes downcast.

Fulk poured himself more beer. Some of the soreness was soaking out of him. He had time to contemplate the strange turn of fate that had brought him where he was. A dispute about a wedding, no less.

That sullen hothead, Roger of Hereford, already excommunicated by Bishop Lanfranc for his insolence to the king, had wanted to marry his sister Emma to Ralph of Wader, the Breton-English Earl of Norfolk. The king had forbidden it.

It did not matter to William that the young Earl of Hereford and his sister were the children of William Fitz-Osbern, to whom William owed much. And that Ralph of Wader had been of indispensable service in helping William beat off an invasion of the Danish fleet. William did not want the two young earls, landholders and powerful in their own right, allying so closely through marriage.

But while William was in Normandy, de Wader had married Emma anyway. Fitz-Osbern and de Wader then had held a great wedding feast in Exning, in Cambridgeshire, inviting not only the restless Bretons of Wader's camp but also the Saxon prince, Waltheof, and most of the north.

The English were there in great numbers, nobles, bishops, even Welsh chieftains. Drink was served, tongues went wagging, and reckless Hereford delivered himself of a speech, saying that in refusing to agree to the marriage of his sister to Ralph de Wader, Earl of Norfolk, William had insulted his dead father, Fitz-Osbern, to whom William owed the success of the great invasion.

Fulk had heard the stories of some of those who had been at Exning. All agreed Hereford's and Wader's madness had spread like wildfire. Someone among the English had cried that William was but a bastard and his claims to England were based on the poison deaths of those who opposed him, like Conan, Biota, and brave Walter. But the greatest complaint was that William had not lived up to his promises to the men who had fought his battles—that he had given them only war-ruined lands that the sycophants who surrounded the king in London did not want.

The wedding feast had broken up with the Saxon prince, Waltheof, pledged to the insurrection, Roger of Hereford departing to call up his army, and Ralph of Wader to assemble the Bretons and other Norman-hating troops.

No wonder, Fulk thought wryly as he stepped out of the iron bath pot, that William was testy about marriages. If nothing else, the Fitz-Osbern-Wader wedding had brought him a war.

Warm with the fire and, for the first time that day not frozen or aching, he stood while Aubrey dried him off with a woolen blanket that still smelled of horses.

"Leave it," Fulk told him as the squire started to call for more knights to remove the kettle. He gave the boy a pat on the back. "Get to bed. I'll tend to it later."

God in heaven but he wanted his own rest, he thought. Not able to hold back a yawn, he went to the bed and looked down at his bride.

If he'd thought to find her fainted, or silently weeping, he was bound to disappointment. She heard his footsteps and opened her eyes. Their silvery-gray irises, finely rimmed with black, were alert and wildly defiant.

Fulk had been bound as a prisoner several times and knew how the body hurt when fettered. A cloth gag in the mouth was better than a leather strap, but it made the tongue dry as a desert and prone to swelling. If you fought the gag, it stretched the jaw hinges to an exquisite agony. There'd not been a whimper out of her.

Half Breton, Fulk thought as he looked down at her. He was not fond of Bretons, who lived in hedgerows in their dank part of France and wore skins and furs like savages.

De Bais had told him the girl had fought like a tiger and screamed like a virago while they chased her through half the keep. She had to be gagged so as not to deafen them all or further frighten the wits out of the greasy old monk.

He hadn't time to tend to her, Fulk allowed, as he eased in beside her and drew the blanket over both of them. He would, in his own time. At the moment he only wanted to rest his bones in a bed, enjoy the softness of it, and close his cold-ravaged eyes.

He would see to his marital duties after that.

In a few seconds he was asleep.

Sometime in the night a peculiar smothered, choking sound woke him. With instincts honed by a soldier's alertness, he came awake with a snap. Not moving, Fulk accustomed himself to the place where he lay.

In a bed, he told himself. He'd been sleeping on the frozen ground for a month and had almost forgotten what a bed could feel like. Castle Morlaix, he remembered. He was surprised at the quick, pleased feeling that gave him. A castle. Now his.

Gradually, he became aware that an inert weight was rolled against him, bulky and curiously unyielding. The source of the muffled sounds.

Jesu, the woman!

Fulk jerked up in the bed, blankets scattering. The fire still flickered brightly, so he knew he had not slept that long. But the devil take it, this was his wedding night. How could he have done such a thing?

A hasty examination told him the girl's gag was still in place. Her eyes were closed. His heavier weight had pulled her down against him, and her face had been resting against the bedding. Trussed as she was, she couldn't turn. It was possible she'd not been able to breathe.

Fulk touched her arm where the sleeve of the woolen gown was pulled back. The flesh, although smooth, was cold.

He swore under his breath. This was not so good. If his bride died in her wedding bed, smothered or strangled by some misfortune with the cursed bedcoverings, King William would have his head. There were no witnesses to swear that this was not convenient murder but merely his own carelessness. Wincing, Fulk knew William the Bastard would have his new baron exquisitely tortured before he was hanged, and confiscate everything—castle, title, the troop of knights. With fumbling hands, he loosened the gag. His fate rested with this Welsh-Breton female who had turned unearthly pale.

The cloth ball rolled out of her mouth but her eyes did not open. Fulk rolled her on her stomach and worked at the knotted ropes binding her hands. He heard her moan.

"Now then, demoiselle, hark to me." His voice was hoarse. "Are you alive?"

No answer. Her arms flapped listlessly as he lifted her to yank away the woolen surcoat. Was she breathing? Cursing himself a thousand times, Fulk bent his head to her pale lips, but could detect nothing. If she moaned she must still be alive, but he was not so sure. She could be breathing but dying; he had seen that on the battlefield.

He groaned aloud. It was Satan's own devilment that here he was on his wedding night, trying to revive his bride, whom he had nearly murdered while sleeping with her. And, curse it, she was still a virgin! What a tale that would make to bring back to London.

Hurriedly, Fulk laid the girl down and rubbed her hands and wrists. Little hands, delicate wrists, but cold as a corpse. He chafed them roughly.

Should he massage her limbs also? he wondered. If her other extremities were as cold as her hands she was surely half-dead.

With more haste than skill, he shook her out of the bliaut and shift until he had her stripped to her underdrawers. After a second's hesitation he peeled those off, too.

Holy Mary, Fulk thought, staring, so this was what he'd married. Lesneven's spinster was the best thing by far he'd found in Castle Morlaix. Her form was exquisite, girlish: high, pretty breasts with thrusting pink, virginal nipples, a sweep of tiny waist and curving hips, a light ruff of dark pubic hair. Here was no aging, unweddable spinster, but a lovely maid, flawless silky skin, a body endowed with enchanting grace. Her long legs were perfection.

While Fulk gazed she twitched. A shudder ran through her.

Hurriedly, Fulk slid down in the bed to send some of his own naked warmth into her. He rubbed wherever he could touch, regretting his sword hand was hard with calluses. With the other hand, he pulled the coverlet over them.

For long moments he held his limp bride pressed against him as he did his best to massage some life back into her. He found her soft, rounded bottom and resisted the impulse to linger as he pummeled it thoroughly. Fulk ran his hand up her backbone and across the back of her neck, and could feel her flesh heating. When he raised himself up on one elbow he could see patches of fiery pink skin. Cursing his strength, he wondered if he would leave bruises.

Nor was he unaffected by all this, Fulk discovered. He'd become stiff as a poker.

Her color was better, bruised or not. The smooth ivory of her face was tinged now with pink. The tangled black fan of her hair spread across the bedcover, the shadow repeated in eyelashes against her cheeks. She had a narrow nose and full, pouting mouth—he couldn't resist touching it with his finger. A strong, clear-cut jaw belied her faint look of a pretty child.

That jaw told the story. This was no maid but a woman. The Lady Alwyn was at least past her fifth and twentieth year. Age had not improved her disposition, either, Fulk knew; from the moment he'd seen her in the chapel she'd been a bundle of wildcat fury, barely restrained by the ropes. He could still hear her furious shriek echoing when he'd removed the gag.

He saw her eyelids flutter. Now he was certain she was alive, and would not die. His problems were just beginning.

She opened her eyes and looked up at him.

Bemused, Fulk regarded her, uncertain how unconscious she'd been while he'd roughly attempted to put some breath back into her.

What did she see? he wondered. He was a battle-worn knight two years shy of thirty, one of King William's loyal captains now suddenly made a baron and given her castle by royal decree. To her he would appear a hard-eyed stranger with short-cropped russet hair, not as handsome as Geoffrey de Bocage to whom women always gravitated, but already aroused and wanting her. Lying naked beside her in her bed.

It was for him to make the best of it: he could not stay idle there all night. Softly, he lifted his hand and cupped one small, smooth breast. He saw her eyes go wide as his fingertip stroked the hard bud of her nipple. She jerked, not taking her eyes from his, and grabbed at his arms.

Ah, he thought, it was not going to be as bad as he'd thought. At least she had not screamed.

26

"We are married," he told her. It was not the most intelligent of remarks, but it got to the heart of the matter.

He saw her bite her lips. Her hands rose between them, ready to do battle, and the corners of her mouth turned down. Before she could open it to shriek, Fulk clamped his hand over her lips. Not gently. Almost without thinking, he raised the other hand, making a fist.

It was impressive, the clenched hand held up before her face: glistening sword scars ran in grooves across his knuckles, and the thumb was bent where it had been broken by a blow from a mace in the Avranches.

Her eyes twisted, mutely, to look at it.

Fulk said nothing, nor did he lower his fist. Let her think it over.

After long moments, he saw her close her eyes. Then a drop, a tear, appeared glistening under black lashes, and slowly ran down the side of her face. She went limp under him.

"Come, it will not be all that bad," he told her. He regretted the gesture, but he would not endure more defiance and screaming; he was too damnably tired. And the truth of the matter was that he was already thinking about what was to come. Almost unwillingly, a hot rush of excitement flared in his vitals and made him painfully harder.

Slowly, he bent his head and put his mouth on hers, careful to draw back at once if she bit. She trembled, but did not resist, her lips tightly closed. He moved his mouth from side to side until the pressure made first the lower lip, then the upper, open to him. Her breath was sweet, and so was her taste. Fulk found himself suddenly flushed, and knew it was not the Welsh beer he had drunk. He had already decided he would have to be gentle with her if she remained calm. After all, it was her first time. But he had not counted on his own lust nearly getting the better of him.

When he nibbled her soft little breasts she made a gasping sound and tried to pull his head away, her fingers locked in his hair. That inflamed, and surprised him, as he had not been that long without a woman. Ah, but she was sweet, *sweet*! More hurriedly than he'd planned, his hand crept between her legs.

She fought him with fluttering, protesting hands, French and Welsh words mixed together breathlessly. Her voice was husky.

"Shhh," he told her.

He kissed her again, and this too was more than expected. The little mouth opened, resigned, and let him do what he wanted. Now it was he who was breathless. Worse, he could not tear himself away from the kiss. It devoured him. In return he devoured her. He broke for a breath, then went back again. He was amazed that the Welsh girl so aroused him. Still a virgin, she was doing absolutely nothing. She didn't know a thing, and he was about to burst. Her hand brushed his bare hip and he shuddered, violently.

"What?" she cried.

Fulk pulled back. He shook his head to clear it. He was not going to be able to do his duty properly if he kept this up. Was it the warmth, the bed, after being so long in the cold? No, it was more her smooth, silky body, her wary, expectant trembling. He'd needed a woman more than he thought.

Breathing hard, Fulk looked down into her face. Her expression was that of one bravely facing an unknown terror. He almost laughed.

"Demoiselle—" She was no longer a demoiselle, he reminded himself; she was his wife. He would fix that in a moment. "Madame, do you know what I am about to do?"

She didn't answer. Saying a prayer for her instruction by someone, sometime, his fingers stroked the tiny bud in the warm, fleshy cleft between her legs. He needed her wet.

Her expression became even more abstracted. Still she said nothing.

"My lady?" Fulk's need was pressing. It fairly shouted at him, a pain that was near to torture. But his bride's eyes were fixed, unseeing, on some point over his shoulder. He kissed her again, his hands stroking her belly, her smooth legs. He kissed her breasts with growing intensity.

"Stop," she breathed.

"No, no." His words were hurried. "I need to make you my wife."

Not for King William, now, but for himself.

He lifted his body over her, his hands eager for her satiny flesh. It was not going to be too bad for her; he'd promised himself he would see to that. He inserted one finger into the tight, slippery channel of her femininity and felt her go rigid. He stopped for long minutes to let her become accustomed to it. He knew he was going to hurt her and cursed himself for the impossibility of it all. Abruptly, Fulk sat back on his heels. He saw her avert her eyes. Well, he was as aroused as a rutting goat; somehow she would have to accommodate him. Gently, he pushed her legs apart with both hands.

"Put your arms about my neck," he told her as he lowered himself to her. He did not know whether she did or not for in the next moment he thrust into her in haste, felt the hot tightness, and the barrier break.

His mind afire, Fulk thrust all the way in and held himself still. He couldn't think. God's wounds, but this was tearing him apart! He would never deflower another virgin as long as he lived. Who would have thought it would be this way?

When he moved, the girl sobbed, softly. He held himself back, gritting his teeth.

Surely he'd imagined it, when she moved. He could only think, with the part of his mind that was still working, that she didn't know what she was doing. Shuddering, her eyes tightly closed, she squirmed against him. Fulk held himself stiffly, half blinded by sweat and passion.

Now she put her hands about his neck, as if clinging to something that could save her. He heard her gasp. He was certain that she did not know what she was doing.

Holy Cross, neither did he.

He imagined his pounding hurt her, but it was her fault, as she kept moving with clumsy uncertainty. He felt himself buck, lifting her, all his good intentions thrown to the winds. They slid to the edge of the bed. He held her in an iron grip, dimly fighting not to lose control.

He reached his peak in a roaring red haze. If he hadn't thrust his foot over the edge of the bed and braced himself they would have fallen out of it.

When it was over he collapsed against her, groaning and struggling for breath. He didn't know if she had reached her peak or not. Since she'd been a virgin, probably not. It occurred to him that he didn't know why he was worrying about it.

Fulk drew her up against him and held her while he fought for breath. Lustful minx. She'd put her arms around him and, for a few awkward seconds at the last, almost matched his frenzy. He found it beyond belief.

He wondered if she would be ready to take him again that night. Would she be too sore? When she had calmed somewhat, he would find out. Then he was reminded of the marital bedsheet, the proof of the bloodstains.

He lay back against the bed, holding the still-trembling girl in his arms, recalling the deficiencies of his marrying. A cursed brutal affair, there had not even been a wedding feast, and virtually no witnesses—certainly no one but his own knights to testify in the morning if her virginal stains were displayed. The thought repelled him. He'd be damned if he'd do that; it was none of his knights' affair.

Then he thought: perhaps he should bundle up the coverlet where they lay and send it back to William.

He tried not to laugh. Still struggling to get his breath, he stroked the top of the girl's head as she lay beside him. He'd be on his way to Chirk before dawn, to rout out

Hereford's rebels. Now was not the time to fret over what had or had not been done—the act was out of the way and it was legal. The deed was accomplished.

Wife. The woman beside him was his wife.

God's bones, last month, last week, *yesterday*—he hadn't even wanted to be married.

Llanystwyth

Chapter Three

WHEN IT RAINED IN SPRINGTIME ON that side of the Welsh hills, it flooded for days on end. The villeins waited despairingly for the land to dry enough to plow and seed, for a late planting meant a late harvest, which would lead to famine in the hot, lush days of summer. By Lent, some of the sokemen of the valley had already begun to build dykes to keep out their swollen branch of the river, which would flood even more as the water came down from the mountains to threaten their crops.

It was about food that Alwyn had come to see Geoffrey de Bocage.

She crossed the stones of the castle yard, skirting the places in front of the keep where straw and other trash from the stables had backed the drains up into puddles. She was wearing her second-best clothes, a blue woolen court gown of her mother's and a red velvet cloak that had been one of her father's wedding gifts. They became her, even if the gown was snug and somewhat short about the ankles. She was slender, but far taller than her mother had been.

Alwyn grabbed her underskirts as the wind caught and

dragged them across a puddle. She was still of two minds about the rich clothes. She had only put them on because when she was dressed for work with the castle women, the captain of the Norman knights treated her as though she were no better than one of the servants. To the Normans, she was only the hanged Breton traitor's daughter, anyway, the means by which they claimed Morlaix castle.

It had seemed like a good idea that morning to come begging a favor dressed as befitted her station, although asking anything of Geoffrey de Bocage was bound to be difficult. Alwyn stopped, one hand propped against the wall of the keep, to shake the water out of her shoes, as the raucous wind whipped her skirts around her ankles, then billowed them out again. She would be a ruin, she told herself, before she even got to the ward. But the castle was full of sick children, the last of the flour had been used, and the cook was grinding their store of dried beans to make bread. If they did not get seed corn for planting their situation would be dire.

The villeins called winter the devil's own season, plagued by sickness and famine. This year the butler had stolen most of their stores and they had a garrison of gluttonous Norman knights to feed. In late winter Alwyn had sent old Dunstan, the priest, to the monasteries to see if spare food could be bought. He hadn't come back for weeks, having gotten lost somewhere in Chirk on one of his drunken excursions. It was a marvel to her that even in famine times Dunstan still could find anything to drink. When the priest eventually returned, the answer from even the rich Norman chapter houses was what Alwyn had expected: what food there was, was being fed to their own people.

Discouraged, she leaned against the wall. She disliked asking a favor of the castle's Norman knights, but she felt as though she was the only one now who cared: God and all the holy saints knew she had never been able to interest even her father in the affairs of Morlaix, except for the levies of money and the men he'd wrung from it.

Curse all men, Alwyn thought, they were a plague to women. One learned to expect nothing of them. She had been given more than her share: a father who had not even seen her properly betrothed, much less wed, his ruthless steward who had left the castle beggared, and— even though she had fought like a madwoman against it— a Norman forced on her as husband whom she did not now even remember clearly. If any of them had ever given a care to the welfare of Morlaix, Alwyn could not see it; she had even to dress up like a peacock to talk to her husband's knight about how to keep them from starving.

A gust of wind caught her coif and she grabbed at it. She was coming unraveled. So much for her desire to look her lofty station. She should have summoned Geoffrey to her, not the other way around.

Not that he would have come.

Across the yard, a young squire carrying helmets saw Alwyn and stopped short, his eyes wide. He turned and bolted up the stairs.

Alwyn bit her lip. She knew the knights regarded her as scarcely better than an oddity. Castle garrisons were great gossips, with the knights having little to occupy their time with besides practice swordplay, dice games, fights among themselves, and rides about the countryside on endless forays, looking for trouble. She was sure they had discussed her endlessly the months they'd been there, told the story of how her father had treated her, a spinster, and how her current estate had been bestowed on a Norman knight who had not prized her enough in the four months since they wed to send her even a husbandly message inquiring after her health. This even though she knew Geoffrey de Bocage received his couriers; she had seen them riding to and from the castle often enough.

Doubtless too the Normans had heard how she had

withstood her father's chamberlain, defending Morlaix's people from his wickedness until he fled with what there was still in the castle to steal. All of it greatly exaggerated, she thought irritably. In the winter, some Cymry story-teller traveling the marches had composed a song of the lady of Castle Morlaix who was more righteous than Saint Brigid, more beautiful than Saint Anne of Warslow, and braver than Saint Agatha, who had been pierced with a martyr's arrows for her pains. By now, Alwyn was sure, the Normans considered her a virago.

She waited by the entrance to the ward a full quarter of an hour before Geoffrey de Bocage came stamping down the steps, pulling on his surcoat as he came. His cropped red hair was tousled, and he looked as though he had been wakened from sleep. Or a tumble with a girl, she thought uncharitably.

"What now?" He stopped short, his eyes widening. "God take us, what a transformation." His gaze traveled up and down her. "Madame, do you honor me with an audience? Should we go into the hall and sit down?"

Alwyn grabbed at her cloak to pull it around her, thinking he must pay his women with food to go to bed with him; it wouldn't take much, they were all so hungry now they would bed even Normans. She would have to remember to ask the cook to watch and see which of the women came to the ward, and speak to her.

He gave her a look that was openly lecherous. "Your husband should see you now, milady—you are always fair, but now by the saints, you are beautiful. My cousin would be more eager to return home if he could but see you this way."

Alwyn regarded him warily. They had come to know Geoffrey de Bocage as a man of foul moods; he hadn't concealed his rage at being left behind with the castle garrison, a nithing duty for a valorous knight, while his cousin waged war for William and covered himself, for all they knew, with fortune and glory. The knights' captain

38

was cruel to the villeins, reckless with his men, and a devil among the castle women. He would even force the scullery girls, unless she warned the cook to be vigilant.

"It's about the food again," she told him. "We are down to nothing."

He leaned against the wall of the ward, his arms crossed over his chest. "If you would stop feeding this riffraff that comes to the castle, we would do better. Half the starvelings are the enemy's, you know, come to see who will take them in."

Alwyn shut her lips against a sharp retort. The castle hadn't fed strangers in weeks; Geoffrey had given orders himself to turn back all but the Morlaix villagers from the gates. She kept her eyes lowered, knowing from long experience that if she showed anything but simpering meekness she would not get what she wanted. "It is the hunger I've come to you about," she murmured. "You know I would not bother you, Sir Geoffrey, unless it was important."

He picked up on the word, his mood shifting. "Hunger? What hunger is that? Is it the sort of hunger, milady, that —dare I say it?" He stepped closer. "I alone can assuage?"

Hastily, Alwyn backed up a step. Holy Mary, she had not expected this. She wondered if he had been drinking. He stood grinning at her, his half-buttoned coat opened enough to show an expanse of muscular bare chest. She had to admit he was handsome. She told herself she did not care what this Norman knight did, sleeping in the ward in the daytime, lying with a woman, if she got what she had come for.

Geoffrey was said to resemble her Norman knight husband, Fulk de Jobourg. She had no way of knowing if this was true; the man with whom she'd spent her wedding night was a phantom, she could hardly remember his face. But the castle people said one could take them for brothers.

Try as she might, she could not recall her husband that clearly. Although she plainly remembered their wedding night; how could any woman forget what happened to her in her marriage bed? Her husband could have been as tall as this knight or taller, well made—to her eyes he had looked all muscle and nakedness—with dark red hair bowl-shaped, cropped high in back in the Norman style. The face she did not remember so well; she thought he had dark eyes. God knows he had been more than enough for a maiden still intact, and surpassingly lustful. He had mounted her endlessly, seeming not to get his fill of her until she was so stretched and battered that she could no longer take him. And even then he had insisted she fondle him while he lay beside her. She had not slept at all that night, tightly held with his big body around her, staring into the darkness thinking on what she had felt. And whether it was best to try and forget it. He had gone before dawn, without waking her, and had left not even a piece of his clothing behind to tell that he even existed.

God help her, if Geoffrey de Bocage resembled his cousin Fulk de Jobourg, then she could only say that she did not care much for either of them!

She said, "The famine is driving the villagers to eat the seed grain. You need to send Hugh de Yerville to impound it so that we can put the corn away here in the castle. If we don't do this now," she pointed out, "there will be no crops in the summer."

He cocked an eyebrow at her. She knew saying that Hugh de Yerville should go was not the way to flatter him. All the castle knew they disliked each other, but Alwyn did not want to send Geoffrey to the village any more than was needed.

"What you tell me is no surprise, lady." He smiled again, silkily. "But so like Wales, where nothing is done properly. Tell me—why was the corn left in the village in the first place?"

Alwyn studied the wet hem of her dress. She had been

so certain he would do this for her since the Normans were as hungry as everyone else, and the villagers would not give up their seed corn without armed knights.

"The grain is the villeins' share," she explained, "it is theirs as their part of the crop. But this year the castle will have to use their seed for our own planting."

He looked disdainful. "By the saints, I don't see why you have not done this before. From now on, every year, you should take all of the villeins' share and hold it here. When you have the seed you can also levy fines for any transgressions, and take away part in payment. This is also the way to make additional profit from your fields. As for their debts—"

"Holy Mary, at the moment they are starving!" These Normans seemed to think only of wringing all they could from the villeins, and punishment. "I only ask you to send de Yerville and some knights to the village to bring back the grain. Nothing more."

His frown deepened. "Tell me, by whose order do you send me, now, on this business?"

Too late, Alwyn cursed her wayward tongue. She did not want the knights' captain to think she wished to command him. Or worse, that she dared assume the authority of an absent husband. But she did not want Geoffrey de Bocage to go to the village. The last time they were there his knights rode their horses through the kitchen gardens, tearing down fences, and Geoffrey himself had been roughly amorous with the good-looking wife of the butcher. In the past, there had been rapes and thieving. Some weeks ago the knights had driven out the Saxon tanner and his family, saying he would be replaced with a Norman. But a Norman had never come, and now the villagers were without a tannery to take their hides.

She tried hard to think. She knew she must be womanly and serve his Norman pride to wheedle him into doing this, but God and the saints knew she had tried her best. She had even searched the Welsh country as far as the vale of Llangollen, but there was not any spare grain to be found anywhere. She could not even borrow from her cousin Powys, because his people were no better off than they. But she could not mention that.

"Only a few knights will do." She tried a look of appeal from under her lashes. "You do not need to bother yourself with this, it is beneath your attention, but it can be done in half a day. A few of your knights can take some of the stable knaves and a wagon."

He was not fooled. "Milady, if you swear this is important," he told her loftily, "then I will think on it."

Think on it? "Holy Mary, it is seed grain!" she burst out. "Are you so ignorant you have never heard of that? Or do they hold back nothing for seed in your Normandy?"

He pushed away from the wall, his face gone stony. "I have heard of it, yes. My father has over a hundred hides of good land. But that does not make me a farmer."

He had her entangled in her own words, and that was not what she wanted. "I did not say you were a farmer," Alwyn said quickly. "Please, sir knight, do not find insult where none is intended. I have only asked you a simple thing, to send some knights to get the grain because the villagers will not give it up willingly."

But the damage was done. "Madame, you insist too much; it does not become you. If you still live in this castle it is only because King William allows it, through the husband he has given you. Accept with great thankfulness," he said condescendingly, "that the king has chosen to forget your traitor father. Also, you must remember your position is such that you do not give orders to me, nor any Norman." Before she could protest he went on, "I will go to the village with my men and get what you want. But only because I have other things to do outside Castle Morlaix and it is on my way."

Other things to do? What did that mean? It did not sound like a trip to the village to impound grain.

"I would never presume to order you, sir knight, I only ask what I must!" The devil take him but he was puffed up with his arrogance! Still, it was useless to hate; women always got the worst of it.

Exasperated, she tried wringing her hands. It was not hard to do, she only wished she had them around his neck. "I—we have sick children in the castle," she pleaded, "and overmuch to do. You must forgive me, I am only beset with worry. I did not wish to offend you."

He considered it. "I will overlook it this time," he said finally. "Besides, it is nothing you need to know, anyway." He turned back to the stairs. "But on our way from Morlaix I will see to your matter of the seed."

"Wait," Alwyn cried. The knights were going somewhere and he would not tell her. She knew nothing of what the Normans did in her castle, ever.

But he was gone.

She went back to her room at the top of the keep to change her clothes. As she shut the door and barred it she was thinking she had got her seed grain, but somehow she had lost.

She stepped out of the embroidered overgown and laid it on the bed. It was good to be in her room, a pleasant place by comparison with the rest of the keep. The quarters for the lord and his family had been chosen by her mother. The site itself at the top of the hill overlooking the river's valley was said to be very old: the bards said there had been forts of the Cymry, the old Welsh tribes, there since before the days of the Saxons. Before, even, the coming of the Romans that only the monks knew much about.

It was plain why the room had been chosen for personal use by the lord and his family. It had a wide window covered with a stout iron grille, the only opening in the castle not a narrow slit as proof against attacking arrows. It looked out on the west and the hill country of Wales, from which her mother had come.

Standing in her shift, a muddy stocking still in her hand, Alwyn looked out on the view. She did not know much about her mother other than that she was Welsh and that she had married her father. He had soldiered for pay for Saxon King Edward, called the Confessor, along the king's western border in Wales, and had met and married her. Alwyn did not know how this had happened; her mother was too long dead and her father never spoke of such things. But she had been told by old Dunstan, who had heard from the Cymry priest who married them, that it had not been difficult for Bruse Lesneven, descended from Briton tribes that had settled on the northerly coasts of France, to marry a woman of the same stock and good family in Wales. Alwyn gathered that when she was born her mother had stayed behind with her people while her husband soldiered in the Saxon king's service.

Sometime around then, her father had met the man who was to make his ill-fated fortune, William the Bastard, Duke of Normandy. Bruse Lesneven must have found something in the Norman to impress him, for when he met Duke William again in Flanders at the court of Count Baldwin, where the Conqueror-to-be had married Baldwin's daughter, Matilda, he threw in his lot with him.

Some years later, when Norman Duke William had declared he was the true heir to England's throne and would invade England to claim it, her Breton father, along with many of Baldwin's Fleming mercenaries, joined William's army. They were eager for gold and land, eager to loot William's future kingdom. Then King William was crowned in Westminster Abbey and he rewarded Bruse Lesneven with a castle and title. Alwyn's father had come back to claim her mother, and bring her to this place he named Morlaix.

She pressed her face against the iron bars of the window. Her father, a cold man who fought for money, told

few people his thoughts, and certainly not women. But
she had long wondered why he so hated King William.
She knew only that he burned with injustice. William the
Bastard was said to be cruel and treacherous. Even his
sons hated him. And of course the priests of Wales
claimed that the Conqueror was damned, that he would
suffer in the fires of Hell for what he had done to subdue
England, particularly in York and Northumbria, where he
had killed thousands of women and children and burned
and wasted the land.

Alwyn sighed. She had always found the affairs of men
violent and dangerous; yet she had known little else.

The sun had long since passed into the slanted beams
of afternoon. She knew she must finish dressing and go
down to the yard where the stable boys were cleaning out
the winter's muck. But Alwyn stayed where she was,
looking down across the broken curtain wall of the castle
into the green valley of Llanystwyth, which was cut by the
glistening thread of the branch of the river. The heavy
rains of spring had turned the hills a thick, dull green.
Against them, the villeins' plowed fields were muddy
brown strips.

When the bards sang of Wales they sang of emerald-
green valleys and woodlands green as the sea. Since Alwyn had never been beyond the borders of the march
country she had never seen emeralds nor the sea, so she
did not know how green that was. But the spring had
burst the trees into delicate bud, and the marshes at the
river's edge were rank with green growth that was the
color the whole world would turn when it was hot summer. In this wet country, mist streamed from the moun-
taintops like smoke, and when the sun came out it
spawned a sky arched with rainbows.

Wales and England were said to be part of one island
that floated in the sea. If there was water under it and
water around it, Alwyn reasoned, it could not help but be
green. Left alone, her Welsh land was rich and gave great

crops and fed the people well. She had never been able to understand why warring men would want to destroy it.

She turned away from the window with a sigh.

"My lady, that one there." The weaving woman from the village was at the castle to set up the looms now that the spring sheep shearing and carding was done. She pointed. "He hasn't moved since last you spoke to him."

The boy, whose name was Hwyl, stood sulkily in the stable shadows. "I've hit stone," he told them. "Can't go no lower."

"Search for the drain then and open it," Alwyn said. The stablemaster was supposed to be somewhere about, but now that Bedystyr was no longer there to harry him, he found such work overtaxing. The haughty Norman knights would not muck out the stables themselves.

She had come to watch the stable cleaning and see that someone carried the dung down to the gates where it could be left for the villagers to use in their fields. She stood with her face to the wind. When the dung was turned over the air was almost too strong to breathe. Mucking out stables was unpopular work; the Welsh mountain boys who came to Morlaix in the hope that being a stable knave was a step, perhaps, to becoming a Norman knight's squire, would lay down their shovels and disappear if someone was not there. Both Alwyn and the weaving woman wore high wooden pattens and looked like beggars, swathed from head to toe in old clothes.

Across the castle yard some men had come up from the village to clean up the broken stones that had been left at the unfinished curtain wall. A messenger had come from the Duke of Chester's warden saying that they must prepare for a troop of masons in the service of King William, who would once again resume work on the wall. A little pale sunshine trickled through the gusty clouds. Some of the men had taken off their coats to feel the sun's warmth on their backs. Their arms were reddish-brown, the rest of their skin bleached pinkish-white.

Two of the stable boys came out of a stall dragging a full sledge. They went slowly down to the gate. At the other end of the yard Geoffrey de Bocage's knights were saddling their horses. One or two were Angevins; they could hear their voices in different-sounding French complaining about the cold Welsh spring, and the lack of food.

The weaving woman, whose name was Adnia, watched the knights with narrowed eyes. "Glennda says one of them there is the father of her baby. You remember, milady, she was one of the girls them Normans took on Saint Sebastian's Day, when they come to the village."

Alwyn said nothing. That was the worst foray so far. Geoffrey de Bocage and his men had left the miller's yard, which served as a tavern in mild weather, a drunken shambles. And there was no doubt the knights had taken some girls by force. When she'd complained to him he had only laughed and said the knights had paid for what they got.

"Glennda's a good girl," the weaving woman went on, "and no roundheel. She had her cap set for a horse dealer in Chirk, a man of property. Poor Gwilym, her father, he tried to fight them knights off when two of them took off after his girl and run her to ground beyond his cow byre, but it didn't do no good." She shook her head. "It was lucky Gwilym's hands was empty with no tools or a hammer—if a poor sokeman raises a weapon to Norman knights they kill him on the spot." She looked at Alwyn out of the corner of her eye. "Now look, Gwilym's poor Glennda is ruined. Her man in Chirk won't take her with no Norman's brat inside her."

Adnia nodded her head in the direction of the Norman knights mounting their horses. "Since there was more than one that raped her, Glennda'll never know the father, neither."

Alwyn sat down on the edge of the watering trough and

put her hand to the small of her back. It had taken to hurting her lately if she stood too long, particularly on stone.

She knew the weaving woman was waiting for her to say something about the rape of the farrier's daughter, but there was nothing to be said. She had no power over the castle knights and she knew Geoffrey would do nothing. He had been with them that day.

She told herself it would probably happen again. In a small fief near Bangor, some of the Earl of Chester's knights had run wild, not only raping and stealing but setting the town afire. They had chased several youths through the woods for sport, and killed them with hunting spears. The outraged villagers had risen, then, and attacked a troop of Norman knights on their way to Whitchurch, murdering most of them. In an act of reprisal, the Earl of Chester had leveled the village, killing all the men over twelve and scattering the women and children in the dead of winter through the countryside. Few had survived.

"If you are down to stone," she called to the boy inside, "now cover it all with straw."

Hwyl came to the door of a stall. "There's no straw been spread in here the winter." He spoke in Welsh. "S'all dung."

No straw? No wonder the stable floor was so hard-packed. "Where has it gone?" Alwyn wanted to know.

A voice from the back of the stables said in Welsh, "The Man of the Vale came to the barns and took it. They needed it for bedding."

Alwyn started, and looked around. They were speaking Welsh, and she was sure none of the Normans understood. Still, it made her uneasy to have Powys mentioned so openly. The Welsh did not use his name, they called him the Man of the Vale. These days her outlaw relative was a man so secret he was never born, as the mountain people said. He melted with the mists; with so many murders of Normans to his credit, that was wise.

She knew what the boys meant by bedding. It was the devil's own cold in the Cambrian Mountains in winter, and outlaw Welshmen did not build fires. Still, to take her straw from the castle stables without telling her . . .

"No straw then," Alwyn said. She pressed her hand to her aching back. "God knows we cannot levy any in the village, I think they have eaten theirs."

The boys looked at her glumly. It was not too far from the truth.

The knights were forming columns. Geoffrey de Bocage wheeled his mount, leaning out of the saddle to shout orders. The stable knaves stuck their shaggy heads out of the doorways.

The Normans looked all the same in their hauberks that covered them in overlapping scales from shoulder to knee. Their swordbelts were slung around their necks. They wore conical steel helmets with a broad nose guard that all but hid their faces. All alike, the mounted fighters were menacing and impressive. They had defeated Harold's brave huscarl foot soldiers at Hastings, and terrorized England.

De Bocage's bright pennants fluttered. The stable boys gaped. The sound of the horses' hooves on the cobblestones was like thunder. Harness and spurs jingled, saddle leather creaked. Behind the nosepieces, Norman eyes stared straight ahead. The knights moved past the stables and across the yard to the gate where the drawbridge was let down. The village men working on the curtain wall dropped what they were doing to watch, their faces showing nothing.

As the line of knights crossed the castle yard, Alwyn shaded her eyes with one hand. The jingle and clank of metal, the arrythmic clopping of shod hooves on the stones, the grunts the knights made to urge on their mounts, made odd, barbaric music. They looked like conquerors. The stable boys were rapt. Geoffrey de Bocage rode past without recognizing her in her old clothes. One of the knights winked at her without turning his head. There was too much noise; a knight said something that she almost did not catch.

Beside her, Adnia drew in her breath. "Monsters," Alwyn heard her hiss. "Rapists—*Frenchmen*! If God wills it, you should all be dead."

Alwyn sat back down on the edge of the watering trough, her heart a queer, suffocating pounding in her chest. She did not know why the knight had spoken to her; she did not even recognize him in mail and the concealing helmet. She thought he was the one who had winked at her.

In his Norman French he'd said they were going to Chester, the seat of Castle Morlaix's marcher liege lord. To meet Fulk de Jobourg and his knights.

Her husband was coming back.

Chapter Four

THUNK! WENT THE BALL AS IT HIT THE table. Made of cowhide and dried gut, the ball rolled erratically from side to side. The cook's little girl squealed as she leaned into its path and tried to catch it, her arms wide over the tabletop like someone embracing a friend.

Abbot Ambrose paused, not attempting to speak over the child's screams. It was plain he was not much used to children or being interrupted; the lines of strain around his clever, deep-set eyes deepened.

Alwyn tried to catch Glennda's eye, but the girl had gone around the table to retrieve the ball from the rushes. The toddler shrieked again, happily. Her feet pushed away from the bench and she flopped on the tabletop and clapped her hands. At the fire, Hugh de Yerville and another knight were playing with the dogs. The big hounds sat back on their haunches, responding to a small piece of bone dangled above their heads with deep, rasping barks. Like everyone else in the castle, the dogs were hungry.

"We have been well aware, my daughter," the abbot continued, "of the lack of priests in the Welsh vales. It is a matter of concern not only to all of us, but to the holy archbishop himself."

He patted the front of his habit, a fine merino dyed purple, and smiled. "So many in these marches must have a revival of holy church discipline. Your own parish monk, for one, has kept an irregular household."

Alwyn bent her head over her sewing. She was letting the seams out of her second-best dress, the blue linen court robe. All her clothes were growing too tight. The abbot, gold rings gleaming on a white hand, pushed the small wooden box of cakes toward her.

The cook's child squealed again as Glennda handed her the ball. No one wanted to discipline her, as she was just learning to talk, but the noise was hard on the ears. Alwyn caught Glennda's eye as the girl went back to her seat. Glennda got up immediately, scooped up the child and carried her to the other end of the hall. At the fire, the dogs bayed throatily for the tossed bone, then fought over it when it landed among them. The young knights laughed uproariously.

"Yes, old Dunstan was living with a woman," Alwyn said.

She bit off the thread and rolled up what she had not used, knotting it loosely so it would not tangle, and then sticking it back in her thread bag. The village priest was so old that she could not see how it mattered. Besides, the woman who lived with him kept his house clean, fed him, and helped to keep him sober.

"Exactly." The abbot pushed the box of cakes closer with his long, elegant fingers. "But daughter, such arrangements are not to be condoned. We hope to set a better example of chastity here as true soldiers in Christ."

By *we,* Alwyn knew he meant the Norman church; she had observed their priests often spoke in military terms. Not a few of them fought with the knights. The hated Odo, King William's half-brother, was a warrior-bishop.

She reached for the wooden box and closed the lid with

a snap. "I'll save the rest for the children." She had eaten five honey cakes already. She wondered if the Norman abbot knew how hungry they were. They'd had lentil porridge again for the noon meal and for breaking their fast that morning. Her stomach was growling with gas.

"If he does not have a parish, what will become of him?" Alwyn wanted to know. She rolled up the skirt of the mended gown until she reached the waist. The knights had begun tormenting the hounds again. The noise was deafening.

The abbot's face was bland. "My daughter, reform is never easy. See what an example of a church in disorder we have in Scotland. That must not happen here. King William is urging upon all the Welsh clergy remaining that they subject themselves to a meditative period, and spiritual renewal."

They will shut him up in a monastery, Alwyn thought. She folded the gown's arms carefully and rolled the garment up tight for storage. She gathered they had not yet found Morlaix's Welsh priest to meditate and renew, as the abbot called it. If she were Dunstan, she would journey west into Wales. There was not much for the old Cymry priests now, under the Normans, although she had not found all that much bad in them. They were a good sort, and the small villages, where the more worldly priests did not want to go, would be lost without them. At least the Welsh priests had not been political. From what she was learning, it was hard to tell where the Normans' church began and King William's ended.

"A Christian life is the basis for God's work," the abbot said, watching her, "and none are so important to the holy church as Christ's daughters—good, obedient wives, gentle mothers, teachers to the young of the church's divine authority in God's holy word."

Alwyn pulled another gown from the pile. "We all lead Christian lives here, Abbot Ambrose." She had not been to mass since the roof of the chapel fell in during the

winter. But since Dunstan had been drunk in Chirk for so
long, there had been no one to shrive them, anyway.
"There is not an hour goes by that we do not seek to do
God's work here in the castle."

The huge hounds before the fire fell into a tangle, attacking each other viciously over the scrap of bone.
Shouting, de Yerville picked up a bench and swung it to
drive them apart. In Glennda's arms, the cook's little girl
screamed with excitement.

"Those are my husband's knights you see yonder," Alwyn said, "good Christians all."

The abbot made a steeple of his fingers and smiled.
"Ah, but those whom God has raised to power and influence are responsible for Christian lives in their care," he
said. "This demands of us the sacrifice of discipline, but
the rewards in Christ are many."

Alwyn pulled out a tunic she used in the weaving room.
It was clean but full of lint. She began ripping the seams.
"I am well rewarded, father," she said, not looking up, "as
you see."

He sighed. "My daughter, I was speaking of priests."

Alwyn told herself she could do nothing about the
noise. If the hall was overly crowded it was because the
abbot had arrived unannounced at almost the same time
the troop of masons had come. She had been expecting
the workmen, thanks to the Earl of Chester's messenger,
but she had not been prepared for the abbot of St.
Botolph's monastery and a retinue of his knights. She had
wondered why they ventured so many long miles from
Wrexham, until the abbot told her he had not forgotten old
Dunstan's trip to the monasteries to buy grain, and she
had her answer.

He has come to spy on us, she thought, as she shook
out the linty cloth. We were not important before but now
my Norman husband is the new baron and his knights
hold the castle.

The abbot had brought not only the box of cakes but

also a tub of honeycombs and bale of dried apples. The cook was guarding them with his life in the kitchen. Alwyn felt her stomach rumble again. She was beginning to suspect Abbot Ambrose knew more than she thought about how they could be tempted. They were all thinner, and in the castle many had gums that bled, a sign that they would lose teeth. He could have us all, she thought wearily; cloister the lot of us for life in some strict Benedictine nunnery, for a bowl of roast meat.

"You must find it lonely, my daughter," the abbot was saying as he lifted the lid of the box and took out another honeycake, "left to your duties here while your husband is gone fighting the rebels in blessed King William's service. But to be solitary in one's Christian faith can be propitious." He popped the cake into his mouth. "Like God's priests, women can also avail themselves of the deepest spiritual renovation under the guidance of mother church."

Alwyn was ashamed to take another cake, but the box nagged at her there within reach. She began unrolling the dress. "I'm no lonelier than before, father. My father was much away too, as you may have heard." She saw his face alter. Rebels, even dead ones, were not a good subject. "I have my work here," she said quickly, "which is a blessing. I keep busy, as women do." What else? she wondered. "And serve my husband dutifully, so that he may be pleased with what I have done when he returns."

"Yes, I spoke to Fulk de Jobourg in Chester as he was on his way south." His sharp eyes still watched her. "He is a fine, bold young knight, your husband. They are calling him the king's Sword of Justice for the way he has dealt with the rebels. William values him greatly, as must you," he said meaningfully. "God gives His children their fate to bear, no more, no less. And though you may think you have not willingly accepted this married estate that God has offered you in His mercy, you must submit in holy obedience. And strive to be your husband's dutiful chattel."

Alwyn was tired of trying to think of proper things to say. He was judging her with every word she uttered; if she cared more, she would resent it. Besides, what could she say to him about the circumstances of her marriage, except that she had had to be bound and gagged before she would submit to it? Dutiful chattel, indeed. She noticed he had not censured old Dunstan the priest.

She wondered if she should excuse herself to go argue with the cook about finding something to serve with lentils for evening meal. She had heard the hungry villagers were stewing greens from the marshes to eat. The cook said they were bitter and one could hardly swallow their nastiness, but Alwyn had been thinking it was at least something to put in the stomach.

She rolled up the unmended gown and put it back in the pile of clothes at her feet. The abbot had brought two monks from Wrexham in his retinue. One sat in the middle of the dogs' melee, reading his breviary; the other was asleep, his head resting on a far table. There were also twenty armed knights from St. Botolph's. She had put half the knights in the empty beds in the keep, the rest would sleep on the benches in the hall. The abbot was in her room in the keep. They were short on sleeping space. She would have to bed down on a pallet in the weaving room with Glennda and Adnia.

Beyond the abbot's knights, the master mason sat at the farthest table, his vellum rolls of plans stacked before him. He was waiting to speak to her; the masons would begin their work on the curtain wall in the morning. The builder was lean, not so young as the knights, but not old, either. His skin was brown from working in the open, and he was bareheaded, his long hair sun-gilded. He wore a fine brown leather coat. He was better looking, she thought, than even Geoffrey de Bocage.

"Father Ascelin will act as your confessor here in the

castle," the abbot was saying. "The good nuns of Saint Botolph's cloister will see to the altar cloths and sacred vessels for the castle chapel." He paused to think of something. "Has milord de Jobourg spoke of building a more substantial God's house in the castle yard?"

Glennda had taken the baby back to the kitchen and was now sitting with the young knights. Alwyn beckoned to her.

"A fine stone chapel," the abbot said, "is a meritorious gift for God's work. If your young lord will see to the building of a new chapel, Father Ascelin will gather the villeins to raise a church in Morlaix village."

Alwyn frowned. "There is much work to do with the planting right now." She had no intention of putting the villagers to work building a new church. "Perhaps the villeins can begin it after harvest time."

She had hoped the abbot would leave her the sleeping monk, and not the one with the breviary. If they were to have a Norman priest in the castle she would have preferred the one with the round, pleasant face.

Glennda came and leaned over her. Alwyn said, so the abbot could not hear, "Send the master mason to me in the yard." She stood up. "I must go see the cook about what we are to eat. There is not much here, as you know."

Abbot Ambrose laid his smooth white hand on her sleeve. "We have brought the wagonload of grain you asked for, my daughter, the church's gift to her deserving children. I shall have my knights bring it into the castle."

She had suspected something of the sort when she saw the St. Botolph's knights on the road with a horse and dray. She wondered if she should kneel and kiss the abbot's rings. She decided against it. "We are deeply grateful, father." She was surprised her voice shook. "As you doubtless see, it is much needed."

The abbot let go her arm. Alwyn turned away, pushing Glennda ahead of her. "Go down to the village," she told the girl, "and get some of the marsh herbs the villagers eat. I want to show them to the cook."

The castle yard was full of men and horses, and squires dashing about importantly. Hugh de Yerville's men stood examining the knights of St. Botolph's monastery, who wore tunics over their mail of woolen so fine it rippled like silk. Each knight's back had a splendid violet satin Saint David's cross and their breasts were decorated with Abbot Ambrose St. Les's family device of lilies and serpents. Their polished helmets glittered like silver. A chased edge of gold ran down the sides of the nosepieces. They wore gauntlets of lavender leather. Alwyn heard one of Hugh de Yerville's knights asking, too casually, how they handled a mace. A St. Botolph knight produced one and swung it about in a series of deft feints and blows almost too quick for the eye to follow. The Morlaix knights' faces fell.

The master mason came through the crowd carrying a roll of vellum under his arm. When he got close enough to Alwyn he bowed, graceful as a courtier.

She had already been told the builder's name, Master Ian. Someone had said he was a Scot from Fifeshire. It was true, when he spoke Norman French there was a rough sound to the words. The troop of masons had set up their camp outside the castle and there were women with them as well as wagons and dogs, a veritable traveling village. But the master mason was staying at the miller's house.

He spread the plans against a platform of boards that had already been set up, holding down one edge with his thumb to keep the vellum from rolling up again.

Alwyn bent her head. She could not make head or tail of the drawings. They did not even look like a curtain wall to her, only a web of straight lines and marks that she guessed were numbers. She was surprised that the master mason flattered her by showing them to her. She took a very long time looking at them, appreciatively, so he would not be offended. She wondered what was in the other vellum rolls.

"It must all come down," he told her. "It is useless to build on what is already there, it is out of line." He frowned at his drawing. "Not from the original stonework, but the standing of the wall, unfinished, for so long a time."

She looked at him sidewise. The master mason's eyes were on the drawing; he spoke with easy authority. She supposed few people gainsayed him, knowing as little as anyone did about masonry. She saw that he had black lashes, long and curly against his cheek when he looked down, and his mouth was thin and graceful. She suddenly felt his body through her clothes, even though they were not touching. A warm rush in sensitive places slightly alarmed her; she had never felt such a thing, just standing next to a man.

She moved back a step, and put her finger at the bottom of the drawing where there was something she recognized. "Holy Mary, is that an eye? What is that under it?"

He smiled, amused. "A pyramid, an ancient monument such as they have in Egypt."

The eye was bigger than the pyramid; it seemed to rest on its point. The little picture was strange, but she liked it. "It looks like the eye of God."

He looked at her quizzically. "It is a masons' mark, for those who know it."

She lifted her head to look at him. She was not wearing a coif and the wind blew her hair across her face. When she brushed it back, his blue eyes followed her hand. "Who has set the approval?" she asked. The master mason might speak with authority, but she had little. "I am sorry to be so ignorant."

"The Earl of Chester." His head was turned to her and now their faces were close; they stood almost shoulder to shoulder. "Hugh of Chester has seen the plans. Also, I showed them to your husband when I met him there. But they were seen first in London by King William's commander of fortifications, Eustace of Torel. The charter to build came from Torel, as this castle," he reminded her in his curiously burred French, "is one of the king's."

She had been watching his mouth as he spoke. After a moment she realized he was waiting for her to say something. Alwyn heard a noise and looked across the courtyard. The wagon with their grain from St. Botolph's was coming, escorted by more of the abbot's sumptuous purple knights. Standing in the windy yard she felt strangely flushed, and the sun was not even that strong.

"Can you build a whole castle?" She was baffled that he had taken the trouble to explain the plans for the curtain wall to her, as though her opinion counted. She wondered if he often spoke to the ladies of the king's castles and explained the masonry to them. "That is, not just to repair, but to build from the start?"

He began to roll up the drawing. "Yes, some few. None so early tested as Norwich." He looked rueful. "There is a triumph of castle building I have been hard put to defending, as I did not know it would withstand my own king's engineers so well."

Alwyn did not know where Norwich was. He had built a castle that had withstood King William? "When was that?"

"You have not heard?" When she shook her head he leaned against the platform, and crossed his feet. "You know of the rebellion of the Earl of Hereford, Roger Fitz-Osbern, and the Earl of Norfolk, called Ralph de Wader, and his Bretons?"

When she nodded, he went on. "When William of Warenne and William Malet defeated Ralph de Wader in a pitched battle at Cambridge, the rebel fled to Norwich, a castle new-built under King William's order. But when Warenne and Malet pursued him, this treacherous Breton took a ship to Denmark where it is said he is even now begging King Svegen to come to his aid and mount an invasion of Danes. De Wader left his wife, Emma, sister to the coconspirator, Roger Fitz-Osbern, Earl of Hereford, behind to hold Norwich Castle for him."

He stopped, to see if she followed him. Alwyn said quickly, "Yes, I know of Hereford and Ralph of Wader." She did not think she should tell him that her father had been a Breton traitor, too.

"I have seen the father, William Fitz-Osbern. He is dead now, but there was never a more steadfast knight. He was William's right arm, and they say that the Conqueror would not have mounted the invasion without him. Emma is Fitz-Osbern's true spawn—more so, I think, than that madman brother of hers. With Emma's husband gone to plead with the Danes to help him, Warren and Robert Malet came up with the king's army to besiege her in Norwich Castle. At first they thought it would take no time at all against a woman, but the castle is new and strong, if I do say so myself. After the first month, the castle still defied the king's army. So all of William's engineers and siege masters were summoned with stone-throwing engines and battering rams and sappers. They hammered Norwich. They mined it. They pounded the castle both in the day and by dark night, thinking that if the structure did not break to pieces and fall, at least Emma would surely surrender. Or that the men she led would overthrow her and give Norwich over to William's forces."

Alwyn's mouth had fallen open. She couldn't believe what she was hearing. To think that a woman would defend her castle against the might of the Conqueror's armies. "Did she surrender?"

The master mason stared at some spot in the distance. "Norwich Castle is strong. When I built it with Medric the Fleming, we knew it would withstand a mighty siege. But we did not know a woman would give it the first testing of our faith in it. Lady Emma de Wader withstood the siege for three months, and even then she did not surrender.

They say William raged, but knew he was bested. He had known Emma Fitz-Osbern since she was a babe, and she has showed she is brave as any man. The castle had not fallen, neither had the lady surrendered, and her men were still loyal. She asked and got favorable terms for herself and her men and they marched out of Norwich Castle and she sailed to Brittany, where she is now safe on Ralph de Wader's lands. The Bretons in the rebel forces were only punished by being made to give up their lands in England and quit the country within forty days. With the others, it was far different. They say the Saxon, Waltheof, will lose his head. Roger, the Earl of Hereford, is already in William's prison."

Alwyn knew what the master builder was saying was true, as no one would go to such lengths to invent such a tale. But a woman had withstood William the Crippler, the dread Conqueror of England, and all the siege machines his knights could bring against her? It was a thing such as she had never dreamed of.

This was a woman like herself, a knight's daughter named Emma Fitz-Osbern. If newly married she was not old; Lady de Wader had led her men, knights and men-at-arms, and the castle folk, they had not deserted her or betrayed her even under a terrible siege. Emma had held fast and won against King William and all that he could put against her.

Alwyn turned, still full of the marvel of it. She would have walked into the scaffolding had the master mason not caught her arm. She looked up at him.

"It must be a very great castle." She was struck with the truth of that, too. That Master Ian would be proud something he had built could withstand all King William's army.

His eyes twinkled. "And a very great woman."

She thought that was a strange remark for a man to make. She was still thinking on it as she made her way through the horses and knights in the yard and back to the hall.

The abbot looked down at his plate of lentils and greens with polite interest.

"It is what the villeins have been eating," Alwyn said quickly. She had to raise her voice to be heard over the noise of a packed hall at evening meal. "At this time of year I am told by the best sources that there is strength in the herbs the villagers pick by the river."

The abbot pushed the greens around with the silver spoon he carried on a silver chain at his belt. "I have read Catullus's dissertation on the means of a good diet," he told her. "A fine scholarly treatise in excellent Latin. The learned Catullus too recommends wild greens of the field picked in the springtime and stewed to make a salubrious tonic for the winter's weakened body." Smiling, he put the spoonful in his mouth.

Alwyn watched him closely. For a long moment the abbot's expression was still, then it grew very thoughtful. His lips puckered as though he were kissing the air, but not willingly. "Is there salt?" he said in a strangled voice.

Alwyn pushed the vinegar jug toward him. "Try this," she told him.

Down the tables, the knights of St. Botolph's were staring at wooden shingles put before them and small mounds of brown lentil peas and boiled greens. Morlaix's Norman knights doggedly attacked their food in silence. Lentils they knew all too well. Their faces said the bitter green stuff was no more nor less what they expected these days.

Alwyn picked up the greens in her fingers and put them into her mouth. If the abbot had read somewhere that stewed greens were a good diet then she would eat them; the saints knew she could not afford to get any thinner. The cook had offered to quern-grind a portion of the grain the abbot had brought them in time to make bannock bread for evening meal, but Alwyn had had the grain sacks carried to the storerooms. If the bishop wanted bread, he and his knights could eat what they had at home. It was still a long time till Morlaix's harvest.

"Tell me, father abbot," she began. It seemed time to say something; his expression was being noticed. "What do you know of the conduct of manor courts?"

Abbot Ambrose wiped his mouth with the back of his hand, and pushed his shingle away. " 'Sake and soke, toll and team and infangenethef,' " he recited, " 'hamsocne and grithbrice, fihtwite and fyrdwite within borders and without.' " He coughed, clearing his throat, and took a drink of water from his cup. " 'And the penalties for all other crimes which are emendable on the lord's land and over his men.' That is King William's own charter on the courts of manor and castle. Sake and soke may be construed as the right to hold manor court and by such it is usually known. The king upholds such rights, honoring what was just and familiar to the people from the late King Edward's time, but in all manor courts in the king's castles it must be remembered that the lord justiciar is only acting as King William's lieutenant."

Alwyn was trying to swallow her mouthful of greens. It was hard enough to chew them, but they seemed not to want to go down. Perhaps the cook had been right and it was all some plot of the villeins to poison them. She said, "What language was that?"

He looked at her in surprise. "It is English, do you not recognize it?"

"No, here we speak mostly Norman French and Welsh." She saw in the back tables the St. Botolph's knights were leaving. "We do not hear English much."

The abbot was looking more composed. He signaled for his water cup to be filled again. "It is the king's wish to retain much of the Anglo-Saxon systems of justice that minister to the people, but to put it in his loyal lords' hands and not in the vills' or any township moots." He drank deeply of the water and managed to smile. "Tell me when manor court was held here last at Morlaix."

Alwyn was looking at Glennda sitting with the cook's wife and her children. The girl was pretty, with the dark hair and white skin of the mountain Welsh, and her up-turned nose gave her a pert look. She had noted Geoffrey de Bocage's two Angevin knights never looked at her.

"We have not held manor court here for many years," she said. She was thinking she did not know what to do now that Gwylim the farrier had asked geld levy for what had been done to his daughter. The farrier sought justice, but to go to Wrexham for the shire court of the Earl of Chester would bring him nothing; Hugh of Avranches was said to be corrupt and cruel, and his sworn juries would be no better. "If the lord is not present, who else could hold manor court?"

She feared, for a moment, that she had been too forward. But Abbot Ambrose patted his mouth, hiding a yawn. "The lord is always present," he said.

Alwyn looked down the long hall with its noisy crowds. These were her people more than any absent lord's. Her father had never been on his lands enough to stop his chamberlains' thieving nor even to know what his daughter had suffered under it. Now she had a Norman knight for her husband who had taken her father's place. She heard of him only when others referred to having seen him somewhere—King William's knight, a wrathful sword of justice waging war and gaining glory and fame. She still could not even remember how he looked.

She had listened to Abbot Ambrose's lecture on a wife's obedience knowing there was no glory and honor in that; women labored without thanks for men who seldom, if ever, left their warring long enough to come home. They hardly knew what life at home was like.

The abbot of St. Botolph's said she pleased God by being responsible for all Castle Morlaix's people. But God had not raised her to the other things, power and influence; he would bestow those on Fulk de Jobourg. But as his wife and Bruse Lesneven's daughter, she had ministered to these folk and worked by their side and tended their sick and, God knew, was hungry with them, too.

She looked at the near tables where the people of the castle sat eating lentil peas and stewed greens. The Norman knights were not hers and she did not want them. But the tally reeve and armorer, the small band of men-at-arms, the two sisters who carded and spun, the girls for the scullery and the kitchen knaves, all answered to her. And that was not counting the villagers outside the castle walls, and the herders and crofters who lived in the hills.

She frowned, thinking it could not be God's will to let knights go unpunished for plunder and rape. Without a court, injustice grew like gas in a barrel of pickles with the lid fastened too tight.

She was not going to bother asking Abbot Ambrose if he had heard of Emma de Wader, and Norwich.

Chapter Five

THE TWO ANGEVIN KNIGHTS GALloped down the old Roman road from Shrewsbury in search of Fulk de Jobourg. At Dorrington, they stopped long enough to switch to their unridden horses and learn from a troop of the Earl of Chester's knights that Fulk was returning north after overseeing the confiscation of the lands of the imprisoned traitor, Roger Fitz-Osbern. But it was Geoffrey de Bocage the Angevins found first, camped in a meadow outside the hamlet of Owen's Town.

Geoffrey watched the French knights dismount, unshaven and covered with the dust of the road. They had made the distance from Chirk in less than two days. When they told Geoffrey their story, he was properly alarmed.

"So you are determined to return to France? Fulk will not be well pleased at this." The Angevins were wiry men, not as tall as Normans, but they were among their best fighters.

The older one spat into the dirt at their feet. "Pah, what was there for us in this country?" he said, disgusted. "This was not what we were promised, garrison time in a half-built castle in the Welsh wilderness. That is no way to make our fortune—and now we have been dealt insult and robbery! Our pockets are as empty as when we left France, thanks to this uncouth land of barbarians, where women are allowed a thousand improprieties."

"All we ask is justice," the other Angevin shouted.

Geoffrey held back a smile. What had happened at Morlaix was enough to make any man's blood run hot for revenge. He could hardly wait to see how Fulk took the news.

"Come, I will take you myself," he told them. "My cousin is camped down the road, at the stream."

They made their way across the field where the squires were hauling water and laying fires. Bundles of loot from the Earl of Hereford's lands lay piled with the knights' gear. It had been a rich business, bringing what was left of Fitz-Osbern's rebels to heel; Fulk's men had routed out castle guards loyal to the young earl and replaced them with forces sent from the south, deposed Hereford's vassals and sent their wives and families away, installing the king's men as overlords. By King William's order, rebel storehouses had been thoroughly sacked. Wagons loaded with grain and foodstuffs, as well as the earl's possessions, dotted the encampment in the meadow. Fulk's knights had looted the villages, although the villeins knew not one cause from the other; they stood sullenly regarding their losses as the punishment of another remote war in which they had played no part.

The light spring rains were still falling; in the knee-deep grass, the knights had made cook fires under makeshift lean-tos. Geoffrey herded the Angevins toward Fulk's camp.

"It is not to be borne," one of the Frenchmen muttered behind him, looking around. "What are the spoils of war, if one is not allowed to have women?"

Fulk's men were near the river. So many knights traveling with wagonloads of plunder had attracted a Norman jongleur going south. The singer was throwing himself into the entertainment with as much verve as a court troubadour, glad enough to show his bag of tricks for something to eat.

Fulk de Jobourg sat on the ground at the rear of the crowd, using his saddle as backrest and eating bread and cheese from Roger Fitz-Osbern's storerooms. The earl's own gyrfalcon, a great brute of a bird called Hercules, sat with its jesses wrapped around a tree limb. From time to time Fulk tossed the hawk a piece of cheese. The bird was very spoiled; it would eat sheeps' milk cheese from France, but not the hard yellow stuff from English cows.

Fulk was in a good mood. It had been a clean triumph the past few weeks, imposing King William's will on the Earl of Hereford's demesne. If there was any one thing that bothered him, it was the clutter of loot wagons and carts the knights' column dragged behind it, and the hangers-on, including the women. He searched the crowd and saw the Saxon girl standing at the edge, holding her boy by the hand.

Fulk lifted his wine bottle and drank, keeping his eyes on her. He told himself he would have to take her down by the river a little later on, somewhere away from his men. And do something with the child. The boy, about four years of age, was old enough to be something of an inconvenience. The Saxon girl still clung as closely to the boy as she had when Fulk found them on the road with a band of Northumbrians, wandering down from William's desolated north. The Saxon girl was trying to sell the child into slavery to keep him from starving.

A burst of encouragement for the jongleur rose from the crowd of knights. After the singer delivered several verses from the *Chanson de Roland,* accompanying himself on a small drum, they responded with shouts and whistles. The tale, which told of a sacrificed rearguard at the pass of Roncesvalles, in Charlemagne's retreat from Spain, was one all Normans considered their own. They even sang it on long marches.

Fulk finished the last of the cheese and wiped his fingers in the grass. The repertoire was not bad for a roadside show: five jokes, one of them new and fairly funny, and a juggling act with objects snatched from the audience, including cooking pans and some of the knights' daggers. He saw the Saxon girl had picked up the child in her arms to allow him a better view of the jongleur. Heads together, their finespun hair was the same pale shade of silver.

Fulk chewed the last of the bread and washed it down with Hereford's wine. The Saxon girl was a nice piece, if a bit melancholy; she still worried they would let her starve or take the child away from her. When he was busy, which he was more often than not, she had taken to seeking him out so as not to let him forget she was there. And she had encouraged the pale, timid child to come to him in a friendly manner, as though that would somehow secure her place.

Fulk watched her slide the child to the ground and take his hand. She needn't fear, he wasn't going to let her starve. But in his experience these things usually took care of themselves. In France, fighting in William's campaigns, he had found camp followers drifted off after a few months to settle down with some villager for a steadier life.

The jongleur had switched to a *chanson de geste* that had circulated widely since William's conquest. The historical tale told of Emma with the golden hair, the beauteous pearl of Normandy, who had been William the Bastard's great-aunt. Emma had been sent to marry the English king, Ethelred, fittingly called the Unready. Emma's contempt for the man she had to take as husband was no secret, until Ethelred the Unready was killed and a man more to her liking, his enemy Knut the Dane, took the English throne by force. This man promptly married beautiful Queen Emma. William's great-aunt had been twice queen of England and, more importantly for the king's purposes, reminded all of the legitimacy of William's claim to his throne.

The Saxon girl walked along the edge of the crowd with her child and some of the knights turned their heads to watch. Fulk wondered if Queen Emma had been as fair, with her Norman-Norse blood. The sheaf of the Saxon girl's hair, which she wore long and unbound, was almost white. According to the song, young Knut the Viking had been a more lusty husband than Unready Ethelred. And Queen Emma more satisfied.

There was only scattered applause for the song; they had heard it too many times. Fulk stretched out his legs and yawned. No one sang the old sagas from their great-great-grandfathers' days; they were considered old-fashioned. But he for one rather missed the accounts of sea battles and Vikings who died with laughter on their lips as they went to a hero's reward in Valhalla.

Beyond the jongleur he saw Geoffrey de Bocage coming from the road with two knights. The singer announced he would next offer a special regale, a popular ditty making its way through English fairs entitled "La Belle Dame de Morlaix."

Fulk put the wine bottle beside him on the ground. Morlaix? It was just a word, he told himself; he had probably misheard it. Out of the corner of his eye he saw his cousin and the men with him veer off toward the back of the crowd.

The boy launched into the song in his high tenor, singing of the beautiful Lady Alweyn, brave and virtuous beyond belief, who had been imprisoned in her own castle dungeon by her husband's wicked seneschal.

Fulk leaned forward. The singer dwelt on the lady's beauty: lips like coral from the sea, flesh as white as driven snow, and how she languished, hidden in the darkness of her dungeon jail. The knights groaned. Some gave raucous whistles.

"Fulk," Geoffrey de Bocage shouted. He was on the

other side of the crowd; he gestured to the two men with him. Fulk recognized Geoffrey's Angevins who had been left at Morlaix.

Fulk had no time for his cousin. He told himself the song was only a coincidence, a few words, names, that sounded similar. There was a long passage about the wicked seneschal, acting on the orders of the Fair Lady Alweyn's brutal husband, a knight who had married her for her castle and lands. The husband had wed the Fair Lady Alweyn by having his knights carry her, tied hand and foot and screaming, to the altar.

The jongleur had said the ballad of "La Belle Dame de Morlaix" was making the rounds of fairs in the marches and in England. Fulk knew little about such things. But he was obviously listening to some tripe about knights forcibly carrying the Fair Lady of Morlaix to her unwanted wedding. The lady wept and pleaded, but her cruel captor was adamant. He would become her husband and defy a just God by serving her shamefully. Nothing mattered, not even her suffering, as long as the evil knight gained her castle and lands. The husband went off to his battles, leaving his seneschal to oppress La Belle Dame de Morlaix even more by locking her in the castle dungeon.

Fulk got to his feet. He'd drunk more than a little of Hereford's wine with his dinner and it was possible he misunderstood.

The songmaker went on with his tale. In the midst of one of his battles, the husband was rebuked by a vision of the Holy Virgin, who told him he must repent, and make a pilgrim's journey many miles on his knees, to a holy shrine of St. David's.

Fulk stared about him, disbelieving. His own men were listening like sheep, openmouthed. Whether it was about his own castle and wife, or merely some troubadour's crackpot fancy was of no consequence. He needed only to pull the jongleur down from his perch and send him packing.

His cousin came up with his Angevins. "Fulk, a moment of your time," Geoffrey called.

The singer's clear voice, carrying in the warm evening air, related how the pious Alweyn of Morlaix, herself on the way to St. David's shrine, found her husband, sick and rightly starving, by the side of the road. A few of the squires wiped at their eyes as the jongleur sang feelingly of the Fair Alweyn taking her penitent husband in her arms.

Fulk whirled on his cousin. "What?" he snarled.

The Frenchmen exchanged looks. The older one stepped forward. "My lord, 'tis of your demesne I wish to speak, since in garrisoning these past months, Cherecourt and I—"

Beyond them, the Fair Lady Alweyn was redeeming her husband with her holy love, thus assuring him of a place in heaven.

Fulk lost what remained of his temper. "Spit it out, man!" The damned song was practically naming him, calling him a miserable pilgrim in sackcloth languishing in his wife's arms. He could see his knights nudging each other.

The Angevin looked aggrieved. "Milord Fulk, I bring news such as you may not want to hear. It is not only our loss that prompts us, but concern for your own affairs, as your lady wife has taken it upon herself to usurp your rightful duty at Castle Morlaix. She has conspired with the Earl of Chester's abbot, Ambrose Saint Les of Saint Botolph's, whom all know as Hugh of Avranches's spy, to assure a cartload of grain, which she sore needed so as to feed the castle." Heedless of the expression on Fulk's face, he plunged on. "We do not know what was promised the abbot and through him, Chester, but your wife has allowed the abbot to put his man, another spy named Ascelin the priest, into the castle under guise of serving as her confessor so that all and sundry are under his constant watch, including the garrison of knights."

"The worst is," the other put in, "that the lady has

challenged my lord by holding manor court, in which she allows that she will judge cases and administer justice like the lord yourself."

Fulk was hardly listening. He gathered his cousin's Frenchmen had some complaint about the way they'd been treated. One was mouthing something about wanting money.

Fulk reached out and grabbed him by the front of his tunic. Startled, the tethered gyrfalcon behind him rose, beating its wings and chirping. "What the devil is this about money?"

Geoffrey stepped between them. "Fulk, she *fined* them."

"Ten silver pence," the Frenchmen said together.

His cousin went on. "And when they could pay only six coins between them she confiscated their plunder, even Penicord's sword and mail. Against the debt, she said."

"The devil take it," Fulk shouted, "I can make no sense of this!" The knights nearest them turned to look. "What makes you think I owe you money?"

The Angevins were deeply affronted. Did Fulk de Jobourg not understand he was being betrayed by his wife, she was playing the Judas with the Earl of Chester, Hugh of Avranches, who had no reason to love Fulk de Jobourg, who was King William's man? As for themselves, they had been swindled, cozened, and mocked, dragged before a woman acting as a judge in a false manor court and accused by baseborn liars of violating a villein's daughter.

"You tell me my wife is conspiring behind my back with priests? She held manor court of her own in Morlaix Castle?" When they nodded, he snarled, "And for what?"

The Frenchmen looked at him as though he were simple. "We were wrongfully accused of rape, milord. The court's witnesses were only a plowman and a smith, even a boy, the swineherd, who said he saw—"

"Rape?" In spite of himself Fulk's voice rose again. "Who in God's name was raped?"

Both Frenchmen shouted back, waving their hands. Fulk gathered his wife had taken it upon herself to hold manor court and had granted the allegedly raped girl's and her father's claim for geld levy, as the girl was now pregnant.

"Jesus God." Fulk couldn't believe his ears. "The farrier's daughter has a bun in the oven and she claims both of you did it? I'm told there can be only one father, even in Anjou."

"The court was a mockery," the taller Angevin shouted back. "How is a woman to judge a court of law? Such a thing is only heard of in this uncouth country of the mad English where women are allowed to do such things!"

Fulk looked around for something to kick, found the leather wine bottle and booted it away into the meadow. This was no more nor less than what one could expect from the damned Bretons. While he was subduing Hereford's domain for William, his treacherous wife was undoing everything at his back. Manor courts. Fining his own knights. And, if what the Frenchmen said was to be believed, intriguing with Hugh of Avranches, no doubt to overthrow him and win back her castle by some foul plot. God's wounds, there was no end to perfidy!

"Break camp." He untied the hysterical falcon, upside down in its jesses, and pushed his way through his knights. He called for his squire, Aubrey, and Geoffrey de Bocage.

"Pay them," he barked, jerking his thumb in the direction of the Angevins. "Send them godspeed to France and good riddance."

"Fulk, consider—" Geoffrey began reasonably.

"Attend to your own men!" Fulk handed Aubrey the struggling hawk. "We will be on the road going north within the hour. I have other things to do."

He went off looking for the jongleur.

* * *

They broke camp in confusion and cursing. As was to be expected, the baggage wagons held them back. It was midnight when they got to the roadside cross that marked the fork to Lydham. The rain persisted, the night so black the columns were hard put to keep order. Horses balked and knights dismounted to lead them, slipping in the mud, encumbered by their mail. The wagons and carts wound away out of sight in the dark, and Fulk cursed them. He rode up and down in the wet, his voice grown hoarse with shouting. Every few miles he got down to put his shoulder to a wagon wheel to help the drovers haul it out of a mudhole.

At last Geoffrey said, riding up, "Holy Mary, get back on your horse, Fulk, before you break your leg or an arm. That is all we need in this mess."

The wagon came free of the ditch in a shower of mud. Fulk stepped away, wiping his hands on his clothes. Leaning down from the saddle to peer at him, Geoffrey told himself Fulk was a driven man, not only from the Angevins' tale of what had happened at Morlaix, but also, he gathered, galled by some strange dissatisfaction with the jongleur back by the river.

Two drovers boosted Fulk back into his saddle. He wiped his face with his hand, smearing it. "How far to Wrexham?" he wanted to know.

"Too far. We will have to stop before dawn, Fulk, the men and beasts will not go much farther."

His cousin grunted. They rode together down the column of knights, their horses shoulder to shoulder.

"It is too dark to see, Fulk," Geoffrey shouted. "We must find higher ground to stop and place the carts and wagons. The knights are growing surly."

"Christ's bones, let them be surly and rot." Fulk jerked the hood of his mantle forward, shoulders hunched. "Only Christ and the saints know if I still have a castle at

Morlaix. I may find Hugh of Avranches already at my table and the gates locked against me, thanks to that deceitful bitch King William gave me."

Geoffrey turned in his saddle. He had never seen his cousin so wroth.

Carefully, he said, "Ah, Fulk, you have not seen your wife these days. She is surpassingly beautiful, headstrong and high-spirited. All the countryside talks of her. She is no longer Lesneven's spinster, but a woman married, sure of herself, in full bloom. A little compassion, Fulk," he advised, as the other man shot him a burning look. "Women are but weak and susceptible creatures. They grow heady with a little power."

As his cousin glared at him, Geoffrey lowered his eyes with an expression of regret. "Like the rest of us, you will find it is not easy to say nay to your wife. She—ah, has worked her powers on me too, I confess."

Fulk reined in his horse. "What the hell's this?" His eyes narrowed, suspicious. "What damned powers worked on you?"

Geoffrey averted his head. "Fulk, God help me, it was not my wish to look on my cousin's wife with anything but the most chaste and pure respectful—"

Fulk grabbed at his reins to haul them to a stop. They sat knee to knee in the road, the horses' heads tossing.

"Stop mouthing at me, damn you." Under his hood, Fulk's face was dark with anger. "What's this puking 'chaste respectfulness'? What are you trying to tell me?"

"Christ forgive me, but I have committed a sin!" Geoffrey blurted out. "I love her, Fulk. When you see her, you will know it is difficult for any man to resist your wi—"

Fulk had reached across his horse's neck and seized him by the throat. "Have you been in her bed?" His face was rigid. "Damn it, I'll kill you!"

For a wild moment Geoffrey considered his cousin might squeeze the life out of him there in the Wrexham Road. "Sweet Jesu," he wheezed, "how can I speak?"

The iron grip relaxed a fraction. "I'll kill either you or her," Fulk ground out. "Or both. I am in no mood to be particular."

Geoffrey pried at his fingers and coughed, clearing his windpipe. "Would I cuckold my own flesh and blood?" he croaked. "I might love your wife, man, but I swear it on Holy Mary and all the saints, I haven't touched her—I hold my adoration of your fair lady from afar!"

"The hell you do." Fulk released his cousin with a shake that nearly unseated him. "I don't believe you. Any woman's drawers are fair game to you, I've seen it."

Still rubbing his throat, Geoffrey tried to look contrite. "Forgive me, cousin, for my unruly passion, but I swear it is chaste." He threw him an artful look. "For God's sake, Fulk, I couldn't help it. I can only throw myself on your mercy and ask your forgiveness."

Fulk had turned away. He spurred his horse forward. "Bullshit," he said over his shoulder. "We will settle this when I see how things stand at Morlaix."

Geoffrey watched his cousin's retreating back. His throat was dripping blood where links of his mail had ground into it. He was lucky Fulk hadn't made him a mute. The faces of the knights in the column were avid.

But all in all, he told himself, it had worked. What the Angevins had told Fulk was bad enough. But he was sure the barb he had planted would fester.

Chapter Six

"THERE HE GOES AGAIN," THE WEAVing woman said. She watched Father Ascelin climb over the rubble of stone at the door of the chapel to lift his hand and ring a small silver bell. "It's a disgrace, these lazy castle folk are so taken with Norman ways now," she said, pursing her lips. "Nobody tells time by the sun anymore. They wait for this monk to come out and ding-a-ling his thing so they can know the hour."

All the women laughed. They were sitting on the grass before the keep, carding wool from the spring shearing. The April sunshine, the first of the year, made the day too fine to stay indoors in the smoky hall.

Glennda, the farrier's daughter, lifted her pert nose. "I don't think he's got a thing to ding-a-ling. They are different, these Norman priests. Not lusty like the Welsh fathers."

The women looked at each other. "Or Frenchmen," the cook's wife said dryly.

Ringing his bell one more time, the priest went back inside the chapel to say his prayers. No one joined him.

"Well," Alwyn said quickly, "it would do none of us

harm to go to chapel. I have been to lauds, but Father Ascelin holds mass even before dawn, and I do not much like praying in the dark."

The farrier's daughter, her face flushed, was staring at the cook's wife. Glennda was now showing a slight bulge at her middle, but it hadn't kept her from the younger knights' benches at meals, and the other women gossiped.

"It's all changing now," the weaving woman said with a sigh. "These Normans are a plague on the land, more so than even when the old baron was here, God rest his soul." She crossed herself, and the other women did the same. "Over at Chirk, the earl's bailiff is putting out the Saxons, freemen and villeins both, and bringing in Normans to settle on the best land. Some of these Frenchmen are not even farmers, or soldiers by the looks of them, just landless riffraff from over the sea. But you can't say anything; the Normans think nothing of stringing up a body for twenty lashes if you but look at them crossways."

The cook's wife nodded gloomily. "They'll be in the valley next, you mark my words. They'll send in Norman land robbers and throw out the good folk what's had their farms since Prince Rhiwallon's time. We've already got the plague of their Norman merchants, like the one that came here after milady held manor court." She turned to Alwyn. "Those were not Normans but Jews, milady, they mean no good. I don't know why you bothered to talk to them. And the girl, dressed like the gentry in all that fur and velvet."

Alwyn hid a smile. The cook's wife had never seen a Jew, only heard about them from the villagers, who'd heard about them from peddlers and people from other villages. Who had probably never seen Jews, either. She believed the wool merchant and his daughter when they said they were Normans from King William's own town of Falaise. They had only come to the Welsh march country that winter, the merchant with a charter from King William to settle in Chirk and establish his wool trade. He'd just built a house and it sounded rather grand, two stories, with many windows. The merchant's daughter had been dressed in a gown of Flanders cloth with fur trim and a long red velvet cloak. She carried a pen and ink pot and a roll of paper and wrote down everything her father said about weights and the price he would give for grades of wool. When he was through, the girl rolled up the paper and gave it to Alwyn, who hadn't been sure what to do with it. Father Ascelin was the only one in the castle who could cipher and read. She hadn't wanted to let the abbot's priest have it, though, and she had taken it to her room and put it in the bottom of her clothes chest.

Now, she rolled the wool down the teeth of the carder and watched the fluffy roll of batten drop in her lap. The weaving woman was right; everything was changing. Many Normans, and even French and Flemings, were coming into England to settle on the land. In some places the results were as bad as what William had done in the ravaged north. Saxons and even some Welsh were being turned out of their farms, desperate for work and a place to live. Many of them were only looking for shelter, but the Morlaix villagers, who did not have enough for themselves, drove them away. Some went into the mountains and became outlaws like her cousin Powys. And now there was even a Norman tanner in the village, as the knights had promised. In the castle the Norman priest served mass, ringing his bell at dawn for lauds, terce at mid-morning, sext at noon, and none in mid-afternoon, and in so doing had changed their days without their knowing it. Now some of the Welsh men-at-arms and the kitchen knaves came for last prayers at compline. Mainly, Alwyn gathered, as there was little to do with their time after dark.

"I think it's nice to have mass said again," she said. "Although the chapel still needs cleaning out. It does stink with the floor full of thatch and mouse dirt from the roof when it fell in."

She had attended lauds when the priest first came, and had found the church full of knights at that hour, sleepily yawning and scratching themselves. Prayers by their own priest were something the Normans were accustomed to, perhaps even liked; they were fond of referring to themselves as Christian knights. They made Alwyn uneasy, unshaven, fragrant with musky male sweat. She had taken to going to terce at mid-morning, which was better. The chapel was deserted, the morning's work under way, and by then she had breakfast comfortingly in her stomach.

"The priest wants a new church," the cook's wife said. "I've seen him talking to the master mason about it."

The weaving woman pulled out an armful of wool from the shearing bag and set it down before them. The shearing had been washed but was full of small bits of dried dung. She picked at it, carefully, for the carders. "Master Ian's got enough to keep him busy, you see how he gets his men up early and works with them all day, going up and down that wall out yonder to see that what they do is done right. Besides," she added, looking at Alwyn, "when the villagers come, all they want to know is when Master Ian's going to call their boys back from the quarry."

Alwyn said nothing. The whole valley had rejoiced when the Angevins had ridden away with empty pockets after manor court. The villeins were still talking of another court for their store of grievances when a press gang had come from Chester with the earl's order to levy the village folk to work in the quarry, cutting stone for the masons to use at the castle.

Alwyn hadn't known what to do. She was not popular with the priest or the captain of the garrison, Hugh de Yerville, for holding manor court to settle the farrier's claim for his daughter's rape; they made it plain she had gone beyond her duties as Fulk de Jobourg's wife and acted far too boldly. But when the Earl of Chester's press gangs came, the villeins had looked to her to save their men somehow from the dreaded quarry work. On the other hand, as the quarry master pointed out, the masons working in the castle needed their cut stone. The village women wept and pleaded with her not to send their sons to the quarry, but the men were hard-pressed replanting the grain and couldn't be spared. She had wrangled for hours with the master of the quarry gang and finally they had settled on six half-grown boys from the village. With her heart in her mouth, she had watched them go. It was not long before some of the villeins went to the quarry and came back saying the boys were greatly overworked and ill-fed, and the miller's son, a sweet-faced youth, was sick. The men were angry. They felt she should do something about it.

Alwyn had wondered many times if the manor court had been a mistake. Justice had been served: Glennda and her father had money for their outrage, and the villagers were satisfied that the castle could give them justice. But both the Norman priest and Hugh de Yerville now treated her curtly, while Morlaix's people had come to regard her as their protectress who could do anything if they but argued and pleaded enough.

Alwyn packed the rolls of finished batten in the basket at her feet. "The masons can't build a new church," she reminded them, "they're making the castle wall. Besides, who's to pay for it?"

The cook's wife said, "Well, that fancy abbot from Chester isn't going to give the money for it, you can be sure of that. Did you see his knights, the finery they wore?"

The farrier's daughter looked dreamy. "Oh, yes, his knights were dressed like lords. Purple is a lovely color."

The cook's wife laughed harshly. "So's spoiled meat."

The weaving woman said, "Now there's a man for you, that master mason. The butcher's wife seen Master Ian taking his bath, and she says her eyes fair rolled out onto the floor when she got a good look at his you-know-what."

The cook's wife snorted. "She never saw the man taking his bath. Peeping around the door when he was putting on his britches is more like it."

Alwyn murmured, "Hush."

The master mason was not far away, going along the wall among his men, his vellum rolls tucked under his arm. He was not wearing his leather jacket. A full-sleeved white shirt clung to his broad shoulders and was tucked into his belt. The masons respectfully put down their tools when he approached. Alwyn had noticed even the villeins came up to the castle to watch the master mason at work. There was no doubt the Scotsman was a master builder; she had never heard his men challenge him, even in jest.

He still came to her to speak about how the work was going, and charmed her with the way he sought her opinion. She was amazed that he explained the reasons for such things as the deep footing of the outer wall to discourage sappers if Morlaix should ever be besieged. He'd also been pleased to find Morlaix had not one but two wells, both of them within the thick stone walls of the keep.

They were not dug wells, Alwyn had hastened to point out, but spring-fed, which was vastly better. He hadn't been surprised. In the old days, he told her, many of the old Cymry forts were built over springs. The wild Welsh also picked free-standing hillocks, or mounds, like Morlaix, from which their wooden forts would dominate the countryside.

On the back of one of his sheets, the master mason had drawn Alwyn a picture of a Cymry fort with its earthen mound which he called a motte, and the wooden tower a bailey. Morlaix was no different from this motte and bailey plan of the ancient Welsh, except that when Morlaix's curtain wall was finished it would have a portal gate and tower for defense, and the ditch around the castle would be dug deeper so that it could be flooded.

Morlaix's water supply had set him to thinking. A few days later he called for Alwyn to come up on the wall walk with him where they could see the masons at work below. He had changed his plans. He was devising something called a water defense.

Master Ian had spread the plans out for her. Standing beside him, Alwyn had listened to him explain that the mighty Norman keep was vulnerable, even strong as it looked, as an army could send sappers tunneling to undermine the tower's square corners. The presence of so much water was a great find; conduits could be built under the keep that would flood any miners' tunnels before they breached the outer walls.

Alwyn had stared at the plans for drowning soldiers in their tunnels. To send men digging under the earth of a castle was frightening enough; she thought of water rushing along, trapping helpless men with no way of escape. She wondered if she could bring herself to kill anything.

He'd been watching her. "War is not something women love, is it?" he said softly. "Only men are fascinated with it. And with sacrifice, and death."

Alwyn shuddered. "You do not seem like that."

He thought about that for a long moment. "No, I am no lover of war and destruction, my trade is all that is opposed to such pursuits, for in building and constructing all is harmony. What is in balance is true. Look, I will show you." With a long sun-browned finger, he traced the scheme of the outer wall. "To make a fortification like this, the builder must obey mathematical systems of order. Stonework follows nature's flow, supported by air and the earth. What is not true, what is in error, will fall down.

"So it is in life," he said, looking down at his plans. "What works against God, what is not in harmony with Him, destroys us."

Alwyn stared. No one had ever spoken of such things to her.

"Then all this warring is against God and nature," she exclaimed. "You just said this, that men love war and sacrifice and death. From what I have seen, it is all they think of."

He shrugged, resigned. "It is difficult to change the nature of men, which the priests call sinful. Or so they tell us. Look," he said abruptly, "the compass, which all masons use, tells us the way we should follow."

Holding the tool, two sharpened brass spikes joined at the top with a bolt, he drew curving strokes on the vellum. From the opposing curves he made the all-seeing eye Alwyn had seen before. Above it, the same two strokes again joined to make the simple body of a fish, head and tail. He put in a dot for the eye.

"These are the signs of the Mystery." His eyes were intent upon her. "Do you know what the fish, *ichthus,* stands for? It is what the early Christians drew on the walls of the catacombs when they were persecuted and driven underground, in the darkness, as a sign to others that Christ, love and harmony, still lived."

Love and harmony. Alwyn looked at the signs closely. These did not mean war and murder and rape such as Normans loved. It was a revelation. It even sounded faintly dangerous.

With a start, Alwyn realized the women about her were still talking about Father Ascelin's desire for a new castle chapel, the cook's wife noting that the master mason never went to mass. Nor did his men. Sleepy from the sun and daydreaming, Alwyn only half listened to their chatter.

"The guild of masons is very secret," the weaving woman said. "They don't tell others the skills of their trade, they travel around raising castles and churches and such like, staying to themselves. You see how they come here to Morlaix with their whole town traveling with them, that's the way they are, standoffish and deep. They say," she whispered ominously, "they have dark ceremonies and make their apprentices swear on terrible oaths never to tell what they know. That way there's no fear of anyone stealing their craft."

The cook's wife leaned forward. "I heard they worship secret signs and the Devil. My old mother told me that. If you anger them or do one of them ill they will leave one of their signs on your door, scratched into the wood, and your house will be terrible cursed."

The farrier's daughter gasped. "What will happen?"

"You'll never know a moment's peace," the cook's wife told her. "Things will fall from the walls that no hand has touched. There'll be noises to shake you out of your bed in the night. The doors will go out of true and you can't close them—why, the whole house will fall down after a while. And everybody what has lived in it," she added, triumphant, "will die."

Alwyn said, "The last time you said that, it was about the charcoal burners who camped in the marsh. You said they put signs on doors too and everyone inside would die."

The women turned to look at her.

"That was different." The cook's wife pursed her mouth, displeased. "Charcoal burners is different from masons, they don't do the same things atall."

The talk died out. Adnia had brought a drop spindle to amuse the cook's baby, who was jumping in and out of the wool bag, squealing. The weaving woman attached a length of batten to the stone cylinder and began to twirl it, twisting it between her thumb and forefinger until it became a growing, somewhat lumpy line of thread.

The sun was hot on Alwyn's bare head. She sat with her hands in her lap, eyes closed, thinking about the master mason. It was to be expected the women would gossip; he was surpassingly good-looking. A few days ago Alwyn had dreamt of him, something that made her ashamed to think on it, the dream was so blatantly lustful.

God and the holy saints knew what put such thoughts in her head, she'd surprised herself!

In the sun, her face grew even warmer. When she thought about it, a mason, even a master guildsman who built castles, would be considered baseborn. But Master Ian's manners, his knowledge of the world, showed that he was well educated. In many ways his conduct put him far above any of the men she had known, including her father, who'd been a knight and noble baron.

She tried to tell herself she should stop thinking about him. That after all, she was married. That was such an improbable idea, being some distant, unknown Norman knight's wife, that she almost laughed. She saw the Scotsman against her closed eyelids, suddenly, tall and brown with the sun.

Her dream had been a revelation, the first time in all her life she'd dreamed of having sex with a man. She hadn't known she'd been capable of such a thing. Master Ian had been walking toward her through a glade of greenest woodland. And he was totally naked.

If she had still been a virgin, she would not have known how to picture him. But now she was able to see him in perfect detail, his body sun-gilded, the heavy shaft of his sex stiff against curling gold hair.

In her dream, at the sight of him, Alwyn had shamelessly lain back against the soft, springy grass, lifting her arms to him. Master Ian fell to his knees before her. He bent his golden body over her, raining fervent kisses on her face, her throat, her shoulders and breasts. He was trembling with hunger for her; Alwyn moaned as he caressed her, every tongue-wet kiss sucking her nipples into such fire that she was wild, crying out. His hands finally lifted her to take her in one hard thrust, plunging deep within her.

Right then, at the moment of ecstasy, the dream changed. Alwyn had looked up to find Master Ian's face no longer there above her but someone else's, shadowy and dark, instead. The groans, the unsparing lustfulness of the body plunging into hers belonged to her Norman husband.

From a distance, the cook's wife said, "Milady, wake up, he wants you."

Alwyn opened her eyes. The master mason stood at a distance, waiting. Clumsily, she sprang to her feet and managed to shake the wool battens out of her skirt and into the basket. She felt warm and disheveled; her hair had come unraveled and a braid, fuzzy with lint, spilled over her shoulder. She tried to plait it back up but could not before the master mason approached her and bowed gracefully. Alwyn had expected him to take her hand to help her over the mason's clutter, but he did not touch her, conscious of the women watching. Instead, he turned his back and started off toward the new portal tower. She hurried to catch up with him.

They climbed the stairs to the top of a wall that looked out over the road to the village and the river. There was a slight breeze and it pulled at Alwyn's loose hair.

When they were out of earshot he said, "I have some new plans just drawn. They will keep me here longer than expected."

He sounded lighthearted. But when he spoke of his leaving, it seemed so portentous they stood staring at each other.

"New plans?" They were talking about one thing, but it was really something else. Alwyn told herself they were keeping a proper distance; from the ward you would only think they were talking about what the masons were doing.

"I have made you a gift." His voice was soft. "You remember I talked to you about the water defense, and the use of the springs under the keep?" He put his elbow on the parapet, and looked down at the men working below them. "There is something else which can be added that is useful in times of siege, but not always possible to make. I have been thinking about it, calculating Morlaix in my head."

Alwyn was distracted by their bodies being so close, when what they were saying was ordinary enough to be overheard by anyone. She tried not to look into his eyes. She tried not to think of him, naked, in her dream.

"From the bottom of the keep," he was saying, "hidden conduits will run from the springs under the ward so that any sappers' tunnels can be flooded even before the curtain wall is breached. One sluice will go all the way to the river. In this way the castle will always have an exit unknown to any who might besiege it." He turned to her, his eyes in the bright sunlight like blue lights. "The only trick is to stay out of it if it is about to be flooded. I have thought of it for many days, for the way into the passage in the castle, and at last it came to me."

Alwyn was fighting her runaway senses. "What came to you?"

"In the new church." His sudden, pleased smile dazzled her. "I have asked for permission to build a new chapel from the abbot of Saint Botolph's, whom I know, and he has pledged the money. I have several ideas for the plans, as the church must be quite small. Like a lady's jewel box."

"A new church?" It was all she could do not to lean into him, waiting for him to touch her. But the mention of the abbot of St. Botolph's struck a strange note. She said, slowly, "Does the abbot know of the plan, also, for your secret passage to the river?"

She saw his smile fade. He looked down at her. "It was customary," he said, somewhat stiffly, "in the building of Egypt's pyramids and other monuments of the ancient world, to kill the master builder so that he could not reveal their secrets. In the centuries since then, masons have become famous for their silence, otherwise we would be many times dead." He looked away over the wall to the blue-green Welsh mountains. "Milady Alwyn, I persuaded Ambrose Saint Les to give the money for Morlaix's chapel for the glory of God, and he did so because he knows me and my work. There will be only two people who know of the entrance to the passageway in the chapel— you and I."

Before Alwyn could say anything, he whipped out a piece of cloth from his pocket. Drawing out his compass from his leather mason's bag, he drew the eye again, and the strange fish. Under it, he made the letters IGM. Then he handed it to her.

"That is my mark, that of the master builder. And my promise to you that everything I have said is true." Without looking at her, he said, "If you meet me in the hours between compline and matins, I will show you where I plan to make the entrance to the sluices in the new chapel."

Alwyn stared at him. He was not like any other man she had ever known; his physical beauty made her tremble. But there was so much more. His words, his soft, caressing voice mesmerized her; she was just beginning to realize the power of what she felt. How much did he know, or guess about her marriage to the Norman baron of Morlaix, who was never there to be a husband? She wondered what it would be like to have him kiss her. To lie in his arms.

Below them on the road to the castle gate, there was some commotion. The masons called up to them.

Looking down, they could see a knight courier galloping furiously toward the castle, his long gonfalon with the device of a griffon streaming out behind him. The hot sun picked out the polished surface of his hauberk and helmet like sparks.

Master Ian backed away. "Is that not the banner of Fulk de Jobourg?"

Alwyn didn't know. She leaned over the parapet. The wind whipped the banner. The knight's horse strained under him, kicking up the dirt. The griffon was ugly, with a leopard's head, goat body, and feet with talons. The knight was close enough to look up and see her above the gate. His expression under the helmet and noseguard told Alwyn one thing.

The messenger was Fulk de Jobourg's, she had no doubt. He had the look of an avenging angel. And only for her.

The last time he had ridden up the road to Castle Morlaix, Fulk remembered, he was in much the same condition: overdue for sleep, saddle-weary, and in a foul frame of mind. Then it had been snowing. Now the day was unseasonably warm, but luck was with them and the dismal English rains had stopped. All around, the fields that spread across the sloping rise were greening with crops. A verdant burst of leaves had begun to obscure the gray stone pile overlooking the valley but not so much they couldn't see how the castle had changed.

His squire reined in beside him. They sat regarding the portal tower and the curtain wall that now encircled the keep. Behind them, the column of knights came to a halt. A murmur ran down the lines.

"It is very fine," Aubrey said softly. "And much bigger than I remember."

Geoffrey de Bocage came cantering up. "Jesu, Fulk, that's solid work there, better than anything we have seen in all the marches! Whatever else your wife has done, she has managed this well."

Fulk only growled in answer. The curtain wall was being done by King William's order; the scheming slut he'd left there had nothing to do with it. To his eyes, the very stones issued an insolent challenge. He would be more satisfied, he told himself, once he was inside, and brought the damned place to order.

He turned in his saddle. "Break out the pennants and

form up a double column. Look sharp, already there are gawkers on the wall there, waiting to see us."

Geoffrey rode back down the line, shouting orders. Galvanized, the squires galloped back and forth fetching swords and cloaks. The knights pulled on their helmets, backs straightening. The banners popped as they took the wind, color sprouting among the rows of lances.

Fulk fingered his stubble. He had more than a night's growth but there was no time to remedy that. Behind the knights, the wagons, drovers, their boys, and the women stretched out to the rear like a traveling show: they were all the worse for hard travel and looked it. But the devil take it, they would give this nest of snakes a taste of how a Norman baron approached his own castle. He would make them all shake in their shoes.

"Aubrey," he told his squire, "blow us a blast on your horn, and keep at it until we are inside the yard."

The boy gave him a strange look. "Fulk, I do not remember what your lady looks like. How will I know her?"

"Shut up," Fulk told him.

He leaned over his saddle and reached for the Earl of Hereford's hawk. Hooded, bells jingling, the big gyrfalcon lifted its feet and groped its way onto his wrist. Fulk raised his other hand high over his head, then thrust it forward. The column of knights began to move.

Chapter Seven

HE WAS FINALLY THERE. ALWYN wished she could stop trembling, but in God's name who wouldn't shake from head to foot to meet a husband one hardly knew?

The spinning sisters met her at the door to the keep with the armorer's wife and a crowd of scullery maids. "Your husband, milady," the spinners twittered excitedly. "Oh, milady, your husband is coming!"

"God and the saints," she answered, "how can one not see an army approaching?" She followed the armorer's wife up the tower stairs. At the landing she remembered to send the scullery girls back to the kitchen with a message for the cook to start the fires. She went into her room and closed the door.

Alwyn leaned against it, breathless. Adnia and the farrier's daughter had already pulled out her clothes from the chest. "The red gown," she told them. "I have already let out the seams."

This was a moment they'd known would come, and yet they were hardly prepared for it.

"So many men," the armorer's wife exclaimed, "such a fine company of knights, and even baggage trains, no doubt filled with plunder!" She pulled Alwyn around to unlace the back of her dress. "It would seem Milord Fulk de Jobourg has many more knights than when he left the Morlaix. How do you suppose this has happened?"

The weaver woman pushed her out of the way. "Now, milady, don't tear at your clothes like that. You must look pretty and honor us before your lord husband and his men."

The other woman seized Alwyn's braids, combing the hair free with her fingers. "Yes, you must remember you are a noble baron's daughter, related to Welsh princes on your mother's side."

Alwyn shivered. "What are you doing? I am not a maid, to wear my hair unbound!"

They shushed her. "You are going to look beautiful," the weaving woman told her.

They settled the red gown over her head. Already the knights' horns sounded closer. The armorer's wife stood back to watch. They had found a silver circlet, something of her mother's, in the chest. Glennda pushed it down on Alwyn's forehead. It was fancy, with small red stones set into the silver but it was too tight, as were all her mother's things. Alwyn pulled it off and threw it on the bed.

Adnia brought it back. The women seemed united in an unspoken pact to have her dressed in all the oddments of splendor they could find. "You must wear it," the weaving woman said, pushing it down on her brow.

"The silk shoon." The armorer's wife was tugging at her foot.

Alwyn stood on first one foot and then the other as they changed her shoes. The weaver woman stepped in front of her to pinch her cheeks to make them red. The gown was too tight, the laces even tighter; she could hardly breathe.

The winding of the horns told that Fulk de Jobourg and his men were almost at the gate.

"Ah, look at her," Glennda said.

Alwyn's hair streamed over her shoulders and fell in back to her waist. The gown's color was like bright blood. The skirt was too short and the gold thread in the embroidery across her bosom scratched. She could tell from their faces how she looked.

They were right, she thought, as the women tugged at the gown's wrinkled skirt to make it settle, she was a baron's daughter, she had to honor her people. She decided she wouldn't mention holding manor court right away, perhaps not even for a week. With luck, she would not have to tell about the village boys and the quarry levy for at least as long.

"I will stand in the yard," she said, "with the men-at-arms behind me." She had never done this before. "I think we will greet them just inside the gate."

"You must give them something," the weaver woman told her. "You must meet your lord with a gift of welcome. It is the custom."

A gift of welcome. It was too late to open some of their hoarded beer just for a cup, and a dish of meat was out of the question, as the castle was still short of food. There was a gold ring of her father's but it would take too long to find it. Besides, a gold ring might be too grand; she didn't know her husband all that well. She remembered the abbot of St. Botolph's, and the wooden box still hidden somewhere in the kitchen.

It was only a token, she told herself. "Yes, there should be a welcoming gift," Alwyn agreed. "I will offer him a plate of the abbot's honeycakes."

The villagers had begun to stream up the road to the castle, following the double column of the knights. A gaggle of village boys raced ahead, almost under the horses' hooves, to reach the gate, where two of the men-at-arms chased them back. The wall walk above the portal gate was crowded with castle people. The column of knights advanced at a hard trot, pennants whipping, the blasts of the squires' horns echoing away into the valley.

Fulk kept his eyes on the new portal. Just beyond the arch, in the sunshine of the yard, he could see a woman in a crimson gown. A line of Welsh and Saxon men-at-arms flanked her.

That was his wife, he knew, even before he could see her face. He felt a surge of wrath. The place was thick with crowds, villagers coming behind them on the road, and she was going to brazen it out in front of them all.

She had gall, he would concede that.

Fulk dug his spurs into his horse. The destrier, surprised, put down his head and tried to buck. Fulk reined him in. Fighting the bit, the big gray lunged forward. They burst at the gallop through the portal gate and hauled up in a clatter of hooves before the slim figure in red. Fulk held the shying horse, glaring down at her.

She stepped forward, holding a silver plate up to him in both hands. The castle people had run from the destrier's charge, but she hadn't backed a step. "Milord," she said, clearly, "welcome to Morlaix."

The horse snorted, tossing his head. Fulk held Hereford's gyrfalcon high on his arm, and leaned to look into her face.

Here, he told himself, was an obdurate, white-faced bitch for you. After what she'd done with Hugh of Avranches, with the Angevins and some damned manor court, she dared stand up to him like this? She was no sweet, tender maid—he remembered the way she'd screamed and fought in the chapel that night, needing the gag and the ropes.

In the next moment he remembered her silvery eyes with their black rims. Black hair, long and loosened, fell down from a silver circlet set with red stones. And that face, he thought, staring. The cool, full mouth. He remembered kissing it.

Sweet Jesu, it was no wonder his cousin had some complaint about how she had worked her wiles on him. He couldn't shout at her where they were, in front of everyone. Nor could he strike her, much as he wanted to.

"Milord," she said again, holding the plate up to him.

"I greet you, madame." Grim-faced, he reached out for the gift on the plate. Whatever it was, it crumbled before he could get his fingers around it. Some sort of cake.

He made a pretense of putting the crumbs to his mouth. "God keep you, and all in my demesne." He was prepared to say anything to get it over with. He wanted to get her alone.

Geoffrey de Bocage and Aubrey came up as the column of knights guided their horses around Fulk into the yard. Someone in the crowd on the wall walk cheered. A few of the squires blew their horns in answer. There were more cheers. Nothing was going to happen, after all.

Fulk bent from the saddle and said, so low that only she could hear, "I paid those damned Angevins twenty silver coins for what they claim your donkey court did to them." He saw her look, startled. "But that is nothing, milady, considering the grave offense you have given me. I want to hear from your own lips what you have intrigued with Hugh of Avranches and his scheming abbot."

She did not look so cool now, he thought, satisfied. Around them, the castle people surged toward the knights, eager for news of what they had done southward.

"We have brought baggage with us," he said, raising his voice over the din, "and much food from Hereford's stores. Get some people to see to it." Restless, the gyrfalcon on his wrist twisted its hooded head and half opened its wings. Fulk tightened his grip on its jesses.

The woman in the red dress looked up at him. He saw that she was pale. "Milord, I know nothing of intriguing," she said indignantly. "I do not know what you are talking about. As for—"

He cut her off. "I have brought a leman with me. I want a room found for her and her boy in the keep."

Touching his spurs to the destrier's flanks, he rode off to the stables.

Alwyn stared after him.

Her first thought was that she still didn't know what he looked like. Sitting on his great horse, he was some image of a Norman knight wearing a stained white tunic over mail, a rude and implacable shape holding a brute of a hawk, his head and face hidden by helmet and metal nosepiece. In one breath he had accused her of tricking the knights who had raped the farrier's daughter and scheming behind his back with the Earl of Chester. And then in another he'd made clear he had a woman with him and he wanted her to be in a room in the castle.

It took her a moment to understand. Then with a rush of outrage so great it made her head pound, she knew there could not have been greater affront.

It had been insult, astonishing, calculated *insult*, every word of it, as she stood with a welcoming gift in her hand, his wife, and the chatelaine of this castle. Holy Mary, it was a mercy the people around them had not heard. Enraged, she realized that was what he intended.

"Milady." It was the tally reeve, who acted now as Morlaix's butler. "The Norman knights have told me there are wagons to be unloaded."

She turned to stare at him.

The evening meal. The thought cut through the red haze of her rage. They needed what food the wagons had brought to feed this great crowd of knights. She counted in her head, quickly. There were so many that some would have to be fed outside in the ward; the hall would not take all of them.

"Milady?" the tally reeve said again.

Worse, she would have to sit with her Norman husband at evening meal, listening again to the insults he growled under his breath at her, while no doubt his leman sat at table somewhere, watching and gloating. After all these months, this was how she was rewarded.

If her father were alive he would kill him, she told herself. No knight dealt deadly affront like that, not even to a woman.

The reeve was regarding her anxiously. "Milady, have I —have we—done something? You have but to say it, and I will see to it."

Alwyn did not hear. Her husband, a total stranger, had sat on his horse and loftily accused her of vile things. In front of everyone he had treated her like a slut. God rot him, she did not need anyone to avenge her! She would take care of it herself.

"The wagons," the reeve reminded her.

"The cook," she said. "Call the cook and the kitchen knaves. When the wagons are unloaded, put aside what the cook tells you he needs." If she had her way, she would poison every Norman within the walls while they sat gorging themselves. "They are wise to bring their own food," she told him. "If it were my choice, I would put them all to eating what we have been eating these weeks. Those cursed weeds from the marshes and lentil peas."

The door to the upper room in the keep was wide open. Going in, Alwyn stumbled over the clutter. Someone had brought in a knight's gear: lances, a tall kite-shaped Norman shield, even a saddle, and thrown them down on the floor. Rope-tied bundles of what looked like spare clothing were tossed on the bed. A youth came running up the stairs with a painted wooden stand and stood waiting for her to tell him where to put it.

"Milady, it is for milord Fulk de Jobourg's gyrfalcon." He was a good-looking youth, slender, with curly dark hair and dark eyes. He added, with obvious pride, "The hawk was formerly the Earl of Hereford's."

Alwyn pushed the bundles to one side and sat down on the bed. A hard pulse still beat in her temples and her neck and shoulders felt as if they were in a vise. There was just so much one could endure. Did he think to leave his hawk and gear in her room, while he slept with his woman elsewhere? The whole castle would know about it before nightfall.

"I am his squire, Aubrey Fitz-Peverell, milady," the boy said. He looked around. "I will put things to order if you will but tell me where."

Alwyn lifted her head. The Normans were turning everything at Morlaix upside down. Her room was no longer hers, not with his belongings piled all over the floor. "I am not going to have a hawk in my room," she said. "This is not a stable, and I do not tend to animals."

It had occurred to her that if her husband did not sleep with his woman then he would sleep here, with her, in her bed. Holy Mary, did she want that? She would be as much invaded by his naked, arrogant body as by his belongings, which filled up her room. "Where is your lord?" she wanted to know.

The boy put down the painted stand and rested his arm on it. "He is below, my lady, with the wagons brought from the Earl of Hereford's estates. He and Geoffrey de Bocage see to the treasure's safe disposal."

Perhaps she would not see him until the evening meal. He would have to sit with her then. "Take that thing back downstairs," she told the squire. "I am still chatelaine here. I will decide if I wish hawks and other animals living with me."

The boy looked surprised. It was obvious his orders had been otherwise. But he picked up the stand and went out and closed the door.

As she crossed the ward, Alwyn saw the Saxon woman. It was not hard to know who she was; she was the best looking of the women who had come with the wagons: tall, with a fall of fair, unbound hair. She was dressed in a rich blue tunic with a large silver brooch pinned to the shoulder, and she wore several silver and gold neck chains. The finery did not look new, more like loot from Hereford's castles, but they were her husband's gifts, Alwyn supposed. She noticed the Saxon had a small boy by the hand.

Alwyn stopped for a moment in the lee of the wagons, feeling ill. Sweet heaven, but she had a blinding headache. It did not pay to be this angry. Nor was her humiliation any less with the sight of her husband's leman and child. She could not tell if the boy looked much like Fulk de Jobourg or not—God rot it, she was still wife to a man she had yet to see clearly! She was so vexed she wanted to scream.

The Norman priest, Father Ascelin, came across the crowded ward, his thin cheeks sucked in. From his expression Alwyn knew he wanted to ask questions.

"Ah, daughter," he began, "I am loath to see you sore affronted, if this be your burden. Now, it is not for me to speak, perhaps, so soon—"

"Then don't," she snapped. The Norman priest had hardly spoken to her these past weeks. It annoyed her that he thought she did not know the game he played.

Squinting from the pain in her head, she pushed past him and went into the hall.

Alwyn sent one of the kitchen knaves for wine. The kitchen was full of casks from the castles of the defeated Hereford. What the boy brought was clear and tasted good. It had been a long time since they had had drinkable wine at Morlaix. She finished one cup and started on another. The servers were just setting out the food when Fulk de Jobourg and Geoffrey de Bocage entered the hall.

One of the knights had seen that Alwyn's father's chair

had been set for the new baron. Alwyn sat on the bench with the rest of them, Hugh de Yerville on her right. At the tables below were the castle folk, the men-at-arms, and more of the new-sworn knights who had come from the south.

They filled up the place, noisily. A barrel of beer from the wagons had been opened in the ward; even the Morlaix villagers had helped themselves before they were driven out and the gate closed.

Alwyn did not see her husband's leman among the tables. She poured another cup of wine, telling herself it would not have made any difference. She watched Fulk de Jobourg make his way to the high table with Geoffrey de Bocage. He had taken off his hauberk and wore the padded undercoat over a shirt that stopped at his knees, cross-gartered hose, and horseman's boots.

She might have known, she told herself. Fulk de Jobourg was not as handsome as his cousin, but he was taller, wide in the shoulders, cropped and clean-shaven in the Norman style. He had a wide mouth, narrowed eyes in a face that was closed, resolute. She supposed he was not bad-looking. It came as a surprise that he was young; she had imagined him older.

"I will not have your leman in my castle," she burst out as he came to the back of the table.

He sat down and waved for a squire to pour him some wine. "You make much of nothing," he said, not looking at her. "And it is not your castle."

She drew back, eyes wide. "That woman is an insult that I, as your wife, do not intend to bear!"

" 'Wife,' " he said under his breath. "God's bones, is that what we call it? I know you not, madame, except that you think yourself the lord here, that's what I know. I will speak to you about these things." He lifted his dark eyes to her, scowling. "But the devil take it, I will not now."

Down the table, his knights exchanged looks. "My lady," Hugh de Yerville called. He held up his cup. "This fine wine is from Roger Fitz-Osbern's own stores. You must tell us what you think of it."

A server put a platter of salt pork before them.

"Do not eat that until I talk to you," Alwyn said between clenched teeth. "If you do not get rid of your leman and child I will go to the nuns at Saint Botolph's and ask sanctuary. I will denounce you to the abbot and to the king's brother, Bishop Odo. Holy Mary, I will denounce you to the pope!"

He speared a large piece of baked pork with his knife and put it on his plate. "The boy is not my child. They are Saxons I found on the road. Ask Geoffrey."

Alwyn looked at Geoffrey, who gave her an innocent smile. "Geoffrey would not tell me if it were a lie, I know him!"

"You know too damned much." Fulk broke off a piece of bread and used it to push the meat into his mouth. "I am not so stupid I cannot see Ambrose St. Les's new priest here, and you can't deny you have traded for grain from Chester. The garrison was quick to tell me how you got food when I was gone. My cousin has lost two good knights from what you know. And you have not yet told me how you intend to get my villeins back from the Chirk quarry."

Alwyn looked down the table at Hugh de Yerville, who shrugged. So he had told him.

"The Saxon is a good girl." Fulk wished now he had settled the matter before he got to Morlaix. He took a large drink of Roger Fitz-Osbern's French wine and rolled it about in his mouth. "She can stay in the village."

Alwyn stared at him. In the village, where he could run down to the Saxon when he pleased? "No, she will not! I will send her away!"

Only the front tables could hear what they were saying. At the back, some knights and men-at-arms were already drunk and singing.

Alwyn lifted her voice. "I will not endure that woman

living where you can go back and forth to her! I am your wife!"

He put down his bread and meat and looked up. The cook had come to the high table with a kettle of stewed apples and stood waiting to serve them. The knights busied themselves with their food.

"Yes, you are my wife." He turned his head and studied her, eyes hooded. "Though as you remember, madame, through no damned choice of mine."

Hugh de Yerville leaned past Alwyn. "Fulk, for God's sake," he said.

"No, let him." This was Geoffrey de Bocage. "She has worked enough siren's wiles on us. A certain honor is required, even from women."

Alwyn turned from one to the other. "What is all this? What is this thing I am accused of?"

Down the table Goutard, one of the garrison knights, said, "Nay, milord, it is a lie, all have been careful of your honor, we will speak for that."

"Lie? What lie?" Alwyn clenched her fists. "In God's name, what are you saying?"

Fulk pulled the bowl of apples to him, spooned some into his mouth and nodded to the cook, who beamed.

"Spiced, milord, with cinnamon and clove." The cook bobbed, wiping his hands on his dirty apron. "I had thought the spice too old. It has lain locked in a cupboard a long time—since the last baron."

"No, it's good," Fulk told him. He wiped his mouth with the back of his hand.

Alwyn stared down the table at the Norman knights. She was under attack for more than holding manor court and whatever they thought she'd bartered the abbot for the wagon of grain. Frightened, she thought of the master mason. She'd done nothing, she told herself. Geoffrey de Bocage was staring at her, steadily.

Fulk de Jobourg scraped the bottom of the bowl with his spoon and put it aside. "I am not going to judge you now, but I promise you I will listen, madame, to what you have to say with a fair mind." He beckoned to the kitchen knave who had returned with a filled ewer of wine. "As for my leman, since you say her presence here affronts you, I will give her to you, and you may do with her as you wish. But I warn you, since you are so jealous of your wifely duties." He paused, watching the boy pour the wine into his cup. "I do not intend to sleep alone."

The knights stopped eating. Geoffrey put his arms on the table. "Fulk, if I may say—"

"Shut up," Fulk said.

A server came and collected the empty bowls.

Alwyn got to her feet. Her cup turned over, splashing red wine across the boards and down her dress. "What are you saying to me? That if you cannot have your leman in your bed, your wife is as good? Mark you, if you can tell the difference, which I doubt, I am no roadside slut to be so used!"

"Sit down," he said, not looking up. "If you are not a slut then mind your damned deceitful Breton manners, if you have any."

Alwyn looked about her. The hall was quiet. The faces of the castle folk turned to her.

"If you do not know the difference between your whore and your wife," she shouted, "then you will sleep in your bed alone. For as God and the saints are my witness, I will not be there!"

She turned away, but he scraped back the chair and sprang up, seizing her arm. Someone at the back tables cried out. To a man, the Norman knights stood up, hands on their daggers.

He yanked her to him. "You have a lesson to learn, madame, about how you would speak to me. I will be dealt with courteously, damn you, and you will be respectful of my good name."

She tried to wrench her arm away. "Your good name? You nithing Norman robber, I am not your whore! You saw when you first came here that I must needs be bound and tied and dragged to a priest to marry the likes of you!"

He gave her a warning shake. "Shut your mouth, I told you!"

She was beyond caution. "What am I accused of?" she yelled. "That I got food for us while you were off plundering and burning English land? Consider that we have had a fine taste of your Norman knights and what good they do here!"

Fulk had as much contempt for men who beat women as for those who struck children; there was no honor in such unequal contests. But this one deserved it, he told himself. He hit his wife a blow on the side of her head with his open hand. Even so, it was enough to send her reeling. If he hadn't had her by the arm, she would have fallen.

At the middle tables, the Welsh bowmen rose, making an ominous noise. The rest of the castle folk sat, unmoving and unsure. Hugh de Yerville's garrison knights climbed over the benches to stand before the high table.

Fulk shouldered past them, pushing her in front of him, hands under her elbows. "Is it mayhem, you want, harridan?" he shouted. "Do you hope to raise a mob against me, here in my hall?" When she tried to stop, gripping a table with her hands, he jerked her free. "When we are alone I will give you all the riot you want!"

The knights flanked them as far as the ward, leaving them by the stables as Fulk dragged his wife, kicking and struggling, across the grass to the keep. Behind them, the hall was silent.

Chapter Eight

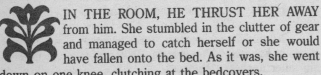IN THE ROOM, HE THRUST HER AWAY from him. She stumbled in the clutter of gear and managed to catch herself or she would have fallen onto the bed. As it was, she went down on one knee, clutching at the bedcovers.

"Tell me," he shouted, "what you have done with my cousin Geoffrey de Bocage in my absence."

He did not trust himself to touch her, convinced that she had tried to start a brawl between the knights and the castle folk. Suddenly, without warning, she scrambled to her feet and launched herself at him.

Her body met his with considerable force. "Your *cousin*?" she screamed. With both hands she clawed at his face. "You dare dishonor me with that accusation?"

He moved to fend her off. But the tactical element of surprise was with her: she clung like a leech once inside his guard, scratching and shrieking furiously.

He could do no more than catch her by the back of the hair to hold her away from him. Too late, he discovered some obstruction behind his feet. He lost his balance and fell backward over the saddle some fool had left on the floor. Then his shield and lances tumbled over and came down with them.

God's wounds, she would not let up, he thought, amazed.

Once, while hunting, he had gone down under a wild boar, not all that heavy but every inch of it writhing, murderous muscle. It was much the same now. She was strong for a woman; a lucky thrust of her knee in his belly knocked the breath out of him. It was all he could do to keep her fingers out of his eyes.

"Stop it," he roared. A lance had his right arm pinned, the long shield crosswise on top of it. Somehow she was on top of both, her long hair flailing in his face. He tried to get his free hand under her chin.

He was in combat with a woman, Fulk realized, astounded. His hellcat wife, who had him down on his back, gouging and punching. The absurdity of it confounded him. What woman would think to do such a thing—to attack a knight of his strength, who with one blow could snap her neck and kill her?

"Thief, murderer, Norman despoiler," she was yelling. "You struck me!"

"I'll strike you again, bitch," he shouted back. "I will beat you until you cry for mercy!"

He managed to shove the shield away. Her knee was right in his groin. He maneuvered carefully, half blinded by the dark cloud of her hair. His groping hand found the back of her gown. Desperate, she tried to bite him.

It did not take much strength even with his left hand to pull her off. He heard the cloth of her gown rip as she tried to claw her way up his body. He held her wrists and got to his feet, dragging her with him.

"Are you crazed?" he bellowed into her face. "Are you possessed by some demon, madame, to act thus?"

"Norman bastard," she screamed. She tried to kick him.

He could see she was beyond reason. Holding her by

the back of the dress, he hit her another smack on the side of her head. The wild howling stopped. She spun away and fell to the floor. She lay there, stunned, the gown like spilled blood around her, dark hair hiding her face.

Fulk stood over her.

The laces in the front of her gown had broken and her breasts tumbled out, full and white against the red cloth. With black hair and silvery eyes she was all vivid color. In spite of himself, he felt a satisfactory surge of lust.

No matter what he had said, he had no desire to strike her again. It only seemed to make her worse. He couldn't believe it when she got to her knees, then unsteadily to her feet, breathing hard.

"Beat me, damn you—*kill* me!" She flung herself at him. "That's what you want, to murder me now you've got my castle!"

He caught and held her at arm's length. "What damned nonsense is this?" he demanded. "Are you drunk?" It was the only thing he could think of.

She gave him a wild look. Quick as an adder, she bent her head and sank her teeth into his wrist.

"Sweet Christ!" He shook her loose, feeling blood trickle down his hand. He had never seen any woman in such a murderous temper. "Tell me what you have done with Geoffrey de Bocage," he growled.

"What *I* have done?" She looked up at him, panting. "Do you mean, is it the same thing I have done with the abbot of Saint Botolph's, and the Angevins who raped a girl in the village?"

Fulk stared down at her. Her bared breasts heaved, her hair tumbled around her, she was full of sensuous fire. Inwardly, he cursed. He was finding that when a woman was beautiful enough, she could say anything and make one want to believe her. God's truth, he hated marriage.

"The Angevins swore your donkey court was a mockery," he told her. "And that you held it only to set yourself up in my place, and steal their money."

She stopped twisting in his grip. "So that was what they told you? Your brave knights had not even the full fine. I took one's sword and his mail to satisfy the farrier's demand. It was only just; the farrier's daughter carries a babe from that rape."

He snorted. "Aye, I am familiar with villeins' cries of rape. But what's usually produced is someone else's brat." He released his grip on her arms. "No one holds court here but the lord," he warned her. "See that you remember it."

She'd told the story differently from how the Angevins had it. He supposed she would have another story to explain away her conniving with the abbot too, for the grain. The pit was bottomless.

He watched her closely. "My cousin has confessed to me that he nurses a passion for you."

She abruptly sat down on the bed and gathered the gaping bodice together with one hand. "Geoffrey de Bocage nurses many passions," she said sullenly. "The scullery maids and the village girls will tell you that."

His eyes narrowed. "Geoffrey has said nothing to you of this?"

"Why should he? I care not what your knights do as long as they do not fight and bother the women." She looked up at him. "Is this what he told you, that he has a passion for me? And that I return it?" To his surprise, she laughed. "Then he would plow a field already sown, milord. I am more than four months gone with your child."

Fulk started. Was that even possible? To cover his thoughts he walked across the room and stood looking at the window. The sun had gone down and he could see nothing out there but the shape of dark Welsh mountains. He turned back again.

"Madame, what happy news," he said evenly. "And this marvel happened in just the one night I spent with you?"

To her credit, she looked puzzled. "That is what I told myself, but the women say it is not unusual. At first I could not believe it."

He stood looking at her, hands clenched in his belt. He had expected more tales, but not this particular story. She might be lying about carrying his child. About everything.

After a long moment, he said, "It is not mine."

Then he went out of the room and slammed the door behind him.

Alwyn rubbed her face. The flesh stung where he had struck her. She wondered if it would make a bruise. In the morning everyone in the castle would know that her husband had beat her for defying him over his leman.

Fulk also thought she had betrayed him with his cousin, and clearly, he dealt treacherously with his enemies. God's love, she had not known he regarded the Earl of Chester as an enemy.

She pulled her knees up and rested her elbows on them, cradling her burning cheek in her hand. Inside her the child turned, a quick, butterfly stirring, reminding her that in a few months she would be heavy and clumsy, not so able to look after herself. What was to become of her? If this Norman turned her out she had no place to flee to, no one to turn to. Everyone's fortunes were uncertain in these perilous times. Perhaps, she thought, she should have been more cautious about his Saxon. But even so, she could not have let him keep his woman there in the castle. She would be mocked all through the countryside as a dishonored wife. There would not be even a stable boy who would obey her.

She needed time. She could not let herself be cast out of her own castle. Even if the villagers would take her in, or a merchant's household in Chirk have her as a servant, she would still be a woman accused of adultery by her husband and worse, out of favor with King William, who had ordered the marriage. There would be many who would be afraid to have her, even as a scullery wench.

Desperate, she considered the master mason. There was not much hope. The Scotsman was not highborn. Besides, he had never said anything to her, he had given no indication that he cared for her. There was small chance he would want her, carrying another man's child.

She rested her chin on her knees and groaned. Holy Mother, but this was a torment. Did he justly believe that she was with child by his cousin? If so, it did not say much for her, that she would bed with Geoffrey de Bocage, who would sleep with any slut who would spread her legs for him.

There was not much in all this that she could use to any advantage; it had been that way from the beginning of this accursed marriage.

She thought hard. Fulk de Jobourg needed a child. If he was wary of the Earl of Chester, he could hold Morlaix more strongly with an heir. Even a girl child would be an heiress; he could marry her off and make an alliance with some high noble family if she were pretty.

The fire had died down in the hearth and the room was chill. Alwyn put her feet down and slipped them into her shoes. The Saxon girl had started it all. It was still not too late to do what she should have done at evening meal.

The sergeant of the men-at-arms found the Saxon and her child sleeping in a wagon by the kitchen house door. So he has not come to her yet, Alwyn thought. She stood nearby as the man-at-arms pulled the girl out of the wagon. The Saxon held the boy tight in her arms but did not struggle. She wore all her gold and silver, but the linen gown was crushed and wrinkled. Her eyes widened when she saw Alwyn.

"This is not right," the Saxon said. She put her arms around the child to shield him.

"Woman, watch your tongue." The Welshman pulled her around to face the light. "This is the lady of Morlaix you see."

The cook came to the open doorway. When he saw what they were doing, he turned back inside.

Alwyn looked down at the waxen child with his thumb in his mouth. Strands of silver hair were plaited at his crown to keep it out of his eyes. His hands were clean, but he had been shoeless for a long time; the soles of his feet were like horn. Another Saxon princeling, she thought; you had only to look at them to see they were not serfs. She wondered if the Normans knew.

The woman lifted her chin. With her face and eyes, and her nearly white hair, she was comely. The men-at-arms pressed close, staring.

"You cannot do anything to me," the Saxon said. She clutched the boy to her. "I will speak to my lord Fulk. He protects us."

One of the stable boys brought up a horse that had been unhitched from the wagons.

"He is not your lord anything," Alwyn said. She motioned to Malluch, one of the men-at-arms, to put the boy up on the horse. "If you do as you are told no one will hurt you."

When Malluch bent to take him, the boy screamed. "Milord does not care for you," the Saxon girl cried, "he told me so!"

Hwyl went to the horse's head and seized the bridle. Malluch set the child up on the horse's back. He held him there with one hand. Howling, the boy tried to slide back down.

The Saxon lunged to the side of the horse, making it shy. She tried to push Malluch away. "Where are you taking him?" she cried.

Impatient, Alwyn said, "Oh, you are going, too."

Hwyl would take them into the hills to her cousin Powys; a man from the village had already been sent with the message. Powys would see that they passed through kinship tribes to the north coast of Glamorgan. From there, boats would take them back where they had come from, to the lands of Northumbria. With the gold and silver Fulk de Jobourg had given her, the Saxon would have enough to keep from starving this time.

"Here, stop crying," she told the boy. She handed up a napkin filled with meat and bread. He stopped screaming and took the bundle. He began worrying the knot in the cloth with his fingers.

"The child needs boots," Alwyn said to Malluch. "He cannot walk the mountains in Wales barefoot. Even in summer."

Two of the men boosted the Saxon up onto the horse's back. The girl leaned down. "You are going to kill us!"

Alwyn stepped back. "Why would we kill you? We will only do that if you ever come back." She moved to the horse, taking its bridle. "Hwyl has some money. If you do not act the fool, there is enough to buy you a husband where you are going."

The stable boy led the horse across the grass to the portal gate. The sounds of the Normans singing and breaking things inside the hall filled the ward.

Two knights came out of the darkness of the arch. They wore mail and were bareheaded and one carried a wine bottle.

The first guard took a torch from its wall bracket. "Who is there?" Lifting it, he examined the Saxon girl and the boy. He grinned.

The knight with the wine bottle said quickly, "Ah, milady, you can't do this."

The other knight pushed him out of the way. He had been in the hall at evening meal. "It is milord Fulk's lady wife, is it not?" He moved the torch so that it shed its light over Alwyn. "Let them pass," he said.

He stepped back to let the horse into the arch. Its

hooves clopped loudly as it stepped onto the planks of the drawbridge.

"God in Christ," the knight with the wine bottle said, "do you see what they are doing?"

Laughing, the other knight pulled him back inside the portal gate.

"The boots," Alwyn called. "Find the child some boots."

Hwyl waved his hand that he understood.

On the horse's back the Saxon girl hunched over the child, arms wound around him. She didn't look back.

The noise of the knights celebrating their sack of Hereford's lands went on into the night. Alwyn took off her gown, changed into a nightdress and climbed into bed, but she could not sleep. Neither, apparently, could anyone else. As the hour grew late, Normans came outside the hall to fight each other or fall over things in the dark. Footsteps charged up and down the stairs in the keep. Doors slammed. The dogs in their pen by the armorer's smithy barked without stopping.

More knights came out and went to the stables and got the horses and raced them up and down the ward, then out through the portal gate and back again, shouting and whooping like boys. Children woke up and cried. A new baby somewhere added its reedy squalls to the din. Alwyn sat up in bed. In the kitchen yard she could hear the cook shouting, voices answering in Welsh. After a while she heard the priest's bell and guessed Father Ascelin had decided to say matins to draw some of the knights into the church. She lay back in bed, staring up into the darkness, hoping the knights would not go down into the village.

Gradually the noises died away. Footsteps climbed the stairs to the barracks on the lower floor. Someone stumbled up the steps that led to her room. Alwyn got out of bed to bar the door, but there were warning shouts from below and running feet. Whoever it was, was dragged away.

She lit a candle and went back to bed. The stone walls were always cold, even in summer, but she did not want to get up and relight the fire. She held herself still, hands at her sides, willing herself not to toss and turn. At last, when she was beginning to feel sleepy, she heard Fulk de Jobourg come up the stairs.

He had been drinking, but was not unsteady on his feet. Once inside the room, he pulled off his padded coat and threw it on the chest, then went to the basin, poured water from the ewer and washed his face. When he lifted his arms to shed his shirt, the top of his hose slid down, hanging on his hipbones, showing a flat belly. He poured more water into the basin and washed under his arms. Finally he undid the laces of his hose and pulled them down and took both hands to wash his groin. The light of the candle sent long shadows on the wall.

Alwyn watched him from under lowered lids. The water glistened on the skin of his shoulders and chest. He was big, narrow hipped, his legs well muscled and long. Her breath grew short. She had forgotten what it was like to lie with him, how his body felt. She was shaking again just thinking about it.

Would it be wise now to get up and go to him? she wondered. The Saxon had been sleeping with him; what in God's name did his leman do? She tried to imagine the woman with the long silvery hair putting her arms around him coaxingly. Whispering some sort of invitation. She had heard that when a woman wanted to encourage a man she put her hands on his privates and squeezed and stroked because it was something men liked very much.

She shut her eyes. Holy Mary, she could not imagine herself doing such a thing; her hands were trembling so they couldn't squeeze anything.

He crossed the room and sat down on the edge of the bed. The ropes sagged and groaned under his weight. Alwyn held on to the covers to keep from rolling toward him. He pulled off his boots. Leaning back, he braced his feet and lifted his hips to strip off the hose. Close up, the wine smell was strong.

He picked up the bedcovers and rolled under them. The bed sank on his side. From under her eyelids Alwyn saw that he had propped himself on his elbow and was looking down at her.

"What did you do with Eadgitha?" he said.

Alwyn's eyes snapped open. The knights at the portal had told him. "I sent her away." Her jaw trembled so she could barely manage to speak. "You said I could."

"So I did." There was a silence. Under the covers his groping hand found her thigh. "Why do you still have your clothes on?"

Alwyn looked up. Leaning over her his face was full of shadows, the corners of his mouth turned up. His teeth were not as nicely even as the mason's; one in front was slightly crooked. Under the bedsheet his hand pushed her nightdress higher.

She fought down frantic thoughts. She didn't want him to touch her, she would as soon bed one of the knights below. They were all strangers to her.

His hand moved between her legs. "What did you do with the little boy?"

She stared at him. Did he think she'd had them killed? "I sent them away." She didn't know whether he believed her or not; he thought her capable of anything.

He lowered his head, his mouth brushing her forehead. She shivered, teeth clicking. He paused. "Shhh," he told her. "You are not so far along, this will hurt nothing."

She forced herself not to grab his wrist as his hand thrust into the fleshy cleft between her legs and then pushed farther, into the tight passage beyond. It was an invasion that made her gasp.

This was worse than she imagined, to have his hard touch on her and in her. He began to move the two fingers

118

that stretched her, stroking in and out. She stiffened as waves of feeling radiated into her belly. Every nerve in her body flinched, but she was growing wet. Suddenly he was over her, his mouth on her mouth, his tongue pushing between her lips.

She would not fight him. He had not kept his Saxon leman to humiliate her and in return she had agreed to be a willing wife. But she didn't remember anything like this on their wedding night. A choked sound broke from her.

He lifted his head, breathing hard.

The child is yours, she wanted to scream. What was he going to do with her? Take her to bed, use her without ever speaking to her of anything? She found she had seized his wrists, regardless. Her heels dug into the bed.

She felt the muscles of his arms quivering against her breasts. He was lustful now, desire shaking his heavy body.

"This is still new to me," she burst out. "I still do not know how to do it."

He looked down at her. "God's wounds, then be still and let me." His shoulder pressed down against her as he shifted his weight in the bed. His hand was on her breasts, circling and kneading, fingers pulling her nipples into hard buds. She cried out when his mouth went to them, wetly tugging. She squirmed under him, lifting her hands and letting them fall. The uneasiness in her body was now an uproar. Between her legs she was aching fit to burst. Still his fingers goaded her, in and out. She couldn't lie still.

"Aaah!" His mouth was right in her ear, roaring with breath. He moved himself against her, powerful, urgent, pushing her knees up. The fingers were gone, and something hard and big took their place, prodding her. "Take me in your hand," he gasped, "guide me in."

When she only stared, he reached between their bodies and took her hand and uncurled her fingers, placing them around him. His flesh felt burning hot.

"In," he said, pushing against her. "Put me in you."

Her hand let go of him. He pushed in anyway. Big, relentless, he filled her carefully, the weight of his body behind each long thrust. She was overwhelmed with the feel of surrender. She fought for air, her heart pounding. With a growl his mouth descended on hers and he thrust his tongue into it. His hips moved in a push that took her completely.

Alwyn cried out, heaving her body under him. She stuck her fingernails into the skin of his shoulders. She reared up, following the fire deep inside her.

"Sweet Jesu," he groaned.

She couldn't shake him loose. Where he moved in long, measured strokes it burned, and she strained for something that would not come. She was wild. He tried to hold her, careful of his grip as she flung herself against him. She heard the sounds he made, bursting from him. He was drenched in sweat.

"What is this you do to me?" His voice was hoarse. His arms wrapped around her tightly as he raked her, shuddering. Then his mouth seized hers and his tongue thrust in. It muffled his loud bellow of release.

She found herself pushed up the bed and against the wall as his body bucked, and bucked again. He groaned loudly, twitching. After a time he subsided, his weight pressing her down. She was flooded with wet. She still burned tight and hot around him. Limp now, he was sliding free.

Alwyn lay still under him, filled with a raging that made her want to scream. She felt his mouth kissing her lips, caressing her wet hair. His hand pushed her hair back from her face and he looked into her eyes. "Are you well?" He was still breathing hard. "I did not hurt you?"

No, she was not hurt. If anything, she could not understand why it had stopped. She wanted to throw herself out of bed and pace up and down the room, shrieking. For what, she did not know.

She licked her lips. "No, you did not hurt me."

"Well, then," he said. His hard face lost its concern. "Ah, Holy Mother." He rolled away from her and lay on his back and rubbed himself, stretching. "What you do to me," he said to the ceiling.

He twisted his head to look at her. His mouth was blurry with kissing, his eyes were dark and hot. His dark red hair stuck up in sweaty spines. He smiled, smug. "The night's not over, wife."

While she still stared at him he got out of bed, only slightly staggering, and went over to the chamberpot.

The night's not over, Alwyn thought, as he turned his back to her. That was what he had said. She put her hand between her legs and cupped her puffed, throbbing cleft.

Well, there was still hope. For something.

Marchawg

Chapter Nine

FATHER ASCELIN PULLED THE LONG sheet of parchment toward him and wrote across the top: "God's Blessings on This Third Day After Pentecost in the Year of Our Lord 1076." Then he put down his pen and took up a small knife and carefully began to scrape away the old message below.

The sheet of sheepskin was from Father Ascelin's own monastery of Bec in Normandy and had been prepared with a quality not to be found in England. His correspondence with Brother Bertram of St. Botolph's over the past months had used the same parchment sheet over and again without, except for a few thin spots where a knife had slipped, perceptible wear.

He blew gently at the writing surface to clear away a drift of stone dust that had come in the open window. The masons were now at work on the last stages of the castle chapel. The chink-chink of their hammers against the stone hardly ever ceased. By harvest time, they had told him, all would be finished. The side walls of the chapel had already been raised and now they were working on the arch beams of the roof.

Father Ascelin's cell at the back of the church was small but well lit by a window from which, when the shutters were open, he could view the busy center of Morlaix Castle—the grassy sweep of the ward, the portal gate, the entrance to the keep, and the knights' barracks.

His new quarters did not fit the strict mandate of Benedictine living, though it was only sparsely furnished with a table upon which he could lay his writing materials, a candlestand, a narrow priestly bed, and a chamberpot. The window violated the rules, but the masons had cut the opening and framed it with dressed stone before Father Ascelin could correct the error, and he had let it stand. He hadn't realized how much his soul had suffered, sleeping at night on the benches in the hall with kitchen servants and young squires crowded out of the keep.

Carefully, he lifted the palimpsest and blew away the ink that had once been Brother Bertram's letter to him. That done, he laid the sheet down on the table and picked up his goose quill and dipped it in the ink pot.

Bending his head, squinting slightly, he wrote in severely vertical letters: "To the Glory of God in the Sky and His Heavenly Hosts and Christ His Beloved Son, the Earthly Domain of His Blessed Servant King William of England by Whom His Grace He Rules and Duke of Normandy. And His Abbot Ambrose St. Les of the Cloister of Saint Botolph and to Whoever in That Demesne This Message Should Come."

The scholarly Latin was perfect for the letters Father Ascelin had been sending from Castle Morlaix since he arrived; if they fell into other hands no one would understand them.

He wrote: "There has been little activity here since last I have written and all remains undisturbed except for some unrest in the village and surroundings over the granting of the right of manor house and lands to the knight of the castle garrison, Hugh de Yerville. Of which I have written before."

He paused, thinking no one would have foreseen such a fury over the establishment of a knight's holding. Here at Morlaix one had only to look about to see the benefits of a Norman administration: buildings were cleaner, people better ordered, even attendance at mass was expected. At least among the knights. Even mealtime was at last regulated by civilized ranking: the lord and his wife, knight captains, honored guests, and the castle confessor seated at the high table, knights and other soldiery immediately below, then the armorer, tally reeve and the like, followed by the common folk and women and children to the back.

With so much sensibly accepted, the outburst in the village over de Yerville's new estate had been a surprise. What concerned the earl's bailiff was that Fulk de Jobourg was Chester's vassal, and the grant of land properly one only the earl could give. Except that the new baron of Morlaix, being King William's man, had made it plain he took casually Chester's claim of lordship in his valley.

Father Ascelin was running short of space on the parchment. He reported the chapel was nearing completion but without the master mason known as Ian of Scotland. He had departed, his masons said, for York. Father Ascelin had learned that guild work took this Ian, whom they seemed secretly to call the grand master, to York, for meetings with the members of the joiners' guild.

Father Ascelin was aware of the church's concern that these guilds should be closely watched, to guard against the heresy of secret rites. The mason's guild perhaps more than any other.

He paused again, the feather tip of the pen at his lips. An excess of noble attributes in a person baseborn always led to a desire to wrongfully challenge one's betters. Father Ascelin could see the appeal of this master mason for a certain young wife. The occupants of Castle Morlaix would have had to be blind as moles not to see Lady Alwyn and the mason together on the wall walk, while the husband made himself absent in the south, entertained by a Saxon mistress. Providentially, the Lady Alwyn had displayed a righteous spirit, confronting her lord husband and banishing his leman, as noted to Brother Bertram before. And, as also noted, the mistress of Morlaix was with child.

A shadow fell at the window. Father Ascelin quickly covered his parchment and got up. The new butler's wife stood outside, holding the babe he had so recently baptised. She carried a plate of his midday food. Marcus, Father Ascelin thought, on the feast of the Evangelist. Naturally, they called the babe something else in Welsh.

The woman had a broad, ruddy face. She looked at him expectantly as she handed him the plate. Under the covering white cloth, Father Ascelin could smell baked bread. He hoped she had remembered the cheese.

"Hold up the child," he said, keeping the plate in one hand as he leaned out of the window. The butler's wife had been churched after the birthing. The rest was God's will, he told himself resignedly. Here in Britain, men took their wives in an indecently short time, ignorant, or indifferent to the civilized custom of not using a woman for at least a twelvemonth, after the child was weaned.

He made the sign of the cross over the babe, who seemed to be asleep, and recited a blessing in Latin.

"He's had the colic, father." The butler's wife looked dotingly at the swaddling in her arms. "Not a good night's sleep to be had in days, I'm that worn out. And there's been a fever. The castle babes are not thriving like they should in this rain and heat."

"He has his share of health, my daughter." Father Ascelin was no judge, and certainly no surgeon. "The babe seems well." He closed the shutter before the butler's wife could say more, and went back to his table and sat down again.

He picked up his pen. He told himself he should be cautious when describing the state of things between the lord and mistress of Morlaix. Fulk de Jobourg was a lusty young knight and one could not judge him too closely,

while the Lady Alwyn's looks and bold spirit, Father Ascelin thought, would serve her no better.

Father Ascelin wrote that he would respectfully call Abbot Ambrose's attention once again to problems of vile
pagan practices, known as Midsummer Eve. Here, even
as in Normandy, young men and women commenced dis-
gusting revelry at dusk with lewd dances, decked with
garlands of flowers. There was unrestrained drinking of
beers and other potions, clothing was discarded, all culmi-
nating in a rush to the forest to couple indiscriminately.

It was an abomination, Father Ascelin wrote, for those
who called themselves Christian to behave in such a manner, and worse, that they were said to be recognizing
some swine goddess, supposedly of fertility and childbirth, whom half the participants could not remember, nor
yet even name.

Father Ascelin was not interested in the name of the
unknown Welsh goddess. He wanted to see only that the
village girls were not subjected to such evil practices. Or
delivered of the crop of infants that in years past inevita-
bly appeared nine months after Midsummer Eve. Which,
Father Ascelin knew, he would have to admit to the Holy
Church by baptism.

He finished, and rolled up the sheepskin. He drew a
cord about it and through it, and then sealed it so that it
could not be unrolled without breaking the wax.

Actually, he did not have to worry. Their messenger
from Morlaix who would carry this to Wrexham—where a
monk would take it to St. Botolph's—was reliable enough.
By now he had too much at stake to risk the ultimate
reward he hoped for.

Father Ascelin got up from his table and stuck his head
out his window. Several knights were lying about on the
grass in the ward, talking and taking the sun. One of them
had saddled his horse and it stood before him, head down,
the reins touching the ground.

After some discreet movements, Father Ascelin caught

the knight's eye. The other stood up, brushed his knees with his hands, and led the horse down the wall to Father Ascelin's cell. The knight had been waiting for the parchment for some time. He drew the horse up in front of the priest.

Father Ascelin handed the letter through the window and the other man slipped the roll into his sleeve. The knight quickly dropped to one knee and bent his head.

Father Ascelin leaned out the window and made the sign of the cross over the knight, murmuring a traveler's blessing. "The same brother," he told him in a low voice. He did this often enough now, the knight went to Wrexham and back at every chance. Father Ascelin suspected a woman. "He calls himself Olibef. At the same place."

Geoffrey de Bocage stood up, took his helmet and pulled it down on his head. When it was in place, he led the horse to a clear spot on the grass and swung himself into the saddle. Then he turned the horse's head and rode off toward the gate.

The summer was hot, more so than it had been in many years. On either side of the river the villeins' strips of land planted with millet and wheat were thigh deep and heavy headed. Thunderclouds shrouded the valley, high purple towers with bottoms black with water; most evenings the castle road turned to mud. But it was a good year, a miraculous one. The villeins could only pray for dry weather to come to Morlaix in time for harvesting.

Alwyn took off her cloak and laid it over the pommel of her saddle. Almost immediately one of the knights kicked his horse up to hers. She waved him away before he could tell her to put it back on. The rain made her gown stick to her breasts and her growing belly, and did not improve her appearance, but it was better than steaming under the wool cloak. Besides, she was uncomfortable enough. Her

mare would foal in the autumn and, round as they both
were, the knights had made joking remarks on their way
to the village.

In the millers' yard, men were sitting under the shelter
of the oak trees drinking beer. When they saw the knights
they ran off into the rain. The miller's wife came to the
door.

The miller's wife was fat and wore wooden clogs, her
blue dress covered with an apron.

"Welcome, Mistress Alwyn," she called. "Come in and
I will find you a drink and something to eat."

A young knight named Janville lifted Alwyn down from
her mare. Her belly brushed him and he stiffened. He set
her on her feet, holding on to her as if afraid to let her go.

She pushed him away irritably. "Holy Mary, I won't
break," she said. The other knights laughed. They turned
their horses to shelter from the rain under the trees. The
miller's wife looked after them, her lips pursed.

"There's no beer," she said. "We're fresh out." She
stepped aside to let Alwyn pass into the alehouse kitchen.

It wasn't true, they had just seen the villeins drinking.
"They don't expect any, they are my husband's knights."

Alwyn bent her head to pass under the lintel. The ceiling of the miller's house was low. Cattle and swine were
kept in the front of the house; the miller and his wife slept
above in the loft. Their son, the boy who had returned
sick from the quarry, lay on a pallet by the storeroom
door. He lifted his head and looked at Alwyn, then
dropped it back on the pillow.

The miller's wife bustled about. "Gwynn's so much better, milady, it's God's blessing it is to have him back,
thanks to your good lord husband, may the angels protect
him and keep him safe." She bent to cover the boy's
shoulders with the blanket. "He eats like a *bleidd*, a wolf,
now, don't you, darling? And before, when he first came,
he was a terrible sight, all skin and bones."

The boy did not look all that well, Alwyn thought. His

face was gray except for two spots of red on each cheek. She put the medicines she had brought, tincture of fox-glove and a tonic of leeks and honey, on the big wooden table. The kitchen was pleasantly warm and the air smelled of baking bread. She sat on a bench by the oven. The miller's wife brought a cup of buttermilk and a slice of fresh bread spread with jam, and sat down on the bench next to her.

"Ah, but you're carrying high." She reached over to pat the bulge under Alwyn's damp gown. "It's a boy, mark you, when the babe rides as high as that."

"God willing." Alwyn set down the cup. Buttermilk made her queasy, but she was always hungry. She stuffed the bread and jam into her mouth. "It's what my husband wants," she said around it, "a boy." That was no lie; a boy was what men always wanted.

"Ah, then, call on the Holy Mother to give your sweet lord what he wants," the other woman said, "you can do no better. I pray to Our Savior Christ every day to bless Lord Fulk for what he did at the quarry. When you have a son of your own you will know what it meant to my man and me to have Gwynn back. And not dead of the whip, and the starving they put him to there."

She got up to bring Alwyn another slice of bread covered with plum jam.

"I do not blame your lord for what happened after," the miller's wife said, sitting back down. "About the land for the manor." She lowered her voice, looking to the door, although there was no one there to listen. "They were wrong, these men here, to stone the castle knights and burn a wagon. The Normans do no more than the Saxons have done here before, seizing what they want." She shrugged her fat shoulders. "Or even old Prince Rhiwallon, in your father's time."

Alwyn nodded, her mouth full. The miller was not one of the men who had rioted, so he had not been lashed or tied to a wagon for a day and a night. Fulk de Jobourg had ordered the punishment. It was a different story with the mothers of the village boys. They would bless him forever.

After the work was completed and the boys had not been sent home from the quarry, Fulk had gone to the masons' camp. He learned that Ian the Scotsman had gone to York. He took twenty knights and rode to the Chirk quarry to find for himself why Morlaix's levy of workers had not been sent home.

The quarrymaster claimed the Morlaix youths had probably run off if they had not come back to the village. While the quarrymaster was lying to Fulk, one of the knights had found the miller's son on a pile of rags in some nearby rocks.

Alwyn had heard the story in several versions. One had it that her husband had throttled the cheating quarrymaster on the spot and tossed his body into the quarry. Another that he had picked up the man and thrown him into the pit to drown. The most truthful seemed to be Aubrey, the squire's—that Fulk had seen the miller's boy carried in the knight Goutard's arms, and had hit the quarrymaster such a blow on the head that the man flew over the cliff and into the water. Then Fulk had forbidden anyone to go to his aid.

Alwyn believed Aubrey's story. She was all too familiar with her husband's famed blows to the head.

The miller's wife bent her head to whisper, "There should never have been an outcry in the village, milady, over the young knight's taking their land. They all know Norman justice, they do. But they have been listening to the Man of the Vale, these people here. He tells them the Normans will come in such numbers now that they will drive the Welsh off the land, like they do with the English. He tells them the only just thing to do is to come and join the rebels in the mountains."

Alwyn licked the jam from her fingers. She did not doubt that; it sounded like Powys. "It was wrong to tell the people here something that would only get them cruelly punished."

The miller's wife snorted. "Well, too late now, they've found that out." When Alwyn straightened, her hand pressed to her back, she said, "Are you uncomfortable now, dear? That's a big babe you carry by the looks of it."

Alwyn grimaced. The babe was big. She had heard that more than once. "There is a midwife in the mountains I would like to see. They say she is skilled. Better than the one here in the village."

"Oh, aye, that's wise," the miller's wife agreed. "Hygwidd's Marve is getting old and can't see, and she's overfond of her beer, for another. If it was storming or such, you would have a worry that she could climb the road to the castle, she's that shaky."

She got up from the bench and went to the pallet. She stood looking down at her boy, satisfied he was sleeping. "Has the priest said aught to you about bringing the village girls to the castle on Midsummer Eve?"

Alwyn looked up. Father Ascelin had been in the village many times the past few weeks preaching against Midsummer Eve and its vile pagan ceremonies. She had never been to Midsummer revels herself, it was mostly confined to the village. But from what she'd been told by the spinning sisters and the scullery girls, on that night young men and young women decked in flower garlands and carrying branches of rowan and holly danced in the fields around an *oddeith,* a bonfire big as a hill. And as the night wore on, there was drinking around the fire, with the result that clothing was discarded and young men and women rushed off to the woods to be by themselves.

It had been years before Alwyn, the baron's daughter, understood what that meant. She'd been a woman grown before she'd made the connection between Midsummer Eve revels and the crop of village babies that made their appearance some nine months after.

"Henwas Hwch." She hadn't thought of that in years. It

was from the old religion, before the priests, and meant the old woman of the pigs, a giant sow who made women fertile and came to them in childbirth.

The miller's wife nodded vigorously. "Aye, and they call her Dagda too, I heard that when I was a girl. Dagda and Henwas Hwch. But whatever, it's the old goddess." She went to the ovens, opened the door and stuck in the paddle and turned the loaves of bread. She closed the door again, her face flushed. "This priest says all the girls what's young enough to still be thought of as maids will have to come up to the castle on Midsummer Day. He's going to bring them into the chapel and keep them at prayers until all has stopped. That would be, mayhap, at sunrise."

Alwyn had heard something of the sort. The cook had come to her, complaining, about having to feed the village maidens. She smiled. "Do you think the girls will come?"

The miller's wife returned the smile, dimpling mischievously. "Ah, milady, all of them girls will come just to prove they've still got their maidenhead! On the other hand, it will be hard to miss Midsummer's fun. This priest has his work cut out for him."

Alwyn got up. The rain was coming down even harder. She thought of the knights outside.

"Take some bread with you, milady," the miller's wife said. "And some of the jam."

Alwyn shook her head. Behind them, on his pallet, the boy coughed. The miller's wife turned, her expression changing. "They say he has stone dust in his lungs," she whispered.

She stood aside to let Alwyn out.

Chapter Ten

BLINDING OR CASTRATION. OR BOTH. That was the penalty. The two Welshmen squatted on the riverbank, their hands tied behind them, their hunting bows at their feet. Fulk doubted they understood French. They'd probably never heard of King William's forestry laws.

The knights had laid the killed animals out in two rows with a smaller row for the birds, none above the size of larks. The roe was freshened, Fulk saw, disgusted, her belly mounded high as she lay on her side. Flies were already collecting around her eyes. She had been dead for some time.

Guy de Bais came up on his big roan and galloped into the riverbank clearing, a villein hanging onto his stirrup. The man dropped free, gasping, and went down on one knee in front of Fulk. His eyes slid to the captive Welshmen on their knees, shaggy heads bowed.

It was threatening to rain again. There was a roll of thunder in the hills. Guy de Bais dismounted, pulling down his cloak from his saddle. He threw it around him as he strode up. "His name is Gwawl," he said. "I pulled him from his bean patch yonder."

Fulk said, "Get him to ask about stolen sheep."

The villein said in Norman French, "Oh, milord, I do not know these men, I have never seen them before. They are strangers to these parts."

Fulk said, "Dammit, I've not accused you of anything."

The villein hesitated, frightened. Then he got to his feet and went to the hunters. He stood in front of them, speaking in Welsh, presumably asking about stolen sheep. The youngest hunter stirred, eyes agleam, and tried to move his bound arms.

The hunters were undersized even for the Welsh, their faces covered with black beard. Their bodies were bare except for leather kilts, their legs wrapped in deerskin. The boy was about sixteen, wiry, well muscled, already a man. The older one was squat, his arms full of scars. He wore a chestful of chains, bone pieces, the usual magic pouch on a string. He knelt with his shoulders forward, back rounded, weight on his heels.

The villein was right. They were hill men, hunters, strangers to the valley. Fulk had ridden out that morning looking for sheep thieves. In the forest on the west side of the river, one of de Bais's knights had found the dead roe. Then, beating up the riverbank, they had flushed out the tribesmen.

They probably knew nothing of sheep. Hill people did little herding. Venison, not mutton, was to their taste. Besides, for sheep stealing they would be hanged. What they had done, killing the king's game, would make them yearn for such a merciful death.

Fulk said, "Ask them why they have killed so much meat."

The village man went to the boy and grasped his hair to pull back his head. He spoke into the boy's upturned face at some length. The boy shut his eyes.

Fulk considered stripping the boy and flogging him to see if the other hunter could be persuaded. But he doubted it would work. The mountain Welsh endured pain as steadfastly as Danes.

Unexpectedly, the other hunter said something.

The villein let go of the boy. "Milord, this man says he has many children and they are starving. The spring has been wet and hunting poor."

Fulk wondered if the boy was his son. A father was honored among these wild Welsh if a son was brave enough to die; they would make no effort to save each other, even under torture. "He lies," he said. "They plan to salt this meat and sell it."

The villein repeated what he had said. The hunter lifted his head, pale eyes measuring Fulk. He was young, not old, with a broad, flattened face, and a short nose. His expression said the forests belonged to the Welsh.

Fulk studied him. The devil take it, he did not need to mete out the king's bloody justice over a slaughtered deer; he needed to find Morlaix's sheep thieves. The herds were being drained; that was a matter that needed his attention, not this.

Also, the Earl of Chester's bailiff sat in Wrexham with a summons for Fulk de Jobourg, regarding the complaint of assault and ill treatment by the Chirk quarrymaster. Fulk did not intend to go to Wrexham to acknowledge the quarrymaster's complaint, nor did he intend to admit any sort of vassalage to Hugh of Avranches. Most especially he did not need a pair of hillmen to charge and send to the Earl of Chester's shire court to be tried.

But now here were these damned Welsh hunters. He had to get rid of them somehow.

It was said that William loved to hunt the deer of the forest as much as he loved his brothers. Perhaps more so. In England, now, there was no worse offense than to poach what the king judged belonged to him, not the conquered.

Fulk stuck his thumbs in his belt, frowning. They had just put down a disturbance in the village and punished the ringleaders. It was a bad time to deliver justice, particularly of this sort. "Tell them," he said, "what the penalty is for hunting in the king's forest."

The knights began to dismount. De Bais tied his reins to the lower branch of an oak tree and stood at a distance, arms crossed over his chest.

Nervously, the villein looked around him, then let out a stream of Welsh. The two hunters watched, unblinking, as Gwawl passed his hand before his eyes for the blinding. He did not need to gesture for the rest. The boy lifted his head to look at the other man.

Beyond, a knight said something. One of the younger knights paled and turned away.

Under his breath, Fulk cursed. Abruptly, he strode over to the boy.

Leaning down, he shouted into the boy's face, asking his name in French and demanding to know about stolen sheep. The boy flinched. Fulk lifted his foot and kicked him, hard, in the ribs. The boy rolled to one side, curling up in pain like a hedgehog.

Fulk bent over him, his hands on his knees. "The boy's simple," he said. "One of God's unfortunates." He shook his head sympathetically. "You can see he doesn't understand a word."

He straightened up and motioned for Guy de Bais to come and haul the boy to his feet. His second-in-command stared at him, disbelieving, as Fulk bent and cut the boy's bonds and pulled him up by one arm.

The boy staggered to his feet, holding his broken ribs. The flesh around his mouth was gray.

"Set him loose," Fulk said.

De Bais still held on to him. Impatient, Fulk jerked the boy out of his grasp and gave him a push. The Welsh boy ran a few steps, stopped and looked back. The other hunter sat with his shoulders hunched, unmoving. The boy turned and ran into the woods.

"Now to the other one," Fulk said. "King William's summary law."

De Bais was still staring at him as Fulk dropped to his knees and took out his dagger. He rolled the hunter over on his face and cut the bonds at his elbows and wrists. The little Welshman lay with his face in the grass, trying to flex his hands.

The knights gathered around. The sky was dark with the approaching storm. A few drops of rain began to fall.

Guy de Bais said, "Holy Mary, Fulk, do you mean to do it now?"

"Yes," Fulk told him. "Kneel on his hands."

The hunters had been caught at the edge of the clearing, on the slope of the riverbank. As Fulk rolled him on his back the Welshman's legs slid higher than his head, his hair trailing in shallow water. The wind had churned the river into waves that slapped the side of the bank.

De Bais tried to shift the Welshman's shoulders onto the grass, but Fulk stopped him. "Leave him," he said, in a low voice, "it will be over quick enough."

The hunter lay still. Fulk knelt on his legs. He looked down into the sun-browned face. Blinded and castrated, that was the law. But what was a man without his cock, and his eyesight? A dumb and fumbling piece of flesh, not to be considered human. And better off dead. Their eyes met and locked. Fulk wondered if the mutilated ever killed themselves. Sweet Christ, if they cut off *his* privates he knew he would not want to live.

When he cut the string that held the kilt, the hunter's legs jerked convulsively. Guy de Bais knelt on the Welshman's hands, breathing hard. Raindrops were falling steadily. A crack of lightning showed over the mountains.

The Welshman had a thick mat of hair that extended like black fur down the inside of his thighs. Taking the soft pouch of the genitals in his hand, Fulk cut into the sac with just the tip of his knife. The hunter drew in his breath with a hiss. He thrashed in their grip, trying to escape. As the knife prodded deeper the Welshman screamed, his feet kicking wildly. He arched his back, wrenching his arms from de Bais.

As Fulk had known, they couldn't hold him; the river-bank was already running with water. When Fulk quickly shifted his knees, the hunter came free and slid down the wet clay like an otter. They saw his feet, flailing, as he went in head first.

Fulk jumped up. Whipped by the wind, the river eddied and churned in brown waves. The hunter's head bobbed above the surface and then went under and came back up again. He went downstream, swimming hard.

The knights stood silent, watching the river. No one moved.

"Drowned," Fulk said, over the noise of the rain. "We have just seen God's merciful justice done." He faced the river and crossed himself righteously. "Praise be to God."

Several knights turned and looked at him, puzzled. After a moment, most of them crossed themselves. The villein, Gwawl, stood staring down the river, his jaw slack.

Guy de Bais followed Fulk back to the horses. "Fulk, what have we been doing here? You didn't order a fire built for the blinding. Nor the hot irons."

"I would have, after I gelded him." Fulk untied the reins from the tree branch and pulled the stirrup forward. "And had God not intervened." He stuck his foot in the stirrup and hauled himself into the saddle.

"God?" De Bais looked up at him angrily. "I saw you cut him!"

Fulk was riding a big gray, not his destrier. He had to kick the horse with his heels to get him to move. "At worst yon Welshman has one dangling nut," he said over his shoulder as the horse walked away, "but I would doubt he is cut even that much."

Guy de Bais stood staring after him. The villein, Gwawl, turned back from the riverbank, walking among the horse-men.

Fulk watched the villager as his horse passed under the trees. He's thinking about it, he told himself. They will all think about it in the village, and talk. It was what he wanted.

He'd taken no hunters prisoner for the Earl of Chester's justice, and he'd carried out the king's bloody law. Well, in his own way.

And it was no damned manor court, Fulk told himself, pleased.

The showers thickened. Persistent thunder rolled in the hills. By mid-afternoon the weather had sunk into slate-colored twilight.

When the knights entered the courtyard they found naked children dancing in the rain. Women rushed to shoo them out of the horses' way.

Fulk dismounted and gave the big gray to Aubrey to lead to the stables. A messenger from the earl's bailiff was waiting for him in the hall. The second time in a week. Fulk walked away toward the keep. The messenger could wait in the hall as long as he wanted to. He was accepting no summons as the vassal of Hugh of Avranches.

When he entered the room at the top of the stairs, he saw his wife sitting in the middle of the bed, darning his shirts. He was surprised that as rounded as her belly was she still managed to sit with her feet tucked under her. The candles were lit, shutters closed against the rain. There was a fire on the hearth. An embroidered hanging from one of Hereford's manor houses covered the wall behind the bed. After a day in the wet, he found the room pleasing.

He pulled up a stool and sat down on it to pry off his boots. Outside, the rain drummed on the stones. A gust of wind down the chimney blew smoke into the room.

"Come help me with this," he said, lifting his arms.

His wife slipped out of the bed. She crossed the stone

floor in her bare feet. He bent forward and she seized the sleeves of the mail shirt. At the same time he grasped the neck with his hands. The hauberk was heavy. When it came free she stepped back under the weight. He stood up to take it from her, and laid it on the floor beside the stool. She turned and went back to the bed.

Fulk watched her with narrowed eyes. She wore a loose linen dress of a pale color that clung to her hips and her legs. Her hair was unbound, it swung loose down her back. She swayed gracefully when she walked, and looked very girlish in spite of the bulge of the child.

How many men had dallied with her? he wondered. He would say one thing for her, she did not flirt openly with the knights like the wives he had seen at King William's court. And she was not friendly with Geoffrey, for all his cousin's love-smitten stories. Geoffrey was a liar and a troublemaker; Fulk did not know what to believe. He thought about her intriguing with the abbot of St. Botolph's through the priest.

She climbed into the bed again and picked up her mending. Her dark hair fell forward as she lifted a shirt and bent and bit the thread.

Fulk was finding a deceitful woman's mind not easy to fathom. When he was with her, his wife was singularly ungiving, holding herself separate even in intimacy, mysterious. It could truly be said that he knew her no better now than when he'd married her. But there were times when he could not keep his thoughts from her. His errant mind went to the sweet secret between her legs that was hot and willing, even though her temper was uneven these last months of carrying the child. He thought about her soft white thighs, her firm breasts that filled his hands.

He peeled off his shirt and wet hose. Naked, he crossed the room to stand before the gyrfalcon's painted perch. He used his shirt as a towel to dry off his shoulders and arms. "Hercules," he said coaxingly to the bird. "Do you wish to hunt, old fellow?"

The hawk was unhooded; it swiveled its head, fixing him with a mad yellow eye. The stink of droppings on the floor under the stand was strong.

Fulk studied the hawk somberly. Unmanageable thoughts of his wife most often came when he was alone with her in their room. That, he supposed, was natural. But lewd wanderings also seized him at meals in the hall, when she sat next to him. Or the imagined feel of her mouth, soft and wet with his kisses, cropped up in his head when he was speaking to villeins about their fields. He told himself lecherous visions were bound to sap one's daily vigor; on the other hand, he was already stiff and hurting just thinking about it. God's wounds, his wife was pretty, but he had never had a woman intrude on his senses this way.

Fulk tweaked the bird under his beak with his knuckle. The gyrfalcon cocked his yellow eye, then neatly bit it.

He had reasoned that his wife was in his thoughts too much because she denied him nothing; in no way had he lessened his demands, and yet she kept to their agreement to serve him in bed as well as any whore. He knew she feared that if she did not, he would turn her out.

He stuck his bleeding finger in his mouth and sucked on it. What she did not know was that it was not his plan to publicly accuse her, now, about the child she carried. With all that was at stake here at Morlaix, he would be a fool to start a scandal that would race across the countryside to London and William's court. And imperil a marriage that, after all, the king himself had ordered.

He walked to the bed and sat down on it. No, it served him best to put up with her scheming for the time being. What he needed to do now was to bring order to his fief, and strengthen his grip on all that he had.

"The bird bit you," she said.

He brushed his feet together to get rid of any dirt before lifting them to the bed. His body tingled from riding in the cool rain, then brisk toweling in a warm room. He was suddenly aware how fine it felt to be doing nothing on a stormy summer's afternoon. His shaft stood up between his legs, hard and expectant. He pulled a shirt out of the mending pile and covered himself with it as he lay back in the bed.

She snatched the shirt back and spread it in her lap. She put her elbow on it as she threaded the needle. "I never saw anyone stick his finger straight at a hawk like that. Even children know they will always bite."

Fulk reached over her and picked up the pile of his shirts and threw them on the floor. He saw her draw back, mouth open, as he pulled the remaining shirt from her hands and tossed it after the others. He rolled her under him and covered her mouth, his tongue separating her soft lips. She made a murmuring sound at the back of her throat.

Her hair lay like silk against the pillows. He scraped his fingers through it, his nostrils filling with scent of the dried lavender she used. He nuzzled her throat. She did not move. Her hand rested lightly against his shoulder.

He broke the kiss, lifted himself on his elbows, looking down at her. She would not resist what he was doing, but he knew there were times when she didn't want to take him. He supposed she was not so comfortable now, with the growing size of the child.

However, he had shown her how to do other things. He took her by the wrist and guided her hand down to him. When her fingers closed around him he took a ragged breath. He wanted to see her breasts. He pulled down the neck of her gown, working the fabric free of one shoulder. She was beautiful, her breasts larger, even more sensuous, traced with pale blue veins. His lips found them, making wet lines across the milk-white skin.

She made a choked sound as his hand rucked up her skirts and pushed through her drawers to her sweet, hot cleft. He stroked it. "Do you like that?" he said hoarsely.

She turned her head away. He pressed her to him, his

hands on her hips, holding her so that he could lick a brown-pink nipple, then suck on it strongly. She trembled, moving her fingers on his hard shaft, playing with the ridges of the burning head. The scent of her skin, the flower smell of her hair, intoxicated him.

He thrust his hips toward her and pushed his knee between her legs. She cupped him in her hands. Her fingers moved between his legs to stroke skin so sensitive he groaned. Abruptly, he let go of her and pushed her head down against him, her mouth trailing his belly.

Her hair spread across his thighs. Fulk inhaled, grinding his teeth in exquisite torment. Her mouth touched the tip of his cock, then her warm tongue slid the length of it and probed bursting flesh beneath. He suddenly saw a picture of the tip of his knife running under the hunter's sac, bright blood welling out from the lips of the wound. He heard the Welshman's scream.

She lifted her head, surprised. Her lips were red from kissing and licking his shaft. But he was growing soft in her hand.

Fulk sat up and took her by the elbows. He pulled her against him. He lowered her to the bed so that he lay curved around her. She trembled, then lay still.

He was thinking that de Bais had not been fooled. His knight knew one didn't administer punishment for hunting in the king's forests by cutting out testicles as one would geld a boar, or a horse. The whole thing came off, Jacquot himself, and one looked like a butchered woman. Men cut like that usually bled to death.

He put his hand on his wife's stomach and something moved under it, a part of the child, it felt like a foot or a knee. She waited, tense against him.

Fulk rubbed the flat of his hand over the spot. Perhaps it was the babe's head. He put his face against her back. Under the gown her skin was warm and sweet-smelling. He lay around her. The calm feel of the room and the rain slowly came back. He closed his eyes.

He felt her stir. She said, "Do you want me to bind up your finger now?"

Fulk didn't answer. He was getting to know her games. He pushed his hips against her gently.

He was growing hard again.

Chapter Eleven

IN THE WARM SUMMER DAYS BEFORE Corpus Christi, they began the year's cheesemaking. There was such a glut of milk that even the cook agreed it was waste to feed any more to the pigs. The kitchen yard soon stank of whey dripping from bags of curds hung up in the sun, a curiously unclean smell that stayed on everyone's hands and clothes. It was a bumper year because of the heat and the rain. The grain was thickly headed, even the hens were still laying heavily though they were approaching midsummer. The ward was ankle deep in grass. The stable knaves turned out a few of the knights' horses each morning to keep it cropped down.

The abundance of eggs and milk after so much winter starving was wondrous at first. Then it grew wearisome. After two solid days of the cook's blancmange one of the knights had come to Alwyn, a gleam in his eye, to ask when they were going to eat lentils again. She had sent him away with such a cross-grained retort he had burst out laughing.

The kitchen folk, the spinning women, and even some of Malluch's men-at-arms were set to preparing food for storage. Morlaix was still short of grain as the corn harvest was months away, but there was such a supply of early vegetables in the marcher country that there was no market for their cabbages and onions. And it did not pay to make the journey to sell them in Wrexham as there was a glut there, too.

When there were so many nets of onions hung in the storeroom that the rafters looked as though they had sprouted, the rest were laid down in brine to pickle. Great heads of cabbage, the best crop in years, were chopped and salted and packed in barrels. They would eat pickled cabbage and pickled onions the greater part of the winter, but at least it was there. With so much pickling, salt became scarce. A peddler with a wagonful who had come from Chester asked outrageous prices, but Alwyn told the butler to buy his whole stock of salt blocks without haggling. In the midst of the heaviest work Glennda, the farrier's daughter, went to the village to stay with the midwife and have her baby. Then she left to marry her horse dealer in Chirk.

The news was a shock. At first they all thought Glennda's babe had come early. But then the gossip was that it was full term. The rape had taken place before the feast of Saint Agatha. There was much counting on fingers.

"Now, the French knights raped the girl," the butler's wife said, "there's no doubt of that. You remember we had manor court, milady, and the witnesses, to prove that was so."

No, they had been cozened from beginning to end, Alwyn was sure. It was a sad conclusion to what once had been the glorious justice of manor court—just another village girl who could not keep her legs together. The farrier's daughter had made fools of them all. Furious, Alwyn sat down on a pile of onions in the kitchen and wept. The women chopping cabbage put down their knives and gathered around.

"By God and all the saints," she cried, "if I had her here, the lying bitch, I would strangle her! She's made a mockery of everything."

The little scullery girls stood around, moaning sympathetically.

"Now, if you ask me," the cook's wife said, "I would say our Glennda didn't know she was carrying the horse dealer's child. It was that early when the Frenchmen took her by force."

"You should be pleased, now, Mistress Alwyn," the weaving woman pointed out. "Glennda's well-off if she saves her silver pence and don't squander it; the geld levy makes a fine dowry. And her new husband's that proud of his babe. It looks just like him."

Alwyn shooed them away. She didn't believe a word of it. Neither would her Norman husband when he heard. The knights would call the manor court trickery. And say that she had falsely accused the Angevins. They thought the worst of her anyway, a hanged Breton rebel's daughter. There was no way, she supposed, despairing, that the story could be kept from them.

She could not get out of her mind what the farrier's daughter had done. Even while she was working, the child she carried was active, and tired her greatly. It seemed as though everyone was against her. Fulk de Jobourg was in the mountains, harrying outlaws that were stealing Morlaix's sheep. Alwyn had sent the usual messages to her cousin Powys to warn him. The Man of the Vale cut the flocks, but judiciously; they had agreed on that years ago. She was sure the Norman knights would never catch him.

At night she couldn't sleep. At last, to ease her mood, the women took her with them to a traveling show that had come to the village. Milord Fulk was away, they told her, and no one would know. Besides, too much fretting over something that could not now be helped would hurt her own babe.

The women wrapped her in an old harvester's gown and put the cook's wife's wooden clogs on her feet.

"You're still much too pretty," the butler's wife said. "Someone will know you." She wrapped Alwyn's head in a scullery girl's kerchief and pulled it down over her eyes. With Alwyn in the middle, they set out for the village.

It was a long walk. As they trudged down the castle road and passed over the river bridge, the women talked of Hugh de Yerville's new bride who was coming from Normandy when the manor house was built, and of the Jews now living in Chirk, the wool merchant and his clever daughter who was also his clerk. They did not mention Glennda. Alwyn busied herself with terrible thoughts of what would happen when the story reached Fulk de Jobourg.

The entertainers' tent was no more than a lean-to, open on three sides, set up behind the empty butcher's shambles. There were no seats; everyone stood. Underneath the shaky top that sheltered them from a warm drizzle, the villeins' wives were close packed, sun browned, with broad faces and the blue eyes of the Welsh, looking all alike in homespun clothes. Many had children in their arms. Some looked at Alwyn out of the corner of their eyes.

Alwyn had no doubt the villeins' wives too had heard what had become of the farrier's daughter.

A tall man, lively as a grasshopper, came out from behind a flap in the rear of the tent carrying a patched rebec with a very bent neck. He was dark skinned, with a head full of black ringlets. He wore a long, loose gown like a priest's made of many strips of satin, velvet, and gold-flecked cloth, and gold rings in each ear. The wizard's gown was very dirty. It would be hard to keep such finery clean going as they did, from village to village. When the man smiled, his dark face was pointed, foxlike.

Walking up and down at the front of the tent, he made a speech about the village that sounded like a speech he would make about any village where he pitched his tent. He told jokes and said that Morlaix's goodwives were famed throughout the marcher countryside for their good cooking and hard work and their children's handsomeness. Some of the younger women giggled, believing it.

Then he sang a bawdy song about a virgin and a lusty young plowboy, accompanying himself on the rebec. It was a song for women, scandalously full of what went on when one made love with a man. The entertainer winked and laughed as he sang the verses. At the end the virgin tricked the plowboy after he had seduced her, and stole his ox.

While he sang, a dark woman in a gown made of the same motley came into the tent and passed among the women. She told fortunes, the man announced, and would be glad to take their barter in return for telling them the secrets of the future. Her name was Madhamet Osiris.

Alwyn stood behind the weaving woman and the cook's wife, the scullery girls around her. In the damp air they reeked of sour milk. One of the spinning sisters paid Madhamet Osiris a new cheese wrapped in leaves for her fortune.

The man told another joke.

A couple came to the village midwife, he said, and were unhappy with the baby she had delivered to them a few months ago. Look, the husband said, taking off the babe's cap, this child has red hair and my wife and I have hair dark as the night.

Now the midwife, he went on, hoping to avoid the usual trouble when people came to her like this, thought hard. Finally she said, "I must ask you some questions, as this is a most unusual situation, seeing this redheaded babe when both of you have black hair. Has there ever been a redheaded person in your families?" When they both shook their heads, the midwife looked solemn. "Now I must ask you," she said, "how often do you go to bed and have sex?" The husband looked at the wife, and the wife

152

looked at the husband. "Well," the man said, "not more than once a year." The midwife clapped her hands together, relieved. "Just as I suspected," she cried. "That explains it all. This child is not redheaded. What we are seeing is *rust*!"

The villeins' wives barked their laughter. The fortune-teller was now holding the butler's wife's hand, her head bent over it.

The man turned abruptly, his bright gown glittering and swaying, and picked up the rebec again. He began a song about King William. Alwyn could hardly listen. First Glennda, now a traveling entertainer's joke that was not funny about redheaded bastards. Her back had begun to pain her from so much standing, and the wooden clogs hurt her feet.

There was another song, the man announced, about the courtship of William, Duke of Normandy, and Matilda, daughter of Baldwin, the Count of Flanders. The Welsh women murmured. Even from the title, "The Wooing of Queen Matilda," they could hope it was spicy. The tent quieted to listen.

Alwyn pressed one hand to her back. If it was true, the story sounded as bad as her own marrying. The Countess Matilda of Flanders had lost her heart to a fair young Englishman named Brihtric, who had visited her father's court on a mission for the English king known as Edward the Confessor. Brihtric was so handsome, so startling fair, he had been given the nickname of "meaw" or snow.

Young Duke William of Normandy was also wooing Matilda, but his courtship was not going well. He much needed an alliance through marriage with the powerful Flemings. When it became plain that dainty Matilda favored the Englishman, Brihtric, William the Bastard grew so angry that as the Lady Matilda was returning from mass in Bruges, he rode across her path, hurled her ladies aside and yanked her from her saddle. He then threw her down from her horse so that she fell in the mud of the street.

The village wives gasped. The butler's wife, who was having her palm read by the fortune-teller, looked up.

After William's rough wooing, the singer went on, Matilda retired to one of her father's manors, at Lille, and would see no one. It was said she wrote many letters to young Lord Brihtric. Perhaps hearing of this, William of Normandy was more determined to have her. And to have the Count of Flanders as a father-in-law. Secretly, William rode to Baldwin's manor at Lille where Matilda was hiding, stormed through the reception hall, defying the servants to touch him, and then into the women's apartments. Matilda met her raging suitor bravely, but William was past reason. He seized petite Matilda by her long hair and dragged her around her chamber. When she struggled and screamed he struck her repeatedly, then flung her on the ground at his feet.

The dark woman who told fortunes had finished with the butler's wife. She came to Alwyn and seized her hand before Alwyn could pull it back. Her black eyes intent, she said, "I will tell your fortune, pretty miss, for a copper."

Alwyn had no money and nothing to trade. "Ah, let me," the weaving woman said, turning around. From her skirt pockets she produced the broken half of a farthing.

Alwyn tried to pull her hand back. The scullery girls nudged her toward Madhamet Osiris. The fortune-teller held on to Alwyn's hand. Her grip was dry and smooth. She pocketed the weaving woman's halfpenny and forced Alwyn's fingers apart.

She peered into her palm. "Ah, there is a man who loves you, a good man, but God will not let you have him." She looked at the child bulging Alwyn's skirt. "And the one whose child you carry denies you, beware of him," she said in a harsh voice. She grabbed the other hand and looked into it. "There is the dark man, the man in the mountains, go with him."

She folded Alwyn's fingers into a fist and covered them with her hands. She looked into her face. "You are pretty, but you look above your station, girl. Your knight lover will disavow you, and even the child."

The weaving woman shouldered the fortune-teller to one side. "Pah, that's no fortune." Her voice was loud. "If I thought I could get it, I would ask for my copper back."

She took Alwyn's arm. The singer had begun another song. They moved through the crowd quickly. The castle women followed, talking about what the fortune-teller had said.

Outside, the air was fresh in spite of the butcher's shambles nearby. The setting sun peeped through the clouds.

One of the spinning sisters said, "Pay no attention, milady, to all that. Last year at the Chirk fair I was told I would find a husband within a sixmonth. And you see how well that has served me."

Alwyn's back was hurting and the babe kicked her fiercely. It had been a mistake to stand so long. It felt good to walk.

They went down through the middle of the village, taking care to jump the open drains. Past the miller's house, toward the castle road. The air was still warm. On either side the fields were solid with oats and barley, thick wheat beyond. The wooden clogs had raised blisters on both Alwyn's heels. She took them off. The earth was wet and slippery under her feet.

"Did you hear what he sang about King William's wife?" the butler's wife said.

The spinner said, "About young Brihtric dying?"

Alwyn took off the big kerchief. "I did not hear that part. The fortune-teller was talking."

"Oh," the butler's wife said, "after all those years, to remember that. He is a cruel man, the Conqueror. These Normans do not give up their vengeance easy."

"What happened?" Alwyn asked.

Adnia said, "He found him, Lord Brihtric, and clapped him in jail, King William did, when he conquered England. It was some twenty years later, but he hadn't forgotten. Lord Brihtric was arrested, the singer said, in Hanley, which is in a place he called Worcestershire. 'Twas only a few months too before he died there in his cell, poor Lady Matilda's handsome young lover."

"Oh," Alwyn said.

Somewhere in the village the cows waiting to be milked bellowed softly.

The women walked along in silence.

"But he loved her," the butler's wife said at last. "That was the end of the song, that no matter what he married her for, King William grew to love his wife dearly. Of all those he has around him, he trusts and loves the queen the most."

They walked faster. The castle road and the river were in sight. Alwyn was thinking it was a good thing that Glennda was now in Chirk. If she'd still been in the village, she would have sent Malluch and some of the bowmen to get her. Then she would have locked her in the keep.

"If I had a bit of cheese to trade," one of the scullery girls at the rear said, "I would have had my fortune told, too."

The butler's wife turned to look over her shoulder. "It was a fraud," she said, "and a trickery, you mark my words. They were thieves. I felt a tug on my belt when she was telling my fortune, and if I hadn't held on to it, she would have had my purse."

The Earl of Chester's bailiff came on Midsummer Eve day. They had some warning. A knight dallying with a girl in the miller's ale yard saw the troop of knights approaching, carrying the standard of Hugh of Avranches, and mounted his horse and galloped up the castle road to bring the news.

Alwyn had been washing with vinegar water to get rid of the odor of cheese. Quickly, she got out her red gown, combed her hair, and put on some gold pins of her mother's. She was breathing hard when she ran down the stairs to the ward. The earl's men were just coming through the portal gate. She drew herself up to welcome them.

One of the knights jumped down to help the bailiff, but he got off his horse by himself. He looked more a fighting man than a castle reeve: stocky, with heavy black brows, a face jowly with middle age. He wore a hauberk highly polished. There was a sword and mace strapped to his high-pommeled saddle. He looked greatly approving when he saw her, a woman heavy with child.

The Earl of Chester's knights dismounted. They were well outfitted, their horses particularly fine. Alwyn bent her knee in respect before the bailiff.

"My name is Osbern Tirell, milady," he told her, "bailiff for the liege lord here, Hugh of Avranches, the Earl of Chester." He hauled her up by the hand. "I knew your father."

She was surprised that he would mention it. Most people did not now speak of her father, especially his former friends. She was startled when the earl's bailiff put his arms around her and kissed her cheek. She held herself stiffly, aware of her bulging middle, relieved when he let her go and stepped back.

"I had hoped to find your good lord husband here." He looked around. "But I am told the baron of Morlaix is in the hills seeking outlaws. That disappoints me," he went on, before she could speak. "I have a writ, a complaint by my lord earl's quarrymaster, that he has been ill treated by your lord."

Osbern Tirell was not tall. Alwyn's eyes were on a level with his. She wondered if he could see shock in them.

Sweet Mother Mary, she had not heard anything about

a writ! She knew Fulk de Jobourg had not sworn fealty to
Hugh of Avranches. But then some vassal knights did not
do so in these times of shifting allegiances. Hugh of
Avranches had only been Earl of Chester since the city
had fallen.

A wagon rumbled over the drawbridge and came under
the portal gate. It was filled with the village girls coming
to spend the night in the castle. The earl's bailiff turned,
interested, to watch.

Geoffrey de Bocage's knights rode in escort, laughing
and calling out to the girls. When they saw Chester's
knights and Osbern Tirell, they quickly put on their helmets.

Father Ascelin came hurrying from the church. When
he saw the bailiff he veered toward him.

The bailiff said, "Ho, Ascelin, is this your flock you're
saving from sin?"

She was not surprised they knew each other.

"It is the Devil's own night." The priest shot Alwyn a
look. "Does your business bring you here for a time?"

The bailiff smiled and shook his head.

Chester's knights had dismounted. They stood in a circle, holding their horses' reins, listening. Alwyn gestured
toward the great hall. "Tell your knights to stable their
horses and we will offer them our best hospitality."

Father Ascelin moved toward the wagon with the Midsummer maids. Alwyn and the bailiff walked toward the
hall, trailed by the Earl of Chester's ten knights.

In the hall the cook brought out trays of blancmange.
When Chester's knights had scraped their bowls clean,
the cook, who had been watching from the door, summoned the kitchen knaves. They came with more trays of
custard.

"This is elegant fare," Osbern Tirell said, pushing his
dish away.

"It has a been a bountiful summer." Alwyn motioned

for the knaves not to bring any more food. "With God's grace we will have a dry spell for harvest."

The bailiff gave her a keen look. "Yes, Morlaix's crops are fine; we passed through them for miles. You have opened up new fields here, they are better even than I remember under the old baron, your father."

Alwyn could not remember if her father had sworn fealty to Hugh of Avranches. She thought he did; she remembered he had paid knights' fees and taxes.

"We fought with the Conqueror," the bailiff was saying, "Bruse Lesneven and I. We were there when William faced Harold Godwinson. That was a day, at Senlac. No one there will ever forget it."

Alwyn stared down at her hands. She did not know when Fulk de Jobourg would return with his knights. They had been gone four days. She knew they had only one wagon and supplies for no more than five. She did not want the bailiff there for Midsummer Eve. The castle would be shut, the drawbridge drawn up. Father Ascelin would keep his village virgins safe inside.

"I was the one who sent the village boys to the quarry," she told him. "Earl Chester's quarryman came here, to Morlaix, and set a number for the quarry that was hard to meet. It was plowing time and the Morlaix men could not be spared."

Osbern Tirell smiled. "Dear milady, no one holds you accountable. It is not necessary for you to explain."

She looked up at him from under her eyelashes. "Oh, but I must. I cannot rest easy that someone else should take the unjust burden of what I have done. For it all began then, when there was a levy against the Morlaix men for their yearly work at Chirk quarry. To understand this complaint from the master of the quarry, you must have my testimony as to what he and I agreed on, is that not so?"

He studied her. After a long moment he said, "Yes, that is so."

She told herself first she must make a great story of it to convince him. She had to tell of each boy, whom he was related to in the village, how long his people had been there, and whether he was a villein's son or the son of a freeman. All were obliged to pay their work levy to the lord of Morlaix. Every small thing was a help.

She told Osbern Tirell, her father's old friend who had fought with him at Senlac, how hard it was to send the village boys to the quarry when they were not equal to the work of men. And how, after much bargaining, she had allowed one third more than the agreed number to go on the quarrymaster's word that many more boys would make the work he wanted. She had gotten his promise that he would not beat them.

When she had done all this she told him of the miller's son. It would not take long to go to the village and see the boy. Osbern Tirell could judge for himself whether her husband had been right to be so wroth with the quarrymaster.

Chester's knights had left the hall. The kitchen knaves were putting down fresh rushes and wiping the boards clean for the evening meal. She had not asked the bailiff to stay the night and wait for Fulk de Jobourg.

He sat back on the bench, observing the red gown, her hair, the gold pins of her mother's fastened in the dress.

He nodded finally. "Yes, I will see the boy in the village if it will not take long. I am returning to Chester. To do that I must make Chirk township by nightfall."

She had gotten what she wanted, she thought, relieved. When he saw the miller's son, Osbern Tirell would see that if there was any blame it was hers. She would gladly take the punishment if that ended the matter. Even better, she would get the bailiff and Chester's knights out of the castle before the priest and his girls began their Midsummer Eve vigil.

Chapter Twelve

FULK'S KNIGHTS CAME UP THE CASTLE road just as the last wagonload of Father Ascelin's Midsummer maidens crossed under the portal gate and hauled up by the church. Hearing the lookout call, the priest hurried out of the church, where the first group of maids were being watched by the butler's wife, and rushed to get the newcomers out of the wagon. He shooed them ahead of him into the hall, where food had been prepared. Then he scurried back to see how things were going in the church.

Father Ascelin had not been prepared for so many girls seeking the Church's protection on Midsummer Eve. If one took them at their word, there were more maidens in the Llanystwyth valley than in all the marcher country from Wrexham to Hereford. Many in four wagonloads did not look at all familiar, and he prided himself that he knew most of the village. He told himself these were the daughters from far-flung shepherds' crofts who were doubtless better off in Morlaix Castle on Midsummer Eve than exposed to whatever demonic pagan revels took place in their wild hills. He viewed with surprise one or two blackened, savage-looking females mixed in with the rest. The only thing he could think of was that these strange creatures could have come from the tribes of charcoal burners that seldom came out of the forests.

Alwyn was overseeing the cook in the hall when she heard the lookout's hail. She came running out into the ward, holding up her long skirts. For a moment she feared the Morlaix knights had passed the Earl of Chester's bailiff on the castle road. She knew Osbern Tirell had gone the village way; from the mountains, Fulk de Jobourg surely would have taken the track from the west. But her heart was pounding when the first knights came clattering over the drawbridge.

There were thirty-odd knights and their horses. The stable boys and squires darted among the animals, seizing bridles. The knights cursed tiredly. A knight with a blood-stained tunic swayed in his saddle. Another, a young knight Alwyn did not know, rode before Goutard, who held his arms around him to keep him from falling. They had taken prisoners. Outlaws, bearded men in filthy rags with their arms bound behind them, crouched on their knees in the supply wagon bed. Father Ascelin hurriedly pushed the last group of women toward the church. The butler came running out of the kitchen house, pulling on his coat. Alwyn shouted to him to tell the cook to come out and look after the wounded knights.

Fulk de Jobourg sat in the middle of the ward, his destrier's feet braced, its big head drooping. He watched as the priest herded the girls into the church and his wife came running up, only to stop short at the sight of him.

He glowered at her. She wore her hair down for some reason, a black cloud down her arms. In her red gown and jewels she looked foreign to the dirt and horses and cursing knights.

He sniffed the air. "Christ's wounds," were his first words to her, "what's that stink?"

* * *

The wounded were carried into the hall. Alwyn did not like the look of the young knight; the boy, no more than eighteen or nineteen, was bleeding freely. Two of his friends laid him out on a table. The cook shrugged. The boy had a bad wound in the side; if it had not hit his vitals, mayhap he would live.

When she came back from seeing that the church was locked with the women inside, she found that the cook, the knight Goutard, and Fulk de Jobourg had bound the young knight up with cloths to ease the bleeding. They left him stretched out on the table in the back of the hall for his friends to look after him. There were three of them, all from Coutances in Normandy. The other knight had a broken arm. When the cook set it, he fainted. He was carried off to the knights' quarters on the lower floors of the keep.

In a few minutes, a squire came into the hall with a message that Milord Fulk wanted his bath. Alwyn sent four kitchen knaves to fetch it for him. She went out into the ward where it was calmer. The horses were inside the stables and the prisoners in the wagon had been pulled out of the way behind the kitchen. The outlaws were filthy and covered with blood. All were wounded.

She went around the wagon, peering at them. She did not recognize any of them as Powys's men, and was relieved. She sent one of the stable boys to fetch the cook to dress the outlaws' wounds. Then she told a squire to fetch them water to drink. When the squire turned away, busy with other tasks, she screamed at him till he obeyed.

Inside the church, the priest had set the women to singing psalms. The racket set one's teeth on edge. She found the tally reeve and some of the kitchen boys rolling a keg of beer out the storehouse door. They set it up in the middle of the ward. "It's for the knights," the tally reeve told her. "After this sortie in the mountains, milord Fulk said they should have it."

She knew what the beer would do, but she had no say

over the Norman knights. She told the tally reeve to break out a small portion for the men-at-arms, too.

The night was warm and wet. Water halos circled the torches on the wall walk and on the buildings in the ward. Alwyn walked to the portal gate. The night guards stood watching the valley and the beltane fires. There were bonfires on every hill at Midsummer Eve, for which the villagers had been gathering wood for weeks. The fires burned brightly, although it was hardly dusk.

More than a few of the castle people had gone down to the village for Midsummer night: the scullery girls, even a few of the Welsh bowmen, Adnia the weaver, the two spinning sisters, the cook's unmarried sister-in-law. Alwyn thought of the stout weaving woman with her heavy legs. She could not imagine any of them running naked in the woodlands, their hair down and streaming, hoping for sex.

One of the portal knights came to tell her to move back. Two night guards worked up the drawbridge. The chains' grinding shriek overrode the women's voices in the chapel. The wooden beams that barred the planks of the gate slammed down like thunderbolts.

For better or worse, they were locked in for the night.

The stairs in the keep were wet with spilled water. Alwyn picked her way over slippery stones. Inside, the bath, full of dirty water, stood in the middle of the floor.

Her husband stood at the basin, shaving. He wore only a linen towel around his waist. Across his back, from shoulder blades to the bottom of his ribs, was a purpling red bruise that looked as though a horse had trampled him. He said, without turning his head, "How fares young Soverville?"

He meant the young knight in the hall. She went to the bed and sat on it, pressing her lower back with one hand. "Not so well, I think."

He pulled down his lip with one hand and scraped it free of stubble. "He'll have his luck if he lives the night. These damned fools who have just come from Normandy think caution is cowardice. He chased an outlaw into the woods and his friends were waiting for him. He took a spear in his side."

Alwyn did not know whether to lie back down among the pillows or continue to sit up. Her back hurt either way. She pulled off her shoes. The young knight was so handsome he was almost pretty; it would be a shame if he died. She wondered about his family in Coutance, what his mother felt when he went to fight in England. Below, there were noises, then a crash. Women's voices singing psalms shrilled over the clamor. The boy should be out in the woods, Alwyn thought, with the girls on Midsummer Eve. Not lying bleeding to death in the hall.

Fulk slung soap against the basin with his razor. He held the other side of his mouth with one finger and scraped. "The priest is mad, to bring those women here," he said around it. "They came because he said he would feed them. They're not going to sing prayers all night in the church." He turned to her, wiping his face, his eyes hooded. "Why are you wearing that dress? And why do you always look like that?"

"My back hurts," she said.

He crossed over to the bed and sat down on his side of it and used the towel to wipe his feet. "Holy Christ, I'm bone-weary." He threw the towel on the bed. "This is not going to stop the sheep stealing. These brutes we took don't know what a sheep looks like." He swiveled his head, frowning. "What the devil is that stink? Has no one cleaned out the ditch?"

Alwyn leaned back on her elbows. The child was a mound in front of her eyes. In that position her belly muscles pulled tight. It felt good. She looked at his bruised back and thought: Perhaps someone knocked him from his horse and it stepped on him. He couldn't get up and it stepped on him and stepped on him.

"We're making cheese," she said. "There are too many cows freshened. The grass is so plentiful we are glutted with milk here at the castle. It is the same in the village, and you can't even give butter away at the market in Chirk." She sighed. "Cheese keeps for the winter, so we are making a lot of it. Milk always stinks when it's aging."

He had turned to look at her. "Is that what you do here," he said, frowning, "make cheese?"

She stared at him. Still propped on her elbows, the babe reared up under her dress. "Holy Mother of God, what else should I do?"

Dark eyes studied her. "Ladies of the gentry make things." He looked up at the Hereford tapestry. "They weave and embroider. Don't you know how to sew?"

She hauled herself up to a sitting position. She scraped her hair out of her eyes with both hands, to see him better. "Sew? I sew your shirts! I sew the holes together in your underdrawers! That's what I do when I am not making stinking cheese!"

Angry, she would have thrown herself out of the bed but he caught her and pushed her back against the covers.

"I don't want you to touch me," she cried. She threw his hands away.

He bent over her, the muscles in his bare shoulders coiling. He put his hands at the sides of her head. "Come, be sweet, you can take me. You are not that far along." It was the same voice he used to coax his hawk. "You are not more than six months gone."

Alwyn stared up at him. Ah, God, the garrison knights had already told him. No gossip in the castle ever escaped them.

"Tell me, wife, whose child is it you carry?" he said softly. "Or, like yon farrier's daughter, is that a secret?"

Far away, there were shouts. Knights in the quarters

below answered. They heard the sound of running feet down the stairs.

Alwyn couldn't speak. The words stuck in her throat. He would not believe them, anyway. She watched, helpless, as he leaned over until his face hovered just above hers. He reached down and put his hand on her belly, fingers spread. He pressed it gently. "That babe is surpassing big for six months, is it not?"

She shuddered. "The women say it is very big."

He bent his head. His mouth found her cheek and the line of her jaw, tracing it with his lips. "Oh, do they?" His lips nuzzled her hair. He said, right at her ear, "If you deliver this big babe miraculous early, I will kill you."

Footsteps came up the stairs and paused. There was a soft knock.

Fulk lifted his head, scowling. "Sweet Mary's tits." He rolled off the bed, picked up the towel and held it before him. He yanked open the big wooden door. Guy de Bais was standing there. His short coat was half buttoned and he was barefoot.

"Fulk," the knight blurted out, "you must come down." He looked past him to the bed. "The women are out of the church!"

The two men charged down the steps, Alwyn right behind them. Fulk and Guy de Bais ran out into the ward. She stood on the last step to watch.

Someone had rolled out two more kegs of beer from the storeroom. Alwyn wondered if the butler, who had the keys, was still alive. It was mayhem. The kegs lay beside the first in the center of the ward. Only a handful of knights were still drinking. The rest were chasing Father Ascelin's maidens up and around the ward and through the stables and into the kitchen yard.

She heard Fulk curse.

There were women in the church but the psalm singing

had stopped. She saw how they were getting out. The women were climbing through the open roof, helped up by those still inside.

The noise was enough to deafen. The women screamed. Some were running and singing and casting off their clothes. The knights chasing them were laughing like maniacs. Two women flung off their gowns by the horse trough and, naked, jumped into it and splashed each other. Outside, on the castle road, Alwyn could hear drumming and singing as though revelers were coming up from the village.

It was a night with a risen full moon. Bright light bathed the ward. She saw a naked man striding about, shouting orders. She looked again. It was Fulk de Jobourg without his towel. One knight dragged a woman into the stairwell, shoved her up against the wall and coupled with her. They were close enough to touch. The man panted. The woman's moans were loud. Alwyn shut her eyes. When they were through, they ran out into the ward again.

She moved to the doorway, hidden by shadow, her hand covering her mouth in amazement. Fulk de Jobourg was right; the women were not going to be shut up the night in Father Ascelin's church singing psalms. Madness had seized them all. Bodies coupled on the grass, in the kitchen yard, by the great hall. Knights ran along the wall walk above, looking for women. She saw Malluch and another bowman by the beer kegs. Their arms were around two of Father Ascelin's maidens who were drinking cups of beer and tearing at the men's clothes at the same time.

By the portal gate, Fulk, shouting, drove the night guards to the winch of the drawbridge. As the knights strained at the wheel the chains began to grind.

Alwyn put her hands over her ears. In spite of the noise one could hear the beat of drums and singing outside. The drawbridge came down with a bang, bounced, then sank back in the dirt.

Some knights in mail began to push the crowd toward

the gate. They jumped back out of the way as yelling naked men and women surged out onto the castle road and met the villagers. Drums beat wildly. Rowan and holly branches waved in the crowd like a moving forest. Men and women clasped each other and screamed with laughter.

She saw Fulk shouting to the knights to drive the crowd back down the road. Like a many-legged beast, the naked horde began to flow down the castle road toward the river and the trees.

Inside, calm settled over the castle abruptly. For the first time, she could hear wakened children crying. A woman was shouting, angrily, in the sleeping rooms over the stables. Outside, the drums and the singing got farther and farther away.

Before the portal gate, Malluch picked up a black-clad figure and set him on his feet. Father Ascelin looked as though he had thrown himself in front of the crowd, to stop them. His face was covered with dirt and his habit was torn. He staggered, confused. The Welshmen turned him in the direction of the church. The priest went to the steps and sat down and covered his face with his hands.

Alwyn walked out into the ward.

Fulk de Jobourg strode across the grass. Guy de Bais ran to keep up with him. A knight from the portal guard joined them. "Count every knight," he was shouting.

Beyond, some castle folk were going about picking up discarded clothing. The armorer's wife, in her nightdress, stood holding a candle, directing them.

Her husband stopped short when he saw her. The moonlight gleamed on his bare skin. With his broad shoulders and long legs, he towered over the others. She stared at him. He was far better endowed than any of the men she had just seen.

She looked away, quickly. He came to her and took her by the arm. "If you can look at it, you can do something about it," he growled, and shoved her toward the stairs.

* * *

When they got to the room she got in bed and he put out
the candles. They could still hear noise in the ward. It
would take forever for people to go back to sleep. He got
in beside her and pulled her to him and said, "God's
wounds, you're like ice. Do you lack sense to put something on when you go out?"

When she stiffened, he rolled her over on her side,
away from him.

"Where does it hurt?" He put his hands against her
back.

She thought it over. "Below there," she said finally.
"Low, in the curve."

He rubbed her. His probing fingers spread and kneaded
deep in the muscles. He seemed to know where it hurt
and how to ease it. She had seen knights pummeling each
other's bodies after sword practice, to get out the ache.

After a few minutes, he said, his mouth against her
cheek, "Is that better?"

When she nodded, he pulled her to him. He took her
hand and guided it to his shaft. "Gently," he muttered
when she grasped him.

He turned her face up to him in the darkness. His arms
went around her. He seized her mouth hungrily.

During the night, the young knight died. It went almost
unnoticed when it was discovered the prisoners had escaped. De Yerville and a group of ten knights galloped off
at once to search for the outlaws.

The rest of the knights carried the body down to the
graveyard by the river and buried it there. Afterward, the
young knight's three friends left to go back to Coutances.
Bad-tempered, Fulk paid them off. The knight with the
broken arm wanted to go to Wrexham and stay with his
brother's family until it was mended.

The knights who came straggling back from the village at dawn were fined and set to doing base work cleaning out the stables and the castle ditch. Afterward, they selected an emissary to go to Fulk to complain of sorties against common sheep thieves that brought little honor, and the lack of plunder. Snarling, Fulk threw the emissary down the stairs of the keep.

The butler gathered the kitchen knaves to clean up the ward. The cook was out of sorts and fought with the tally reeve over the custody of the storehouse keys. Alwyn went down to take the keys herself and settle the quarrel. Then she got out clean bed coverings from the linen press and went up to the room to change the bed.

When she came in, Geoffrey de Bocage was sitting by the fireplace, drinking wine. Fulk de Jobourg stood by the window. He whirled on her.

"You damned intriguing, back-stabbing slut!" he shouted. "I ought to cut out your foul treacherous tongue!"

He threw his cup of wine at her. It hit the wall behind Alwyn and splattered red over the linen she was carrying. She opened her arms and let the linen drop to the floor, uncaring. "Greetings, Geoffrey," she said. "What lies have you been telling about me again?"

He gave her a crooked smile and leaned back in the chair. "I never lie about you, sweetheart."

Fulk stamped over to the table and threw rolls of vellum across it. "Now may the damned fry in hell, where's the thing? The noose around my neck she so well placed, God rot her. The writ from this snot-nosed provost of Chester's."

Alwyn sat down on the bed, heavily. She looked at Geoffrey. "Now what have you done?"

He looked at her complacently over the rim of his cup. He was as handsome as ever. "I have done nothing, sweet lady, the honor is all yours." He looked at Fulk. "The Earl of Chester's provost sends a summons. He says you testified to his bailiff that this fief has always granted the earl's levy of men to work each year in the quarry. That you took the bailiff to see one of the workers as proof. Hugh of Avranches is well pleased with this assent. He only wants his vassal, Fulk de Jobourg, to come to Chester now and swear fealty."

Holy Mother! Alwyn licked her lips. "Where is the summons? Get the priest to read it."

Fulk strode to her and grabbed her arm. "Will you listen?" he shouted into her face. "You are not the lord here, and we do not need to call Chester's spy to read it. It's a summons, damn you. I have skirted shy of Chester since William granted me this place and now you have put my arse in it!" He shook her by the arm until she slid from the bed to the floor. "You dealt with that cursed bailiff as you held manor court, you presumptuous bitch. There is no end to your damned conniving cleverness!"

He stood over her, fists clenched. She put her arms across her belly to protect it. "My father swore fealty to Chester," she yelled. "What is the matter with that?"

He turned from her. "Your father was too stupid to stay out of traps. I am King William's man."

Geoffrey watched them. "Ask her about the women," he said.

Alwyn stared at them. Surely they were not going to blame her for that. The prisoners they took looked to be more English from the north, starved and burned out, like the other outlaws that hid in the forests. Father Ascelin did not know all the women who came to the castle. She still did not think that women, even outlaws' women, would be so brave as to come to Castle Morlaix on Midsummer Eve and help their men escape.

He leaned down, his hands on his knees, to glare at her. "You see how she plots to destroy me," he shouted. "She can look like that, but it's in her eyes, the deceit." He straightened up. "It's like living with a snake."

Geoffrey put down his wine. He came over to stand beside him. "I know what I would do with her."

Alwyn bent her head. She was frightened. She had a babe now, and she had to protect herself. She should have worked this better, she thought. He always wanted to lie with her, he wanted her to give him sex day and night, she should never have told him she didn't want him to touch her; she knew now she should have given him all that he wanted, and more. She tried to think. How was anyone to know Osbern Tirell would turn the sick miller's boy so neatly against them? Holy Cross, it was a spider's web of plotting, just to live like this!

"Leave it," she heard him say. "I'm sick of it."

She heard the door slam as they left.

Her husband did not come to the room that night to sleep. Alwyn banked the fire, slipped into bed and waited, but he did not come.

Later, she heard the drawbridge go up, the bars at the portal gate come down, the castle being secured. Someone drove a wagon across the ward to the stables. Fitfully, she slept. Once when she woke up she heard voices, but it was only some knights on the stairs of the keep, going to their quarters, and she drifted off again. It was nearly dawn when she woke for good. She could not go back to sleep; she was dreaming too much. She dreamed she was crying out in a storm, lost; fighting a flood in a boat on the river, sending servants for things which they never found. She got out of bed, the stones of the floor feeling damp to her bare feet, and went to the window.

The moon had set and there was nothing to see but the faint gleam of the river and, dimly sensed, the humid strips of grain ripening in the fields, the darker blot of the woods beyond.

She rested her chin on her elbow. The woods had been full of people on Midsummer Eve. It was a good thing crops were laid by and work was not hard; the villagers who had been out all night had come back in a stupor. She wondered what it would have been like, running through the forest on Midsummer night, coupling with anyone who wanted to take you. Those who had been out of the castle would not talk about it. The weaving woman even denied she'd gone.

Her husband and his cousin thought she'd had something to do with setting the outlaws free, although there was no proof that this had happened; someone in the castle might have done it. They accused her of everything. Like living with a snake, he'd said. And Osbern Tirell with his smooth manners, his listening air, had betrayed her, too. She'd only taken him to see the miller's son because she had some foolish thought that she would plead a good cause, that her husband would come to trust her as they said King William had come to trust his wife, Matilda. Now there was no one she could turn to.

Her husband might kill her yet, she thought, shivering. Geoffrey de Bocage had planted doubt in his mind about her babe. If he truly thought the child was someone else's, there was no reason to keep her.

I'll pray to God to help me, she told herself. There was no need to wait and go down to the chapel. She could pray right there, standing up, looking out on the valley and the place she could not leave.

She closed her eyes. Oh God, she thought, show me a way out of this.

Chapter Thirteen

THE MASTER MASON RETURNED TO Morlaix Castle the day after the feast of Saints Peter and Paul. One morning, on her way to the storehouse with the cook, Alwyn saw him standing with Father Ascelin, directing the last work on the roof of the church.

The masons were dismantling the scaffolding now that the outside was mostly finished. As the men carried down the timbers and piled them in the yard, the chapel's shape was gradually revealed. It no longer appeared, as had the old church, as a random outbuilding attached to the castle wall. Instead, it was now a perfect small structure, freestanding, built of Glamorgan gray stone in the Roman style it was said the Normans used everywhere in Britain with their great spate of building. The master builder had left his mark. The chapel reflected a marked gracefulness, something unmistakably Celtic and Welsh.

Alwyn was sure the master mason saw her. As the mistress of Morlaix she could not call to him in front of everyone, nor could she go to speak to him without some excuse. She turned away, fighting strange, hopeful feelings. He was only the master mason, a craftsman builder.

But she had longed for him in her desperate moments; she had even dreamed of him in a way that revealed all too plainly where her secret thoughts lay.

She knew she was a great fool to entertain such a dangerous fancy. She was ungainly, almost seven months gone with child, irritable, sorely pressed with work. Not pretty. Not happy. Not what any man possessed of his senses would want. And she was married to an unloving, untrusting Norman knight who did not let her forget the hard facts of their marrying; in much less than three months she would birth his child. It was lunacy to think of anything else.

Still, he was there. Every morning when she came to break her fast and attend to the chores of the day, he was at the church working with his men. She told herself that Master Ian of Scotland, for all his fine manners, was a workman without power to help her in the hard world in which they lived. She was surprised that she was attacked by such a wild sense of yearning. For him. For tenderness. For something. The Welsh had a word for it. *Hiraeth.* A longing for that which is not to be found in this life.

She looked for him when she came in and out of the ward on errands. He was not much changed. When he climbed the scaffolding to where the masons were laying the last shingle over the nave, the sun struck his gilded hair and his fine white shirt. She could pick him out from the others easily. She wondered what business had taken him away to York. The masons would be gone by harvest time. The abbot's clerk came from St. Botolph's to pay them every week, and he had told the butler that they would break their camp by the castle road after the feast of Saint Matthew.

By then, the summer would almost be past.

The castle was empty of all but the masons finishing the church. The cheesemaking had stopped as the calves grew big and accounted for a greater share of the milk. A spell of warm dry weather had sent the weavers and spinners to the village to dye new cloth. A horse fair camped on the river between Morlaix and Chirk. In the long summer evenings, the garrison knights went down to gamble and look over the horseflesh. Fulk de Jobourg had gone to Chester, a trip of many days, to swear fealty to Hugh of Avranches as his vassal.

It had not been a happy departure. The knights were not eager to swear to Chester as liege lord over Morlaix. King William was in France, subduing his son Robert and his rebellious allies; there was no counsel from London except a late message to concede to Chester's demand with discretion.

It was decided that they would make a brave show of it. They would go to Chester and do homage, but with the best trappings, showing unyielding pride. Before they left, a knight from Falaise stood up at evening meal and told the story of Hrolf, the Conqueror's ancestor, the first Viking duke of Normandy. When brave Hrolf and his men were made to pay homage to the king of France by the custom of kissing the king's royal foot, the old Norseman haughtily refused. But he chose one of his men who, just as unwilling to so demean himself, promptly seized the king's foot and amid gales of laughter jerked it up to his mouth so that the king fell flat on his back. Shouting, the Morlaix knights pounded their tables in agreement. They would not kiss the foot of Chester, either.

The castle had been thrown into a frenzy of work. The armorer was busy for days polishing and repairing weapons. Horses were groomed by the stable knaves and then groomed again by the knights, who had all received white tunics sewn with the device of Fulk de Jobourg's prancing griffon. Guy de Bais brought the gonfalon to Alwyn to be repaired, as it was frayed from the wind and hard wear.

"This needs mending, and Milord Fulk says you are skilled in needlework," he told her. The knights now treated her coldly. The story of the dispute with the earl's quarrymaster and what had become of it had gone through the castle and countryside.

Alwyn turned the seams of the banner and sewed linen strips inside to strengthen the edges. The griffon was an ugly beast. She thought of adding flowers or vines curling about it as she had seen on some pennants. But when it was finished, she gave it back to the knight as it was.

On the day they left, Fulk de Jobourg called together Hugh de Yerville, head of the castle garrison, Malluch and the men-at-arms, the butler and the tally reeve, to leave his orders as to what should be done in his absence. To his wife, he said nothing, but merely touched his finger to his helm and nodded, before turning his mount toward the gate.

Holy Cross, that did not bother her, she told herself. The bed was empty at night; she missed the feel of a body next to her. But he had called her a snake. She told herself it was not worth worrying about.

A few days later, she was with the tally reeve, counting the sacks to be ready for the new harvest of grain, when a kitchen knave came in. The master mason respectfully asked to see Morlaix's lady before the church. The masons were taking down the scaffolding from inside, should milady now care to view it.

She stopped what she was doing and went out into the ward. Master Ian was standing at the church steps, looking down at the ground. When she came up he bowed low and motioned with his hand for her to enter the church.

She told herself she could be as cool as he. But her heart was racing. The church was dim inside. Without the sun through the roof it was serene, different, a holy place. And with the ceiling scaffolding gone, one could see at last the arching vaults, like opened stone flowers, that marched one after the other up to the nave.

"We have made groined vaults, milady, and they are exceeding strong." His voice came from behind her. "It is still a small church, it will not hold more than forty souls, but the transverse arches are not only high but stilted, so as to provide a level top. Upon the levels rest the horizontals supporting the peaked roof. It took some time in the doing, but you will not find better or stronger in the west country."

Alwyn walked down the apse. The floor was still cluttered with boards from the scaffolding. Her eyes went to the high arches above. The old chapel had been dark as a tomb. Now she could imagine this perfect little church with many lighted candles, the altar with an embroidered cloth, all crowned with the heaven-reaching ceiling. A long time ago he had told her it would be a jewel box and it was.

He went on talking in a rapid voice. "You will find the design lighter than Norman tastes. I have seen the new cathedral at Jumièges, and there is much there to admire in the new Norman style. Still, it is the churches that I have seen in Paris that influenced me here." He touched his fingers to a fluted pier in the wall. "In the monasteries, they still have the writings of one called Vitruvius, who wrote on proportion and design. The Carolingian builders knew of them. As you know, harmony is everything."

He walked ahead of her, gesturing. The dim light caught gold glints in his hair. She was struck by the subtle grace of his body. "But there are two churches that are known as l'Abbaye-aux-Hommes, and l'Abbaye-aux-Dames, the church of the men and the church of the women." He spoke with his back to her. "They were built by King William and Queen Matilda as gifts to the church to expiate their marriage. There were many who were opposed to William's marrying Count Baldwin's daughter when he was still only Duke of Normandy. Including the Lady Matilda herself. Various parties, some say Matilda's mother was with them, went to the pope, who was persuaded to forbid the marriage. Some four years the ban lasted. But then the Conqueror married Matilda in defiance of the pope's ban. Later, these churches were what they were obliged to offer for forgiveness."

He stopped. Someone had come into the back of the church. He said in a different voice, "This is my gift to you."

Alwyn clasped her hands to keep them from trembling. She knew now what he had been saying. All this explaining the little church to her. He looked calm, but he was as tremulous as she. He would not even look at her.

She turned to look over her shoulder. She saw the priest there, watching them. She was suddenly struck with their peril.

She lifted her eyes to him. He looked as though he wanted to put his arms around her. "Ah God," he breathed, "I knew you were lost to me the first time I set eyes on you. It was madness even to think of it. And now you carry his child."

Eagerly, she stepped to him. He put up his hand to stop her. He turned away.

"Now milady," he said, "you must see the altar work, which is particularly fine, and the back of the nave."

She followed him as if in a dream. They approached the altar. She remembered to genuflect. He stood watching her as she went down on one knee and then hauled herself up with an effort. When he swiveled his head to look to the back of the church, the priest was no longer there.

"The entrance to the sluices." His voice was heavy with feeling. "Do you recollect the water defense of the castle we talked of, and the springs under the keep? The work on the tunnels has been done through the chapel all these months, while we were rebuilding it, so that it will remain secret."

Alwyn wondered when he had spoken to her about the springs under the keep and the sluices to trap any besiegers. She had forgotten.

He saw that she had. "In God's name, remember what I tell you now. It may save you someday."

She followed him around the back of the altar. At the back wall there were two recessed arches flanked by the fluted piers. The capitals were carved stone roses. She had never seen anything like them.

"Here," he said. He put his hand on a stone pillar. "When you pull out this small piece, remember it is the latch. Once the latch is opened, the stone swings out." To show her, he swung out the stone column from the wall. "It is counterweighted, meaning it will not grow stiff for many years. Then you must bring in someone to fix it."

The space was narrow, a vertical hole sliced in the stone. Alwyn could see she would not fit into it, big as she was.

He was thinking the same thing. "The passage is steep going down, there are no steps, and it is not high enough to stand upright. In the sluices, one must crawl on hands and knees. It was not hard for the men to bring the tunnel under the curtain wall. As I made it myself, I knew the configuration and where to find a way through. But it took much labor for the masons to dig out as far as the bank of the river, which is the best exiting place well away from the castle. And bring the dirt back up through the floor of the chapel and hide it in the building work each day."

She didn't know what to say. "We must find a way to reward them for their work."

"They are well rewarded. The abbot of Saint Botolph's has paid them, although he may not know the particulars of all that he has paid for." He looked down at her, his blue eyes like lights. "I wanted to show you this. Every castle has a secret way, some better than others. This one will work." He hesitated. "The troop of masons leaves here soon, to go to the north. I will go to Scotland. The king there wishes to build a church as grand as any Norman cathedral, and I am commissioned for it."

He was telling her that he was leaving and this time he would not come back. Suddenly she wanted to throw herself on him, feel his fine strong body under her hands, plead with him to take her with him. She knew if she begged him he would. It was that which stopped her. His words to her when they had first come into the church had been that she was lost to him the first moment he saw her.

They were thinking the same thoughts. "Do you know who I am?" He hesitated, then said, "I am called the grand master of the lodges. Not many know of this, and to some it means nothing. But I am a mason's son, and my father's father was a mason before him. I have studied in France, in the lodges there, and have drunk and argued with the students of the Paris universities. I have been to Rome and seen true marvels in building. I speak the tongue of the Flemings, of the Scots and the English, the French of many districts, the language of Italy, and I know the geometries and can read some Latin. I am not an uneducated man, for all that I work with my hands."

"It does not matter," Alwyn cried.

"You know it does," he said. "I am, as you and your people see it, baseborn."

"Please—" she began.

He put his finger over her lips. It was the first time he had touched her. "No, there is no need to speak of it. All I need from your mouth is this."

He drew her to him and covered her lips with his.

It was a soft kiss at first. Then he deepened it with the touch of his tongue in her mouth. She was swept with an intense feeling that was like nothing she had known before. She followed it, hungry for him, straining for his mouth, the bulk of her swelling belly between them.

The wonder of Master Ian's kiss faded almost as soon as it began. The heavy reminder of the babe and all that was real pressed against them and held them apart.

He backed away, his mouth wet, his eyes dark.

What could she say to him, after all? She was filled with despair. They were both trapped in their lives. They could never have each other. She was so desolate she could not weep.

"Come," he said. He was breathing heavily. He did not hold out his hand, nor did he touch her again He stepped in front of her and led her from the chapel.

She sat on the grass in the ward in the afternoons with the women, sewing clothes for the babe. The masons still worked on the last of the roof scaffolding. Their chisels chipped with a drowsy noise like the locusts below in the river trees.

She could not help watching the master mason as he worked. The priest, she noted, watched Master Ian, too.

If he didn't love her, Alwyn asked herself endlessly, then why had he kissed her? She jabbed the needle fiercely in the babe's new clothes. He didn't want her, that's what he had said. He was only a builder, he had nothing to give her. If they went away together, all Christendom would revile them, an adulterous woman and her baseborn lover. Her husband would search for them, maybe kill them. It was his right to do so under the law. The master mason was the finest man she knew. She had asked for God's help and He had given her nothing.

She was due to deliver the babe when cool weather began. It seemed as though the terrible summer would never end.

In this lying-by time before the work of the harvest, the villagers came to the castle for the year's tallying and to declare their service for the coming twelvemonth. Alwyn moved to the hall with her sewing to sit near the tally reeve and the priest and listen.

This year, they had Father Ascelin to record the work each sokeman and villein and their families were expected to do for the lord of Morlaix. In addition to the lord's service, the tally reeve with his sticks counted how many acres of peas, beans, wheat, oats, and barley there were now to be gathered, and how many strip fields for the villagers would be ploughed for the winter.

She was glad she sat with them. There were still disputes over the land that had been given to Hugh de Yerville for his manor. She wanted to hear what the villagers said.

Feeling still ran high in spite of the punishment of the ringleaders the past spring. Then there was the manor house itself. A group of masons from the castle was finishing the foundation, but the villagers were levied to do the rest—the half-timber walls and the roof. When young de Yerville's bride came and they moved into it, Alwyn thought, Fulk de Jobourg would have his own vassal.

The hall was crowded. There were villeins, cotters too poor to buy their own oxen for plowing, and free sokemen and their families overflowing out into the ward. A villein called Dyved One-Eye and his brother-in-law, Maredudd, who also helped the smith, loudly complained that they did not have time to give to the raising of the Norman knight's manor house. And without the acres that had been taken from them, their families would go hungry next spring. The smith's helper would not leave the table where the tally was taken until they heard him out.

The tally reeve was testy. "You will cry all the more," he shouted, "when you see the new taxes the lord of Chester will make us groan under come this time next year."

Alwyn stitched a sleeve of a small shirt, then turned it and began the other. The villeins said the same things Fulk de Jobourg had said. They feared the reach of Hugh of Avranches, and the liege lord's share they thought would be wrung from them. They were probably right.

Watching Father Ascelin, she was thinking that although they had written records, now the priest was privy to them. Truly, if one wished to believe it, the priest was Chester's spy. She supposed it couldn't be helped.

She was somewhat surprised that none of the villagers had appealed to her to seek justice in their behalf, although she was sitting close by. When he turned away from the tall table, the smith's helper muttered that he would look to the lord of Morlaix when he returned, to hear him out.

Alwyn thought, It's because I'm big with child. They think I will have nothing more to do now but give it suck and look after it. She really didn't think they preferred to go to Fulk de Jobourg and not her.

The wool merchant from Chirk and his daughter came up the valley to the castle before noon prayers.

It was time for the midday meal and Alwyn supposed they would take it with her in the hall. But the merchant, whose name was Simon Belefroun, politely declined. He had brought his daughter, who rode a fine white palfrey, two servants and two pack mules, and would feed his people in the ward if she would give her gracious permission. Alwyn saw no reason not to. She left them there.

She came back later and saw that the stable boys had gathered around to watch. The wool merchant's servants in neat black tunics and hose had unpacked a table and stools. They spread a linen cloth and served a meal of white bread and red wine, a plate of cheeses and ripe pears.

Simon Belefroun and his daughter, whom he called Sophia, were richly dressed. He wore a long green satin coat trimmed with velvet that touched the ground, and a hood to throw back in warm weather. His high shoes with pointed toes were fine red Cordoba leather. His clerk daughter wore a coif over her hair that was trimmed with fine gauze the same gold-peach color as her cheeks. Her blue linen gown, slashed at the sleeves and skirt with red and white, billowed about her as she sat eating. The merchant's daughter had dark eyes with deep-set, carved lids and black furry lashes. Beside her, Alwyn felt drab and swollen in her everyday dress.

Simon Belefroun offered her wine in a cup. She sat down on one of the stools to take it.

The wool merchant had come to talk about brokering Morlaix wool. The Saxon dealer, Wolfrung, whom Alwyn had always liked, had been gone from the marches for many months. It was no secret the Norman traders had driven him out. She gathered there were many Norman merchants now in Chirk and more coming, from England and from France. Business was so good, Belefroun told her, that he was bringing a distant cousin from Falaise to assist him. Alwyn did not want to talk about next year's shearing; it was too far away. But he assured her that in Falaise it was the custom to buy the wool crop several years ahead.

She shifted to a more comfortable position on the stool. It was pleasant sitting in the ward in the sun. The hall was always smoky and dark. "I will think about it," she told him. She didn't know why he was eager to have her wool so far in advance. "I will contract with you after harvest."

The merchant's daughter gave her a sharp look. "Can you grant this alone, without your liege lord's permission?"

Alwyn tried not to dislike her. "I have done it for many years. Rest assured I will do it again this harvest time."

"My daughter means no disrespect," the merchant said. He looked pointedly at Alwyn's middle pushing up under her gown. "But milady may be otherwise occupied with God's blessed tasks."

Holy Cross, they were just like the villeins. "God's blessed task is selling wool," she snapped. If they thought by having a child she was going to give everything over to the man who had put it in her, they were mistaken. "I will pray to Our Blessed Father to make me capable of it."

The girl opened her mouth to speak, but her father stopped her. "Well, milady." He looked around to see if there was anyone to hear. There were only his black-clad servants and the masons on the church roof. "There is something else."

His daughter stiffened in her seat and looked away. Alwyn watched her, curious.

"I am a merchant, lady," Belefroun was saying, "it is not our destiny in life to look above our station, even though we may possess more of God's earthly goods than some of those of noble blood." He looked at his daughter. "To be somewhat rich is not to be wellborn."

Somewhat rich, Alwyn thought. She knew they had money in plenty. A wool exchange in Falaise and, from what the merchant had said, in Bruges in Flanders as well. They were always dressed as though going to a king's court.

He said, "You see, my daughter is a Jewess. Her mother was one, a beautiful woman, God save her. By the laws of that religion a daughter is as her mother, a Jew. You see my position."

Alwyn had turned to look at him. "Your position?" She turned back to the girl. She was seeing a Jew at last. Sophia gave her a frigid look.

"The young knight," the merchant said. "You must tell your lord that he cannot address his suit."

"I do not want him," the girl said. "It was none of my doing."

Sweet Jesu, they were talking of one of the Morlaix knights. She was intrigued. The wool merchant wanted her to tell Fulk de Jobourg so that he would discourage this knight, whoever he was. Tell him that his interest was in vain because the girl was a Jewess.

But a rich one, she was thinking. Besides, what did it matter? The merchant's grim-mouthed little beauty was well dowered, she had no doubt of it. If Sophia wanted her

Christian knight, one supposed she could convert to the church.

"He is a handsome and valorous knight of good family," the merchant put in quickly, "of glorious prospects in the future, that is certain. So this is a delicate matter."

Ah, he hasn't got any money, Alwyn thought, delighted. It was like a troubadour's tale. The Jewish beauty with her account books and cleverness, and the lovelorn Christian knight who didn't know her true blood. She wondered if the chit really cared for him. For all her looks, one might guess clerk's ink ran in her veins.

"Who is the knight?" she wanted to know.

The merchant looked at her, surprised. "Why, milady, this is the reason why we have come to you. The valiant knight is your lord's very own cousin."

Geoffrey. She burst out laughing. Startled, father and daughter glared at her.

Sweet saints in heaven, Alwyn thought, trying to compose herself, she did not wish to offend the poor people, but Geoffrey did not want to wed the Jewish beauty. He only wanted to get inside her skirts.

She straightened her face. "I will talk to my husband when he returns from Chester. Since the knight is his kinsman, he will point out your fatherly misgivings."

"More than misgivings." Simon Belefroun frowned. "When she weds, my daughter will make an excellent match. She has a great dowry. But no hint of scandal must touch us, milady."

"Oh yes, I quite agree." She was thinking, Perhaps it is the money Geoffrey is after. What a jape! She would swear that if they should come together, Belefroun's Sophia would be more than a match for Geoffrey de Bocage.

"I will talk with my lord husband so that the knight will bother you and your daughter no more." She stood up. "Godspeed, until I see you past harvest time about next year's wool."

She lasted until she got into the stairwell of the keep. Then she burst out laughing again.

In his cell behind the church, Father Ascelin went to his table, pulled up a stool, and took up his sharpened goose quill to write.

The message was simple enough. Father Ascelin did not worry about its reception when it reached its destination. The problem was the messenger. The one who usually carried his letters, the cousin of the lord of Morlaix, was with Fulk de Jobourg in Chester for the swearing of the oath of fealty to Hugh of Avranches.

It was necessary, then, to summon some other knight there in Morlaix Castle, pay him for his trouble, and send him to a point that would not be open to suspicion. A holy place. He had decided the chapter house in Wrexham would be the spot. Brother Belknap there would see that the message was forwarded, unopened, to the abbot of St. Botolph's, with all due speed.

This time, Father Ascelin wanted Abbot Ambrose St. Les himself to see his letter, it was that important. It was, in fact, what they had all been waiting for.

Outside, the noise of the chisels at their finishing work suddenly ceased. The voice of the master mason conveyed some order. Then the noise started again.

Father Ascelin had listened intently. When the sounds resumed, he turned his attention back to his letter. He carefully scraped the ink from his last message from the abbey, blew away the dust, then dipped his pen.

On the prepared surface of the sheepskin he wrote: "The Antichrist has returned."

Chapter Fourteen

THE COLUMNS OF KNIGHTS, FOUR abreast, came through the village at full gallop, scattering chickens and villeins like leaves. By the time they reached the castle road, the lookouts on Morlaix's battlements had time only to see that the banners were those of Fulk de Jobourg and the abbot of St. Botolph's, before they made their hail. There were no trumpets blowing. The galloping pace did not slow.

The first group thundered across the castle drawbridge and into the yard, hauling up in a flurry of shouted commands. Fulk de Jobourg, the Morlaix knights, and the knights from St. Botolph's threw themselves from their saddles. The abbot's purple-clad knights made straight for the church.

The priest came running out to meet them, pointing up to the roof where the masons were working. Two knights scrambled up the ladders to seize the master mason. They took him by the arms and dragged him down to the ground. The other masons quickly threw down their tools and followed.

The yard continued to fill with horses and men until it

could hold no more. The rest of the long column halted on the castle road below. In the courtyard, two monks on palfreys dismounted and made their way to the church.

Two St. Botolph's knights forced the master mason to his knees on the grass of the ward. They tied his hands behind his back. A black-gowned monk unrolled a parchment and began to read, the clamor drowning out his voice.

At the sounds Alwyn had run from the hall with the women mending winter clothing. "Oh, God save us, they've got Master Ian," one of the women cried.

Alwyn squeezed between knights and horses. She found a Welsh man-at-arms and stopped him. "Tell me, what is it?" she cried.

He gave her a harried look. "Milady, they've arrested the mason, that's all I know."

Arrested him? "God in heaven, why?" Frantic, she pushed at a wall of knights at the front. She recognized one of Fulk de Jobourg's men. "Fitz-Alayne!" She grabbed the back of his tunic and he turned to her. "What are the abbot's knights doing here?"

Beyond him, she saw the purple tunics of the knights from St. Botolph's standing in a circle around the man on the ground, shutting the troop of masons away from him. The man they were holding was Master Ian. His face was bleeding.

"They came with us from Chester, milady." The young knight hesitated, looking around the crowded yard. "You should see your lord husband. He can tell you best what this is."

She turned away from him, shoving at the backs of stable boys. "Give way, give way," she told them. "It is your mistress, I will know what's going on!"

The body of a big knight in mail loomed in front of her. He seized her arm and turned her around. "Get back," he growled at her, "this is none of your affair."

She started to give him a sharp answer and saw that it was Fulk de Jobourg. She tried to get around him to see. "God in heaven, what are they doing to the masons?"

"They've arrested their master." He turned her around again and pushed her toward the back of the crowd. The knights parted to let them through. "The monks have charged the lodge master with heresy and Satan worship."

She was too dumbstruck to resist as he pushed her across the ward. "Heresy?" She could not believe it. "That is madness! I will swear an oath on it, he has done nothing!"

"Stop shouting." He gave her arm a shake. "You can tell me what you swear when we are alone."

They mounted the stairs in the keep. At the top, he threw aside the wooden door and strode across the room.

"I had naught to do with this; they joined us at Wrexham." He put the helmet on a stool. His hair was sweaty, stuck close to his head. His face was streaked with dust. "The two monks have a warrant for the mason's arrest. Bishop Odo has had the grand master followed from place to place. The last was York."

"Oh, no." She put both her hands to her mouth.

He gave her a sardonic look. "Oh, yes. The church charges he holds secret meetings among the guilds, and preaches that all men are equal, be they villein or king."

She thought of the time she had seen him in the chapel, the priest watching him. He was kind and good; he was not a heretic. She had a fearful thought. "Holy Mother, what will they do to him?"

"They will take him to London to the ecclesiastical courts. It is a matter for the bishop, Odo."

She shuddered. Odo was as savage as his half-brother, William the Crippler, an ungodly man who had many mistresses and bastard children. "God in heaven, what will they do if they find him guilty?"

He shrugged. "In Odo's courts everyone is guilty. As to what they will do, they will drown him, or burn him, whatever." He took off his mailed gauntlets and laid them together on the bed. The leather-lined fingers stayed curled as though his hand were still in them. "First they will torture him, to make him confess."

She sat down on a stool, abruptly. She did not feel her legs would hold her up any longer. "I cannot believe it, that this would happen," she whispered. "They are mad, all of them. The master mason is a simple man. He has not preached any heresy." She lifted her eyes to him. "He has done nothing of that sort of thing here; the people like him."

"They like him." He sat down on the bed, staring at her. "They told me at the abbey that you favor him with your great liking, too."

She recoiled. So they were spied on, it was true. "Who told you? More of these priests? They lie! He has never—" She stopped. She could not say the master mason had never touched her. He had kissed her.

He studied her, narrow-eyed, seeing guilt in her face. She would rather he shouted at her, even struck her. She was filled with dread. In God's name, what had they told him?

"I have spoken to him, nothing more than that!"

She could see he did not believe her. He was obsessed with what he saw as her treachery. Nothing she had ever done had made him think better of her. But she could not let an innocent man die.

Desperate, she fell to her knees in front of him. "Oh God, I plead with you! Do not let them take Master Ian to London to kill him. It is all lies, mad lies, these coils they weave. These monsters, they will weave them about you, they will destroy anyone. The master mason is innocent, he is not a heretic! Help him to escape!"

He sat with his open hands on his knees, watching her.

"Damn you, weren't you listening? I have nothing to do with this. It is a church matter."

"God send the church into infernal hell!" she screamed. He was going to let them kill him. She could see it in his eyes. "It is all lies! What do you know they have found?"

"Oh, they have told me. The abbot himself says that in spite of your great liking for the mason they have not called you an adultress. Or charged you with mortal sin. In that you have talked to this man, invited his attention, they only call you misguided. They continue to regard you highly. That is," he added, sarcastic, "so you may still serve their interests here, naturally."

"Stop it, stop it!" She grabbed his knees and pressed her face against them. Somehow she had to persuade him. She could not let them take the master mason to London and torture him to make him confess. Why did they say he was a heretic? He was more Christian than any of them!

"Listen to me." She licked her lips, thinking hard. "They will not take him away tonight. He can escape, you can help him to escape. You can send some of the knights to help him, in the dark."

He pushed her hands away. "Your favor is wondrous, madame, to bring you to your knees to beg for your lover's life." He thrust her away from him and she sat back on her heels. "Would to God I could attract it in the same measure. But I am only your damned misbegotten husband."

He stood up, his back to her. "I am sick of this torment. I can rid myself of this treachery, I can send you to a convent."

She rolled to her knees, no longer weeping. "You will not send me to a convent." She took hold of the bed and hauled herself to her feet. "This is my castle. I was born here. You will not send me out of it!"

"It is not your castle." He did not lift his voice. "It was no longer yours the night I wed you. That was King William's intent. And I will send you to a convent, an it please me, before or after this brat of yours is born. There is naught you can do about it."

He pushed her out of the way and went out.

She waited until she was sure that he had left the keep. When she went to the door and opened it there was a young knight standing there. Surprised, she almost closed the door again.

The knight put his fingers to his forehead in salute. "Milady."

"What is your name?" She didn't know it, there were so many knights at Morlaix now.

"You will stay inside, milady," he said.

She knew who had told him that. She drew herself up. She was not going to let them imprison her in her room. "You fool, I must go down and see about the food." She picked up her skirts. "You wish to eat evening meal, do you not?"

He tried to block her way. "Milady, Lord Fulk has ordered me to keep you here."

She put out her arm and pushed him aside. "There are twice a hundred knights to feed in the ward. No one would think of that if I am stuck in here." She started down the stairs. "But they would soon come for me after this great crowd has gone unfed for a while."

He followed her down the steps. "Milady," he begged. But he did not try to stop her.

She skipped into the ward and made for the kitchen, running. A thunderstorm was breaking. Lightning flashed as she crossed the grass. A hard burst of rain drenched her as she passed the place where the St. Botolph's knights were guarding the master mason.

One of the wagons had been pulled up by the stables. Master Ian was tied, spread-eagled, to a wheel. His shirt was gone. Someone had lashed him and left him with a bloody back. He hung, arms tied by the wrists to the spokes, his head bent, as the rain poured down. She could not tell if he had fainted. Two St. Botolph's knights stood in the stableyard door out of the wet, watching the prisoner.

She turned and went down the ward to the kitchen house. Inside, the cook had already started the fires; they roared under the stewpots. The kitchen was filled with steam and noise. The cook was beating one of the kitchen knaves around the ears with a spoon.

When he saw her, he pushed the boy away. "Ah, glad I am to see you. Here I am with an army of wolves to feed and you have not given me the keys."

"I need a fire here," Alwyn told him. She kicked some of the rushes toward the hearth. Fire backed into them quickly, eating at the grease.

"Milady!" The cook rushed forward. Flames danced across the rush-strewn floor. "Jesus help us!" He stared at Alwyn as if she had gone mad.

She kicked more rushes into the fire. The flames sprouted up as high as the cook's knees. The kitchen knaves, shrieking, ran for water.

She seized the cook by the arm. "Keep it burning," she hissed at him. "Let the knights outside put it out."

His eyes widened.

"Do you understand me?" she cried. "Let the knights come to put it out!"

Nodding, he rushed to stop the boys coming with buckets from the water butt.

She took a knife from the table where the knaves had been chopping turnips and stuck it in her sleeve. As she passed the fireplace, she picked out a stout billet of wood and tucked it close against her skirts. Then she went back outside.

The wind blew rain in sheets across the yard. Night was coming. The storm made it darker. She went into the back of the stables and found Hwyl.

She held her finger to her lips. Some St. Botolph's knights were playing at dice just inside the door. "Saddle my mare," she told him in a whisper. "Do you have an old cloak?"

He ran and found one for her inside a stall, filthy and speckled with straw. She put it around her. Now she knew she looked like everyone else.

She told him, "Bring my mare out to the wagons, but not too near. And wait."

She went outside and stood looking at the master mason tied to the wagon's wheel, his legs stretched out before him. Rain beat off his shoulders and head and ran down into the puddles around him.

Smoke was coming from the kitchen door. Inside, there were shouts and screams of fire. The abbot's knights came out of the stable behind her. One of them cursed. They started for the kitchen house at a run. Atop the portal gate, the night guard rang the alarm bell. Knights from the keep began to empty into the ward. Alwyn saw Hugh de Yerville, and Geoffrey's red head in their midst.

The drenching rain did not halt the fire. The kitchen house burned merrily. Flames sprouted like red flags through the boards of the roof. The cook came bursting out, shouting, with the kitchen knaves following him.

There were two St. Botolph's knights guarding the master mason. Stepping out of the shadows, Alwyn cried, "Oh, help us! My mistress is trapped in the hall!" She pointed to the crowds around the burning kitchen.

The taller knight looked at her. Then he handed the other his sword and ran off. Alwyn tossed back her hood and stepped up to the guard.

He peered at her through the rain. "Ho, you're a pretty little thing. Don't be afraid for your mis—"

She hit him across his middle with the billet of wood. He doubled up and fell to his knees. She hit him again on the back of his head. It was a hard blow but his helmet caught most of it. Groaning, he staggered to one knee to get up. She hit him again. He fell forward onto his face in the wet grass.

She dropped the wood and shook the knife out of her sleeve. She knelt beside Master Ian.

"I am going to cut you loose," she whispered in his ear. "Can you hear me?"

He lifted his head, his eyes glazed. Alwyn cut the leather bonds and they fell away from his wrists. His arms came down from the wheel. He drew in his breath, in pain.

"Are you bad hurt?" She crouched and put her hands into his armpits to haul him up. "You must walk. We have only a few moments to do this."

As she strained to lift him he lunged, staggering, to his feet, nearly knocking her over. She held him up. His skin was cold as a corpse. Blood ran over her hands mixed with rain.

"The chapel," she told him. They stumbled toward it. The babe made her clumsy; she sobbed with the effort. He was getting some strength back in his legs. At the church door, he stretched out one hand and threw it open. "Where's the priest?" he croaked.

"I don't know." She wondered if the priest found them would she have the courage to kill him. She still had the knife.

He was walking better. It was not so hard to guide him down the church and around the altar. At the back she pushed him up against the stone columns and let him go. She leaned against the wall.

Now, thinking what was before him, she cried, "Holy saints, you cannot manage it. You said yourself, you must go on hands and knees in the tunnels." Tears rolled down her cheeks. He was free and it had come to naught. "It is all dark down there and you have not even a candle."

He put his arm against the wall. He rested his head on

it. She heard him laugh, weakly. "Dear lady, I have the sluices all in my head. The dark will not matter."

She looked around. "Where is the latch?"

He straightened. His hand groped over the stone, finding the piece. He pushed and the stone column opened, a wedge of blackness beyond.

He turned and looked at her with burning eyes. "I will not come back. This is my last sight of you."

She stared at him. She had not thought of that.

"What I feel for you." He reached out and cupped her cheek with his palm. "Tell me that it is returned."

"Yes, yes, I care for you," she cried. "God keep you safe. There are knights on the road, watch for them when you come out at the river."

He gave her a strange look. He started to say something more but she pushed at him with both hands, in a frenzy to get him out of there. "Dear Christ, get in! Do you want them to kill you?"

"No." He stepped to the opening, turning sidewise. "Remember me," he said.

The blackness swallowed him.

Alwyn pushed the stone back in place. She came around the altar. She pulled her hood back up and walked the length of the church, listening to the furor outside.

The ward was packed with people fighting the fire. She hurried along with the cloak held to her, the hood hiding her face. The kitchen house was lost. It stood as an eerie framework of burning timbers. A bucket line of knights handed water from the well. The rain had stopped. They were wetting the roof of the hall to keep it from catching. Men-at-arms held the crowd back.

Fulk de Jobourg was in there somewhere. She kept her head down, keeping to the shadows around the wagons. Beyond the stables, Hwyl moved in the dark. He stepped out and handed her a handful of reins.

Her mare nickered, thrusting her soft muzzle into her hand. Alwyn put her foot in the stirrup and the boy boosted her up to the saddle. She turned the horse's head toward the gate. In the confusion she could gallop through; no one would stop her.

She leaned down to the boy and said in Welsh, "Tell me where to go to find the Man of the Vale."

Henwas Hwch

Chapter Fifteen

THE WELSH KNIGHT DISMOUNTED, tied his reins to the branch of a tree, and sat down on the grass in the miller's ale yard. Emrys wore his thick curling hair long in the old style, green and blue ribbons braided in the forelock to keep it out of his eyes. His body armor, a sleeveless shortcoat, was boiled leather studded with iron bosses. His sword, short and leaf-shaped, hung from his belt. Resting his back against the oak tree, he stretched out his legs to wait.

One of the three Norman knights sitting at the table was now the lord of Morlaix. None of them wore armor or carried swords, but six mailed knights from the castle stood guard under the trees.

The markedly handsome Norman with the loud laugh Emrys passed over. As he did the narrow-faced knight in the green velvet coat. The man at the end, he thought. The one who slouched, half turned on his stool, arm resting on the boards of the table. He was listening to the churl before him, explaining how the oxen were shared for plowing.

Emrys studied the young baron of Morlaix. He was bigger than the other two men, broad shouldered, with the powerful sleek strength of a swordsman. He looked the typical Norman with his long nose and bowl-cut russet hair.

"And if to pay this," the churl was saying, "I must sell my ox, then how am I to plow my fields for the crops that will pay next year's share to the castle?"

The man beside the lord of Morlaix leaned to the one in the green jacket and said something behind his hand. The baron turned to them, frowning. The red-haired man sat back on his stool. He said in French, "They hate castles, Fulk. It is the same in France. They do not like the knights' forays or their way with the village girls. Nor the levies to support them."

The knight in the green coat said, "It is different with a manor. There I will be working with them."

Fulk de Jobourg said to the churl, "You do not need to sell your ox."

"Then my lord, how do I pay this new levy?" The soke-man was a big man with a bush of blond hair; he looked more English than Welsh. "When we tally my shares this year I will have less than last year, and that was a bad year, not a good year like this. How can it be so?" He turned and gestured to the woman holding a child in her arms behind him. "With this levy I cannot feed my family next spring, and my wife is carrying again."

Fulk looked away. "Sell your ox to the new manor knight, Hugh de Yerville, and he will rent it back to you for the plowing. You will produce on shares, with so much for him and so much for the castle, and keep your portion."

The churl clenched his fists. "It is not my portion, it is the share for my lord of Chester. To pay this I must give up my ox to the manor lord?"

Fulk regarded him, thinking if he had to pay Hugh of Avranches, then they had to pay the lord of Morlaix. That was the way things worked. In Normandy, his father's land had a reeve who saw to the business of the fields;

God knew his father never had time for it, he was busy with one noble war or another. Fulk vaguely remembered his mother doing some of this haggling with their tenants. He was finding it took the judgment of Solomon.

"Reduce your levy by one sixth." He turned to de Yerville and said, "Mark it on the stick for Laess the sokeman, less one-sixth Chester's levy."

Geoffrey leaned forward. "We should have brought the priest to write this down."

"No." Without looking up, Fulk waved his hand in dismissal.

The sokeman stared at them, stricken. "I have lost my ox," he said as he turned away. "I have nothing."

De Yerville bent to speak to Fulk. "That is the fifth ox I have acquired. I will need a herdsman to care for them."

"At the rate we are beggaring the freemen, you will have plenty." He looked at the sokeman walking away. "If this one is right, they will work for their food." Or leave the village, he thought privately. Three freemen had gone so far, even before the harvest. The rumor was, to the south looking for a better place. Or to the west, to join the war-ready Welsh.

Geoffrey laughed. "At least we do not condone slaves. The Saxons were rotten with slaves for all their pious mouthing."

Fulk grunted. "We are making our own slaves. We squeeze the freemen until they become villeins and the villeins are tied to the land, so what is the difference?" He said, "Who is the next?"

Some sokemen who had been waiting turned away. In the time they had been standing in the miller's yard listening they had learned the year's share for the castle was larger, and on top of that was the share for the Earl of Chester. Beyond, a crowd of villeins had come to the ale yard just to watch. They squatted in a half circle close enough to hear the baron and the new manor lord. The villeins' lot was not like the freemen's: the castle lord took all their crops and gave them back some portion to live on. They wanted to hope that this year it was not less than last, but it did not look promising.

"Would to God we had King William in England," Hugh de Yerville said under his breath. "The king would put a rein on the greed of Robert of Coutances and Odo. And through them, these earls."

Fulk watched the sokemen join the other man, Laess, in the road. They stood talking, gesturing angrily. He said, "From what I'm hearing there will be little help from William."

The Conqueror was in Normandy, fighting his battles. But it was said that William was growing fat and could not hold his own, that for the first time he was knowing defeat. He was sorely needed on the English side of the Channel. In London, the court was a debauched scandal and the king's half-brothers, Bishop Odo and Robert of Coutances, ran wild, plundering the land, gathering great wealth. Even Normans were being oppressed. But it was unlikely that there would be another revolt so soon after the Bretons'. That had been too bloodily crushed. Still there were rumors that the Welsh were massing under Prince Rhiwallon and Dyved ap Gwythyr.

Geoffrey looked up. "Hah, we have a wild monk coming. What is he doing here?"

Fulk saw the fat miller's wife coming forward with a ragged friar, tall, gaunt, and barefoot, his brown sackcloth habit so frayed it flapped about his calves. His head was shaved bald. Something in the set of it, the hawk nose and pale eyes, made one think of a fighting man.

The miller's wife said, bobbing, "Milords, you know me. I am Lleu, Ton the miller's wife. We have a sick boy, you remember he was in the quarry when you—"

"Yes, yes," Fulk broke in. He did not particularly want to hear all that again. "What business have you that you bring this friar?"

The woman turned to look. "Oh, he is not a friar," she said, "he is an Irishman."

Behind his hand, Geoffrey laughed. Fulk turned to him and his face smoothed.

"His name is Bran," the miller's wife said, nervous. "Please, milord, give permission for this holy man to stay in the village and tend to my son. He has not much strength, my boy, and I am at my wits' end to nurse him. In this six months since he went to work in the quarry he has grown no better and a little worse, God save us. This fine holy brother, Bran, is from Kells monastery in the land of the Irish. He says he ranges wide over both Wales and England; he does not stay with the brothers but walks the roads seeking God and doing His good works and he has some gift as a healer."

Once started, the miller's wife could not stop with her worries for her son and the particulars of his weakness. She pleaded for the monk to stay in the village for a while and heal her boy.

Interested, Hugh de Yerville asked the monk, "What medicines do you use?" The village needed a good herbalist.

The Irishman fixed him with a look that was as gray as the winter sea. He said, "Nothing."

"Nothing?"

"I come to do Christ's holy work of the Gospels." His voice was strong, somewhat rasping. "I am not a surgeon or a leech."

Geoffrey leaned over the table to de Yerville. "A wandering Christ healer. There are many of them among the Irish. They are all lunatics."

Fulk studied him. For all his gauntness the monk was a big man. "You have carried a sword."

The monk shifted his eyes. "A long time ago."

Fulk was not displeased. If one had to have priests, this monk was better than some. "Don't preach in the village," he said, "we have a Saint Botolph's priest here. Confine yourself to whatever you do to heal."

The monk gave him another bleak look. Quickly, the miller's wife took him by the arm. He allowed her to steer him away to the back of the crowd.

"Who is next?" Fulk had seen the Welsh knight under the trees. He was in no hurry for that meeting.

Geoffrey rapped his hand on the table. "Who is next?" he repeated.

A woman had come up from the village road, dragging a girl by the hand. It was always the women who came at the very end, Fulk had noted. They hung back until the men had finished their business. He had learned to watch out for them. Women's affairs were not so important, but they were often tricky, and not by chance. He'd found himself trapped by some sharp-tongued villager's wife more times than he wanted to remember.

The woman pulling the girl toward the table was old, and she was missing most of her teeth. The girl wore a dirty woolen shirt that reached to her knees. "I am next, milord. Marve is my name, Hygwidd's woman." She pushed the girl forward.

"It's the midwife," Hugh de Yerville said.

Geoffrey ducked his head. "She sells girls when she can get them."

The girl before them was about fifteen, not ugly, but only pretty in that she was youthful and well grown. She was some villein's daughter with a big body, long legged, long waisted, with ripe swaying breasts that thrust out under the woolen shirt.

"Milords," the old woman said, looking at Fulk, "if you be wanting a rare piece to bring comfort the cold nights that's comin', and tell stories and maybe sing to you a little, this be a serving girl of good stock, one of them from the north what's hungry enough to be agreeable. Ain't you, girl?" She gave the girl a sharp tug by the wrist. "Don't be shy, tell these good lords your name."

The girl looked up. Her face was rather broad. A thick upper lip lifted over good teeth. She was not afraid. But she did not look too bright, either.

She said, "Edda."

"Serving girl?" Geoffrey looked at the others.

"Ah, but she's a rare one, truly fine," the old woman insisted. "She comes a long way intact, fine gentlemen, I paid a good price for it, straight from her father, who was in Chirk to hire her out, like. And you'll get your money's worth."

Before anyone could stop her she had stepped in front of the girl and yanked up her shirt with both hands. The girl had nothing on underneath. Hugh de Yerville sucked in his breath.

They were looking at truly beautiful white skin, newly washed. The girl had rounded thighs, the hint of buttocks as firm as pumpkins, and where her legs joined she had been shaved in the Saracen style. In the place where one usually saw dense pubic hair, her plump flesh folded together whitely like freshly baked bread.

"Holy Mother." Geoffrey too was staring.

"There, you see her, brave lords!" The old crone was triumphant. "A virgin girl, sweet and untouched."

"A *what*?"

Fulk's voice made them all jump. He leaned forward, both hands on the table.

The woman still held the girl's dress up. She looked over her shoulder. "No lie, milord, I swear it on my mother's grave. But the proof of the pudding is in the eating."

Geoffrey guffawed, his head thrown back. The old woman, heedless, kept talking. Hugh de Yerville stared at them, appalled.

The villeins could not see, as the girl's back was to them. But the knights, to one side, scrambled over each other for a better view.

Fulk got to his feet. He looked down at his cousin. "Was this your idea, damn you?"

Geoffrey covered his face with his hand. "Fulk, I swear not." He started to laugh again.

"Swear me nothing, you stupid swine." The old woman, seeing Fulk's face, stepped back hastily. The girl smiled vaguely. He glowered at her. "Sweet Mary, look at her, the damned girl's a lackwit. She has no idea what's being done." He turned and shouted, "Get me that Irish monk."

Hugh de Yerville said, anxious, "Fulk, what are you going to do?"

"The monk's just got a new servant, by Christ. Get her out of here," he barked to one of the knights hurrying forward.

"Fulk, the Irishman's a mendicant friar," de Yerville protested. "They have no servants."

"He has one now." As the castle knight led the girl away, Fulk bent a black look on the old woman. "Ask me to pay you for her," he growled. "Ask a price for your virgin lackwit, whoremonger."

The old woman backed up a step, her hands waving in front of her face. She had lost all her bustling assurance. "Oh no, milord, I wouldn't think, now, of doing such a thing. Simple the girl may be, I'm not saying no or yes to that, but if she is, it's not so much as would keep her from pleasing a man. Some men like the girl a bit unknowing, you know? I meant no trumpery, as God is my witness! I'll swear to that on the Holy Book or a blessed relic of a saint's bones if the good lord can find one."

Fulk leaned over the table. "I said, damn you, do you want money for her?"

"Oh no, sir," she cried, "bless you, that's fine, you've given her to the church in a way if you've given her to the Irish monk, haven't you, just like a little nun. And if it's a good sum out of my pocket now that I will sore suffer for when the winter's on us, and I need a bit of money to buy wood to keep my old bones warm, I'll say to myself what I paid for her was worth it. The girl's in good hands now as a dear Irish monk's servant, thanks to our generous lord."

Abruptly, she turned and bolted for the road. The villeins hooted at her as she passed. The knights laughed.

Geoffrey said, "It is a long winter ahead, cousin. I'd think hard before I'd give such wondrous comfort away to the care of an Irishman. Even a monk."

Seeing Fulk's face, Hugh de Yerville said quickly, "I think that the old woman was thinking of your comfort in a good sense, milord. Since, God keep her well, you do not have your lady wife with you now."

Fulk sat back. "No, that I do not." He looked at the knight waiting under the trees. "Although I see the Welsh have come again to try to bargain to give her back to me. Now," he said, lifting his voice, "where is the next one? Or is that the last of it?"

Geoffrey craned, searching the crowd. Hugh de Yerville nudged him. "Under the tree, to the left of the horses. The one with the colors in his hair."

Geoffrey said to Fulk, "Do you want us to stay with you?"

Fulk shook his head. The Welsh knight was getting to his feet. "No, if it was anything of importance they would have brought her."

Hugh said, "We will be nearby, if you call."

Fulk put his hands before him on the table. "It does not matter, it is all talk. They take years with it, these Welsh."

Emrys started toward the table where the baron of Morlaix sat. He was a good speaker, but it was hard to approach those who thought they had claim to what was, after all, Welsh, and to know what to call them. They were only robbers.

He had decided to call this Norman Morlaix, which was the French name they had given to the valley. But all knew it was not that; it was the Cymry place of

Llanystwyth. The prince's messengers who had been sent did not call the Norman a baron when they spoke to him, they called him *morchawg*. The horseman. Emrys had been told that these Normans thought it a term of respect.

"Greetings, *morchawg* Morlaix," Emrys said. He did not go down on one knee. He had gathered from others the prince sent that the Norman did not expect it. "I, Emrys, knight of Gwyddelwern, speak for Prince Rhiwallon of Glamorgan and Colwin Rhyl and all northerly lands of the Cymry, who sends his greetings under God, and greetings to you also from his kinswoman who is now his guest, the Princess Alwyn, your lady wife."

Fulk said, "You speak good Norman French."

Emrys smiled. "I have traveled in your country of Normandy, and also in Bretony, *morchawg*. It is a good tongue to speak."

Fulk studied him, eyes slitted against the sun. "You have been here before."

"It was my brother," Emrys told him. "You spoke to him at the last half-moon concerning the prince's message. Which was, at that time, that he would return your lady wife to you only when the Normans give up the valley of Llanystwyth and return over the sea to Normandy."

The other man only said, "I have a castle here, given to me by the Conqueror, King William of England. He is not going to give it up to any of the Welsh. Nor am I." He stretched out his feet against the grass and looked down at them. "I am pledged to hold this place for King William, who owns all lands beyond this valley to the west sea and including all Wales. Now, as I told the last messenger from the prince, I also demand the sheep and cattle that have been stolen from King William for many years, and which I expect the prince to return. Or pay the price for them." He said, almost indifferently, "You may go back to him and tell him that is still my answer."

"Oh, *morchawg*, the prince has no sheep or cattle from this valley," Emrys said. "You must talk to some other one about that. I am sent now to say that the prince will consider a ransom for your lady wife." He paused. "It is said you rightly place great value on her."

The Norman looked up.

Emrys met his stare. It was no secret that the Earl of Chester desired this fief of Morlaix. It had been given to this Norman knight by grant of King William, but the king was in France, fighting rebellious subjects. In England, his earls grew stronger every day.

This was only a young knight, Emrys told himself. A warrior favored by his king, but surrounded by enemies here in the marches. For him, a wife who had blood kinship with the Welsh people was important if he wished to hold what he had.

"Prince Rhiwallon sees that it is soon time for the Lady Alwyn to bear her babe," he went on. "A woman belongs with her husband at such times. For in such circumstance, away from him and expecting a birth, there may be others not so kind and compassionate as my lord who would wish to come and claim her now, in order to benefit from possessing her. And my lord cannot guarantee her protection."

Fulk said, "Tell me who Rhiwallon suspects will come and seize my wife from his princely care."

Emrys spread his hands, smiling. "Tell me who are your enemies."

The man at the table stood up, angry. "You are not speaking for Prince Rhiwallon, damn you, you are speaking for someone else. The outlaw Powys, who holds my wife. Go back and tell Powys I will burn more villages like the two I burned and sacked when I first found the Lady Alwyn was with him. And I will go across the mountains to the next vale and find villages and destroy them, also."

Emrys looked pained. "Powys ap Griffyd is a noble prince of Wales, *morchawg*, and kinsman to my lord Rhiwallon. To speak of one is to speak of both. By right what is here in Llanystwyth belongs to Prince Powys; this has been the land of his blood always."

"But not my sheep, by the Cross, and not my wife! Tell your shirtless Welsh bandit I demand the return of both. Or my knights will ride out to war against him and burn the mountains he hides in."

Emrys said, "Nevertheless, I have been told to speak of a ransom."

The other Normans moved closer. The big knight swept them back with his hand. He leaned across the table. "No ransom." He bit down on the words. "Tell Powys my answer is that my Norman knights will drive him out and slaughter his people and burn his houses and destroy all he has until he brings back what is mine."

"It is a ransom such as befits the noble station of Lady Alwyn." The knight came around the table at him. Emrys backed up several steps. "A mighty one, all to be paid in gold."

"Instead of gold I will send him one of your ears, Welshman." The *morchawg*'s dagger was in his hand. "Then you may carry it back to Powys to say I have answered."

Emrys looked at the knife. He said, "Well, then, if that is the way you will have it, I will tell Prince Powys your response."

The Norman lord of Morlaix put the dagger back in his belt. "Tell him if he sends another messenger, that messenger will also bring my wife. Or he will not live to go back to him."

Emrys shrugged. There would be another messenger, he was sure. And doubtless as long as the Lady Alwyn was held hostage, the Norman would talk to him. *"Morchawg,"* he said, "one other matter. Do you mean to sell the girl that was here? If so, I will offer for her."

He could see by the expression on the Norman's face that he would not consider that, either.

Emrys gave him a pleasant nod, and walked back to his horse.

Fulk watched the Welsh knight haul himself up to his high-pommeled saddle and ride out of the miller's yard. On the road, the villeins stood aside as he kicked the horse into a gallop. He went westerly, into the mountain road.

They are dandling me, he thought. They had not talked ransom before. And now Powys was threatening him with Hugh of Avranches. Who was, at this time, in London with the king's half-brothers, Robert of Coutances and Bishop Odo. While the king was fighting in Normandy, it was said Odo and Robert were slicing England up between them.

Geoffrey came up. "There is nothing new?"

"No, there is nothing new." He gestured to the miller, who went into the alehouse and came back with a brimming cup. "By now he will have moved back into the mountains again so that we will have to penetrate deep to hurt him."

"What did he say of your lady?"

"Nothing." Fulk finished the ale and gave the cup back to the miller. They walked to the knights holding their horses under the trees. "We will harry them again in two days as far west as Glyn Cieriog."

He disliked taking heavy war-horses into the mountains. The Welsh used surefooted ponies, even their knights. Worse, there was no plunder to be had. With nothing to sack, the knights fought over the girls and slaughtered the livestock. Discipline broke down quickly.

Fulk swung himself up into the saddle. He ducked his head under the branches of the trees as his horse moved out of the yard. The leaves that brushed his head and face were yellowing. All through the valley floor the ripening grain was gold tinged with green. It was no longer summer.

She is due sometime now, he thought. He wondered

what they would do with the babe. If the outlaw Powys would kill it. If it was his, mayhap that was what she wanted.

Perfidious bitch. He knew she was pleased with her schemes. It was because of her that he was forced now to raid the Welsh in the mountains. And get for his pains a threat by this snot-nosed bandit Powys, for whom she'd foolishly betrayed him these past months. Powys, it seemed from his messages, would be glad to betray her—perhaps to deliver her to the Earl of Chester, should her own husband not be willing to pay a ransom.

He supposed to sit in Hugh of Avranches's court in Chester and connive against him from there would please her; Christ and the angels knew she had caused him enough disasters. At least now he knew for whom she'd been spying.

The night the master mason escaped he had thought she'd gone with him. Both of them run off to be lovers. After all, what was he to think? There was no doubt as to who had cut the mason loose from the wagon: the knight she'd cracked over the head had told of a pretty maid who'd caught him by surprise. Black hair, pale eyes, white skin. It had been his hellcat wife, no doubt of that. Then they'd found her horse gone from the stables, although all the knaves, even with a lashing, swore they knew naught about it.

The two of them gone. His wife and the baseborn builder. He'd been maddened beyond reason. He'd gone forth in the darkest hours of the night with Morlaix and St. Botolph's knights to sweep the countryside, vowing to kill them. He'd ordered the camp of masons and their families held prisoner until his wife was found. He'd scoured the village, routing out those she visited, coddled, and befriended. And found nothing. A fortnight later, a messenger had come from the abbot saying the known heretic Ian of Scotland was safe now beyond those borders and thought to be at the court of King Alexander. The church, Abbot Ambrose had written, was petitioning the Scottish king for the grand master's return to stand trial for heresy and witchcraft before Bishop Odo in London.

Two days after that, the first of the Welsh messengers arrived from over the Cambrian Mountains to tell him his wife was being held among her own people somewhere in Glamorgan. She could only be had back, they said, for the return of the valley of Llanystwyth to its rightful lord, Prince Rhiwallon, and his kinsman Powys ap Griffyd of Wales.

It had all been a mockery, the pleas for the mason's life; like all else it was deceit. The Scotsman was not her lover. Since he'd been the baron at Morlaix, perhaps before then, she'd been helping the Welsh outlaws steal from the fief, spying for them and her true lover, her hidden lover, the Welsh bandit Powys.

Fulk guided his horse to the head of the column. Hugh de Yerville moved up next to him. On both sides of the road, fields of grain moved in the wind like a golden sea.

In Chester, when he had gone to swear fealty, his knights had gone down to the stews to bathe and sample the whores and he'd gone with them. But at the last, bathed, steamed, and shaven, he'd stayed out of the whores' booths. His knights had railed at him mercilessly. The truth of it was he had not been all that tempted. The women were not as clean or as fair-looking as his own wife. And he had told them, why pay for poor-quality goods when one can get better for nothing?

Not for nothing, he knew now. He had paid bitterly for whatever feeling he had for her. It was some satisfaction that she was now knowing treachery from her own; those for whom she'd betrayed husband and home were now going to betray her—using her, Powys's messenger was now telling him, in their own schemes.

De Yerville cantered up beside him. "Pray God to bless

us with a dry harvest season, Fulk." He gestured to the fields. "This is a rich harvest, if we can gather it all."

Fulk kicked his horse out in front. De Yerville's head was filled with his manor land; he talked as though the fields were already his.

He was thinking it was not for the villeins to concern themselves with whether he did or did not have a woman. He would lie with a woman when he wanted to. One only missed a woman, anyway, when one was in bed. The warmth of her body, her soft breast to cup his hand, the firm, pillowing curve of her bottom if he wished to pull her to him, was comforting in the night. But it was a small pleasure with a large price.

The truth was, he could not remember when he'd played the fool so well. This hanged traitor's daughter had witched him: when she grew large with the child, he knew she did not much want to take him. But he'd found he could make her hot enough for all that. The sweet button in the flesh between her legs opened her to his touch, made her reluctant desire rise. Now he knew it was all a lie. Whose child was it? He hoped the outlaw Powys pondered it, too.

Fulk tightened his grip on the reins. Startled, his horse tossed his head, fighting the bit, and he kicked it savagely.

The Welshman knew what he was about, to play him like this. She was a deceitful viper; throttling was too good for her. But for all of that he could use her. He saw the trouble with the villeins; she was born there, half-Welsh, she was one of them, and the villagers always had some business or other with her. Hugh of Avranches could well use her, too. Fulk knew now why William had given her to him. If there was anyone in Christendom who was a master of the uses of marrying, it was the king.

The knights' horses cantered down the path between the villagers' cottages, scattering pigs rooting in the drains. A squealing sow dashed under Fulk's horse, and it shied.

He reined it in, cursing, and rose up in his saddle to look back.

"Get someone to go for the swineherd and get these accursed pigs," he shouted. "How can we have meat for the winter if we trample the damned things?"

Chapter Sixteen

CARADOG WAS A WARLIKE YOUNG chief who liked his people around him in the old style, when everyone lived in the chief's hall. Even the crofters came into Caer Caradog twice a week with their families and slept in the big outer yard. At night there was harping, sometimes dancing. On this particular night, Caradog's wife, Gwenavy, who was expecting another child, came and sat with Alwyn.

"Look at them jumping about," the chief's wife said, envious. Gwenavy had a crowd of women to take care of her children, but there was always a baby in her lap, crawling over the mound of her belly. "Big as sows we are, poor things," she lamented, "sitting here side by side. We've had our pleasure now, and we're paying for it." She crinkled up her face. "You see no one is brave enough to bounce us around out there in a dance."

Alwyn picked over a dish of currants they were sharing. "I don't think it's a matter of courage." She paused to pry a piece of fruit from her front teeth. She was always hungry now; it was embarrassing. "Men are brave enough except when it comes to a woman nearing her term."

Caradog's wife nodded. "Yes, that is so." The baby jumped up and down in her foreshortened lap, and she lifted him, wincing, and held him away. "Caradog, now, won't sleep with me as he says I'm too big and crowd the bed too much. So he sleeps with his knights. But the truth of it is he fears he will have to get up some night and go down to the hall to fetch the midwife, as he did the last time." She popped a handful of currants into her mouth. "Such shouting and cursing, you would have thought he was the one having the babe."

Alwyn held out her hands. "Give him to me." She was fairly sure this one was the boy; the children were all so close together she was never sure. Although she was but seventeen, Gwenavy was carrying her third.

Caradog's wife was redheaded and very pretty. She wore fine silver chains studded with garnets. Her silk gown was heavy with jeweled pins and her hair was dressed in the style of the northern mountains with many braids twined with strings of glass beads. Everyone at Caer Caradog was well dressed, including the crofters, but the fort was riddled with fleas. Gwenavy's babies were covered with angry red spots. Although the women greased them with lard to keep the vermin away, it attracted the dogs, who were always licking the children if someone didn't drive them off.

Alwyn was glad they were only stopping at the fort, and that Powys had not brought her there to have her child. They were on their way to the nuns at St. David's priory. And late enough, considering she was due any day by her reckoning. They had been delayed while Powys skirmished with the earl's knights at Caergwrle, then went north to raid for cattle. It took more days to herd the cattle south to a valley for safekeeping.

She ate another handful of currants, watching the couples circle the floor. She was sharing Gwenavy's bed in the chief's room in the wooden tower. She supposed she could endure a few more fleas. In Powys's camp in the hills she had suffered so much from the cold that she would have given anything for a hall with a big hearth and roaring fire like this one.

The harpers changed their dance tune. A rebec and viol joined them. Men—knights from Prince Rhiwallon's court —crowded onto the floor. Gwenavy gave her a poke with her elbow. "Look what they are doing now. This is new, this dance, from France."

With Gwenavy's baby jumping up and down in her lap, Alwyn could hardly see. "I thought the Welsh did not copy from the French."

Gwenavy shrugged. "Caradog rails against it. But Welshmen fight now for King William in France. They bring such things back with them."

A tambour measured the beat. The couples linked arms. A few knights without women danced with each other. The dancers lifted pointed toes, stepping high. On the beat they turned to each other and bowed, their heads almost touching.

The baby's head grazed Alwyn's chin. "What kind of dance is that?"

"It is called a dalliance." Gwenavy put her hand to her mouth to talk behind it. "You walk, then step and pause. Then turn to your partner to flirt."

Alwyn made the baby sit down in her lap. She gave it a currant. "It doesn't look like flirting to me. If anyone made a face like that and stuck it in mine I would slap him."

Gwenavy screamed with laughter. Some of the dancers turned to them, affronted.

Across the hall, Powys looked up. He was standing with a group of hill chiefs. Alwyn smiled at him. Her cousin wore his hair long, trailing his shoulders, and there was a spark that seemed to leap from his blue eyes. That was Powys's trick, that blazing look. Women swooned for it.

The baby in her lap hauled himself to his feet again. Her

arms were growing tired. She saw Powys bend his head to the chiefs. They clustered around him, gesturing.

Powys was a slender man, but full of strength; she had seen him at swordplay with his men. In the mountains they called him a Welsh hero. When Caradog's harpists sang of Kilhuch and Gawain in the evenings, they sent him meaningful looks.

She supposed it was only Powys's due. She had grown into womanhood with the legend of him: Prince Powys the great rebel, Prince of the Cymry, ally of nearly all the Welsh lords who would have him do their fighting for them while they sat safe in their halls. After all the years she had helped him, it had seemed right to go to him for help.

She saw the looks the chiefs sent her way. I am notorious, she thought. I am the woman who ran away from her Norman husband, defying even the Conqueror. When they had arrived at Caradog's fort, the gossip had been obvious. But there was nothing between Powys and herself; they had known each other as children. Besides, who would want to steal a pregnant woman?

She saw Powys leave the chiefs to speak to Caradog. He started across the floor. When he reached the high table, he reached over it and seized her hand. "Come and dance with me," he said.

Caradog's wife laughed, delighted. "Now we have a hero. Powys is the bravest man in Wales."

Alwyn made a face. She was wearing a long, loose gown lent by one of Caradog's sisters that did not hamper her jutting front. "Powys, I am as unwieldy as an ox team. And just as light on my feet."

He pulled her up from the bench. "Come, they are playing a Norman tune. You must show us how it's done." He drew her toward him with both hands. "And this dalliance."

"You are mad." She allowed him to lead her out on the floor. "Can a mountain flirt?"

Ahead of them two couples lifted their feet, then bent over as they pointed their toes. The farthest couple hopped into the rear of the old chief of Llanarmon, who turned and roundly cursed them. The younger man only laughed.

There was no singer, only harps, the rebec and horn, but Alwyn recognized the song. She had heard Morlaix's knights bellow it enough in the evenings when they were in a mood to sing. Or riding, when they took her to the village.

> *Fair is her body, bright her eye;*
> *When it smiles her mouth is kind to me;*
> *Between the earth and heaven high,*
> *There is no maid as fair as she.*

When they turned to each other for the dalliance, she found Powys watching her closely. "Why do you look like that?"

She grimaced. "Like what?"

"You were sad."

"No, not that." She hopped on one foot and pointed her toe. To show him it was nothing, she hummed the melody under her breath.

Caradog's hall was as big as Morlaix's. There were more than a hundred people inside, many of them wild herders and their wives who did not dance, but stood gaping. Caradog's chiefs stood at the far end, near the door. They talked, heads together, through the racket.

Powys looked down at her as they turned for the dalliance. Blue eyes under straight black brows gave him an intent, passionate look that drove all the Welsh women mad. The married ones as well as the maids. "Does it make you sad now to be with the Welsh, instead of the Normans?"

He was teasing her. "Don't look at me like that, I have enough women here who hate me. Why don't you pick one of Caradog's sisters to dance? They are slim, and skip about most lively."

He seized her hand again and they moved forward. "I will look at you as I wish. You are by far the most beautiful woman here."

"God and the saints, you have strange tastes." She lifted her pointed toe and hopped a little, heavily. Across the floor, two women watched her, disdainful. "Look for a fat woman to take my place, then, if that is your pleasure. This babe will not take much more of this jouncing."

She would have walked away but he held her hand tightly and skipped forward, taking her with him. The drum beat loudly. He stopped and turned to her.

He said in a low voice, "The chiefs are telling me that I should have wooed you before this Norman rode from the south and forced a marriage on you. That you would be carrying my child now, not his."

She stared at him, dumbfounded. "Well, it is too late to think of that."

His eyes glittered. She had said the wrong thing. "I will be glad," she said quickly, "when tomorrow we start for the priory at Saint David's wells." They danced a few steps, her heart beating heavily. Why talk to her of such things now? "We do not want to linger here; I am too close to my time."

He gave her an enigmatic look. "Tomorrow Caradog and I go hunting."

She stopped short. She didn't want to dance anymore, she was filled with a feeling of dread. The line of men and women parted, going to their right. She was suddenly looking at a new partner, a young Welsh knight with curly black hair and ribbons plaited in it.

"Luck has not deserted me," he said, catching her hand.

She followed him. She didn't want to dance, she needed to go someplace and think. In the back of the hall, all the Welsh chiefs were watching.

They brought their heads together in the dalliance. "I

don't know why you think luck has favored you." She tried to think of something to say. "Unless this is your pleasure, to gallop about with imminent birth."

He put back his head and laughed. He was good-looking, dark like Powys, with white teeth. "They say there is none here so witty as the Lady Alwyn." They pointed their toes and hopped. "I am Emrys of Gwyddelwern, Prince Rhiwallon's knight."

As he pulled her along, Emrys said so low she almost could not hear him, "I have seen your husband, the Norman *morchawg*."

She stumbled and caught herself. They were at the end of the hall. They turned, passing Caradog with his chiefs.

"I was sent," he said, in the same low voice, "to talk of ransom with him as Prince Rhiwallon's emissary. The *morchawg* wants you back. He has burned two villages of Powys's saying that he will do more if you are not returned to him. But he will not ransom you."

She almost tripped again as she swung her foot forward and pointed her toe. Sweet Jesu, why was this knight telling her this? Caradog's fort was full of intrigue; she'd been stupid not to see it. "My cousin Powys is taking me to the nuns at Saint David's wells," she said.

He looked down at her. "Everything has a price. It is wise to know your friends."

She knew what he was saying. Or she thought she did. They were not looking to ransom her, but something else. Desperate, she racked her brains, trying to think of what her cousin had said to her.

They came down the room slowly. Gwenavy watched them from the high table, the fat baby jumping and clawing at her hair.

She said to the Welsh knight, "Did Prince Rhiwallon say to tell me this?"

They came to a stop as the music ended. He took her hand and lifted it to his lips. "If I were your husband, lady,

I would want you so that the price, if it were ten thousand pieces of gold, would be as nothing."

"You have not answered me."

His eyes were hooded, distant. "When you need Prince Rhiwallon's aid, send for me."

The dancing was still going on when Alwyn and Gwenavy crossed the fort's inner yard, full of small fires with the herders and their families gathered around. It was growing cold in the high mountains. The grass underfoot was rimmed with frost.

The wooden tower was old. One could see why the Normans in England were replacing wood with stone keeps. Alwyn suddenly thought of the master mason. She wondered what her life would have been like if somehow she had gone with him. To live as a mason's wife, forever traveling about. She knew how that would have ended.

Gwenavy carried a bowl of red plums with her. She climbed into the bed with the baby on one arm and the bowl tucked under the other. She settled herself, her feet drawn up under her, and put the baby to her breast.

Alwyn climbed into the bed and Gwenavy moved over to make room. They settled their big bellies between their legs. The chief's wife handed her the bowl of plums. "You could see Emrys of Gwyddelwern wanted to dance with you," she said. "They say he is Prince Rhiwallon's bastard, handsome like him. The prince looks after his children, the girls, too; he gets them good marriages."

Alwyn stuck a plum in her mouth. These were men's games. She felt sick, like a mouse in a trap. She didn't know if the plums would stay down.

They were not going to the nuns at St. David's wells. In the morning I will go hunting with Caradog, Powys had said.

Gwenavy reached for the dish. "Whenever he has an

interest the prince sends young Emrys. Caradog is always telling me, be careful what you say in front of him."

"I need to use the chamber pot," Alwyn said.

Gwenavy put the child to the other breast. "I should wean this one, with another coming so close. Go outside," she told her, not looking up, "there is a board across the outer wall you may sit on. Take the end or they will see you in the yard."

Alwyn went outside. She lifted her skirts gingerly. The jakes emptied into the outer ditch. It was cold and windy enough not to smell it. Suddenly she stood up and turned and threw up what she had been eating, out into the black void of the night. She leaned against the wall, dizzy.

She had not known Powys claimed Llanystwth Valley as his by ancient right. He was being told he should have wooed her before King William sent Fulk de Jobourg to marry her. God in heaven, it was easy enough to see how Powys's mind was working!

She had thought he would help her, and all the time that was what he had planned.

When she went back into the room, Gwenavy had finished nursing her babe. With a growling noise, he filled up his napkin. The chief's wife scrambled out of bed, carried him to the door, and shouted for one of her women to come and take him.

The baby gone, she came back and got into bed. She peered into Alwyn's face. "Are you feeling well? You look pale."

"Plums." She held her hand in front of her mouth. "They do not agree with me."

Gwenavy pulled the bedcovers over them and patted them into place. "Shall I put out the candle?" she wanted to know.

When Alwyn nodded, she put it out between thumb and forefinger. In the sudden dark they lay side by side like young girls visiting, with all night to gossip.

After a while Alwyn said, "How did you marry Caradog?"

The other woman laughed. "Oh, that makes a good story. Caradog saw me at the fair in Colwyn. He was already a warrior the other girls talked about. He followed my father and asked for me. Of course my father would have none of it, I was too young. Caradog went home in a rage. One day I was at the market in Llanerfyl with my mother and my aunt, and Caradog came with his men and snatched me up in front of them. You never heard such screaming. My father came to Caer Caradog with a hundred men and the bishop. There was almost a war over it."

"Did they make you marry him?"

"Holy Mary, no. I wouldn't let Caradog touch me; I was only thirteen. I screamed and cried and made him bring me presents. Some of them I took, some I threw back at him. Oh, I was a terror! When he tried to bed me I screamed my head off and he wilted. I tell you, when my father and the bishop came, Caradog was ready for them to take me back. So I said I would marry him."

Startled, Alwyn said, "You would marry him?"

In the dark, Gwenavy giggled. "Yes, and I made the bishop stay to see the virgin sign on my sheets. It took Caradog all night, I was such a ninny. He got no sleep at all. Now, of course, he is forever at it. My mother wants me to come home for a twelvemonth, my babes are so close together. So that I may have a rest from him."

There was a silence. Unwilling, Alwyn thought of her own husband. "There are other things to do," she said.

"Yes, perhaps, but I think I will go home anyway. Caradog will not sleep with another woman. He has told me so." In a different tone, she said, "When will you go to Saint David's wells?"

She knew, Alwyn thought. Caradog has told her. "Not tomorrow. Powys has said he wishes to hunt."

There was a long silence. Alwyn thought Gwenavy had

gone to sleep. But she turned, restless, her weight shifting the bed. "Alwyn?" she whispered.

She waited a long moment. "Yes."

In a rush, Caradog's wife said, "I do not think I could stand to have my babe taken from me."

She said nothing more. After a while, Gwenavy slept. Alwyn stayed awake, staring into the darkness.

Caradog and Powys and their chiefs went hunting before dawn, on foot. They would hunt all day, Gwenavy told Alwyn. The Welsh knight, Emrys, did not go with them. He sat before the fire combing his hair and retying the ribbons. He watched Alwyn as she played with Gwenavy's children.

After the noon meal, when the chief's wife took the children away to sleep, Alwyn came to where Emrys was sitting. She sat down beside him. "How far is Prince Rhiwallon's castle from Caer Caradog?"

She knew she had said something he wanted to hear. "Two days."

"I have two boys with me. They know the mountains."

He looked down into his cup of ale. "Then I will meet you at the rood oak that marks the end of Caradog's land. It is a pass in the mountains, they will know it."

She smiled at him as though they were talking of other things. "What does the prince offer me?"

He looked at her broodingly. "Lady Alwyn, he will do all for you that you would wish him to."

She waited a while in the hall after Emrys left. Gwenavy did not come back. Then she went into the yard and looked for Hwyl and the boy from the village. She found them in the stables playing at dice with Caradog's horse boys. When she caught Hwyl's eye, she motioned for him to meet her outside.

"Can you get the horses?" she wanted to know. "I must leave before the hunters return."

He was excited. She hushed him, looking around. "Prince Rhiwallon's men will meet us at the oak tree in the pass. The knight, Emrys, said you would know."

He nodded, wary.

"How far to the east?" she asked him. "To Morlaix?"

He went very still, eyes gleaming. "Two days," he whispered back.

She had thought they were farther into Wales. So that had been a deception, too. "The chief here, Caradog, will think we have gone with Prince Rhiwallon's men. He will follow Emrys. Yes," she told him, meeting his look, "I will do it. You will not have to deliver this babe on the road."

He dropped to his knees and would have kissed her hand but she caught him in time.

She turned away. By her reckoning she was due anytime. But do it she would.

Chapter Seventeen

BY THE TIME THEY REACHED MORLAIX village, Alwyn was bleeding. She thought her waters had broken hours before; she was riding with both legs to one side of the saddle as she could not bear to ride astride. If that racking pain was labor, then it had begun when her waters broke.

As they came through the village the dogs smelled the blood and followed them, barking. The miller came out of his house, a cudgel in one hand and a torch in the other. When he found out who it was he dropped the torch in his excitement. The miller's wife crowded behind him in the doorway.

"Bring the midwife," Alwyn managed.

The miller's wife gave a low cry. Clutching her blanket, she ran off into the darkness. As the horses plodded along, the miller ran ahead of them with the torch. The villeins, half awake, spilled out of their huts. Gwylim, the farrier, ran up beside Alwyn's horse. "Let me take you in the wagon, milady."

She shook her head. If she got down from the horse, her strength would leave her. She did not want to have the baby in the village.

She wanted to go to Morlaix. It was something she said over and over to herself. She must have looked mad. Pains wracked her like someone pounding on her bones. The whole village had turned out; a mob ran beside her with lighted torches. Some of the women were crying.

A cold night storm had come up. It swept toward them, wind shaking the trees. Alwyn shivered. A villein ran up to throw a cloak around her.

The horses plodded up the castle road. The Welsh boys were sodden with weariness, not able to hold up their heads. Some of the village men ran ahead. The drawbridge was coming down. The horses did not have to stop and wait.

Torches were already lit on the portal gate. Seeing the crowd, the knights rushed out as though being attacked. Fulk de Jobourg was in the midst of them, a white nightshirt flapping around his bare legs. He carried a drawn sword.

The village people surged around the horses, carrying them into the ward.

Seeing her, Fulk de Jobourg began to curse. The horse came to a stop. Dropping the reins, Alwyn held out her arms to him.

He threw down the sword. He came up to the horse and seized her under the arms and lifted her from it. He started to set her on her feet. When he saw the blood he took her up into his arms again, and strode across the ward. The villagers and the knights followed them in a crowd.

Guy de Bais ran ahead up the stairs ahead of them. Everyone was shouting at once. Fulk took the stairs two at a time. Alwyn bit her lips to keep from crying out.

She looked up at Fulk as they entered the room. His face was harsh by torchlight, his eyes shadowed. She was surprised at how familiar he was. She burrowed against his chest, trying not to weep.

Villagers and knights crowded in behind them. He laid

her on the bed. Alwyn gasped in pain. Fulk had not said a word to her from the moment he had picked her up. She thought crazily that he had a right to kill her if he wished. But then she had never thought to come back. "They were going to take my baby," she tried to say.

He stared down at her as though she were speaking another language. She tried again in Norman French. She grabbed his arms with both hands, holding herself up from the bed.

"He wasn't going to take me to the nuns at Saint David's." Another spasm racked her. It was a moment before she could get her breath. "They were going to take the babe from me!"

She let go of him and sank back on the bed, not sure he had heard her, there was so much noise. The room was full of people. Women rushed into the room carrying a sack of wool. They split the sack open and began to stuff the clean wool under her to soak up the blood. Alwyn cried out that the new shearing was ruined, blood never washed out of wool. No one listened.

A young woman pushed forward and leaned over her, speaking French. She was in a nightdress, blanket thrown over it. Her dark hair was long and loose. Alwyn knew this was Hugh de Yerville's new bride. It was no place for her. She screamed for someone to take her away.

The tally reeve's wife put a hot drink to Alwyn's lips. It was nasty-tasting, hard to swallow. She was immediately dizzy. The pain was still there. In a few minutes, muddled, she floated in a stupor, not able to speak.

The women stripped her of her bloody gown and pushed her knees up, bracing her heels in the bed. There was another gush of blood. Fulk de Jobourg drove the knights from the room. The women gathered around, looking between her legs. Their voices beat in Alwyn's head. The weaver woman pressed on her belly, trying to turn the babe. Alwyn screamed.

Fulk de Jobourg came back to stand by the bed. He

folded his arms over his chest, staring down at her. The weaving woman said, wiping her hands, "It's a big babe with a big head. And it has a shoulder up. It needs to be turned if she's to bear it at all."

There were voices on the stairs. The crowd parted and the old midwife hobbled in. Fulk met her at the door. "Goddamn you, you old whoremonger, it's past time you got here!" He pushed her toward the bed.

The old woman stopped and looked between Alwyn's legs and shook her head. Then she came to the head of the bed and bent over her. Alwyn saw her face growing large as a full moon as she kept bending into hers.

"Milady, can you hear me?" she shouted. With both hands old Marve pushed on Alwyn's belly. Somewhere, far away, Alwyn heard the screaming of a woman in torment. The old woman straightened up. She said, "The babe's too large, it won't come out. You should call the priest and let him shrive her."

Fulk de Jobourg took the old woman by the arm and dragged her across the room. People fell over themselves to get out of their way. He opened the door to the stair and threw the midwife outside.

Some mailed knights came into the room. They stood, shoulders touching, trying not to look at the bed.

"Get the monk," Fulk shouted. "The mad Irishman. Get a horse and ten knights and find him in the village."

Alwyn hauled herself up in bed and vomited up the foul-tasting brew. It spewed all over the bedclothes. The women rushed about, exclaiming, to clean it up.

She fell back onto soft wool piled around her and tried not to scream. Her throat was so raw she could only gasp. Guy de Bais had come in. He stood talking to Fulk de Jobourg. The lord of Morlaix ran his hands through his hair. Shoulders hunched, he turned away.

Guy sent most of the women away. The room grew quieter. A knight threw more wood on the fire and it blazed up. The weaving woman stayed. So did the butler's wife. After a while, the cook came in with a bowl of hot soup. Alwyn, listless, allowed the weaving woman to lift her up into a sitting position. A second after she drank the bowl of soup she vomited that up, too.

They put her back down and a wrenching pain, like a hand with claws, gripped her. She screamed again. The pains were coming more slowly, each one more terrible than the last. Floating numbly, she stared up at the ceiling. She thought Caradog's wife came and took her baby. She knew it was dead. It was all wrapped up. Gwenavy would not let her see its face. "Hush," the chief's wife said, "you will have a better babe by Powys."

She didn't want Powys's child. She tried to tell Caradog's wife that the child was a Norman, willed by King William himself to exist. But Gwenavy turned her back and carried it away.

At last Prince Rhiwallon himself came and bent over her. He explained that he would only hold her for ransom, not like Powys. And that he did not want her child; he would send it back to its father. Weeping, she thanked him for his kindness.

A strange face bent over her, with strange eyes. The prince said, "You know I cannot touch a woman's body, it violates my holy vows."

An arm came across her from the other side of the bed to grab the prince by his monk's habit. It dragged him over her. The prince had to put his hand on the bed to keep from falling on her.

"You bloody ruined fighting man," Fulk de Jobourg's voice shouted, "I know you've touched women. Think of all you screwed before you took your puling vows!"

Looking up, Alwyn saw Fulk right over her. Eyes narrowed. Hair askew. "You've helped foal horses, haven't you?" he shouted. "Help her birth her babe or I'll rip your eyes out and make you eat them!"

She lifted herself on her elbows. "But he is a monk," she whispered.

A crowd of knights filled up the doorway, jostling each other to see. Fulk de Jobourg was shouting for someone to bring him his sword.

Angry, the monk walked away. He came back with a vacant-faced girl. The monk and the girl bent to peer between Alwyn's propped knees. The monk shrugged. He turned to the girl and made the sign of the cross over her head. The monk prayed over the girl. He said, "You must touch this woman for me and do as I tell you."

Nodding, the girl went to the bed. The monk still looked angry. "This is what you must do." He spoke to the girl as one would to a child. "The babe must be pushed back before you can turn it. When the head is slipped up inside the mother again, reach in and take the babe's hand and push the arm and shoulder against its small body. When the head comes down again, as it will, reach under to the back and stick your finger in the babe's mouth and in this way begin to pull it out."

The monk suddenly reached out and seized Fulk de Jobourg by the front of his nightshirt. They were both big men. They stared into each other's faces. "I will not touch her," the monk said, "the girl will do that for me. Now you must get behind your wife, in the bed, seize her between your legs and hold her so that she cannot move." He pushed him toward the bed. "Hold tight to her."

The monk's girl drew Alwyn's hips forward on the bed. She felt Fulk's weight behind her as he settled himself. She saw his long legs stretch out beside her on top of the bedcoverings, enclosing her. His arms went around her to hold her.

With a sob, Alwyn leaned back against him. There was another wrenching hard pain in her belly. Something moved. She grabbed his wrists.

He was there. She had something to hold on to. Suddenly she knew the babe would come. A great pressure had begun against the bones of her hips as though the key in a lock had been turned. She reared back, feeling him big and solid behind her. It was his babe, after all, no matter what he said. She drew a gasping breath.

Then she screamed.

The monk's girl had pushed the babe's head up into her body. She felt her belly muscles contract with blinding pain. Something was tearing at her. The monk was shouting at the girl. Alwyn screamed until her voice died away. The man holding her tightened his arms around her until she felt her ribs would break. Everything was breaking.

The babe's head butted forth. The women screeched. The knights in the doorway cursed. The monk hovered over the girl. "Keep your finger in its mouth," he was shouting, "and pull down, not up, until you have it free."

In a gush of wet the babe slid out. There was a long, low moan from the women. Two or three fell on their knees and started to pray. The monk's girl lifted up a slippery body and wiped its mouth and eyes free of the caul. Dizzy, Alwyn lifted her head to look. She saw its ribs fill with air. The babe let out a rusty squeaking noise. Its chest pumped again, bones showing. The squeak became an angry bleat. It looked to be a very large child. In spite of its hard birth, it waved its arms and kicked its legs. Its screams grew louder.

Alwyn closed her eyes. She held on to Fulk's wrists, not wanting to let go. The monk gave the howling babe to the women, who were laughing and crying. They carried it off to wash and swaddle it.

Guy de Bais came to the bed and began to pound Fulk on the back. "A boy, Fulk, a boy!" Carried away, he leaned over the bed and embraced him. The knights in the doorway cheered. The cheering passed down the steps into the ward.

A boy.

The man holding Alwyn pried at her fingers. She let go of his wrists. Without looking at her, he shifted and swung one leg to the floor. Then he stood up. The monk's girl kneaded Alwyn's stomach for the afterbirth, the monk telling her what to do. Quite suddenly, a deep darkness such as Alwyn had never known washed over her. As though stunned, she slept.

It was dawn before the women left. They had changed the bed and put on clean coverings and bathed the lord's lady and put her in a nightdress. They had then fussed about, lifting the babe and passing it from hand to hand and exclaiming over it, changing its napkin and putting it back into the cradle while they repeated endless stories of childbirth and colic and teething until Fulk at last drove them out. When they'd gone, he stopped at the cradle to look once more at the child.

One could not tell much from something that size, he thought, bending over to peer at the compressed red face wrapped to the ears with cloth swaddling. But he had seen enough of the child's midnight hair and filmy blue eyes when they were washing it to know it was not his.

He lifted his cup of wine and drained it, eyes on the baby. The master mason's eyes were blue. At least he supposed they were; it went with the fair hair. So could the eyes of the outlaw Powys be blue, to whom she'd fled that night she'd set the Scotsman free. Only Geoffrey de Bocage's eyes were brown.

What the devil did that prove? She could have slept with all of them. Perhaps she herself did not know who the father was.

Behind him, in the bed, the woman fretted and murmured in her sleep. He piled more wood on the fire and sat down again, his bare feet to the heat.

He had seen bravery many times, but this was a queer sort, laboring to bring forth something that might get stuck inside you and never come out, as this one nearly had. Thinking about it, his innards flinched. Though she screamed her head off, she had never given up. Or called for someone to help her.

That was the accursed trouble with her; she was stiff-necked and unmanageable, not at all what a man would want in a wife. She had held on to his hands with a grip that had near numbed them at the last. The child had not started to come until he had got into the bed to hold her.

Well, that had not been his idea.

It was the child that had brought her back, only that, he told himself; she felt nothing for him. She had fled from her Welsh rescuers as she had fled Morlaix, seeking again some place that would work to her advantage. She was beautiful but treacherous and self-serving. All those times he'd set out to catch the Welsh outlaw, she'd been sending messages to him, warning him. And letting him take his cut of the flocks to provision his men.

Well, now that he had her back she would not find it so easy to run off again. She would be a wife to him in all ways, he would see to that, and would serve his purposes —more so, now that he knew the Welsh wanted her. The Morlaix people followed her, castle and village; it had been like an army coming up the road in the middle of the night to bring her back.

A creaking noise, like an unoiled hinge, sounded somewhere. Fulk cocked his head, listening. It grew louder.

The damned child.

He got out of his chair and went to look into the cradle. The thing seemed all mouth, like a cornered badger. A red tongue wagged as it squalled.

Undecided, he leaned over the cradle and studied it. Behind him, the woman in the bed said something in her sleep and cried out.

Fulk reached down and took the noisy bundle in both hands and lifted it. For a time this was what he would have to listen to. He supposed there was a wet nurse somewhere in the castle to give it to and keep it out of his sight.

He carried the thing to the bed. Juggling it in one hand,

he reached down and shook his wife by the shoulder. She slept deeply. Her eyelids quivered but she did not waken.

He put the back of his hand to her cheek and found it hot. The women had done a good job washing and dressing her; she did not look as though she had been through the ordeal of the past few hours. Her black hair was tied in braids and red ribbons and lay against her breast. He smelled the faint scent of lavender. She wore a nightdress, her skin as waxy-pale as the cloth. With her eyes closed he was reminded of the Welsh word, *blodwedd.* Flower face.

The bundle he was holding was making a terrible noise. He shook her again.

"Madame, wake up," he told her. The child's screaming set his teeth on edge. He was sorry he had picked it up.

She opened her eyes and muttered something. He put the howling thing down beside her. "Here, no one has taken your child. Do something for it. I need a few hours' sleep if by great fortune I can get it."

He saw that she was sufficiently awake to know what it was he had put beside her. He sat on the edge of the bed and brushed his feet together, getting rid of the rushes and straw.

When he turned to look at her she had pulled down the neck of the gown and was putting the child to her breast. He watched it as it rooted across her white flesh, screaming. Then, with a sucking sound like a horse freeing itself from a quagmire, the howling ceased.

Fulk leaned forward. The thing had her nipple in its mouth. Had devoured it, in fact; it had disappeared from sight. A dwarf hand pressed against her breast in total possession.

She looked up at him. "Thank you," she murmured.

Fulk looked away. He supposed the thing would sleep with them. It had been a terrible night; he was too tired to lie awake until it was fed and return it to the cradle. He snuffed out the candle and lifted his legs into the bed. The loud smacking noises continued as he settled himself down beside her.

Determined to ignore it, he shut his eyes. In a few moments, he slept.

Chapter Eighteen

"NO ONE FIGHTS A WAR IN WINTER," Alwyn said.

The day was cold and no one seemed to want to go outside. The hall was so crowded there was little room even for the new knights who had come to join in the mountain campaign. Alwyn and Berthe, Hugh de Yerville's wife, had settled themselves on low stools by the fire.

"King William does. He fights in any weather." Fulk leaned his arm on the mantelpiece, warming his front before the roaring fire. "It's not a war, not yet. Only a campaign against the thieving Welsh." He looked down at his wife sitting at the hearth and frowned. "Sweet Jesu, do you have to feed that thing night and day?"

She lifted her eyes to him coolly. "Yes." She pulled her dress together in front and lifted the child to her shoulder. "Besides, it's not a thing, it's a baby."

Berthe held out her hands. "And a beautiful baby, too. May I hold the little love?" Hugh's wife was only fifteen, but the villeins' wives who helped her at the manor house complained of her bitterly. A real Norman, they told Alwyn in Welsh, nothing pleased her.

Berthe laid the child in her lap. For a long second he looked at her, then screwed up his face and bellowed. She lifted him to her shoulder, patting his back. "And he has a fine Norman name, Gilbert." She smiled at Fulk. "He looks so much like you, milord. He even has your generous feet!"

Fulk was not listening. "It's indecent to see you exposing yourself twenty times a day to every lout in Christendom who wishes to watch. I told you to pass that thing to the wet nurse."

"Oh, are they Christendom's louts?" Alwyn said sweetly. "I thought they were your new knights, milord. The ones you are going to use to conquer the Welsh."

He said in her ear, "God's wounds, are you listening to me?"

Alwyn turned away, not wanting to look at him. Since the babe had been born he was more cross-grained than ever. They did nothing but fight. "I will feed the babe in the room in the keep." She thought of all the stairs to climb. Gilbert was always hungry. "Or I will take him into the kitchen."

"No you won't. There's a woman named Uta or some such thing, the cowherd's wife. She has a babe of her own, she can suckle this one."

She turned her back to him and picked up her sewing. They had been over this before. He hated her getting up and down in the night to feed the babe. It always woke him. And he did not like Gilbert to sleep in the bed with them. He wanted to lie with her soon; he was thinking of that.

Hugh de Yerville came in. He bent over and kissed his wife on the cheek. "It's one of the Commandments, not to covet another's babe." When he saw Fulk's look, he gave Alwyn a quick glance.

"We have been to the village again, but God and the saints, Fulk, I believe these serfs will bring out the levy grain by grain. And only after we have threatened to hang their children." Hugh squeezed his wife's shoulder. She looked up at him and smiled. "The miller can give silver, he makes it and more on the ale yard and the mill. But he pleads the sick boy he has from the quarry work. The smith is as bad. I vow, to get what we want this time we will have to have another round of floggings."

Alwyn put down the baby dress she was sewing. "I thought you levied once in the village. Why do you go back?"

Fulk looked over her head. "When you have to beat them every time you want something it is useless. The serfs will hide even more."

"Not if you punish the ringleaders," Hugh said. "We could make an example of the smith. He is spoiling for it, that one."

"Sweet Christ, if we tie the smith to a tree and whip him until he cannot stand up, who will do his work? There are swords to be edged for the new knights coming in, and other work the armorer cannot do here."

Alwyn looked from one to the other. "Why do you want to punish the villagers for not filling a levy so you can fight the Welsh? They are all Welsh!"

"If you do not want to do it, then," Hugh said, "there is only one other way. Get the butler to give over some of the grain you have stored here at the castle."

Fulk looked down at Alwyn. "My butler does not have the key to the storerooms, my wife does. And if you think she will give over any of the food in Castle Morlaix, then you have not seen that she hoards cheese and pickled cabbage the way Bishop Odo does gold."

Alwyn said, "You were not here when we were eating lentils, milord. Besides, it is wrong to make the villagers give up their grain. We will only have to feed them after Christmas when they are hungry and have nothing to eat."

Hugh de Yerville shrugged. "In the winter the villeins can forage. The castle does not need to feed them."

She put down her sewing and folded her hands in her lap. "That may work in Normandy, but do you forget the rioting here in the spring?" Even Berthe was staring at her. Well, she did not care what they thought, it was the truth.

Hugh started to say something but Fulk stopped him. "She is right. There is no need to go against the Welsh if half the garrison must keep an uneasy peace." He looked down at his wife, rubbing his chin. "The levy must needs be shaken out of them by other means."

Geoffrey came up, peeling off his gauntlets. He had been in the tilting yard training the new knights. "Shake what out?"

Fulk said, "Go upstairs and put on that red gown. I am going to take a company of knights and go down to the village. I want you with me."

She didn't look up. "I have no time to go to the village, I have sewing to do. Guy has given me all the banners to mend."

Geoffrey bent over Berthe. "Holy Savior, Fulk, this cub is twice the size he was yesterday. Are you feeding him raw meat?"

Geoffrey held out his hands for Berthe to give him the baby but Fulk pushed them aside. "Bring him, too," he said, looking down at the child. "That's even better."

Alwyn stood up to face him. She thought she knew what he wanted. "I will go with you, but I will leave Gilbert here."

He scowled at her. "I said bring him. Listen to me for once."

She took the baby from Berthe's arms. The blanket slid to the floor. She and Geoffrey reached for it at the same time and knocked heads. She balanced the babe in one arm and wrapped the cover around him. "No, I will get the cook's wife to keep him."

Before he could say anything more, she hurried off across the hall.

* * *

She put on a blue tunic, new made from that year's weaving, with an unbleached linen undergown. Berthe had brought a blue silk gauze scarf from France as one of her gifts for the wife of her husband's liege lord. When Alwyn draped it on the high pile of her braids, the edge fell down to float before her eyes. The rest wafted about her shoulders, so light it was in constant motion. It was the first time she'd worn the silk. It looked very pretty.

When she came into the yard where the saddled horses waited, she saw Fulk de Jobourg's eyes narrow. She thought he would say something about the blue dress but he didn't. They rode out with Geoffrey beside them, the column of knights two abreast.

The day was bright and windy. On both sides of the road, a few sheaves of grain still stood in the fields. By the feast of Saint Andrew, the harvest would be over and there would be merrymaking and dancing around the empty threshing floors. Then winter would come. By that time the knights from Morlaix would be warring with the Welsh in the mountains.

Alwyn lifted her head and smelled the air. The winy odor of apples grew strong as they approached the village. They saw red and yellow piles of fruit mounded high at nearly every hut. The miller's ale yard was full of villagers trying out the new cider. Only a few stayed when they saw the knights; the rest ran into the woods. Fulk spurred his horse among the trees and reined in before the smith.

"You," Fulk said, leaning from the saddle, "I want to talk to you." The miller had come to the door of his house. He beckoned to him. "Both of you."

Dismounting, Fulk tied his horse's reins to a tree. Geoffrey seized the reins of Alwyn's horse and rode forward. The wind lifted the blue scarf around her face. She smiled at the smith and the miller. The smith looked away.

"You must pay your levy in full, not just a part of it."

Fulk pushed his cloak over his shoulders to keep the wind from catching it. He stood, taller even than the smith, his thumbs hooked in his belt. "I have a hundred knights to go against Prince Rhiwallon and his bandit, Powys. I intend to go into their lands in Wales and drive them out, far to the west, where they will no longer prey on what's mine."

"Milord," the miller began, "we have been levied until there is nothing—"

"Now listen to me, damn you." Fulk took Alwyn's reins and pulled her horse up beside him. "Look at her. Rhiwallon and Powys seized your lady and took her into the mountains and held her for ransom. This is what you are being levied for."

Startled, both men looked up.

Alwyn bit her lips, eyes downcast. She thought this was what he intended. He kept her now only to use her; as he would use her babe, Gilbert, too if she let him.

"Held her against her will," Fulk was saying, "until she escaped and found her way back to those she knew would avenge what had been done to her."

Alwyn lifted her head and nodded.

"I want my vengeance," Fulk went on, "on those who would mistreat and dishonor my lady wife. In so doing, they dishonor me. And they dishonor all of you who call her your liege lord's lady."

The burly smith said, surprised, "They kidnapped her?"

"Oh, milord," the miller said quickly, "your lady is most beloved here. We remember her mother, a devout and gentle lady of most generous manner, born here in the valley. It was not long ago—"

"Christ's blood," Fulk said, impatient, "what does it take to put some bowels in you? You saw her the night she returned. She had to run from them. They would have let her have her child by the road."

From the doorway, the miller's wife called, "Aye, and they would have killed her, those devils!"

The men shuffled their feet. The smith said, "Well, it's no secret Powys has been taking his cut of the sheep. Since the old baron's time."

The miller's wife shouted, "God love her, I'd give something for milady Alwyn. She's been good to my boy."

The miller turned and his wife popped back in the house and closed the door. "Well," he said, "I have given all I have, I swore to your knight on it. But mayhap I could borrow a few more pence from my cousin in Chirk."

Geoffrey leaned from the saddle, his face scornful. "Is that all your lady means to you, a few pence?"

Fulk waved him back. "Miller, say what you will give now, we must needs meet the new levy before we can march."

Both men looked into the distance. The big smith was sullen. "What do I have?" he growled. "Nothing. It has all been given before when your knights came to get it. They have squeezed us dry. If I give silver, I'll have to borrow, like the smith."

Fulk lifted himself into the saddle and kicked his horse to turn about. "Good enough. Come to the castle when you have it in hand."

That seemed to settle it. The smith stood with his hands in his belt, staring at the ground.

Alwyn turned her horse to follow them. When she looked back, the villagers had come out of the woods and into the ale yard once more and were clustered about the miller and the smith, talking.

Geoffrey and Fulk trotted ahead. She heard Geoffrey say, "Borrow, my arse. Both will be digging under their pigpens tonight to bring up their treasure, and they will count it to see what they think they can spare. The miller's a rich man." He turned in the saddle to grin at her. "Now, what is the matter?"

Alwyn pulled the blue veil over her face. She looked away as though she had not heard him. Two knights rode up to her, one on each side. They cantered through the village. A woman, her apron full of apples, stood to watch as they passed. In the rear, one of the knights began to sing a Norman love song.

> *Now she is quiet on my breast*
> *And from her new and living nest*
> *She doth not seek to rove.*

The knights in the back joined in the chorus. Geoffrey threw back his head and laughed.

Alwyn sat on the edge of the bed and pulled down her braids with one hand. She paused to shift Gilbert to the other breast. He howled until his mouth closed over her nipple. "I wish you had told me you were going to do that." She shook the hair over her shoulder and began to comb it loose with her fingers. A strand brushed the babe's face and he squirmed, protesting. She brushed it away. "Take me down to the village and tell them Powys carried me off."

"It worked well enough." Fulk sat on the other side of the bed and pulled off the strings of his crossgarters. He stood up to pull off his hose. His head bent as he skinned them down his hips. "I thought that was what he did, Powys. Carried you off."

She cupped her hand over the babe's head. He wriggled, not wanting to be touched. She stroked his shaggy black hair. "I know you are pleased with yourself, you and Geoffrey, to use me like that. If you go back again for such a levy, I will tell them my honor has been avenged enough—and to give you nothing."

He was pulling his shirt over his head. "Don't threaten me," he said, through it. "And don't tell my people what to do."

"They are not your people. Your people are Norman. People here are Welsh." Gorged, the baby let the nipple roll out of his mouth. Before she could get him to her shoulder he belched loudly, and a gush of milk spilled down the front of her gown. "Oh, you are such a pig," she told him. "I have never seen anything eat as you do." She cupped his feet in her hand. He pushed at them vigorously.

Fulk stood barefooted on the sheepskin at the hearth, wearing only the cod strap all the knights wore to keep from chafing in the saddle. She changed the baby's napkin as he glowered at her. His jaw set, he watched her every move.

She went to the cradle and laid Gilbert in his fur bunting and laced it up the front. He made a cooing sound.

"Are you my sweet little piglet?" she cooed back. "Are you my fat little babe with such big feet like the lord's?" With her fingertip she wiped a trickle of milk from the corner of his mouth.

She bent over him, her hand on the cradle, rocking it back and forth, humming under her breath. A log on the hearth popped loudly. He was still standing there, watching her. After a while, the babe's eyes closed slowly, to slits.

Alwyn bent over him, pressing the open front of her gown together with one hand to keep her breasts from spilling out. She drew the woolen coverlet over the bunting with the other. The cradle was near the fire, its wooden sides quite warm. A few feet away, the room was cold. In a few hours, when the babe woke to be fed, she would have to remember to put more wood on the fire before she put him back in the cradle.

"Come to bed," he said. Out of the corner of her eye she saw he had discarded the cod strap. He stood on the sheepskin, upthrust flesh showing what he wanted.

She supposed he had waited longer than some men did with their wives. She dawdled at the chest at the foot of the bed, unlacing the front of her gown. She sat down on it to pull off her shoes.

He got into the bed and pulled the covers up to his shoulders. "Hurry up," he said.

Deliberate, she eased the gown down over her hips and stepped out of it. She knew the bed was cold; she kept on her shift. She climbed into it from the foot and crawled on her hands and knees toward her pillow.

He seized her so quickly she gasped. His hands tore at her shift, yanking it over her head. "Are you mad?" she cried, frightened.

"I'm not going to hurt you." He hurled the shift into the room. His hands worked at her underdrawers, peeling them away. "Did you sleep with your outlaw, Powys," he grunted, "there in the mountains? Or did he find you too big with his child?"

"Holy God!" She fought him with both hands, her legs thrashing against his under the covers. "Is this all you can think of? That I am whoring with other men?"

His mouth slammed down on hers. Both hands on her breasts, he hauled himself over her. She squalled, angry, against his lips. She had a wild thought that he had not been with any other woman, he was so hungry, since last they bedded. His shoulders, his arms shook as he held her. He thrust his hips at her. She felt his sex, hot and hard, prod her thigh.

His tongue bored into her mouth. She put her hand at the back of his neck. She slid her fingers up into his thick, cropped hair. He jumped as though she touched him with live coals from the fire. Between her legs, his hand fumbled for her cleft. His mouth, against her ear, breathed something. She moved her legs apart and then he was in her.

At first he was slow, crowding her until she winced. Seeing it, he rasped words about not hurting her. She shook her head. It was not exactly hurt. A restless itch burned around her stretching flesh.

He thrust into her hard, driving in and out, lifting her hips in his hands to hold her. She dug her heels into the

bed and gripped the damp skin of his shoulders, feeling
him straining. He threw his head back, groaning in bursts.
The bed shook. In the back of her mind she worried they
would wake the baby. Relentless, she pursued the hot
core inside her, wanting him to touch it.

Suddenly he stiffened and pulled out of her. She
grabbed for him. His body convulsed and he collapsed on
her, teeth clenched, body rigid. "Aaagh," he cried. His
mouth found hers roughly, his hands tangling in her hair.
He shook, all heavy muscle, his full weight upon her. She
felt a wet spreading across her belly.

He lay on top of her for quite a long time, struggling for
breath. Abruptly, he rolled to one side. He put one arm
behind his head to cushion it and closed his eyes, breathing hard.

Alwyn's hand groped for the stickiness. She said, "Why
did you do that?"

He gave her the edge of the sheet to wipe with. "They
call it thunder in the meadow. It's to keep you from having another babe too soon."

She gaped at him. With the edge of the cover she wiped
at her crotch. Thunder in the meadow. It was something
men would think of to call it. Her flesh ached. Inside, she
was still hot and trembling.

He put his hand on her back to stroke it, fingers spread.
She shook him off. "Why do you like to do this so much? I
hate it!"

He opened his eyes. "You hate it."

"Yes." She was shivering. "It sickens me. I ache."

He sat up so his eyes were level with hers. "Are you
still aching?"

When she nodded, he pulled her back down against the
bedcovers. His hand stroked down her belly.

She jerked away. "Don't touch me. I feel foul."

Insistent, his hand moved over her thigh. "Oh, so you
are still aching?" She lifted her knee in protest. He thrust
it aside. His fingers reached for her. He held her still while

he found a button of flesh in the folds and stroked it. She tried to sit up, to push him away. He bent over her, blocking the light from the fire. He lowered his head to her and his lips forced her mouth open. One hand gripped her thigh to hold her and his fingers invaded her.

It came in a rush, the darkness confused. The feel of what he was doing to her. Gradually, she gave in to him. The constant stroking sent quivers deep inside her. The ache grew insatiable.

Alwyn flung her arms around his neck. The stroking drove her mad. Writhing, she bounced her hips up and down in the bed, her hands in his hair, on his face. She could only see him as a shadow looming over her. Then the darkness began to whirl. He would not move his hand. Her fingers dug into his arms, scratching.

She fell into a strange void, helpless, her senses bursting. Nothing mattered. When it washed away, she went limp against him. He pulled himself over her and entered her again. Exhausted, she could only moan.

She was asleep when the baby woke. She stumbled across the icy stone floor and took him out of the cradle to keep him from waking the man in the bed. She was naked; she had only to put him to her breast to quiet him. Holding Gilbert in the crook of her arm, she crouched and picked up billets of wood from the bin and threw them on the glowing coals. She shivered. She knew the babe was wet. She got his napkins out of the chest and held them in her hand while he nursed, sitting at the foot of the bed, still shivering.

Her body was sore. Not only in the private places, but everywhere. Bedding with someone as strong as Fulk de Jobourg was combat of a sort; she was not used to it. This time she had found pleasure, he had seen to that. The same way he had used her in the village to wring money out of the smith and the miller.

She shifted Gilbert to the other breast, wincing at the grip of his mouth. He said nothing of his babe, biding his time. But he would have used Gilbert, too. God knows what he had in mind for both of them.

When the babe was finished she put him to her shoulder. He belched, splattering milk. She wiped it up, then changed his napkin, laced up his bunting and put him back in the cradle. The room was like winter. She had done it all without a stitch of clothing, hurrying and trying to be quiet.

Half-frozen, she slid into the bed and pulled the covers over her. Her teeth chattered. The room was dark except for the light from the fire. Beside her, her husband slept, snoring a little through his nose.

Well, at last now she knew the mystery. She had thought it wasn't so much but it was, after all. No wonder people talked of nothing else.

She burrowed farther into the bed and touched a wall of warm flesh. Carefully, she edged against the warmth and closed her eyes. The bed was soft. He was a big man, he made it warm. It was not long before she slept.

The smith was flogged the day after that. Fulk gave the order, and Guy de Bais rode off to the village to see it done.

The smith had come to the castle not with his silver but a tallying of money he claimed was owed to him for past service. The accounts were credited to the long-departed Bedystyr, chamberlain to the former baron, a tally of much work in the forge. There was no way of knowing if the smith's claims were true.

"He swore to pay the levy," Hugh de Yerville pointed out, "and now he defies us."

Fulk drew on his gauntlets. "Lash him. Tie him up as before, and leave him for a day. In this cold, he will soon have the proper spirit."

Alwyn came running as he led his horse across the ward. "I told you, they have given enough, the villagers." She kept step with him. "You are beggaring them! The smith is not rich, he gave all he had."

"Stay out of this. I will have you whipped too if you interfere."

She raised her voice. "If you flog him, I will go to the village and tell them not to pay another levy to the castle. Not for a year."

He stopped, raking her with his eyes. "Damn you, I want you to stay out of the kitchen." He seized her arm and shook her. "If you have business with the cook, send the butler to deal with it. When I come back I want to see you with woman's work. Some decent sewing, sitting in the hall."

She yanked her arm away, rubbing her wrist. "You said yourself that if you flogged him he would not be able to work!"

He swung himself into the saddle. A group of knights waited for him at the portal gate. He set his face. "You are not the lord here. Shut your mouth."

He spurred his horse forward.

She stood watching the knights ride out. Just as angry, she went back to the kitchen.

Berthe came that afternoon. She wanted to see the baby but Alwyn had sent Gilbert away with the cook's wife and her little girl. She laid out the gonfalon to be mended on one of the tables in the hall.

"Did you note there are as many English knights now as Normans," Hugh's wife observed, "who have come to fight the Welsh?"

Alwyn had gone up to the room in the keep to fetch her red dress. She spread it out on the tabletop. "Knights will go anywhere there is a fight. They all want to make their fortunes."

"Yes, I suppose that is so." She looked interested as Alwyn cut the red dress into strips. "That is such a pretty gown. What are you going to do with the cloth?"

Alwyn motioned for her to sit on the bench. "I need you to help me with this." She had been told a Norman girl of good family was skilled with a needle. "I thought I would cover the holes with some decoration. It will look better, anyway, some bright fancy ringed about the griffon there in the center."

"It could not be leaves," Berthe said, judicious, "if you are going to use the red. Leaves are always green, even here, are they not?"

She talked as though England were some alien land.

"Roses," Alwyn said, sitting down beside her. "Red roses. The color is practical, it can be well seen from a distance in battle. I have some green yarn. We can make the stalks of the flowers in which to twine them, thus, all around the beast in the middle."

"Roses," Berthe said. She looked thoughtful. "I have never seen that on a battle banner. What does your lord say to it?"

Alwyn cut a piece for a rose petal out of the red dress and laid it on the table. Then she cut another.

Her lord said he would have her whipped, that was what he said. That she was not the lord here. Before that, when she had pleaded with him to save the master mason's life, he had said he would send her to a convent.

In her mind's eye, Alwyn saw herself giving Guy de Bais the gonfalon on the morrow. Saw the standard-bearer take it as they rode out from the castle. Saw it opening in the wind and streaming out with the ugly beast rampant on a field of red roses. And what her lord would say then when he saw it.

"Oh, he has not heard of it yet," Alwyn said, squinting to thread the yarn through the eye of the needle. "It is my special gift to him."

Chapter Nineteen

A WAGON WITH WOUNDED KNIGHTS came back almost immediately. Goutard, the tall blond knight, was with them. He ordered the most sorely wounded carried up to the knights' quarters in the keep, and Alwyn sent the cook to tend to them.

"They were waiting for us," he told her. His face was red with the cold. He had seen hard fighting; he had not had time to clean the blood from his clothes. "The second valley into Glamorgan, where Powys has a wood fort, they came down on us with few knights but many little bowmen, intending to pick off men on horseback."

Alwyn knew Powys's fort well. She signaled for a server to bring something for the knight to eat as well as drink.

He took a cup of hot cider gratefully. "If it had not been for Fulk de Jobourg, we would have been bested." In spite of weariness there was a lift in his voice. "There is none to beat Fulk in the field, my lady, even caught as we were, not expecting attack so soon. He rallied us and we pushed them back and then secured our position." He threw back his head and drained the cider, then wiped his mouth with a chapped hand. "Pray," he said, "that it does not snow before Christmas."

She held the pitcher for him and filled his cup again. "Why do you say that?"

He looked at her over the rim. "We must have a base camp by winter. If this is the way the Welsh will fight us, from behind trees with bows and arrows, we have a long task before us."

Later she went down to see the smith, who was still in bed. His house was two stories with shed rooms added to the bottom part. The byre was a separate building; his family did not have to live above the animals. But she would not call him a rich man. The place was sparely furnished, full of threadbare children. From the look of her, his wife was expecting another.

Alwyn bent her head to pass under the low lintel. The smith was on a bed in the kitchen where it was warm. He raised himself on his elbows to glare at her. "Bring me nothing," he shouted, "unless you bring me skin to replace what they have flayed from my back!"

Hurrying to her, the smith's wife took the basket. "He is still wroth," she said in a whisper. "He has been sick with a fever from the flogging, and he has missed good work. The new knights who have come had ordered weapons and other things."

Alwyn had brought salves and a dozen apple tarts for the children. She went past the smith's wife to his bed. He lay with his arms outside the covers, muscles straining the seams of his shirt. He had a beard of several days' growth; he looked as though he had been sick.

"You were flogged for defying your lord," she told him, "and not paying the levy. You should have come to me with your complaint. I am the only one who remembers what my father's chamberlain did."

"You would not know of this." His eyes slid away, sullen. "I did much work when your father was warring away, locks, bolts, chains for the cistern, too much to tell. I am owed a fortune."

She doubted he was owed a fortune or he would have come forward sooner. That he was owed for some work was more likely; Bedystyr had robbed them all. The smith had only picked a poor time to defy the lord of Morlaix over it.

"You must make a list of what you remember, what work was done and when. Find witnesses to your work if you can. When you present all this to me, I will hold the lord's court and see what can be done."

He looked up at her. "That Norman lord will not let you hold manor court again."

She could see why most of the village disliked the smith. "Do not tell me what I will not do, I am your lady! Remember, my father was here before these Normans, and he held manor court. When my husband is not here, I will do it again."

The smith's wife came up with the youngest child on her hip. "What ails you, man?" she scolded. "The Lady Alwyn means us well—and she is the only one who does in that castle up there."

Alwyn was thinking she would have the smith's claims written down, it would look more legal that way. But she did not want the priest at the castle to do it. "Is the Irish monk a scrivener?" From their looks they didn't know. "Never mind," she told them. She would have to go down to the village and see for herself.

The Irishman had repaired the hut that had fallen into disuse since the pigherd's uncle died. When Alwyn rode up, the simpleminded girl was in the yard feeding apples into a wooden press, her hair bound up in a cloth, a wooden cross on a string around her neck. She stared at Alwyn, unsmiling.

Alwyn dropped the reins over her horse's neck and slid down from the saddle. The monk came to the door of the hut, his arms dripping water to the elbows.

"What do you want?" he said rudely. "Go away."

"I wish to speak to you." She looked at his wet hands. "But I will wait until you have finished what you are doing."

"I am washing clothes." Up close, she could see he had once been a handsome man. He started back inside. "I have not time to talk with you or anyone else from that castle."

She told him that she was seeking a scrivener. He stopped, his back to her. "I would have someone write a complaint. The smith charges that he did work for my father's chamberlain and was never paid."

"The smith's a troublemaker. The Normans flogged him."

"Wait!" She held out her hand. "Brother monk, there can be a manor court to try complaints. It is the law."

He turned his bald head to her. "Now what is it, woman, do you ask for a scribe, or a lawyer? I am neither. I leave that to Lanfranc and the others."

Even she had heard of Bishop Lanfranc, King William's minister. "Then you can read and write?"

He flung her a look of massive contempt. "Write? I was teaching at Bec when Lanfranc was but a lay clerk." His face changed. He raised his hand, pointing heavenward. "But now I have renounced the sins of a corrupt and violent world. I am a wandering seeker, a lowly penitent preaching the true gospels, living as humbly as Saint John in the wilderness." He lowered his hand abruptly and scowled. "Until your Norman lord gave me this lackwit Eve, yonder, as my burden."

The monk's affliction seemed a peculiar madness. "If you will do this for me," Alwyn said, coaxingly, "I could build you a hospice here in the village. There you would have a place to pursue your healing."

"I don't want a hospice."

"The girl can be your nun."

"The girl is feebleminded."

"Then she will have a true vocation." She was determined he not best her. She could see many uses for the Irish monk. "I will build a house for her. We will get more nuns from Chester and found a nursing order here."

"Will you cease?" He glared at her with pale, furious eyes. "Woman, I do not wish to found an order, gather nuns, or tend the sick in a hospice! My calling in life is solitary. I wish to retreat from the madness and evil of this world, and contemplate only God and His mysteries."

"You can do that here." She was thinking that since the monk was a teacher they could even establish a school for clerks. She needed one in order to get rid of Father Ascelin.

Before he could say more she handed him a cloth filled with the apple tarts she'd intended for the miller's sick son. He looked at the bundle as though she'd handed him a snake. "What's this?"

"Food, what else? You must eat even while you contemplate." She stepped closer and looked into his eyes. "The smith will be on his feet in a few days. I will tell him to come here and speak to you about writing his testimony."

She left the Irishman holding the cloth. The simple girl stood watching her, curious, as Alwyn swung herself up into the saddle. She was thinking hard as she rode out of the yard.

That same week a sickness swept the village and castle, mostly afflicting the children with fevers and congestion. The tally reeve's young baby fell gravely ill. The reeve and his wife spent much time in the castle church with the priest, who confessed them and prayed over the child.

Gilbert too fell sick. With his nose clogged with thick humors he could not breathe enough to take the breast and spent most of the time screaming. The cook fixed a thin gruel that Alwyn was able to scoop into his mouth while he was howling. Some of it stayed down. The whole castle was a misery of fretful, sleepless children.

A wet, cold wind blew down the valley from the north and the sea. It moaned around the curtain walls and the keep like a living thing. The knights and the men-at-arms were sick with deep, rasping coughs. Although no one had yet died, chapel masses were suddenly crowded. Father Ascelin preached against witchcraft and unholy pagan excesses such as had happened on Midsummer's Eve, and which had now brought God's punishments on them. Some of the castle folk stood in the ward in the cold to listen.

By the second day Alwyn's breasts were tight enough to burst and she could not sleep herself with the pain. At night she paced the room with the babe in her arms. Once she dozed, holding him, standing up with her cheek pressed against the mantelpiece.

The spinning sisters came to her with a new puppy from one of the litters in the stables. "You must get out your milk," they told her, "or it will dry up."

The puppy was sleek and fat. When it opened its mouth, smelling milk, the pink tongue inside curled like a trough. Alwyn pushed it away. "I can't do this. Besides, it will bite me." She knew it was common enough among the villeins. But for a knight's wife?

They clucked over her, insistent. "He is not going to bite you, don't be foolish. Your breasts are hard and feverish, the milk is already waning. You must do it now."

She held it in the crook of her arm. The sisters threw a napkin over her shoulders in case someone should come in. Relief came almost at once. When the pup was glutted the spinning sisters carried it off. In another day the mucus in Gilbert's nose was thick enough to wipe out with a wadded cloth. But before she could put her own babe back to the breast she had filled up two puppies. Four times a day.

A few days before Advent, a knight in the purple tunic of St. Botolph's galloped up to the castle. His message was that Abbot Ambrose St. Les was in Chirk, making pastoral visits before Advent, and would beg the same for Morlaix, its master and mistress and people.

This came at a terrible time. There was still much sickness and they were putting down food for storage from the harvest. "Saint Michael and the holy saints," Alwyn grumbled, "now he knows we will have to feed him. And more than lentils this time."

The Norman church asked fasting and penance for four weeks before Christmas, which made the last days until Advent right for feasting. In that season there was plenty of meat: since cold weather they had been butchering swine and culled ewes. The thing was to feast the abbot and his knights, but not lavishly, now that they paid taxes to Chester.

Alwyn sat down with the cook and the butler to see what could be spared. The cook offered oat bread, pickled onions and cabbage, and three kegs of salted pork. For the sweet, she chose apple and suet puddings. "They will have had apples galore wherever they go, anyway," she told them.

"Let them drink the green beer," the tally reeve put in. "'Tis a good way to find out when it is full brewed."

"And have them fill up the jakes?" The cook looked sour. "Fish and guests stink after three days, anyway."

For the entertainment, Guy de Bais's garrison knights would offer a challenge to St. Botolph's in the tilting yard before the feast.

The next day Geoffrey rode in with more wounded from the fighting in the mountains. These knights were not too badly hurt; at least they managed to sit up in the wagon. When they were taken to the knights' quarters in the keep, Alwyn sent for the Irish monk from the village. He came, angry as ever, the girl with him carrying a sack of the things he used in doctoring. Father Ascelin shut himself up in his cell. She had noted the monk and the Norman priest had little to say to each other. Carrying Gilbert, she followed the monk to the keep.

Most of the wounded knights were mere boys. One had lost three fingers from his right hand from a sword thrust. There was not much the monk could do.

"Your fighting days are over, lad," he told him. "Make your way back to France." He sat by the bed of a knight with graying hair who was not wounded but sick.

"I would say to you, also, go back to your home in Normandy." He laid his hand on the man's head. "If you have no money laid by to buy land, that is no dishonor. It is the easing of your soul you must think of now, and a little peace." When the knight shook his head, adamant, the monk shrugged and stood up. "This is for young men, this madness. I have known this life, I know of what I speak."

Coming back down the stairs, she found Geoffrey waiting for her. He was bundled in sheepskins over his mail, so at first she didn't recognize him. He tried to put his arm around her. "You are more beautiful than ever, sweetheart."

She pushed him away. "And you have grown surpassing brave since your lord is not here. Do you still tell him lies?"

He threw back his head and laughed. He had orders to have the smith make a chain and other ironwork to take back to the mountains.

She put Gilbert against her shoulder and covered him from the wind. "You do me no favor, Geoffrey. The smith has not forgotten his flogging. What do you need these things for?"

"We are building our own fort." He strode beside her,

handsome and confident. "The Welsh are learning to respect us. Rhiwallon sends his knights every day to sit in
the passes and watch us raise our motte."

So Fulk de Jobourg was building a base to spend the
winter and fight in the mountains. She supposed she
should be happy to have him away. "Why does not Chester send men to help? Why do Fulk and the Morlaix
knights fight the Welsh by themselves?"

He raised his eyebrows. "This is Fulk's war, his and
King William's. We do not need to share the glory with
Hugh of Avranches."

Glory. Holy Mother of God. "Tell me when you need
these things. I will have to send word to the smith before
you leave."

"Oh, I will not wait for the smith." Now he was smiling.
"I go now to Chirk. When I return will be time enough."

She watched him mount a fresh horse and ride out of
the portal gate. There was no business she could think of
for him in Chirk, unless he went to press his suit with the
wool merchant's daughter.

The abbot came with his knights, forty of them. It was
cold autumn weather and the feast of cabbage and pork
was well received, the apple and suet puddings even more
so. The knights' challenge fight held in the ward was
hugely successful. A St. Botolph's knight broke his shoulder and three of the Morlaix garrison took sizable gashes.
After the meal the sun came out, and the abbot walked
across the ward to inspect the new kitchen house.

"A fire inside a castle is a dangerous thing." He had
been in fine spirits since he came from Chirk and had not
once lectured her on womanly duties. "It is the grace of
God that all here survived it. But from a spiritual view,
one can say the actual fire was as nothing compared to the
spiritual inferno that hellish Satan's messenger, the grand
master, proposed here."

The abbot had talked much during his visit of the master mason, whom he and Father Ascelin seemed to regard as the Antichrist. She gathered the Norman church was alarmed at the prospect of secret associations outside the reach of the holy mother church, and the masons' lodges were said to teach the equality of all men, with peace and harmony the goal of Christian lives. The abbot told her Bishop Odo was determined to stamp out what he called this heresy. In this the king's half-brother was said to have the support of the pope in Rome.

Not once had Abbot Ambrose mentioned the master mason's escape from Morlaix. But he praised Alwyn's feast, and her fine healthy child. He was interested in the presence of the Irish monk in the village.

"So you have Bran of Cluny and Kells here." He looked around the hall as if hoping to find him somewhere in the crowds. "A famous man, he is the scourge of philosophers, the pope's stormy petrel."

She hadn't understood that. "The pope's what?"

"My dear, a figure of speech." Later he'd spent a long time talking to Father Ascelin at the tables in the back of the hall.

It was not what Abbot Ambrose said but what he didn't say that made her uneasy. He told her Hugh of Avranches, the Earl of Chester, had heard of her good works and influence among her people.

She didn't know that the Earl of Chester knew that much about her to praise her for anything. She talked of household things, and when she hoped the baby would teethe. She saw his attention wander. Then she asked if he had fresh news of Fulk de Jobourg's war against Prince Rhiwallon in the Cambrian Mountains.

He looked at her keenly. "A winter war is hard and Prince Rhiwallon most formidable. But your husband is well favored by King William, who has uses for ambitious young knights. Sometimes the king's favor is misplaced, as you remember with young Hereford and Ralph de

Wader. Pray your brave husband will avoid their particular sin."

"Abbot Ambrose, my husband is no traitor." She wondered if that was what he wanted to hear. She hated this sort of fencing; men were always much more clever at it than women.

He smiled. "Dear my lady, I did not say that. Fulk de Jobourg is an admirable knight, King William's own man. My lord Chester is well pleased with Morlaix. This is a fine, strong fief defended not only by your husband's brave deeds but the love that your people bear you. I am told you were born here, is that not true?"

"My father was wed to my mother here." She knew the Earl of Chester would be pleased to have his own man at Morlaix, not King William's. With Fulk de Jobourg away, they were surrounded by wolves. She wondered where Gilbert was; Berthe had taken him to the hall with her. "I pray for my husband's well-being, milord abbot, every hour."

"As so you should, my child. As do we all." He looked down at her benignly. "No tragedy will strike your lord husband. God will keep him safe. In these times of war and uncertainty, you may rely on the love and strength of your friends. I am sure you know who they are."

Mother of God, they were talking about friends again. With the abbot of St. Botolph's, Chester, Prince Rhiwallon, even her cousin Powys, she needed no enemies. She worried privately that they would try to rid themselves of Fulk de Jobourg. The thing was not so mad as it seemed.

The abbot said, "There is no denying your lord husband's skill; de Jobourg is brilliant at tactics. They say the fort he builds at the pass of Glynowestry has blocked Rhiwallon completely."

Until that moment she had not known where he was. He did not trust her enough to tell her. Nor, she knew, did he trust Chester and Ambrose St. Les.

She put her hand on the abbot's arm while they walked

back through the ward. The St. Botolph knights were saddling their horses. Pages and squires ran about loading up the wagons.

"There is a store of Hereford's fine wine here, lord abbot," she told him, "that my husband prizes much. You must let me fetch some for you, to take on your journey."

She could not wait to get away from him. His eyes followed her as she went straight to the kitchen.

While the cook fetched the wine from the storeroom, she sent for Goutard. She sat down at a table filled with pots of pork and pickled cabbage, the remains of the feast, and tried to slow her breathing. She needed to look calm.

The blond knight came into the kitchen, pulling on a quilted coat. When he saw her sitting at the table he straightened, smartly. "Milady," he said.

She motioned for him to sit down beside her. The kitchen was noisy.

She clenched her hands before her on the board. In spite of everything, she was shaking. "You must go to my husband," she said, "and tell him to beware. There are Chester's spies with him. I do not know who they are, but they plan him ill."

Even as she said it, she knew that when the message came to him he would not believe her.

Chapter Twenty

THE VALLEY LAY FLAT AND BROWN with winter grass, smooth enough for the knights to charge full course at the rear of the retreating Welsh, who were going in wild confusion. The way was littered with weapons and baggage Prince Rhiwallon's knights were discarding.

Fulk's squire, Aubrey, came galloping up on his lathered horse. "It is a rout, Fulk," he shouted. "We will smash them here, against the pass!"

On the left, Hugh de Yerville's forces held to a disciplined canter, waiting for the order to charge and drive the Welsh to the end of the vale. They could see the walls of the mountains closing like the neck of a bottle. But not what was at the end of it, Fulk thought. That was what bothered him.

The destrier tossed his head, smelling battle. Fulk reined him in and he fought the heavy chain bit. Behind, the rear columns pressed up against the line in the fore, eager to join in the fight.

Hugh de Yerville pulled to a skidding stop beside him. "I do not know this valley," Fulk shouted. He looked around for their trackers. None was in sight. "Is it blind?"

" 'Ware the Welsh," his knight shouted back. "We are far to the west, that is all I know."

Fulk did not need to be reminded. The field was barely in control. Once the enemy broke and ran it was the devil's own temptation for mounted men not to follow. He could see the right flank still at a gallop, spreading out over the meadow.

From their position on the slope they saw the forces of Powys and the prince emptying down the narrow vale. The right flank of English and Norman knights began to pick up speed. Men-at-arms burst through de Yerville's front ranks, cheering.

Hugh kicked his horse closer to Fulk. The two stallions, mouths foaming, lunged at each other and tried to bite. Fulk hit at Hugh's mount with the flat of his sword. The master-at-arms came running to them.

"Malluch, turn your men," Fulk roared. The Welshman turned and ran back to his soldiers.

Fulk shouted to Hugh to hold his knights and the other man galloped off. He turned to Aubrey. The gonfalon the boy held snapped in the wind. Distracted, he looked up. The things around his griffon looked like bloody fists on green arms. He was told they were roses.

"Hold here, Aubrey, on this hill." The excited squire gave him a glazed look. Fulk cursed under his breath. "Hold the rally point or we lose the field!" The boy nodded.

It was a mistake, Fulk knew, to go after the flank on the right with the hope of turning it back. Such maneuvers courted disaster. But if he did not attempt it, they would lose one third of the field in what he was beginning to sense was no trap for the Welsh but might be for them.

As he started the destrier down the slope, the knight de Bracy and his squire broke from the hill to follow. De Bracy's squire lifted his horn to his lips and blew retreat. At least someone had his wits about him.

The destrier stretched out his heavy legs and labored

to overtake the charging flank. A dismal hope. The right was lost to its frenzy, rushing after the fleeing Welsh. A horse stepped into soft ground and fell, spilling its rider. The knights, screaming the Conqueror's battle cry, "Deux Aide," overrode the fallen man. Leaning forward in the saddle, his sword drawn, Fulk cursed them all.

At the far end the valley became swamp; one could not see it until one was right on it. There was no sign of the Welsh, they had spilled out of the far end of the vale. By now the right flank knew its error. In the soft ground, more horses fell. Fulk kicked his mount into a heaving gallop. The big horse hurtled through low bushes. Too late, he saw the hidden spearmen. They came up under the destrier's hooves as though they had sprung from the mire.

Unable to jump them, his horse reared, pawing the air. Behind him, Fulk heard de Bracy vainly shouting. Hands caught at his bridle. They were all over him, the Welsh, pulling him out of the saddle. He came down headfirst and hit the ground. Instantly, they were upon him.

I am dead, was his last thought.

Alwyn had chosen the miller's ale yard to hold manor court. She picked an escort of only six garrison knights and Guy de Bais, stiff with disapproval. The ale yard proved to be right; the whole village turned out, even a crowd of shepherds from the hills whom no one had seen in years. Berthe de Yerville came from the new manor house to tend Gilbert. The smith and his advocate, the Irish monk, met them under the trees.

She took a seat on a bench at a table the miller had pulled out. She had wanted Father Ascelin to act as the manor-court clerk, but he had gone away on some business to the chapter house in Wrexham, and would not be back for a sennight.

Two knights circled the crowd, pushing everyone back.

Guy de Bais acted as herald. He paced up and down in front, shouting, "The lord's manor court of Morlaix is opened by the grace of God and his servant King William of England, the king's servant Hugh of Avranches, Earl of Chester, and his faithful vassal, Fulk de Jobourg, Baron of Morlaix."

The smith came forward, black-browed and sullen, the big monk by his side. The Irishman unrolled a vellum sheet and began to read from it. Alwyn rested her elbows on the table. After a few minutes she put up her hand.

"That is not Welsh or Norman French," she said.

The monk glared at her. "It is Latin. Court Latin, Vulgate Latin. Latin of the schools."

For some reason, the crowd laughed. Alwyn supposed it was legal. She waved for him to go on. At the end of the Latin, the miller's claims for unpaid moneys were in Norman French, so it didn't matter.

There was also a list of villeins and sokemen at the castle, witnesses who could be called to testify to the work. The first was Daffyd One-Eye, the villein who helped in the forge. Bashful, the man shuffled forward to testify. His friends called out to him, jeering.

There were seven of the smith's witnesses who swore bolt by bolt and link by chain link to the work that the smith had done while Bedystyr was chamberlain. After a while Gilbert, in Berthe's arms, began to scream. De Yerville's wife took him away down the village road and out of sight, but not out of hearing.

Alwyn called a halt in the court to take Gilbert into the miller's house to feed him. Guy de Bais looked annoyed. The crowd wandered to the back. The miller had been told to sell only sweet cider, not ale. He rolled out a new barrel. The villeins sat on the grass with their families and ate bread and cheese, like a fair.

It was past noon hour when the testimonies began again. Geoffrey de Bocage rode up from the village road; Alwyn saw him in the back of the crowd. She had not expected him. He had been in Chirk for three days. He pushed to the front, curious. When he heard a villein testifying to cistern pipes, he broke into a smile.

He circled the edge of the crowd and came and sat down beside her on the bench. "If you are settling money on these louts' disputes," he murmured in her ear, "I will have to remind you that your lord husband is building a fort in the Welsh mountains we must pay for."

"I'm not settling anything. I have told the smith that after his complaint has been heard, I will take the matter to my husband, who will consider the claims." She knew what he would say: that unpaid bills from the old baron's day were none of his affair. She had told herself she would solve that problem when she came to it.

The crowd was rapt, listening to a stable knave describe locks the smith had made several years ago. "It is the best I can do, to promise my husband will consider it. Holy Cross, I have no money, either. But this way the smith will keep on working." When she turned her head, Geoffrey's eyes were right in hers. "That is what you want, isn't it?"

"You must ask Fulk." He looked very serious. "When will this be over? I needs must talk to you."

She wondered if he had gone to Chirk to declare marriage to his beautiful rich Jewess. She tried to imagine Geoffrey in a long-skirted townsman's robe, in velvet and fur, and couldn't. She wondered what he wanted to talk to her about.

"It will not take long," she told him.

Fulk hung head downward across the back of the Welsh pony. He was too big a man for such a stubby animal and knew they intended it that way. The thongs that ran under the horse and bound his hands and his knees, bending him belly-down across it, left him barely clearing the mountain track. As the pony trotted, he jerked his head up to protect his face and eyes. Once his nose hit a stone and began to bleed. On the other side, his feet hit trees hard enough to tear loose hose and crossgarters and flay his legs. To torment him further, the Welshmen running alongside beat him about the head and across the back with the butt of their spears.

Hanging like that, the blood drained into his face. His tongue began to swell. He fought against stupor and lost. When they finally stopped, he was no longer fully awake. The Welshmen cut the bonds and he fell into the dirt and lay there. They kicked him onto his back.

He looked up. They bent over him and he saw they were little tribesmen like the hunters he'd captured on Morlaix land. Dimly he wondered if the one he had cut that day had lived to tell other Welshmen about it.

They dragged him to a sitting position. They hit him across the back of the head with a spear to make him look sharp. They were in a clearing of tall oaks that had already shed their leaves. When he could focus his eyes, Fulk saw a figure that was so magically splendid in that wild place that he blinked. A slender man in black leather studded with silver, both jacket and breeches, stood holding the reins of a black horse. Not an infernal Welsh pony, but a splendid animal with a harness of tassels and silver to match the man's.

The Welshmen began to shout. They hauled Fulk to his feet and prodded him forward with the point of their spears. A shove from the back sent him to his knees, his hands still tied behind him.

The princely figure smiled. He said in Welsh, "Ah, he is a brute, this *morchawg*, a real Norman. He lives up to what we have heard."

The tribesmen laughed.

In Norman French he said, "Greetings, lord of Morlaix. I hope your journey has been a happy one."

Fulk made a noise with his swollen mouth.

"It is not necessary to thank me," the man in black said.

"I am Powys ap Griffyd, prince of these hills. Your Norman liege lord, the Earl of Chester, desires that I kill you."

Laess, the sokeman, stood with his shoulders hunched. "My ox was taken from me to pay the levy for the baron's liege lord in Chester," he was saying. "Now this Norman knight in the manor house has it, and I must pay rental to him for it so that I may plow in the spring."

The crowd made a murmur of sympathy. Someone in the back shouted about the other oxen forfeit to Hugh de Yerville. The line of Morlaix knights that had been lounging, bored, against the trees, now stiffened. A few put their hands to their swords.

Alwyn said loudly, "There will be no more levies this year. I promise this."

There was a ripple of murmurs in the crowd. She knew they had not expected that.

Laess spread his hands. "The Norman now has my ox, lady. I own naught but my breeches and shoon, for all that I have worked for the castle since I was a lad. I am a freeman, not a villein. What I own was mine to keep. That was the law."

Alwyn looked at all the faces turned to her. There was no answer that she could give. The Normans squeezed the land hard. Every peddler and trader who came to the castle was full of stories of cruel taxes and robbery by confiscation. But she was beginning to see that in spite of the hard levy, the earl did not overreach himself while Fulk de Jobourg stood at Morlaix.

"This must wait until the manor knight, de Yerville, returns," she told him, "for nothing can be done about your ox without his agreement. If you pledge manor work to him this coming year, think on how this can be taken as payment for the return of the ox."

The crowd began to shout. In some cases, such work

was frequently for barter, like shares of cloth. They knew the Norman would not agree to it.

"This is a new manor." She raised her voice over the noise. "You must dicker for what you want, even with the manor lord. If you would work and buy back your oxen, then see de Yerville."

Geoffrey had come to stand behind her. "Tell them when you will have another manor court," he whispered.

She gave him a withering look.

She was still thinking on the matter of the oxen when they rode back to the castle. Geoffrey pushed his horse close to hers, to talk.

"Don't turn," he told her, "I don't want the others to see." He meant the knights behind them. Obediently, Alwyn kept her eyes straight ahead. "Nor do I wish to startle you."

Now she turned to look at him. "Ah, you are going to tell me about your handsome Jewess in Chirk. You are going to marry her after all."

She was surprised at the sudden look on his face, contorted and bitter. "Hah! I tell you there is nothing better than a marriage with Jews. You are right at the source of the money they will lend you. It is all they think of."

She couldn't make any sense of that, but she saw the depths of his feeling. "Then you are not going to marry Belefroun's Sophia."

"Marry her?" He turned to her, eyes burning. "I seek fame as a knight, that is all life means to me. You know I do not have money. I will wed a woman who seeks to hold what is her own." In a rush, he went on. "When I say that if I were to wed you, you would hold Morlaix and rule here as you have done today, what would be your answer?"

She laughed. "Geoffrey." She turned in the saddle to look at the line of knights behind them. Berthe rode in the rear, holding Gilbert in her arms. His bunting covered his face. She knew he was asleep.

He said, "People in high places would aid you. This marriage can be annulled. The pope can be made to favor annulment, since you were married by force."

She turned to stare at him. He had not thought of all this by himself. "Annulment? With a babe? Are you mad?"

His face was set. "But your son would be the lawful heir, here. You would be regent and rule for him. No one would interfere."

Her mouth was suddenly dry. For a moment she couldn't think of anything. Finally, she said, "What people in high places?"

His eyes were fixed on her, desperate. She could see he was not too good at this. And yet they wanted him to marry her.

"Fulk de Jobourg does not have to be lord here." That bitter look came again. "It is not a matter of loyalty. Hugh of Avranches is also King William's man."

Holy Jesus in Heaven. She held on to the horse's reins with icy hands. In spite of the wind, the sun beat warmly on her cheeks. Hugh of Avranches was Bishop Odo's man, even a fool could see that. She felt as though the world were collapsing.

The castle road began to slope to the river. So close to home, the horses broke into a jog. She still couldn't think. It was as though her mind worked at a snail's pace, thick and unwilling.

They would let her have Morlaix, to act as regent for Gilbert. And Geoffrey would be her husband.

She thought: if Fulk was no longer alive, she would have to be cleverer than she felt. She was numb with fear.

He was watching her closely. They rode for several minutes before he said, "I would be in Avranches, fighting for Chester. I would not be here."

She stared straight ahead. It was better that they were

on horseback, talking. If she had to sit and look at Geoffrey, she would strike him. She knew they wanted her badly, to promise her all this. Even that Geoffrey would not be a true husband but safely away in France.

Suddenly she knew how badly they wanted to be rid of Fulk de Jobourg. King William's famed sword of justice. That valorous, loyal knight.

She said, "How long have you been Chester's man?"

Geoffrey's face reddened. "These are honorable men. They wish to deal with you honorably."

Mother of God. She didn't dare ask him if they had already killed her husband. She wondered how long Geoffrey thought he would be wed to her, fighting in Avranches.

She said, cautious, "Then through me they can have what they want?"

As soon as she said it she knew the villagers kept peace for her better than they did for the knights. Gilbert was the Norman heir and she could act as regent. That satisfied them all. Abbot Ambrose had been pleased with her this last visit; she should have been warned.

"You would rule here," Geoffrey reminded her.

They thought she would agree, she could see it in his face. She thought of Fulk de Jobourg, the last time she had seen him in his mail hauberk and helmet, the long-strided way he walked to his waiting knights, to go fight the Welsh for King William. She used to dream lustful dreams of the master mason. Now the naked man in her fancies was her husband.

Geoffrey was still talking. At the bend just before the river they saw a knight watering his horse. He looked up as they approached. Behind them, the column slowed.

The knight came forward, both hands out before him to show that he was friendly. He wore leather armor and green breeches, his sword sheathed. She recognized him as one of Powys's knights.

Beside her, Geoffrey reined in his mount. Stepping toward her, the knight said in Welsh, "It is you, Lady Alwyn, with whom I would speak."

She felt suddenly dizzy. She did not think she could stand at that moment to hear what he had to say.

Chapter Twenty-one

 POWYS'S MESSENGER SPOKE THE HIGH Welsh of the princely courts. Geoffrey pressed his mount close to hers. "What is he saying?" he demanded.

She was uncertain herself. But what she could make of it made her start in surprise. She clutched the reins so tightly her mare tossed its head, protesting.

The message from Powys was long but the young Welsh knight had been bard-trained; his memory never faltered. When he was through he bowed. He did not look as though he expected her to answer then. "Lady of Llanystwyth," he told her, "I will be back in two days at this same place."

While they watched, he mounted his horse and turned it back toward the village road. The column of Normans pulled their mounts to one side to make way for him.

Guy de Bais trotted up quickly. Alwyn threw up her hand. "Your lord is not dead." She was still numb; it took an effort to bring out the words. "He is Powys's captive. He holds Fulk de Jobourg for ransom."

The two knights looked at each other. "Ransom," Geoffrey said. Surprise and something else showed on his face.

Guy shook his head. "Milady, that is not good news."

She gestured, impatiently, for him to be quiet. Her eyes filled with angry tears. God's wounds, at the moment she felt like screaming. They did not know the Welsh, these Normans; the Welsh were masters of deceit and their own sort of betrayal. Powys could not be loyal to his own prince; she did not know why they thought he would be true to his bargain with Chester.

Behind them, the knights' voices rose, angry and excited. Her stomach was tied in knots. "We have nothing for ransom. Powys wants the world." She lifted her eyes to Geoffrey. "You know I cannot fight Powys. I have fled from him once."

Guy de Bais stared at her. Geoffrey's face smoothed at once. "My lady, I swear you will not have to do this alone." He looked around and spurred his horse closer. "This is beyond our powers, here, to bargain for your lord's life. Only give me your permission to ask aid from your high-placed friends. With God's grace they are willing to help."

Guy looked from one to the other. Alwyn reached out and touched his arm. "Would to God that they can be of some service, but they have no reason to love us." She bit her lip, undecided. "Holy Mary, I don't know."

Under her fingers she felt Guy tense. She squeezed his arm. She wanted Geoffrey to persuade her.

"There is nothing else for it," he said. "It is a matter for powerful and wise heads."

She held back. Guy glared at her. "Yes, you are right, I cannot do this alone." Finally she nodded. "To ask aid may be best."

"You have charged me, then," he said quickly. "I go to do your bidding." He yanked his horse's head to turn it. The big destrier reared and pawed the air. "Wish me Godspeed."

He spurred his horse down the column of knights. Halfway there, it broke into a leaping gallop. She watched him until he passed onto the road to the village. Then she sat back in the saddle, thinking.

Guy leaned to her. "By the Cross, woman, do you know what you have done? They hold Fulk, these damned Welsh!"

"Only Powys." Geoffrey was on his way to Chester to say that she did not want to ransom her husband. She knew they waited to hear that.

She told Guy what the messenger had said, but not all of it. She did not tell him that the Welsh knight said her princely cousin still wished to marry her. On the other hand, if she did not want to be the wife of a Welsh prince, then she could have her Norman *morchawg* back. The price, however, would be high. The Earl of Chester had offered Powys a great sum for Fulk's death. It was only a matter of besting it with a greater one.

Guy let out a string of oaths. "Chester, may God rot him! He is a traitor behind King William's back. When the Conqueror returns to England he will deal with his half-brothers, and all who connive with them." He stopped, then added, anxious, "Will this Welsh outlaw bargain with us?"

"Powys will bargain with everyone. That is the danger." She was thinking she did not know whether she should go to the village herself or send someone else to raise what was needed. God in heaven, she had just promised there would not be another levy!

The knights watched them, ready for orders. She had been clever with Geoffrey, but this was like the game of chess, each move a trap. Feverish, she counted the ones she could depend on. Guy de Bais. The garrison knights. Malluch was gone with most of his men fighting in the mountains. She wondered how much the Morlaix people would give up for their Norman lord. She realized she was now in the Normans' place, squeezing the villeins.

She said to Guy, "We must send two knights to the village. Tell them to fetch the Irish monk, the smith, and the miller. We will need them to help us raise the ransom."

He looked surprised. "You will do it?"

"Holy Mother, what did you think?" Berthe had pushed her palfrey up the line of knights, Gilbert in her arms. He was hungry and screaming. The girl's face was white. "Oh, milady Alwyn, the knights are saying that the Lord Fulk has been captured."

Alwyn took the baby from her. "If you wish to see your husband again, do as I say." She had no time to be gentle. "Go back to your manor and gather up your household and prepare to move it." She jerked her head toward Guy. "He will give you some knights to help."

Guy motioned for a knight to come up. The knight took her bridle and led the palfrey away. Frightened, Berthe began to cry.

The column stood in the road. The knights were shouting to each other what they thought should be done.

"We must find Hugh de Yerville." She could hardly make herself heard over Gilbert's shrieks. Holding the reins in one hand, she fumbled at the front of her gown. Guy looked away. "Powys's knight did not say that Hugh had been taken. And he said nothing of the others."

Her horse began to walk, wanting to go home. Busy with Gilbert, she gave the mare her head. Guy's destrier moved alongside. "Our knights would fall back to the fort," he told her. He paused, thinking. "We will have a messenger soon, if they survived."

She knew they would need as many knights as they could send to guard the ransom wagons. They did not want to let Powys seize the ransom without returning the lord of Morlaix. Alwyn wished they could attack Powys to punish him for this and kill some of his men.

She freed Gilbert's mouth from her breast. As soon as she lifted him he belched the air out of his stomach and then a gout of milk. Heedless of the mess, his tongue and lips clamped against her other breast.

Her nerves were on edge. She pushed his flailing hands away from her sticky front. "You would not spew back at me," she told him, "if you were not so greedy."

They were all greedy.

She was thinking she would play on Powys's greed and give him so much ransom, even if it beggared them, that he could not refuse. She was already counting the gold and silver in her head. She knew what she would strip, including the chalices, the hanging lamp, and the candlesticks in the church. If Chester's spy, the priest, came back from Wrexham, she would have him chained and locked in the keep.

She tried to tally the cattle and horses they could gather. She added Hugh de Yerville's horses at the manor house. He had brought some fine riding stock from France. Also new cloth, food, and other stores such as an outlaw could use. Thank God in heaven it had been a fat year.

She knew she would still have to go back to the villagers and the castle people for what silver and copper they might have. When Geoffrey reached Chester, they would know her situation. And know the trick she had played when they found she would pay the ransom after all.

Guy sent a knight galloping ahead to the castle with the news. When the troop of knights came over the drawbridge, crowds of castle folk were already in the ward, some of them on their knees praying for the lord's safety.

When she dismounted, the spinning sisters and the tally reeve's wife fell on her, weeping, and grabbed at her cloak. She thrust them away. Guy went to see to horseflesh for ransom in the stables. She sent the tally reeve to look for someone to call in the herders from the hills with their sheep. The scullery girls wandered about, crying.

When they sat down to eat evening meal, they found even the cook was demoralized. The cut of venison was raw on the inside, charred on the out and there was no bread. Nerves raw, Alwyn slapped a kitchen knave and sent him back with the meat.

When the meal was over, she gathered up Gilbert and took him to the keep, glad to be away from them. The garrison knights had stayed late in the hall talking of the ransom and what was to be done with the Morlaix force holding the fort. All were eager to go to their relief. The younger knights sang the *Song of Roland,* the parts about the mountain pass at Roncesvalles and Roland's brave battle. A north wind howled in the ward. The priest was not at the castle to say midnight prayers but the tally reeve rang the bell. The knights got up from their benches and straggled to their quarters on the lower floors of the keep.

Rain began much later. The nights were growing cold. When it was damp, the stone walls of the castle gave off a chill that no roaring fire could fight beyond the hearth. Alwyn tried to sleep, but thoughts of Hugh of Avranches in Chester and what Powys might do with his prisoner crowded each other in her head. She turned from one side of the bed to the other, thinking of how to threaten the villagers, the arguments she would use.

The roar of water in the gutters woke her, and she got out of bed. Someone was knocking on the door to the stairwell below. When no one answered, she lit a candle at the banked fire, threw the bed blanket around her shoulders, and went down herself.

The stairs were dark. The rain drummed on the slates of the tower like thunder. None of the knights had got up to answer whoever was in the ward, nor was there a knight on guard at the door. She pulled back the wooden bar and it swung open. Beyond it, waiting in the downpour, was a black-cloaked figure. He reached out for her.

She threw herself against him with a glad cry. "How have you come here? Have you escaped?"

"Be quiet." His voice was hoarse with cold. His arms went around her, hungry. Her gown and the blanket were instantly soaked. He smelled of sweat and wet flesh, pungent, the way she remembered. Bending, he lifted her in his arms to carry her up the stair.

"I think of this, always." His mouth was against her hair. "All of the day. In the night. Only this." He pushed open the door with his foot. Gilbert was sleeping. He carried her past the baby's cradle, not looking, but that was usual. He lowered her to the bed.

"Ah, Christ, how I want you." He stripped away her nightdress, put his hands against her breasts and held them there. Kneeling on the bed between her legs, he lowered his head slowly and kissed her mouth.

He was cold and wet. Firelit, his face was all harsh planes. She found him beautiful. With a sob she threw herself against him. She opened her mouth to take his kiss. She clutched his thick, ruddy hair, not wanting to let him be an inch from her. She twined her legs around him so that he could hardly draw back to pull off his breeches and hose. She ripped at the lacings of his wet shirt, anxious to see him naked. To have him naked against her.

They fell on each other like brigands. His mouth was all over her. She could not leave him alone. She touched him everywhere. She had forgotten how big he was, how heavy his arms and legs, how it felt to have him want her. He was rough, insatiable. Against her mouth he groaned that he loved her. She matched his frenzy. When he came to his peak he did not pull out of her and she was at her own: only dimly she felt him spill into her, thrashing and shouting. She raked his back with her nails, leaving long scratches.

They could not get enough of each other. In a few minutes they were at it again. When they rested, she put her head on his breast, his arm around her, their legs tangled together. He was strong and tender, his skin smelled good. She ran her fingers through his hair while he told her how much he longed for her. What it was like to be away from her, fighting in the Welsh mountains. He was sick of it. He wanted to come back. To lie with her and be warm.

Leaning over him, she kissed his lips and his eyes, then along the line of his chin and throat. Eyes closed, he smiled. "So you like that," she said. She had always wanted to kiss him like that. They drifted off to sleep, wound about each other like nestling children, his chin resting on the top of her head. When Alwyn woke Gilbert was crying and she had both hands between her legs, holding her cleft. She felt aching and spent.

She got up and picked up the baby and went to the door and opened it. There were wet footprints down the stairs. He had not been there. She had made love with Fulk de Jobourg's ghost. Then she knew she had made the footprints herself, walking in her sleep to open the wooden bar of the door below. The treads of the stairs were wet with blowing rain.

She had dreamed it. A rush of despair so hard it was like an ax hitting deep in her chest swept over her. Her legs gave way. She sat down on the top step of the tower stairs, not bothering to put Gilbert to the breast. She laid him in her lap and listened to him scream as she wanted to scream, legs pumping, his face red and furious.

Suddenly she was crying. There was no one to listen in the middle of the night, it did not matter. She wept with her mouth open, loudly, tears streaming. They fell on the baby and slid off his screaming face.

She got up at last and went back to the bed and lay down in it and put Gilbert to her breast. In the sudden silence her sobbing was loud.

She did not care.

Guy had readied the garrison knights to go out and harry the village for the ransom, but they were not needed. Long before dawn, the shepherds began bringing in their flocks from the hills. By first light, the pens outside the castle gates were overflowing and the armorer had gathered men to start building more on either side of the castle road.

The shepherds brought sheep from Morlaix herds, but also strange, stubby animals with burr-filled coats of a type that few had seen before. Holdbacks, the tally reeve said knowingly, hardy sheep the shepherds bred for themselves. He was surprised they had brought them. He walked up and down the pens, interested, examining them.

Alwyn came down to the ward in a new fur-lined cloak, carrying Gilbert in his bunting. The weaving woman and the spinning sisters carried the baskets she had filled with her mother's things. She had ransacked the chest in her room for every silver circlet, jeweled brooch, and hair fastening she could find. Since Fulk de Johourg had given her nothing, there was nothing of his to contribute. The night before, she and the cook had dragged the castle strongbox from the storeroom. It was never opened. It had been there since before her father began his conspiracies. The leather bags that held the coins were so rotted that when they lifted them they burst. She had taken half the money to bring to the ward and put on the table so that the people could see the castle gave its share. The rest had been put back and the strongbox hidden again.

A table had been put out in front of the hall. The tally reeve sat on a bench with the Irish monk who was to keep the records. The butler and Guy de Bais stood behind them as witness.

The herders stepped forward one by one to touch their foreheads in deference to the castle's lady and declare their part of the ransom. They looked like their own sheep with sheepskin caps, sheepskins for coats, their legs wrapped in shearling. When they greeted her, the tribesmen spoke a Welsh she could not understand.

She said to the tally reeve, "Do they know they are ransoming the Norman lord?"

He looked at her. "The shepherds are saying they give for you, milady, since you want back your *morchawg* husband. Many mention your mother."

The smith shoved a wheelbarrow roughly through the crowd. Cautious, Guy de Bais motioned a few knights forward. Without speaking, the smith upended the barrow in front of the table.

Alwyn shifted Gilbert to her shoulder and stood up to see. There was a pile of forge tools, broken iron for melting, kitchen pots and cranes for the hearth, candlesticks, a brass crucifix, horse bits and shoes. Powys could use the iron and the tools. The smith tossed a small knotted bundle of cloth on the table. The tally reeve reached for it and shook it open. Copper coins spilled out.

"Ah," the tally reeve said. He swept the coins toward him with the edge of his hand and began to count.

The smith hitched up his breeches. "For some," he said, glaring at Guy de Bais, "I will give."

Alwyn said, "Mother of God, is that not the crucifix from the old chapel?"

No one answered her. The ward was filling up with villagers as well as shepherds. The miller was behind the smith. They had been told to come forward first as an example to the others.

"Insolent serf," Guy said. "Hanging is the punishment for withholding levy."

She had always thought the miller an honest man. But as he brought out sack after sack of coins from his padded coat and set them before the tally reeve, she could only guess that the miller had been selling some of his ale in Chirk, if not places farther east. It was a hanging offense too to withhold that profit from the lord.

He looked bland. "Blessed lady, I have borrowed as much as I can," he told her.

Beside Alwyn, the Irish monk choked back a laugh. "What do you wish me to do?" Guy de Bais asked her.

Do? There was nothing they could do. They had de-

manded ransom and the miller had brought nearly all that
he had. If he had more, he was richer than the lord of
Morlaix.

The castle people pressed around them to give their
share. From the crowd hands, the table filled with gold
buttons, silver spoons, hair combs of horn and ivory, a
goblet of Levantine glass, a fancy horse harness, and a
gold-rimmed chamberpot. The Irish monk, fuming, lost
track. Guy de Bais came to push them back in line.

Someone put in front of Alwyn silver pins inset with
onyx and porphyry that had been among her mother's
bride gifts. She snatched them up quickly and put them in
her sleeve. There were things that had been missing for
years from the castle.

"That's my old doll," she exclaimed. She shifted Gilbert
to one arm, but the doll disappeared before she could get
her fingers around it. She managed to grab a carved ivory
pick for the teeth that she remembered the old Welsh
priest used.

The table now held a pile of treasure so big they could
hardly see over it. There were ancient drinking horns,
polished silver mirrors, sacred relics of saints of bone and
wood in small boxes, amber beads on strings and crosses
on gem-studded chains. There were gold rings, and
torques of the old Cymry make. And coins. Alwyn picked
one up. There was a likeness on it of a bald man wearing a
crown of leaves. It looked as though it had lain in the
ground for years.

She had heard stories of peasants' hoards all her life. It
was the castle lords' excuse for wringing them mercilessly, that every villein had some secret treasure hidden
away. God in heaven, she couldn't help thinking, she had
been living in a pack of thieves, as well.

"The knights, milady," Guy de Bais reminded her.

Looking solemn, the garrison knights came forward,
one by one. She hadn't expected them to give but she
supposed it was a pledge of loyalty to their lord. Now she

saw that it was more than that. Some even gave weapons.
The rest was surprisingly like the ransom of the Morlaix
people: trinkets of all kinds for women from plunder, a
dagger with a gold hilt, a belt of French coins, copper
money. She saw, surprised, they were not as rich as the
villagers. But every little bit mattered. Unfortunately,
there was not much left of Hereford's plunder.

The knights were still giving their part of the ransom
when the butler ordered the kitchen knaves to roll the
wagons from the stables. Wool shearling sacks were
brought from the storeroom. The butler stood by as the
boys stuffed them. At the table, the Irish monk totaled his
account.

"Will there be enough?" She looked into his pale eyes,
hoping for a good answer.

He shrugged. "How much is a husband worth?"

"God and the saints." Annoyed, she stood up and put
Gilbert over her shoulder. He was asleep, a much better
baby now that he was no longer constantly hungry.

"It is enough," the monk shouted after her.

At the wagons she asked the tally reeve. "Enough, my
lady? There is overmuch for this sort of thing. Considering it is the outlaw Powys I would save some back. A third
of it, there is that much."

"No. Send it all." She was deeply pleased that the people of Morlaix had stripped themselves for her. She hoped
they would do the same for Gilbert someday if he needed
it. "We will not stint him, the lord of Morlaix. I would have
him know he has a fine ransom, even though the people
have not the same love for him."

"Love? Oh, mayhap that is not so." The tally reeve
looked into a sack of coins and women's jewelry. He nodded for the kitchen boys to tie it up. "There are many
here today who think he is not so ill a lord, milady. And he
is a brave man, if grasping. When they brought in their
share, that is what the people said. As Normans go, God

has let us see it is better to have Lady Alwyn's *morchawg* than take one's chance with some other."

The knight Goutard came up. Goutard and half the garrison knights would go to deliver the wagons to Powys. They knew it would stretch them thin to split their knights' numbers in half, but there was no help for it.

The wagons were still in the ward when the guard on the portal gate called down that there was a Morlaix knight and another rider galloping hard on the road. The cook's wife came to Alwyn quickly and she gave Gilbert to her. Guy and the knights ran among the two wagons, shouting to the drovers to turn their horses around.

The riders' horses came into the ward lathered and blown. One mount stumbled, spent. The stable knaves ran to grasp their bridles. The Morlaix knight, covered with dust, slid from his horse and went down on one knee in front of Alwyn. The other man did not dismount. She recognized the fine black clothes of the wool merchant's livery.

"Milady," the Morlaix knight said. He was still breathing hard. "I have come from Chirk with Simon Belefroun's man, here, who was on the road north to Wrexham. He swears the Earl of Chester sends a great force of men under Osbern Tirell against you."

Stiffly, the servant in black got down from his horse. Guy de Bais swung on him. "How many men?"

"It is a siege force." The man cleared his throat. "My master was there, we traveled north." His eyes slid to Alwyn. "We saw your priest and Morlaix's brother and his company of knights meet them."

She put her hand to her throat. She heard Guy's expression of disgust. It was no more than they expected, and yet it pained to hear of Geoffrey's treachery. Well, at least they knew where Father Ascelin was.

Guy said, "If Chester's force is in Chirk, we have little time." He hurried off again.

"Go to the hall," Alwyn told the knight and Belefroun's

servant. "The women there will give you food and drink."
As they turned away, she looked around the ward for the
miller. She knew he had not left.

The miller was a rich man. She had learned that when
he paid his share of the lord's ransom. He had his ale yard
and his mill. He had the most to lose in the village.

She wished to ask him, first, if he would be the one to
come forward to set fire to it.

Chapter Twenty-two

OSBERN TIRELL RODE UP WITH MORE than three hundred knights and surrounded Castle Morlaix. To open the siege, the Earl of Chester's herald came forth before Morlaix's portal gate, his banner whipping in the winter wind. He blew his horn. The knights, men-at-arms, and Morlaix villagers who had not fled to the hills, climbed to the castle wall walks to look down.

The herald rode back and forth before them shouting that all inside the castle should know that the Lady Alwyn's father had been a Breton traitor, hanged for his treachery against King William. It followed, then, that her supporters had best not expect trustworthiness from his daughter; she would betray them all, as treachery was in her blood. The herald was answered with hoots and jeers. Someone on the west wall threw down a chamber pot. His horse shied as the thing bounced in the grass and rolled under its hooves.

Guy de Bais turned and shouted down for a knight to go find the villein who had hurled the pot. "God's wounds," he told Alwyn, "if we begin by insulting their herald, it will go ill for us."

She leaned her elbows on the parapet and thought she did not see how it could go any more ill for them. She had a husband captive somewhere in the Welsh hills, his cousin Geoffrey was eager to betray them, and now the Earl of Chester had come to bring the wife of his vassal under his power. She said, "Well, the people here do not like insults."

"Nevertheless, that is the usual way in a siege. Chester hopes to make your people doubt you. After a time, when the siege grinds us, they will say more in the hope they will overthrow you and open the gates." He watched two knights searching the walls for the villein who had thrown the chamber pot. "In all truth, we should keep this rabble off the walls. It is not soldierly."

She was thinking of the master mason. All day they had watched Chester's siege machines being hauled into place. Beyond, in the river meadow where their tents were put up, the soldiers were building a wooden tower on wheels. The master mason had told her of what an attacking force could bring to bear against a besieged castle. And that in spite of it, the castle did not usually fall unless its defenders were starving.

She supposed they should thank God and the saints that the storerooms were packed with a good harvest. They had water, too; even with so many people, the wells under the keep gave them water to drink, and enough to flush the ditch into which the jakes emptied. The weather was cold, anyway; they would not be plagued with the stink that brought sickness and fevers.

Beyond Chester's siege camp, the ribbon of the castle road wound over the hill to what had once been the village. She thought she could still smell the odor of burning. It had been hard to fire the houses and byres and a good part of the crops, but with the village leveled and no forage, they had made Osbern Tirell haul his supplies the long miles from Chirk.

The crowd on the walls had tired of their catcalls. The

herald resumed his riding and shouting. Their liege lord, the Earl of Chester, demanded the Lady Alwyn give up the defense of Morlaix. There was no need under God's heaven for her defiance; her liege lord was willing to parley. Much could be hers by Chester's grant if she agreed to the terms of surrender.

The Irish monk had climbed the curtain wall stairs to join them. Alwyn looked at him over her shoulder. "The earl offers to let me rule here, with my son Gilbert as heir," she said.

Guy answered quickly, "Chester wishes you to acknowledge your lord husband is dead."

She turned back. Perhaps he was. Perhaps Osbern Tirell knew it for truth and they did not. She rubbed her cold hands together, shivering. "If I am so treacherous as their herald says, you would not think they would bargain with me."

The wind suddenly dragged at the herald's long banner. He looped his reins with both hands and braced the staff on his leg. The sky above the valley was gray, but it was too soon in the year for a snowfall. She remembered someone had told her to pray that it did not snow. Goutard the knight. For Fulk de Jobourg fighting in the mountains.

She leaned over the parapet with the Irish monk to watch the herald. From what he was saying, one would believe Fulk de Jobourg had no friends. At least they did not count her as one.

The herald waited for an answer. There were only jeers. Turning his horse's head, the herald rode back to camp. Grim-faced, Guy said, "Well, now it begins."

Sudden cheering broke out on the walls. They could see Chester's forces mounting a sortie. Knights in bright polished helmets and red tunics over their mail charged across the fields carrying pennants. A squire followed blowing his horn. The knights raced up and down, turning their horses, shouting their challenges. Behind them, men ran toward the castle wall, bent together under overlapping shields held on their backs. The villeins building the siege tower threw down their tools to watch.

Guy left at a run. Two knights rushed to him along the wall walk, gesturing. Alwyn leaned farther out over the parapet. To her left, one of the men-at-arms shouted to her, "If your lord husband was here, Lady Alwyn, he'd send them Chester lice packing!"

The men assaulting the portal gate flung a ladder against the wall. From above, Malluch's Welsh bowmen took aim and sent down their arrows. Three of Chester's men fell to the ground, screaming. One had taken an arrow through the eye. Covering them with their shields, the attackers picked up their wounded and retreated. Where the three men had fallen there were large splotches of blood on the grass.

Alwyn turned away. One of the men would die, she was sure of it. She could not see the sense, to charge at a stone wall well defended by bowmen, and kill men needlessly.

The monk was watching her. She turned her head. Three more groups under shields were forming below. She said, "Mother of God, why do they keep doing it?"

He gave her a hard look. "Woman, you must expect this. In time, Chester's assaults will grow heavier, more men, more ladders, more breaching machines. Soon they will batter us from the catapults."

She turned her back to him. He was a difficult man and she did not wish to argue. She would not tell him of Emma de Wader and the siege of Norfolk. "I will hold Castle Morlaix, brother monk. I am told a castle will not fall unless those inside are starving."

"Very wise," he said, ironic. "I see someone has advised you. However, a siege can last many months. You will know how to starve by then." She turned to face him again, angry. He met her look with cold pale eyes. "The people trust that you hold this castle for your lord husband, Lady Alwyn. It is Fulk de Jobourg they wait for."

She set her mouth. "Morlaix is mine. The people here are Welsh, not Normans."

"And you are but a woman," he shot back. "Come to me thirty days after you have withstood Chester, and we will talk of it then."

She told herself she could not talk to the mad Irish monk when he was like this. She turned on her heel and left him.

The ward was a mass of people sitting on the ground. Meals were no longer taken in the hall because of the women and children sheltered there; food was handed out through the kitchen during the day and sometimes the night. In the stable yard, some of the villeins had built lean-tos and put their families under them. She knew Guy was right, they had given room to too many, but the people had resisted going into the hills in the winter without food or shelter, and she'd not had the heart to turn them away.

Across the yard, the butler saw her and started toward her, the cook behind him. She did not want to talk to them. She kept the storeroom keys; they would eat sparely until she told them otherwise. She hurried across the ward to the church.

Some knights who did not have duty were sleeping on the porch. She stepped over them. The inside of the church was full. Babies cried. There was a strong stink of food and urine. The miller and his family had made a place for themselves near the nave. Their sick son was well enough to be tending to some of the children. She did not stop to speak to them.

She made her way behind the altar. It was dark there under the arches and quieter. She leaned her head against a stone pier. She saw it was the same one that opened to the passageway to the sluices. Weary, she told herself she needed to pray. She was sure God was not pleased with her. She did not pray to Him much these days and she had not been good to His priest, Father Ascelin, with her sinful thoughts as to what she would do to him for his treachery. Worse, she did not much like His Irish monk, either.

She let her fingers trace the cool stone, thinking of the master mason. Wherever he was, she wished him well. She remembered the night of his escape and what he had said to her, and the feel of his mouth when he kissed her farewell.

Standing there in the darkness in the back of the church, it occurred to her that if she were brave enough to go down through the water passages, she could escape. What the Earl of Chester did not consider was that she did not have to surrender to him. She had thought on it. She could, for instance, appeal to King William himself to be Gilbert's regent at Morlaix. With luck the king would agree. The she would need no husband at all.

A shadow appeared against the light from the outer church. "Milady," the miller's wife said, "the butler and the cook do not wish to disturb you, but they wish to speak to you about the bread."

Alwyn nodded to her.

She knew she was mad to think of escape. She could not leave. She had a babe. The people of Morlaix looked to her. She had a husband. If he was not dead. And if she still wanted him.

She lifted her hand from the stone. "I am coming," she said.

Fulk looked across the mountain clearing of rowans and bare-limbed oaks. On the opposite side, but not out of range of bowshot, Hugh de Yerville stood with six Morlaix knights and a handful of Malluch's men, the number the

ransom party agreed on. But the Welsh had not yet un-
shackled his hands.

The sacks of ransom had been unloaded from the wagons and dragged across the clearing to the Welshmen's
side. Now Powys himself knelt to cut open the last of
them.

"By Saint David, she has emptied Morlaix!" Powys got
to his feet, his hands full of silver coin and women's orna-
ments. "Your lady wife wants you back, *morchawg,*" he
said, grinning.

Fulk grunted. He had the length of the clearing to walk
if they set him free. Malluch's men stood at the ready with
their bows held pointed down in front of them, arrows
fixed to the strings. The Welsh bowmen behind him did
the same.

Tentative, Fulk straightened his back and moved his
cramped hands. He had been fettered since they took him.
He did not know if he had much use of his arms. He felt
someone take his wrists from behind. A knife cut his
bonds. His hands fell down by his side, paining with the
sudden rush of blood into them. He felt his bladder fill
with a rush of excitement. They were going to free him.
Or they were going to make him think he was free. He
worried about the walk across the clearing to join Hugh
on the other side.

Powys stepped in front of him and thrust something
into his hand. His fingers were too numb to feel it. He saw
it was a silver circlet with red stones set in it. It had
belonged to his wife.

"It was the Lady Alwyn's mother's, also." Powys
watched him. "Your lady wife wore it many times, when
she fled to me."

Fulk kept his eyes down. The Welshman could not
leave it alone. All the time he had been held captive
Powys had reminded him of how his wife had come to
him, asking shelter. Fulk knew he wanted him to think he

had slept with her. He said, "My wife returned to me of her free will."

"Hah, *morchawg*, you may brag on that, but I have loved her since we were children, you have only to ask her. For the love I bear her, I give you to her." Powys smiled his crooked, engaging smile. "Besides, she has given more for your ransom than your liege lord, Chester, will pay me to kill you."

Fulk shifted the silver thing to his other hand. If they were going to murder him, they would do it as he walked the clearing.

"Until we meet, Welshman," he said.

The other man gestured. He stood aside. "Tell her that Powys, Prince of the Welsh, loves her greatly."

Fulk did not answer. He started, his knees stiff and unwilling. The sun came down through the bare trees and made patterns on the winter grass. Frozen snow edged the trees. I will get an arrow in my back, he thought. His breath was tight in his chest. Now that they have the ransom they will try to kill me. He kept walking. He was dirty, and had gone unshaven for days. His underclothes felt as though they had rotted. The muscles in his legs ached.

The last few feet de Yerville, reckless, stepped out to meet him. Malluch's men half lifted their bows, their eyes on the Welsh.

"Ah, milord, God save you!" Hugh put his hand on Fulk's arm. "You are well, they have not injured you?"

"Take care." Fulk looked over his shoulder. The Welsh were loading the sacks of ransom onto their horses. Their bowmen stood watching them.

He rubbed his bristled jaw. So she had ransomed him. Stripped Morlaix, the Welshman had said. "How many knights have we left against the damned Welsh? Has Guy sent us no relief?"

Hugh looked at him, surprised. "Fulk, Morlaix is besieged. Chester has sent Osbern Tirell against it. Your lady wife holds firm, but the castle is sore beleaguered."

"Your milk is less because you do not get rest," the weaving woman said. She broke off a piece of bread and put it in Gilbert's mouth. He held it between his lips, frowning. Then he began to suck on it.

Alwyn shifted him to the other arm. She refastened the front of her dress. She was sitting on a water cask on the wall walk by the portal gate. What the weaving woman said about not getting enough rest was true; she had been on her feet since dawn, and now the sun was setting. She took another piece of bread and put it in Gilbert's mouth.

A burst of cold wind blew along the wall. The other woman shifted her seat to move out of it. "It was not so bad, today," she said. "They say their machine was broken, that is why we were spared the terrible stones."

Alwyn thought of the bodies in the ditch. Seven days after the siege began, Guy had come to her to allow him to petition Osbern Tirell to let some of the village people out of the castle. Reluctant, she had known he was right.

They had sent a knight out under a white flag of parley but Tirell had sent back a message that they could let the Morlaix folk out of the castle to be rid of them if they wished, but he would let them go no farther. They could stay trapped between Chester's force and the castle walls, suffering for want of everything, until the siege was ended. That was all he would allow.

"And they call themselves Christians," she had railed at the Irish monk. He had stamped away.

The next morning, the big catapult had been brought up from the valley to hurl heated boulders into the castle yard. When it began, there was no place for the villagers to go. They trampled each other to get into the shelter of the church, the crowded hall, even the kitchen house. The bombardment of the red-hot stones had been terrible.

People were killed in the panic. The Irish monk's girl died this way, crushed against the outer walls of the church. Afterward, the Irishman picked her up and carried her body in his arms to the stables, which were being used as the charnel house.

The siege tower was rolled up. Constant storming of the walls killed Morlaix men every day. The weather was cold and the dead did not stink but they had little space inside the castle walls and needed to bury them. Guy de Bais himself went out under a white flag to parley with Tirell. He came back livid with anger. There would be no party from Morlaix with dead to bury. That too had been refused.

The Irish monk oversaw the sewing of the bodies in wool-shearling sacks. He said prayers over them and then, one by one, they were dropped over the wall into the ditch.

At night, Alwyn thought about the Morlaix dead. She saw the two children killed by the catapult's stones, the seven knights and men-at-arms dead from Chester's storming the castle walls.

One night, when the watchman in the keep heard the sappers tunneling, she told Guy and the Irish monk about the master mason's water defense. The two men went down to the big cistern under the keep with her. They turned the big iron wheels, letting the water roar out into the sluices. Chester's miners had been closer than they knew. The screams of the trapped men were right under their feet. They let the water flow until the cistern was empty. In the morning, they saw Chester's men carrying bodies out of the tunnels. One of the knights on the wall, taunting, shouted down that Chester's men did not need to work to bury their dead, they could throw them into the Morlaix ditch with their own.

Now, every evening, the herald came to ride under the walls and exhort the Welsh and English men-at-arms and the Morlaix garrison of knights to overthrow Lady Alwyn and bargain for terms of surrender. The Earl of Chester, Hugh of Avranches, would pardon all inside Castle Morlaix and allow them to depart with safekeeping. The Norman knights would retain all their arms and their horses. The Welsh and English men-at-arms would be allowed an escort out of the marches. The villagers who had taken refuge inside Castle Morlaix could return to their lands in the valley without fear of punishment. All they had to do was turn over Fulk de Jobourg's wife to his rightful liege lord, the Earl of Chester.

"Watch him, milady," the weaving woman warned.

Alwyn sat Gilbert upright and hooked a gob of bread out of his mouth. He coughed, then wailed for more. She put him on her shoulder. He was growing heavy. He had learned to roll over in the bed and strain to sit up, and his temper was sweeter: he would smile and make cooing noises as long as anyone bent over him.

"What is that?" She lifted her head, listening.

On the west wall, some men-at-arms were singing.

"What do you hear, milady?" the weaving woman said.

She peered through the arrow slit. There was no standing up on the wall walks; Chester's men were too eager to shoot at them. Usually at dusk there was no movement in the siege camp other than the building of cook fires and tending to horses. Night work was left to the sappers. There would not be much of that for a while, she thought, and was surprised at her own bloodthirstiness. She was not sorry about their dead men at all.

Toward the river, the winter trees were like ironwork against the gray sky. There could be horses moving down there. She strained her eyes. Or a glint of light on helmets. It is nothing, she told herself. If Osbern Tirell was bringing up reinforcements, they would not be coming that way. Her heart began to beat, heavy and hurting.

"My lady," the weaving woman said, "what is it?"

"I think someone is coming," she said.

* * *

Hugh de Yerville's scouts ran into a knight in Morlaix colors. Thinking they had found a spy, they grabbed his reins and would have knocked him to the ground, but Geoffrey de Bocage came galloping up. "Hold, that is my man," he shouted. "Tell me, where is Fulk?"

A knight pointed. Geoffrey turned and spurred his horse across the blackened wheat field and hauled up at Fulk's side. Without greeting he burst out, "God's bones, Fulk, I went to meet Tirell as you said and he put me in a house in Wrexham under guard! My own men rescued me." He shifted in the saddle to look back. "Sweet Jesu, but your men are worn. You need more strength. Osbern Tirell has a force of more than three hundred."

Fulk did not need Geoffrey to tell him that with his sixty knights and his cousin's forty, they were thrice outmanned. "Attack now," he shouted back. "The hour and the light is with us."

They could see Tirell's siege forces camped in the meadow. "Hugh and I will make for the castle gate to thrust a wedge between. You will fall on Chester's rear, scatter their horses and wagons and drive them back to the village road."

Fulk wanted no more than that. He did not need to war with Hugh of Avranches. It was enough that he showed that he was not dead, but alive, and would defend his domain. He knew that when he heard of it, Chester, that perfidious liege lord, would appreciate the subtlety.

The sinking sun burst through the snow clouds as Fulk's knights charged full course across the valley's charred fields. They turned their horses along the castle walls to front Chester's men before the portal gate. In their camp, Chester's knights abandoned their cooking fires, crying alarm. Geoffrey and his knights swept through the river woods and came up on their rear. They rode, yelling, through their wagons, scattering the drovers and cooks. The evening quiet burst with charging knights crying for God and Morlaix. The alarm bell in the castle began to ring.

Barcheaded, Osbern Tirell rode among his knights to rally them, but the Morlaix knights were shouting their lord had returned. Chester's men faltered. In a pocket, Chester's men-at-arms fought to salvage some horses and a wagon. The knights retreated slowly down the castle road. Fulk galloped among his men to pursue them. At the river, Tirell's forces regrouped and formed a rearguard. After some confusion they began to fall down the road toward Chirk.

"Christ's bones, Fulk," Guy de Yerville shouted, "when they saw it was you and not your ghost, Chester's men had no stomach to fight!"

Fulk reined in. There were two dead on the ground, both of them Chester's. Five wounded Morlaix knights, two on foot, their horses killed. His destrier set his legs and drooped his big head, spent.

From the rise, Fulk looked down on Morlaix. This was the same place he had stopped those long months ago when he came with King William's order, half-frozen and joyless at the prospect of marrying. But wanting what he saw, nevertheless.

Now, in the setting sun, Morlaix was his own, and Chester be damned. That tune would change quick enough when King William returned. This was his fief, his domain. Here as lord he rested secure. Well-fed. Content.

Then there was his wife.

A few snowflakes drifted down. They fell on his face and lightly dusted his shoulders. In spite of the cold he felt a lightening of spirits. He was in a forgiving mood. He'd been fourteen days as prisoner in a filthy Welsh outlaw's camp and was so dirty he itched, but he was not so mean-spirited as to deny his wife her triumph. She had held

Morlaix for him. That was well done. He supposed she was famous; the people thought well enough of her, as it was.

He was ready for peace between them. There were things he would concede. He would let her hold her accursed manor court, but he would keep a stern hand on it. For the sake of discretion, he would take her brat and raise it as his own; it was no more than what he was doing, anyway. He told himself Powys had not slept with her; in spite of the man's taunting he was sure of it. And there was always the chance it was his.

He looked around for his squire. "Sound the horn," he told Aubrey. "Let them know to make us welcome."

Behind them, Geoffrey rode down the line of knights shouting to come two abreast, smart. Someone broke into a song. The air was cold. The knights' voices were hoarse with tiredness.

He was thinking it had been weeks since he had bedded her. A thing he remembered many times in the mountains. That was the fault of it. Once you thought of a woman in that way you could not get it out of your head.

Hugh came up to ride beside him carrying the gonfalon. The snowy wind lifted it, flapping. Fulk looked up. The cloth flattened in the air to show the griffon, fierce as a demon, surrounded by red and green scribbles. On the walls, the castle people cheered.

They rode steadily forward. The light was fading. "Blow the halloo again," he told Aubrey. "Hurry them to let down the drawbridge."

Hugh frowned. "Perhaps they are having trouble. It has been closed some long days."

Fulk raised his hand for a halt. Where they were, he could look up for the sentry at his position over the drawbridge. No one was there. "The devil take it," he swore. If the winch was broken they would spend the night outside in the cold.

The setting sun cast a gold hue on the castle walls. By

the portal gate they could see black stains from fire and the scars of combat. To the left, some siege machine had breached the top and stones were still missing.

The knights' singing stopped. Fulk threw back his hood, impatient. His destrier, hungry, pulled at the bit and pawed the ground.

The signs of the siege raised his fury. Damned be to Chester, to batter a lone woman and a skeleton garrison while some bandit held him captive. He knew from Geoffrey what they had offered her, how Hugh of Avranches had sought to suck all of them into Odo's schemes. He would give her her due, she had tricked them all. She had paid Powys his ransom, she had squeezed her own people when she had vowed not to have them levied again. And she had done this to win back her rightful husband.

He was suddenly not so sure.

The weasel Welshman had been happy all those long nights tormenting him with how many men valued and loved her. Even, he'd confessed, himself. She could have any man she wanted. Or even none at all.

"Fulk," Hugh said.

Behind them, a murmur grew among the knights. The sun was down, it had grown colder. The snowflakes thickened.

Fulk allowed himself to think the unthinkable. Was she challenging him, now, to oust her? God's wounds, with his own villeins and knights watching, would he needs lay siege to his own castle?

"Blow the horn again," he told his squire.

Chapter Twenty-three

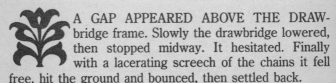A GAP APPEARED ABOVE THE DRAW-bridge frame. Slowly the drawbridge lowered, then stopped midway. It hesitated. Finally with a lacerating screech of the chains it fell free, hit the ground and bounced, then settled back.

"Ah, they have fixed it," Hugh de Yerville cried.

Or she has made up her mind, Fulk thought. She'd made her point; the whole world had seen him waiting in front of his own castle for his wife to let him in.

The moment the drawbridge settled to earth, a disheveled, odorous crowd poured toward them, waving their arms and shrieking. The mob flowed through the column of knights and danced deliriously out into the fields by the side of the castle road. The villeins and their families held their faces and arms up to the falling snow, laughing and crying. The din was deafening.

Scowling, Fulk spurred his horse forward. The crowd scattered in front of him. He trotted his destrier into the ward. The place was a shambles, the grass torn up. There was a detectable stink of a battlefield. He knew they had taken a bombardment from the siege machines he'd seen in the meadow. On the walls, men-at-arms and the garrison knights cheered.

"Berthe," Hugh cried. He kicked his horse forward.

Fulk stood in his stirrups looking for his wife. Eager hands grabbed at his bridle. He was surrounded by people praising him and thanking God for Morlaix's deliverance. Over their heads, he saw her standing on the steps of the church with Hugh de Yerville's bride. Beside them he recognized the mad Irish monk.

Guy de Bais fought his way toward them. He grabbed at Fulk's reins. "God keep you, milord," he shouted, "it was wondrous to see you fall upon Chester like that. Tirell ran like a cur with his tail between his legs!"

Fulk only nodded and pressed his mount toward the church. She was wearing an ordinary gown, somewhat dirty. Her hair was tied up in a cloth. In the mountains, he had imagined her in a red dress.

She saw him now. She stepped forward, then froze.

Geoffrey had ridden up behind him. Fulk knew what was the matter as soon as she saw him. He was close enough to shout, "Forbear, there is time enough to explain later."

But she would not listen. He saw the outrage on her face. He sat back in the saddle and watched her run through the crowd.

Fulk went with Guy de Bais, Hugh, and Geoffrey to clear some of the villeins and their families from the castle and drive them to makeshift shelters in the fields. There were still too many people inside Morlaix. Fulk's knights moved horses from the castle to picket at the river and went back to sleep in their stalls.

The snow continued to fall. At dark, the villagers surged back into the castle for food. They sat in the ward huddled under sheepskins, shouting and singing. Bone-tired, Hugh de Yerville and Fulk stripped naked in the kitchen yard and bathed under freezing buckets of water thrown by the squires. Then Aubrey fetched clean clothes for Fulk from the keep. He reported there were knights sleeping on the stairs and three to a bed in the barracks.

In the hall, room had been made to put tables by the fire. The place was filled with knights, so crowded some of them were sitting on the rushes. He looked and found his wife dressed in a blue gown, her hair tucked up and covered by a floating blue veil. He looked for the child. It was nowhere to be seen. Usually she carried the thing with her everywhere.

"You are looking well," he told her as he sat down. She did not answer. He studied her profile. So it was going to be like that, he thought. Geoffrey came up and sat on the other side.

"Well, you are a heroine," he said, reaching for a piece of bread. "There is no denying what you have done here."

He considered telling her that to withstand Tirell's siege was a brave piece of work, something few women could have done. He didn't want to speak to her in the hall with all the noise and bustle. He was looking forward to seeing her alone. Besides, there had been praise and enough for her; he had listened to nothing else from Guy and the others.

"Sweetheart, don't look so glum," Geoffrey shouted across the table. "You were tested and found faithful."

Put like that, Fulk thought, it didn't ring too sweetly. He poured himself a cup of cider. The year's crop had finally begun to harden. It was potent.

Guy came to stand in front of them. Fulk gestured him to sit but the garrison captain shook his head. "Nay, milord, it was no test." Guy's voice carried, righteous. "You have a true wife, nor is she de Bocage's dupe. I would follow her to hell and back after this siege, and the people here with me."

Some knights around them cheered. Hugh's young wife leaned forward. "Oh milord, there is no one—"

Hugh's hand clamped down on her arm. He said, loudly, "Tirell had the better part of wisdom, Fulk, to withdraw in haste. Now, do we wait to see what Chester will do?"

"He will do nothing." The cook and the kitchen knaves came in carrying platters of roast pork and cabbage and pickled onions. It smelled good. He was ravenous. Taking the spoon, he piled his plate high. "Tomorrow I will send a messenger to Chester to say I have disciplined my rebellious wife. And assure him of my craven vassal loyalty."

Geoffrey laughed. The rest fell silent, staring down at their trenchers. The cook and the kitchen boys backed away.

He scowled. Whether they liked it or not, it was what he would do. Guy and Hugh, at least, would see the sense of it. They would save Chester's face and in return, not being dull-witted, Hugh of Avranches would not soon try again to usurp Fulk de Jobourg's rightful hold at Morlaix.

Out of the corner of his eye he saw his wife stand up. All heads lifted to look at her. She turned to him. "You are detestable." She looked to Geoffrey. "Both of you."

Hugh's young wife jumped up. Hugh jerked her back into her seat. Down the end of the table the Irish monk shouted, "Morlaix! You do not treat your lady wife well!"

Fulk lifted his head. The Irishman glared back. Guy still stood in front of him. "It was she who thought of the water defense, Fulk," he said, stubborn. "And none too soon. The sappers had breached the walls and were under the keep when we stopped them."

"Bah, you are all alike," the monk shouted, leaving, "yours is a wicked, uncouth life!"

From the hearth, the cook quavered, "She would not give up the keys, milord, she was so careful of us. We would have starved without her."

Fulk watched his wife, back straight, sweep through the tables. Some of the knights sitting on the floor got to their feet and stood, respectful, as she went by.

Hugh's wife burst into tears. Hugh put his arm around her. The Lady Alwyn had gathered up her skirts and gone out by the door. The hall was in an uproar.

"Christ's wounds," Fulk shouted, "must we have this at every mealtime?"

He got up and followed her.

On the stairs, he passed one of the castle women. She glared at him. When he came in, his wife was sitting on the edge of the bed, nursing the child.

He said, "No matter how you see it, I am not going to march on Chester for trying to steal my castle and my wife. He would not only trounce me, it would give him my head on a plate to present to King William."

She put her hand on the top of the child's head, stroking it. "Don't shout," she told him.

"Shout?" He kicked a stool out of the way. "I drove sixty spent and frozen knights through the mountains four nights to reach here, fell upon a force that thrice outnumbered us and sent Osbern Tirell and Chester's best men in shameful rout. And what I am told after I have accomplished this miracle is that you have done it all. I am near attacked in my own hall for not conceding the raising of the siege of Morlaix to my saintly wife!"

She looked up at him. She had taken off the blue veil. In the firelight, her face was white. "You were a fool to trust Geoffrey."

He snorted. "I never trust Geoffrey. He only came to me when he was frightened and saw that in the end Chester would use him ill." He prowled around the room, kicking at things. He was trying to think of how to tell her what he had reserved for the last, when he was alone with her. "Geoffrey is all mouth. It was no test." He stopped. "I have been miserable enough. That is what I wish to talk to you about." He looked down at the top of the babe's head. "God's wounds, what have you done to its hair?"

314

She looked up at him with clear, silver eyes. "Oh, the black? That was newborn hair, it fell out." She closed the front of her dress with one hand. "And he is not an it, he's your son." She thrust the babe at him. "Here, take him."

Fulk caught the bundle hastily, before she could let it drop. Unwilling, he cradled the thing in both hands and looked at it, frowning. The small face frowned back, unfriendly.

Suddenly Fulk felt his hands tremble. It could not be, yet he was looking into his own face. He would know that nose, that mouth anywhere. The fuzz of its hair was distinctly ruddy. He sat down on the bed, holding it.

All those months, he thought, stunned, since they were wedded. His cousin, the master mason, the damned Welshman, Powys, none of it true. He told himself he had not really believed it, it was only that she tormented him vilely. The whole time.

He said, "His name is Gilbert."

She had her back to him, poking up the fire. He looked down at his son. Gilbert smiled hugely, then blew a mouthful of milky bubbles. Fulk tried to think of something to say to him. His son. God and the saints, he had an heir. Hugh of Avranches could take nothing from him now.

"I have done nothing but think of you," he said, "at night. Sometimes during the day. Many times during the day, in the mountains, you have filled my thoughts when I should be thinking of other things."

She turned from the fire, the poker still in her hand. She had pulled down her hair and it fell over the front of her dress like a long shadow. She said, "Do you accuse me of making you think?"

"Don't twist my words. This is why I don't talk to you." He sniffed the air. "What is that foul stink?"

She put down the poker and came across the room and took the child from him. She laid the babe on the bed and changed its napkin. He watched her put away the dirty one in a pot with a lid on it and then put on the clean cloth.

She put Gilbert in the fur-lined bunting and laced him up, cooing to him. He listened, interested in what she said to his son. It was another language. When she was through, she carried the babe to the cradle. He followed her, watching as she piled more furs upon him. He stood behind her as she rocked the cradle with one hand, humming, to put him to sleep. He realized she had been doing this, tending his son like this, all these months. All the time he had been gone fighting the Welsh.

When she turned she did not know he was standing behind her and she bumped into him. He was so much bigger he towered over her. He put his hands on her arms. He said, gruff, "In time, you will not be sorry you wedded me."

He was surprised at the expression on her face. She pushed him away. "No, in time I will not care when you ill-use and humiliate me."

She went to the bed and sat on it. "That was a mistake," he told her.

She kicked off her shoes. "It was all a mistake. If not ours, then King William's." She said, her head bent, "I want to leave you."

He stood still, his hands hooked in his belt. Finally he said, "You cannot."

She picked up the brush and started brushing her hair. "No, I cannot. I am carrying your child again." When he started, she said, "It thundered in the meadow to no avail. The crop sprouted, regardless."

He stared at her. "Well," he said, "there were a few times."

"Yes." She turned her head away. "Those few times."

Fulk turned to pace up and down. He wanted to put his arms around her. Another child. In a flash he saw strong sons like those of other knights. Big, valiant boys. Wearing mail, laughing, hunting with him. He thought of little girls. He had always liked little girls. Mysterious, but he liked them. God's wounds, he had to do something.

He strode to her. He said, "I am miserable without you. Don't leave me."

She brushed her hair up from the back, to fall in front of her face. "I said I wasn't going to leave you," she said through it.

Her hands were graceful, white, as she lifted her black hair. Looking at them, he thought of the rings and jewels she had given to Powys to ransom him. And remembered he had brought back the silver circlet. The Welshman's gift to her.

He took her hand in his and pried the brush out of it. He pulled back her hair so that he could see her face. He had always thought her pretty, but he could see it was more than that. Everyone told him she was beautiful. Slowly, he got to one knee before her as she sat on the bed. "I have never talked to a woman of love before," he said.

She pulled her hands out of his grip. "Get up. You're making a fool of yourself."

"A man always makes a fool of himself for a woman," he shouted, "that is only the beginning of it. Look, I am doing penance for my unholy sins on my knees. Is that not what you want? Do you want me to say that I love you?"

She glared at him. "This is beyond belief. You are trying to humiliate me again."

He shoved his face in hers. "Humiliate? That is better than torture. I am chained to this marriage by a lovesick passion worthy of some languishing maid. My knights laugh at me when I will not go to the whores with them, I am so besotted with my own wife."

A silence fell. She looked at him, biting her lip. "That is not true."

"True? The devil take it, I did not want this marriage!" He grasped her knee. It was warm. He rubbed his hand along her kneecap under the gown. "Others have civil arrangements and bed each other and have children and are not so sorry entangled. I only thought when I wed you it would be such a thing. That I would see you only when

I was not campaigning for King William. Every twelve-month, to get a child on you."

"Well, you are doing that." Tentative, she touched his lips with her fingertip. "You are a brave knight," she said in a different voice, "I did not mean to insult you. If you had not come to raise the siege on Castle Morlaix, we would have had to surrender sometime. The monk said so. He was a knight once."

He turned his head to nuzzle her hand. "Nay, I know you too well. You would have thought of something."

Annoyed, she struck him lightly on the cheek with her fingertips.

He laughed. "You would not have surrendered. You would have parleyed with Osbern Tirell and had him with his breeches tied round his knees, offering you everything Chester owns."

"Holy Mother, you are coarse." His hands were at her gown's lacings. She pushed them away. "Where is this civil arrangement? I am not going to bed with you. Nothing is solved between us."

"I am full of civility." He leaned over her and pushed her back down on the bed. He guided her hand down to him. "Can you not feel it?"

Breathless, she said, "I wish to hold manor court."

"Don't bargain with me in bed." He fell back and pulled her over him. "Sweet Jesu, I have missed you. Longed for you. There is no one to torment me, when I am fighting." He pulled open her lacings and put his mouth against her breasts. "You are so soft." His other hand rucked up her skirts. "You are a quarrelsome bitch, I know you will use this weakness against me."

"Always," she murmured as his mouth closed over hers.

From the cradle, Gilbert made a sudden squalling noise.

Fulk lifted his head. "My son." He let her go and she rolled to one side. Gilbert's screams grew louder.

"My son." He got out of bed. He stepped on something, her shoes, and staggered, cursing. He made his way to the cradle and picked Gilbert up. The babe drew his knees up, screaming. "In God's name, what is the matter with him?"

Alwyn sat up in bed and pulled her gown over her head. She lay back and held out her arms. "Bring him to me."

He came to her quickly. Gilbert's mouth was wide open. The noise was terrible. "Is he ill?"

She took the babe from him. She put him to her shoulder and Gilbert belched. "He only wants to be dandled." She watched Fulk strip off his shirt, then his chausses. He brushed his feet, then got into the bed beside her.

Gilbert belched again. The milk stayed down. He smiled, angelic. Alwyn kissed his cheek. "Dandled and petted, my sweet lamb," she murmured, "that's all he needs."

Fulk slid down beside her. He turned on his side and pulled them against him. "So do we all," he said. He kissed the back of her neck. "So do we all."

Epilogue

ALWYN TOOK THE CUP OF WINE FROM the page before he could spill it. They were fostering now at Morlaix and this was one of Prince Rhiwallon's grandsons of the legitimate line, who was only five years old. And mortally afraid of the cook. She had almost not got him to fetch her drink.

She put the cup on the ground by her chair and reached out to straighten the front of his jacket. Like all of the old prince's offspring he was beautiful, with clear blue eyes and curly black hair.

"Do you know the knight Goutard?" Her Midsummer concert of an orchestra of rebecs and horns was playing a lively Flemish tune on the small stage set up by the kitchen house. She had to put her mouth close to his ear. "We are short of chairs and stools," she whispered. "Tell the knight Goutard to see that more seats are brought out for the Earl of Chester's party when they arrive."

The little boy nodded. He raced off to deliver the message.

"He is just a baby," Geoffrey's wife said, watching him go. "I know it is the custom, but it would break my heart

320

to have my Samuel taken from me like that, to live in some castle."

Alwyn sipped at her wine. "Well, you need not fear that," she said shortly. "Since you are not raising him to be a knight."

On the other side of Sophia, Geoffrey lounged, his feet stuck out, his little boy, Samuel, held between his knees. The child was dark like his mother, with her magnificent eyes. He leaned on his father's outstretched leg and plucked at the velvet edge of Geoffrey's long merchant's gown to get his attention. "Papa. Listen, Papa." But Geoffrey was eyeing the tumbling girls who had come with the players.

Sophia was embroidering, something she did very well. She followed Geoffrey's eyes when he did not answer. Taking her scissors, she reached over her son's shoulder and rapped her husband smartly on the head. He turned to her, innocently smiling.

Alwyn put her hand to her mouth, trying not to laugh. Now that Geoffrey had a rich wife, he had grown sleek and submissive. But he seemed happy enough.

She looked across the ward, seeking out her husband. The bright sunshine of Midsummer Day picked out the colors of the crowd dressed for the castle fete. Only the brown habits of the monks from the Irishman's priory in the village struck a somber note. They stood together, the young brothers with their freshly shaven tonsures, their hands in their sleeves. One of them was her new clerk for the manor court. A group of children ran along the edges. She looked for the twins, knowing they were somewhere about. They were enamored these days of Malluch and the Welsh stable boys; when they made an appearance, she knew they would be filthy as any pig herd's child.

The crowd parted to let the children race through. She saw her husband sitting on a stool, talking to Osbern Tirell, little Alys on his lap. Alys was sucking her thumb. Alwyn tried to catch her daughter's eye, to frown at her.

Gilbert stood to one side, his hands hooked in his belt, feet spread, looking down his nose in a perfect imitation of Fulk.

Alwyn felt her heart turn over. Gilbert was seven. Talk of fosterage, Hugh of Avranches had already asked for him. She had a sudden sympathy with Sophia. She could not bear the thought of it, either.

The orchestra finished their tune and left the stage. In the sudden quiet, the noise of drums and singing in the village drifted up the castle road on the warm wind. She watched the two monks. The new chapter house of young Irish brothers had taken charge of the Midsummer Day revelries and planned a maypole dance, an innovation from England, and a feast in the miller's ale yard. Still, these things had a way of getting out of hand. The year before, at nightfall, many young people had slipped into the woods. The Irish prior, Bran, had gone after them to drive them back to their huts. At least some of them.

Bran was in the Welsh hills on one of his long forays preaching to the hillmen. From time to time the famed bandit, Powys, caught the Irishman and sent him back. It was said Bran was now trying to establish a cell of monks at the Normans' fort at Glynowestry, to Powys's annoyance.

Fulk jabbed his finger at Osbern Tirell, arguing some point. She watched him over the rim of her wine cup. The siege of Morlaix Castle was far away. King William was fighting his son again in Normandy, but Bishop Odo and Robert of Coutances had been punished and confined for their scheming. And Hugh of Avranches was as strong as ever in the north. So, Fulk de Jobourg had been right. And she had been wrong.

A harper climbed up on the stage, sat down on the stool placed there for him, and began to tune his instrument. Alwyn put down her cup of wine on the ground and looked to her husband. He seemed engrossed in what he was saying to Chester's bailiff. She knew he had an uncertain temper with harpers. She willed him to look at her.

The harper stood up and announced in both Norman French and Welsh that he was there from a tour of castles in the marches and would sing for them the latest and most popular romances. That included a French ballad newly come from Aquitaine, in France, called the "Romance de la Belle Arlette de Morlaix."

She saw Fulk pause and look up at the stage. Alwyn said to Sophia, "If I must leave you in a hurry and the knight Goutard comes looking for me, tell him to put the seats for the earl's party I asked for down by the stage."

She sat on the edge of her seat, ready to get up. The troubador was singing of a beautiful woman, virtuous beyond belief, who had been imprisoned by a wicked seneschal in her castle dungeon. He had done this on the orders of Lady Arlette's brutal, unloving husband.

Holy Mother, Alwyn thought. She saw her husband had stopped talking to Tirell and was now staring at the harper.

While the lady's husband, the singer sang on, was away at war, the Lady Arlette was fortunately rescued by a handsome young knight, Reginald the Pure, who although he fell in love with the fair lady of Morlaix sadly told her he must continue onward with a troop of knights-errant dedicated to finding the Holy Grail.

"Mamma," one of the twins said, throwing himself by her side. He sprawled across her knees. "Mamma, Alain says I am not old enough to ride a horse, I must ride only ponies."

Her other son draped a dirty arm across her shoulder. "I did not, Mamma, he's a liar," he said, vehement. "I only said he could not ride *big* horses. Like Malluch's. Mamma, I—"

"Hush," she said. She pulled Hugh's arm down from her shoulder. "I am trying to listen."

She kept her eyes on Fulk. Head turned, he was not listening to Osbern Tirell. He was watching the harper.

The musician struck a dramatic chord. He paused and looked at his audience. In the midst of his battles, the brutal and unloving husband was rebuked by a vision of the Holy Virgin, who told him that for his sins he must make a pilgrimage to her faraway shrine, hobbling the distance on his knees. But then a miracle happened. His pious and forgiving lady of Morlaix, on the way to the shrine herself, found her husband sick and starving by the roadside. She redeemed him by her love.

Alwyn saw Fulk half rise from his chair. The harper, innocent of impending danger, sang a virtuoso trill. The crowd was silent, hanging on his next words.

And then, the harper sang, repenting their sins and transformed by their sublime experience, both the fair lady of Morlaix and her now saintly husband took holy orders and retired to a religious life, he to a monastery, she to a cloister of nuns.

Alwyn saw her husband sink back into his chair, looking baffled. He turned and looked through the crowd, seeking her.

They could hear a disturbance on the castle road outside. In a moment, the portal guard shouted down the imminent arrival of King William's servant, Hugh of Avranches, the Earl of Chester.

Alwyn stood up. She gave her front, muddy from the twins' hands, a quick brush. Knights clustered around Fulk to greet the earl and his party when they rode in. They blocked her way; she could not see him. The twins tugged at her, eager to say something. The knight Goutard pushed through the crowd to her.

"Yes, I know," she said to him, "the chairs. Put them down by the stage, in the first row." She took Alain by the arm and pushed him forward. She found Hugh's wrist and handed him on. "Find a knight and tell him to get the boys to the tower for clean clothes."

Suddenly, in front of her, her husband appeared.

He was taller than the men around him. Sun struck his ruddy cropped hair. He was wearing the black velvet coat she had sewed for him and around his neck was a fine gold chain. She loved him. He was beautiful.

"About the harper," she said quickly.

"The harper," he said. He looked around for Osbern Tirell and his escort of knights. Then he looked down and smiled at her.

He had forgotten it. "It's of no importance," she said, taking his arm.

HERE IS AN EXCERPT FROM *NO ROOF BUT HEAVEN* BY JEANNE WILLIAMS—A MAGNIFICENT ROMANTIC NOVEL SET IN THE AMERICAN FRONTIER—COMING IN OCTOBER FROM ST. MARTIN'S PAPERBACKS.

"Make the best of things?" Rawdon's eyes bored into her. "Is that what you're doing, Miss Alden?"

Susanna could do nothing about the blood that rushed to her face but she didn't speak till she had control of her voice. "I'm doing just that, sir, and I'm not ashamed of it."

The silence lasted till they passed a mud house with a partially destroyed roof. The door was gone and a hide flapped at one small window. A few stalks of corn, unhusked, rose from a grown-over patch that had almost returned to sod. Rawdon veered out of the ruts and snapped off the ears. "No use their going to waste. Mrs. Osborn went sort of daft from the wind, their baby died, and they went back to Iowa two years ago."

Susanna repressed a shudder. Had she been foolish to come here? Even without the undefined menace of the school board, this vast plain made her feel as if—as if— She groped to define it. Aunt Mollie used to say that if you could understand what troubled you, you were halfway to dealing with it. Susanna felt as if—the roof and walls of a comfortable house had suddenly blown off and she was left with no roof but heaven, no floor but the grass, no neighbor but the wind.

She shivered, but there was something spacious and wonderfully free about this prairie, something that whispered there was all the room in the world to grow, to be what you couldn't be inside the walls. Susanna's head ached from the pins that had held her hair in place for three days. How good it would feel to pull off the sedate bonnet and let the wind blow her hair!

After one brief moment of shock at the audacity of unpinning her hair in front of a strange man, she tugged the ribbon and, as Rawdon shot her an amazed look, she loosed her hair. Hadn't she come out to lead a new kind of life and along with the hardships of the frontier taste its freedom? Defiantly heedless of this man who didn't approve of her anyway, she threw back her head and laughed into the western breeze, reveling in the way it soothed the chafed places on her scalp and touched the roots of her hair with cooling invisible fingers.

To her surprise, Rawdon's chuckle was almost sympathetic. "Bet that does feel good. Like a horse that's lathered up enjoys a good roll in the dust. Till you did that, I figured you for the perfect schoolmarm."

"Who never lets down her hair?"

His eyes touched her, only for a moment, but their curious light seemed to pierce her, see deep inside, and there was something more, a flash of danger, heady, intoxicating, a feeling she had never had before. She had been only seventeen when Richard kissed her shyly and asked her to wait for him. How many times since then had she wished that she'd been a little bolder, that each of them could have had more than a swift kiss to remember. Startled at the way Rawdon's glance sent her pulse racing, she looked away.

"You bet she doesn't let down her hair, Miss Alden." His tone was almost contemptuous. "She's careful of her clothes, her money, and her reputation."

Thinking of the money pocket sewn into her dress, Susanna nearly winced. "No more than they get paid, teachers have to be careful of the first two," she said defensively. "And any woman has to guard her reputation."

"Then you'd better twist that pretty hair back into a knot because the dust and smoke up ahead looks like a branding crew and Ase McCanless may be there. He's chairman of the board of trustees. Smile at him sweetly, Miss Alden, because if you don't get along with him, you won't last long."

"He's a rancher?"

"You could say that. His cattle range clear down to Texas where he started broke after the war. He wouldn't like homesteaders plowing up what he thinks is his grass anyway, but when they're Yankees, and most are, it really sticks in his craw."

As they approached the pall of dust, Susanna could hear shouts and the angry, frightened bawling of cattle. Some distance from the track, mounted men kept watch over grazing cattle while others roped calves and hauled them to a fire where long irons glowed red. When a calf was wrestled down by two more men, a third applied one of the irons, made swift cuts with a knife, and in a few minutes, the calf stumbled up and made for its mother who licked it tenderly and comforted it with her udder.

These cows looked very different from the sleek Jerseys and Holsteins and Guernseys of Ohio. Most of these had vicious long and curling horns, were rangy and lean, and came in a dusty rainbow of bovine colors—gray, dun, brindled, red, cream, and brown. The man with the iron called one of the herders, gave him the iron, and, appropriating his horse, rode over to the buckboard.

Sweeping off a wide-brimmed hat so soiled it was impossible to discern its original color, the big stranger gave a curt nod to Rawdon before he frankly stared at Susanna. "You the new schoolmarm, lady?" Lean and tough and dark as the leather of his saddle, he had piercing blue eyes and sandy brown hair. About Rawdon's age, she guessed, though it was hard to tell. "No offense," he continued in a lazy drawl, "but you don't look old enough to be traveling around by yourself."

Susanna couldn't keep from chuckling. "That's flattering, sir, but I'm twenty-seven and I've been teaching for years."

Eyeing her with increased caution, he sighed. "Seems Henry said you're from Ohio."

"Yes."

He sighed again. "Well, accordin' to Henry, you had the best qualifications of the teachers who applied—not that many did. Western Kansas isn't real popular. Too bad we couldn't get a Southern lady but I reckon their menfolk won't let 'em go gadding around the country."

"My fiancé was killed in the war," Susanna said icily. "And my father recently died after years of pain from his injuries. I'm willing to answer any reasonable questions about my competency, but when the county superintendent invited me to come, he knew I was what you doubtless call a Yankee."

"Now don't go flyin' off the handle, ma'am. Two of the board want you because you *are* from the North like them. But the main thing is, our kids need teachin' and if you can do that, more power to you." He set his hat firmly back on his head. "I'm Asa McCanless, ma'am, and I reckon you're Miss Susanna Alden. I got to get back to work, but Rawdon, just take her on to the house, and much obliged. Stay for supper and overnight if you want."

"Thanks, Ase, but I'll get on to my place. Cash Hardy's back is paining him. I promised I'd get him some medicine in Dodge and stop by tonight."

McCanless chuckled. "For a doctor who says he don't doctor, Doc, you sure pay a lot of calls. If you ask me, what Cash needs most is a good kick in the pants."

"Oh, he's got some injured vertebrae," said Rawdon. He spoke to the team and they were moving on when suddenly McCanless shot past them, making for a rider on the horizon, a rider whose horse skimmed the plains, tail and mane swept by the wind.

"One of your pupils," Rawdon said. "Ase's daughter. Regular little hellion and made a lot worse by the way he treats her." As the team started, he gave Susanna a grim smile. "You're going to have an—interesting time, Miss

Alden. It's not just Yanks and Rebels still fighting the war, but some of the families have their little problems."

"Would you enjoy seeing me give up?"

"What's it to me? I told you, I've no youngsters and probably never will." He hesitated a second. "I'm—sorry about your father and fiancé."

That had taken an effort. Moved to honesty, she said, "I'm sorry about your hand."

His face went red, then pale. After a moment, he spoke in a tight, hard tone. "My hand, Miss Alden, is absolutely none of your concern. The revulsion it causes, especially to ladies, is perfectly natural. I prefer honest shrinking to pity."

Stung, Susanna could think of no good answer. They drove along, the silence between them heavy and bitter with memories, till what must be McCanless's home came into view.

A wide-porched white frame house dominated a sprawl of sod buildings and corrals. None of the trees planted around the dwelling as yet rose higher than the windows of the gabled second story. This added to the impression that the big house had been conjured up in a place where it didn't belong.

"Here you are at Ace High." Rawdon got down, hitched the team to a post, and impatiently helped her alight. "Why will women wear corsets?" he grumbled. "At least you seem to have the sense not to lace yourself so tight you can't breathe."

"Sir!" His remark was so indecorous that she could think of no retort but a withering glance that only made him throw back his head and laugh.

"Sorry, ma'am. Consider it a physician's observation."

"*If* you go back into practice and *if* I seek your advice, then Dr. Rawdon, you may make such comments."

"I already did." Ignoring her displeasure, he greeted an old man who limped out of a shed and came to help with the trunk. The door of the house flew open and a plump, elderly lady hurried out, catching Susanna's hands.

"Come in, dear," she greeted, her smile spreading to warm shrewd hazel eyes as she took Susanna in with one swift toe-to-top glance. "Fagged, you must be, and wanting a bath, and to stretch out. Your room's ready. Johnny'll fill a tub for you. I'll bring you some nice soup and you won't need to come down to supper if you'd rather just go to bed. I'm Betty Flynn, Mr. McCanless's housekeeper."

She bore Susanna into a carpeted hall and motioned up the stairs. "First door on your right, dear. If you need anything, just call."

Overwhelmed by such a welcome after encountering Dodge City and two Southern men who hadn't exactly lived up to the tradition of chivalry attached to that region, Susanna started up the stairs. Rawdon met her on the landing.

"Thank you for your trouble," she said with cool civility, and made to open her satchel. "I want to pay you for bringing you out of your way—and for having inflicted my company on you."

The landing was dim but that made his eyes more disconcertingly brilliant than ever. "Yankees think they can pay for everything, don't they? I don't want your money, Miss Alden. As I told you, save it for your ticket home."

He gave her a curt nod and was down the stairs before she could move. Dreadful nasty bigoted jaundiced misogynist Rebel!

Whatever the Mason-Dixon school board was like, it couldn't be made up of more difficult men than the two she had already met.

NO ROOF BUT HEAVEN BY JEANNE WILLIAMS—COMING IN OCTOBER FROM ST. MARTIN'S PAPERBACKS